Alison Boulton was born in London. She studied Anthropology and Linguistics at University College London and Creative Writing under Andrew Motion at the University of East Anglia. Like Vincent van Gogh and Kate Butterworth, she once lived in Holland but then moved to the south of France. She is still there, in a rambling old château, scribbling away amidst geese, donkeys and sunflowers.

GW00721763

Also by this author

Tom's Daughters

'The plot is juicy: the death of an estranged father triggers a journey into the past, revealing all kinds of family secrets. ... But the real gem here is the characters. They're ... the kind of people you miss when you've finished reading.' Katie O Rourke, author of *Monsoon Season*

Chasing Sunflowers

ALISON BOULTON

Château du Fraissinet
Languedoc-Roussillon, France

First published in Great Britain by
Château du Fraissinet,
30110 Branoux les Taillades
Languedoc-Roussillon, France.
July 2015

Extracts from the letters of Vincent van Gogh reproduced with kind
permission of the Van Gogh Museum, Amsterdam
Digital edition: Vincent van Gogh, The Letters. Ed. Leo Jansen, Hans
Luijten and Nienke Bakker. Amsterdam 2009

ISBN 9781849147729

Printed in Great Britain by Lightning Source International

Cover photo © Alison Boulton

http://alisonboulton-writing.blogspot.fr
http://french-chatelaine.blogspot.fr
alisonboulton@yahoo.co.uk

For Chris

'A major exhibition of contemporary painting opens tomorrow at the Merle Gallery in Brussels. Attracting critics' attention is a stunning new work by talented Dutch artist Rudy de Jong. De Jong's painting, The Sonnet, *depicts a copper-haired nude reclining on a green chaise-longue. Although relatively small in actual size, this vibrantly sensual work dominates the exhibition. Painted in the style of Van Gogh and emulating his use of strong, contrasting colours, De Jong exploits the emerald background to draw the pale-skinned model almost out of the picture and into the room. Although it has been the subject of considerable speculation, De Jong has remained mysterious about his alluring muse.'*

Chapter 1

'Amsterdam!' Kate exclaimed, spinning round from her station at the cooker so her red-gold hair fanned out behind her. 'Did you say Amsterdam?' She held the wooden spoon aloft dripping a puddle of tomato sauce onto the floor. 'And for how long?'

Sean opened a beer and took a long swig from the bottle before replying. His face seemed to have folded with exhaustion. It was a long way from Suffolk to London every single day. He loosened his tie. This was going to be hard work after all. For some reason he had thought she would be pleased. She had seemed keen enough when he first mentioned the idea and it wasn't as if – he glanced round their kitchen and through the window to the rectangle of mossy lawn with the red and yellow climbing frame – it wasn't as if their life here was very interesting. Usually Kate was the first person to point that out. But now there was an opportunity to change it, to break away and do something a bit different and she was pulling back. He didn't get it. Amsterdam. It sounded great. Didn't it?

'A year, that's all. It's a fantastic opportunity and we could live right in the city. It's clean, lots of trams. People cycle everywhere.' He paused. 'I wouldn't have to commute. You wouldn't have to work.'

'Maybe I like working?' Kate inclined her head, eyebrows raised pointedly.

'You keep saying you don't,' said Sean. 'You keep saying ...'

'Oddly enough I know what I keep saying,' she said, returning her attention to the pan and stirring vigorously. 'I keep saying that my job's boring and it's a strain doing everything myself because you're never here. This, please note, is not the same as saying I don't like working.' She inhaled sharply. 'And by the way, how would we pay for two houses? Right now we can hardly afford one.'

1

'The company would pay. That's what makes it such a great deal.' Sean leant forward eagerly. 'We could rent this place out if we liked, but even without that the gains would easily be more than your wages are now.'

'I'm pretty expendable then. That's good to know.'

'That's not what I meant.' Her husband sighed.

Kate tipped a saucepan of pasta into a colander making sure she avoided his gaze. Of course it wasn't what he meant, she knew that. But a different country... it was a big ask, surely? Five years before, with property prices sky rocketing and the baby due it had seemed like an excellent idea to move out of London, buy a proper house in a real town and make a home for their family. So here they were and it was fine. But there was no particular reason why they couldn't leave it all for a year.

'Spaghetti bolognaise,' she said, handing Sean a piled-up plate.

'Didn't we have that the other day?'

'Nope, that was penne bolognaise. Subtle but important difference.'

Sean grinned.

'Fair enough. It smells good and I'm starving.' He shook a generous amount from a packet of grated parmesan over the meat sauce and lifted a forkful to his mouth. 'I think you've got it just about perfect.'

'Maybe I should move onto something else then. Shepherds' pie, perhaps?' Kate smiled briefly. 'Hang on.' She rose and turned off the overhead light leaving just the soft under-cupboard lamps. 'Nicer like that.'

'Do we have a candle?'

She nodded.

'Good, because I actually stopped and bought...' he leant over and opened his briefcase, 'a bottle of bubbly to celebrate.'

Her lips pursed. 'Which bit are we celebrating exactly? Leaving our home? Our country? Or the loss of my independence?'

'I thought maybe my promotion,' Sean said quietly.

'Is that what it is?'

'Kate, we discussed everything before I applied for the job. I can't just turn it down now they've offered it.'

'Maybe you could commute weekly, lots of people do.'

His jaw tightened.

'Yes, I could, if that's what you want.'

Kate studied her plate.

'Actually, I don't have to come back at all. Would that be better?'

Her chin lifted. Unwittingly, her eyes flicked to the ceiling. Luke's room was above the kitchen. He would be asleep by now, puppy-brown hair loose across the pillow, one arm clutching that toy that was neither teddy-bear nor rag doll but a mini replica of some character from CBeebies, a first birthday present from their friends, Paula and Dom. Incredibly, he was now four and a bit but the battered Igglepiggle continued to be Luke's bedtime companion of choice.

She turned back to her husband, her face softer.

'No,' she said. 'I want to see more of you, not less. I don't want you to have commute and spend hours on the train that you could spend with us.'

Relief washed over Sean's features.

'Hopefully in Amsterdam, there'll be less pressure.' He paused. 'I also thought...'

'Yes?'

'That maybe if you were more relaxed...' He corrected himself. 'If *we* were more relaxed, it might be easier... you know.'

'What?' she flashed. 'So is that what you think? It's my fault? You think it's because I'm too tense?'

Kate let her fork clatter onto the plate and her hands flew up to her face. Sean reached across to rescue a strand of hair that had fallen into the spaghetti and tucked it gently behind her ear.

'No, of course not, it's just that... well, people say...' he stopped as she wiped her eyes and glared at him. 'Oh I don't know,' he mumbled. 'It doesn't matter anyway.'

'It matters to me,' said Kate. 'I wanted a big family. Three maybe even four kids. But there's only ever going to be Luke.'

'We don't know that. And anyway, Luke's great, isn't he?'

Kate sniffed. Of course he was. He just wasn't enough. Everyone Kate knew managed to produce children to order, why not her? Even Paula was now struggling to squeeze her enormous belly behind the steering wheel.

'It's another boy,' Paula had confided, trying not to look disappointed.

'Almost looks like twins.' Kate said, managing a giggle. 'Anyway, it'll be nice for Henry to have a brother, someone to play football with.' She swallowed. 'I'm not convinced Luke's ever going to have anyone to play anything with.'

'Of course he will,' Paula reassured her. 'It's just taking a bit longer, that's all.'

'Amsterdam.' Kate repeated, testing the word. Once she would have jumped at the chance to move somewhere like that. Now, without realising she had become settled. Settled into nothing, she thought. Leaning back against the worktop, she surveyed her kitchen; limed-oak units, shiny taps, all very nicely done. She didn't even like cooking much.

Sean got to his feet with a yawn.

'Shall we go to bed?' He reached out and touched her, lightly, in the hollow of her shoulder.

She shrugged. The champagne had been left unopened. Before going upstairs she put it in the fridge.

We should have just popped the cork and got sloshed, she reflected. Why was everything always so difficult?

In the large bed they lay side-by-side like wooden dolls. Sean stretched out a tentative hand and ran a finger along her thigh. She ignored him. He didn't seem to notice. She turned off the bedside lamp.

'There's no point, you know. It's too late in the month, it won't happen now.'

'I thought you might want to.'

'To celebrate?'

'Okay, forget it. I have to get up early anyway. Got a meeting tomorrow morning.' He turned over heavily and closed his eyes.

Kate stared into the darkness aware of him breathing steadily beside her. He wouldn't wake now until the alarm went off. For her, the transition into sleep came more slowly; a stillness seeping into her muscles like a lethal injection. As she lay, waiting, unmoving, she listened to the wind whistling through the cracks between the window frames.

Might as well go, she concluded. I'm not doing anything much here. I'm thirty-seven. My job's a dead end. And you never know, it might even be fun.

Sean opened the bedroom curtains and placed a cup of tea on his wife's bedside. Luke, his face still full of sleep, staggered into the room and crawled in beside his mother.

'I'll come,' murmured Kate from the pillow. 'Or rather, we'll come. No reason to stay here. It's not a very interesting job anyway. I'm going to expand my mind, tour the museums. Study art.'

'You could learn Dutch,' Sean suggested.

'I'll do that too,' she confirmed. 'And if I get bored I'll sit in coffee shops and smoke weed.'

Sean grinned. Some of the tension visibly evaporated from his shoulders.

'Thanks, babe.' He stooped to place a kiss on the messy silk of Kate's hair, smoothing out a wiry strand of grey that sprang up at right angles to the rest. She opened her eyes.

'I suppose I should get up.'

'Why bother? You're not working today.'

'Well, if we're still here when you get back you'll know we didn't.' Kate nestled further down under the duvet and wrapped an arm around her son.

They were very alike, these two, with their identical hazel gaze and sweeping lashes, curled together in the bed like two halves of a peach. Sean regarded them with some disquiet. It might be better for Luke if they had more children.

'I'm late, must go.' He tousled his son's head. A small hand flew out from beneath the covers and grabbed his wrist. Sean smiled. 'See you later, Batman.' He unpeeled the fingers.

'Bye, Dad.'

'Bye,' said Kate, automatically. 'Have a good day,'

He arrived at the station just as the guard was about to blow the whistle and only managed to attract his attention by waving wildly. He was granted just enough time to jump into the nearest carriage where he leant against the luggage racks and closed his eyes. He hadn't slept particularly well but whatever, she had agreed, that was a huge relief. If he turned down this post after having applied for it he wouldn't be offered anything else for years, if ever. He needed a break, commuting was taking its toll and this was a fantastic opportunity. Contracted overseas to set up the IT side of the deal between his UK bank and a Dutch partner with the option of returning to the UK in a year or two. It was perfect really, like going on an extended holiday. All the excitement of a move abroad but no real commitment. And Kate had been really keen when it was first mentioned. It wasn't as if her part-time job at the estate agency was very challenging and now that the new guy had arrived she would only get the crap houses to deal with anyway.

Worst of all, though, in Sean's view, was that she seemed to have got it into her head that it was his fault the second baby wasn't appearing; the strain of too much commuting, or something. She kept nagging him to go jogging at the weekends. Well, no chance of that. Maybe Luke was their quota and it just wasn't going to happen again. Personally Sean didn't think that was so bad, or it wouldn't be if she would stop mollycoddling the boy and let him grow-up a bit. Hopefully relocating to Amsterdam would break new ground and be good for everyone. He nodded to himself thoughtfully and moved inside the carriage to look for a seat.

*****

'Amsterdam! Wow, why wouldn't you?' enthused Paula as she and Kate sat in Costa Coffee that afternoon sipping huge lattes. Beside them Luke and Henry munched chocolate chip cookies and manoeuvred their model engines round the table. 'How long for?'

'It's just for a year. Sean's going to do the IT stuff for some kind of company merger. The pay's good. We could let the house.'

'Amsterdam's a very romantic city,' said Paula, encouragingly. 'I spent a summer there working as an au pair before I went to uni,' she chuckled. 'Or maybe romantic's not quite the right word. Anyway, it's probably just what you and Sean need.'

Kate managed a feeble smile. 'I think it might take a bit more than a new place.'

Her friend looked sympathetic. 'You never know. Change of scenery, no more commuting, time together...'

'Maybe...'

'Well, if you don't like it you can always spend the entire year stoned. And don't forget all those sexy Dutch guys just standing around to be admired.'

'I'm not sure I'm into sexy Dutch guys,' Kate protested.

'Course you are.' Paula giggled. 'Everyone is. Tall, blond, blue-eyed. What's not to like? Are you excited, Luke?'

'S'pose,' Luke replied, his mouth full of biscuit. 'Mum says there's a zoo with elephants. I like elephants. You can come and see them, Henry.'

Henry glanced up at his mother.

'Can we go and live with the elephants too?'

'No, but we can visit,' Paula assured him. 'When do you leave, Kate?'

'Sean goes in a week or so. We would follow next month.'

'You're letting Sean loose in Amsterdam by himself!'

'Of course,' Kate laughed. 'This is Sean, remember! The guy that comes home and sits in front of computer all evening.'

Paula shrugged. 'If you say so.' She paused as if about to say something, but then pressed her lips shut.

'What?'

'Nothing really. I just remember when Dom was away for a few weeks; he was working with a younger crowd, most of them single. There was, well, a bit of an incident. Nothing serious, fortunately.' She frowned.

'I didn't know that,' said Kate, quietly.

'Nothing to know really.' Paula gave herself a shake and her face creased into a grin. 'Anyway, I don't know what you're sitting here for. Go home and start packing! I can't wait to come over.'

Chapter 2

The sky was heavy with cloud when Sean eased the car into the tight space in front of their apartment. Kate stepped out and breathed deeply. The air smelled of damp trees. At the far end of the street, presumably along a main road, a tram trundled past. Luke clambered out of the car seat clutching his faded Iggle Piggle. A small model train tumbled onto the pavement.

'Don't lose Thomas,' said Sean, picking it up.

'Percy,' Luke corrected sternly. Kate threw her husband a consoling smile as she pushed the car door shut and took her son's hand. Together they stood on the wide footpath, paved with hopscotch slabs, and stared up at the imposing art deco block that was to be their home.

'Mummy, does it sunshine here?' asked Luke, dubiously regarding the grey canopy above them. England had been cold and bright when they left.

'Of course, sometimes.' Kate gave his small, damp fingers a squeeze and with a swift, professional glance inspected their surroundings. The street was quiet and clean and there was a little park across the road with swings and a climbing frame. She could see mothers, or maybe au pairs, sitting smoking on the benches, and with them small, presumably pre-school, children who were playing and squabbling companionably. The sounds floated across to them on the still, heavy air, guttural and unfamiliar. Her gaze flicked to Luke but he didn't seem to have noticed.

'It all seems fine,' she conceded.

'More than fine,' Sean insisted. 'We were really lucky. It's almost impossible to find anything to rent round here. However,' he pulled a large brass key from his pocket and with a flourish inserted it into the lock, 'the owner is going overseas for a year so this place is ours.' The heavy, polished-wood door swung open with barely a squeak. Directly inside was a little porch with a stone floor, a large doormat and hooks for coats. Beyond, Kate registered a long gloomy hall lined with blonde parquet. On the right, steep stairs rose to the bedrooms above. A huge chandelier hung from the ceiling. It didn't look like a house that was much used to children.

She peered tentatively into the dim passage while Sean lifted the luggage out of the boot. Their cases held just a few basic changes of clothes. In a day or two the removal men would arrive with the things they had decided to bring with them – Sean's filing cabinet, the dressing table and silver-backed brushes that had belonged to Kate's grandmother, Luke's favourite toys and DVDs, a few books. Their other possessions, the stuff Kate termed 'the rest of our lives' had been packed into boxes and stored in the attic at home.

But this is our home now, she silently reminded herself. As from Monday, Dr and Mrs Birnie would be living in their Suffolk house while Dr Birnie spent a year directing an archaeological dig that he hoped would reveal new and interesting tendencies in Anglo-Saxon burial patterns. Their two children, Tom and Adele, would be attending the school that Luke had been enrolled in. Kate wondered what Mrs Birnie planned to do during her year in Ipswich.

Perhaps she will bake things like Paula, she reflected, and the kitchen will be properly used at last.

The family paused for a moment, standing like refugees under the chandelier. Then the all-too-familiar notes of Sean's mobile sounded. Pulling a rueful face, he slipped the phone from his pocket.

'Can we explore, Mummy?' asked Luke, loosening his grip on her fingers.

'Of course we can.'

Leaving her husband deep in conversation, his head bent and forefinger pressed into his ear to block out any extraneous noise.

Which means us, thought Kate. They pushed open the doorway at the end of the hall. Light from the glass-panelled back door flooded in and the apartment brightened instantly.

'Mummy, it's the kitchen!' exclaimed Luke. The room had been left in the original style; black and white tiled floor, free standing cupboards and a butler sink with an elderly mixer tap.

No limed-oak units here, Kate thought, biting her lip, but at least there was a dishwasher. From the kitchen the back door opened onto an enclosure the size of a handkerchief, room for a table and a sandpit but that was all. She turned the key and stepped out, followed by her son. They found themselves in a patchwork of gardens surrounded by looming apartment blocks.

'Oh well, at least we have fresh air.' She gazed upwards to scattered clouds laced with a net of black branches; a towering magnolia tree. Luke surveyed the new yard with dismay.

'Where can I play football?'

'I think we have to go across the road to the park.'

'Will Daddy come?'

'I'm sure he will, sometimes.' Kate looked round but Sean was still on the phone. He gave an apologetic wave.

'I'm not sure Henry will like this much.' Luke's face was anxious.

'He'll like the park,' Kate soothed. 'Let's explore upstairs.'

At the top of the stairs another solid door opened onto a huge bedroom that looked out over the gardens.

'A balcony!' Kate's delighted voice resounded like a bell against the white walls.

'I thought you'd like it,' said Sean, coming into the room behind them. He put his arm round his wife and pulled her to him. She let her head rest on his shoulder. They managed to stay that way for a few moments before Luke tugged his father's trousers.

'Can we go and play football now?'

'Not just now. Come and have a look at your room.' Taking the boy's hand he led him along the passage to the room at the front. In the middle of the floor was a cabin bed with a real slide. Luke's face lit up for the first time that day.

'How cool is that?' Sean asked.

'Cool,' Luke beamed, finally dropping his Iggle Piggle and running over to have his first turn. 'Henry will like this, Mummy,' he affirmed. 'When can he come and stay?'

'Not for a while, sweetheart,' said Kate. 'Probably when the weather gets warmer. Did you buy that?' she asked, turning to her husband.

'I saw it in a shop near work,' said Sean.

Kate smiled.

'I want him to come now,' Luke protested.

But his mother was no longer listening. His father had claimed her and was kissing her gently.

'Soppy,' grumbled Luke, going back to the slide.

'We'll be alright here, I think,' Sean said at last.

'I think so.'

'But I'm afraid I'll have to leave you for a couple of hours...'

'Work?' Kate's jaw tightened.

'Just a couple of things that have cropped up. Unfortunately I'm the only techie that really knows the system.'

'Great. You'll be in demand then.'

Kate watched the familiar tired, exasperated expression sweep across Sean's face.

'Don't be like that. It'll ease off after a month or so when everything is set up and it's all more routine.' He regarded her seriously. 'It's a move forward, Katie. I can earn good money here and when we get back we'll have the kind of life we both want. If just anyone could do this stuff then we wouldn't be here.' His arm made a sweeping gesture taking in the enormous bedroom. 'And you and Luke can explore this fantastic city.'

'Just try not to be too long.' She managed a smile.

'I won't be. But if you two fancy a walk then head towards the main road. There're shops and a supermarket up there, I think. I'll text, anyway, to let you know what time I'll be back. Bye, Luke.' He bent to give his son a hug.

'Where's Daddy going?'

'Work, of course,' said Kate.

'Does Daddy have to go to work here too?' Luke asked.

'I'm afraid so,' replied Kate. 'Just me and you again.'

Later that afternoon, after they had unpacked the cases, Kate and Luke walked up towards the larger road that ran perpendicular to theirs. Every few minutes trams rattled past the intersection of the two streets. A constant stream of bikes sped past and to Luke's considerable interest, many carried passengers.

'Maybe we could ride along like that,' Kate suggested.

Luke snorted. 'I can ride by myself,' he said.

Down a side road Kate could see children piling out of a primary school and the familiar confusion of waiting parents. The kids wore jeans and trainers and lots of the girls had straight, fair hair in ponytails that tumbled forwards as they turned upside down on the railings.

'No uniform,' Kate murmured. 'I forgot that children here don't wear uniforms to school.'

'But I'm going to have a red sweatshirt, aren't I, when I go?' said Luke, fingering Percy in his pocket,

'You will when we go back to England but not while you're here.'

Luke's forehead creased and his hand closed tightly around his toy engine.

The main road was busy with shops and bikes and trams. The bustle reminded Kate of London, though without the stink of diesel fumes. They trailed slowly along, gazing into the shop windows; grocers' with exotic fruits, hand-crafted toys, chic designer clothes and a shop that sold enormous pieces of sparkly costume jewellery. Her spirits lifted. This could be okay, after all.

When they got back to the apartment it was almost tea time. Luke insisted on having one turn on the climbing frame in the park before they went in.

Kate watched him clambering up the bars. At the top, he waved. A solitary conqueror. She waved back, swallowing hard.

It was dark when Sean finally texted to say he was on his way home.

'I can stay awake, can't I?' Luke demanded, whizzing Percy round the rim of the bath.

'Of course,' Kate agreed, after all, hadn't that been the point of this move – no more lengthy commuting, more time at home? But another half an hour passed before she heard the key in the front door and the click of the unfamiliar lock.

'He-llo,' Sean called, hanging up his coat and pushing open the sitting room door. The house smelled of meat and herbs. He suddenly remembered he hadn't eaten lunch. Kate was sitting with her feet up on the black leather sofa, reading.

'Hello,' she replied, without glancing up.

'What's up?'

'Nothing.' She turned a page, wondering if Sean could see the almost imperceptible shake of her fingers.

'It doesn't look like nothing.'

She took a breath.

'Okay. Nothing except that it's our first day in Holland and you went out six hours ago saying you wouldn't be long. Luke's fallen asleep. He was waiting for you but he couldn't stay awake any longer.'

Sean peeled off his suit jacket and placed it on the back of one of the curved mahogany dining chairs.

'I had almost made it to the stairs when the boss called me in to check over a couple of things.' He shrugged helplessly. 'On the plus side I'm not as late as when I was commuting to London. It's only fifteen minutes to the office here, as long as I don't travel in the rush hour.'

'But if that just means you stay later at work it won't make much difference.' Kate threw the paperback on the sofa and crossed to the archway that led to the kitchen.

'Katie...' Sean caught her arm and spun her round. 'That's really not the plan, I promise.'

She was horrified to feel tears trickling out from under her lashes and dripping damply on her cheeks. He brushed them aside with a finger.

She looked at him doubtfully.

'And we'll have another baby, won't we?' she asked.

Sean bit his lip. Did it always have to come back to this?

'I don't know. But I think we stand more chance of it happening if we have other stuff going on. I'm not sure it's good to let it eat us up.'

'Eat me up, you mean,' said Kate, taking a breath.

'Yes. But our relationship too.' He looked her up and down. 'I never get the chance these days to tell you how much I fancy you.'

Kate's lips twitched. 'Do you then?'

'Of course I do. You're gorgeous.'

She placed the palms of her hands on his broad chest and looked up at him.

'Okay, after tea you can show me.'

Sean grinned. 'I will. We need to christen that enormous bed.'

Kate drew the curtains across the French windows to block out the lights from the surrounding apartments and stood with her back to Sean, holding the heavy fabric, unable to make herself turn round as he extinguished the overhead bulb and switched on the lamp. She heard the rustle of his suit trousers as they slid to the floor and the jingle of his belt as he picked them up and hung them over the back of the chair for the morning.

Now he would begin to unbutton his shirt, she thought, remembering how sweetly vulnerable he looked in underpants and socks. He would start to be aroused, to want her... Kate waited. His feet padded on the carpet, he reached out and touched her hair.

'Take these off.' He slipped a finger under the waistband of her jeans. She undid the button, the zip, and leant back against him. His mouth pressed hot on her neck. She turned to face him, kicking her Levis aside.

It was months since they had had such good sex, sex where they touched and kissed and didn't rush to climax and the possibility of conception. But still, when Sean had rolled across to his side of the mattress with a lopsided smile, Kate lay awake, tense in the unfamiliar darkness, and knew there would still be no baby.

Chapter 3

'The removal men should be here today,' said Sean, placing the usual mug of tea on Kate's bedside. 'I'll try and get home around lunchtime and see how it's going but I can't promise anything.'

'Lunchtime!' said Kate in dismay. 'And what am I supposed to do with our son while I try to organise the house?'

'Can't he just watch DVDs for a couple of hours while you get on with stuff?'

'A couple of hours. Is that how long you think it'll take?'

Sean's fingers twitched. 'I don't know. Look, I'll try to get back but I have to go just now. I've got a meeting at eight thirty.'

As he passed Luke's bedroom door the small boy zoomed down his slide and sped across the carpet to anchor his father's leg.

'No, don't go. I want to see the elephants today. Mummy said so.'

'Really?'

'Luke,' Kate called, sitting up against the pillows, 'I said the weekend. We need Daddy to take us in the car.'

'We'll go on Saturday,' said Sean. 'I promise.' He gently unclasped his son's fingers and made a dash for the stairs. 'Wave out of the window, Luke,' he called up as he opened the front door.

'So do we think he'll be back at lunchtime?' Kate sang in a brittle voice, trailing into Luke's bedroom as the car disappeared round the corner.

Luke shrugged. 'Prob'ly not.'

'No,' his mother continued. 'No, of course we don't.' Her mouth tightened. 'But we're starting not to care. Once the removal men have left I think we'll go on a tram and explore the city. How does that sound?'

Luke nodded. It certainly sounded much better than staying at home and being cross with Daddy.

By eleven o clock the removal men had been and gone. Boxes, rather than furniture had been unloaded, but there still seemed to be an awful lot of things. Kate eyed them wearily wishing Sean was around. It wasn't that she couldn't do it herself. Of course she could. She could unpack their belongings and make a home for the three of them in this apartment in this city. She could organise school for Luke, shop for food, pay bills, find out how the country worked and which buttons to press to operate its services. She didn't doubt her ability for a moment, but that wasn't the point. This move was supposed to be about them all; her, Sean and Luke as a family – hopefully with the addition of a second child too. That was what he had promised. But two days in and there was every indication that things were going to be pretty much the same as they had in Suffolk.

But perhaps she was being unfair. Sean was bound to be busy at first, wasn't he? She pulled a photo album out of one of the boxes and stuck it listlessly on the bookcase. What on earth had she decided to bring that for? It wasn't as if she had ever looked at it in England. She sighed. Her bad mood was probably just the result of the strain of the move and this whole baby-thing which seemed to run like a nasty knotted thread through everything she tried to do. She extracted the blender from a crate labelled *kitchen*, stood it on the work surface and pushed the rest to one side. It could all go in the cellar - there was no cupboard space in this prehistoric kitchen, anyway. She wiped her eyes with the back of her hands. Sean should have warned her, it would have saved a lot of time.

'Are you okay, Mummy?' enquired a small voice in the archway.

Luke! Kate looked up guiltily. How long had he been standing there?

18

'We should have stayed at home,' she said, letting her hands drop, 'and let Daddy come and see us at weekends.'

Luke shook his head fiercely. 'I like seeing Daddy after my bath,' he affirmed, forgetting apparently, that this hardly ever happened. He picked out his favourite rabbit dish and placed it in a cupboard beside a saucepan.

'We can put this here. Let me help you, Mummy.'

Kate smiled slowly and ruffled his hair. 'Okay. We'll put our best things away, then we'll have lunch, then we'll go and explore.'

'It's raining,' the child pointed out, indicating the damp patch of yard outside the kitchen door.

'That doesn't matter. We can explore a museum.'

'Can I take my bike?' He looked longingly at the blue two-wheeler that had arrived that morning in the van.

Kate shook her head. 'Not this time. We're going on a tram. It's kind of half-bus and half-train.'

Luke's face brightened but he managed a theatrical sigh.

'All right then.'

The tram stop was on an island in the middle of the road and they missed one trying to work out which direction they should be facing. A second came almost at once; a smart blue and white caterpillar. Luke and Kate jumped on excitedly and Kate sat down. Luke stayed standing up, holding on to the pole.

'Sit down, Luke.'

'Why? Lots of people are staying standing up.'

'Maybe they're not going very far.'

'Are we going far?'

'I don't really know. We'll have to listen to the driver when he makes announcements.'

'I like standing up,' said Luke, swinging out as they turned a corner. 'Is that the museum?'

'I think it's a library,' said Kate. 'Do you really not want to sit down?'

Luke shook his head.

It hardly mattered. Museumplein turned out not to be very far at all. They hopped out, holding hands uncertainly. The sky had remained grey, the clouds barely defined, but at least the rain had stopped. In front of them, at the far end of a long stretch of flat grass, the Rijksmuseum stood, ornate and imposing.

Empire architecture, Kate decided.

'Is that where we're going?' Luke asked.

'I don't know. It looks a bit stuffy.' This building would no doubt house the Rembrandts, the Vermeers, the Frans Hals, and they would all need to be taken very seriously. Lots of snow scenes and seventeenth-century Dutch interiors.

'Let's try the Van Gogh museum instead,' she suggested. 'It's a whole building for one special artist. A very famous Dutch artist who loved to paint sunflowers.'

'Sunny flowers?' Luke was intrigued. 'Is that because there's never any sun here?'

'Kind of,' agreed Kate. 'In fact, he left Holland and went south to get more sunshine. It's just there look. We can walk to it.'

'It looks like lots of buildings joined together.'

'Right again. I think they built an extension to make more room.'

'I like the other museum better,' said Luke. 'It's more like a castle.'

'We'll try that one another day.'

Outside the Van Gogh Museum a line of people stood patiently waiting.

'We'll have to queue for a bit,' Kate apologised.

''S okay. I don't much mind.'

They edged forward slowly and Luke amused himself jumping up and down the steps. As they neared the doors, he suddenly squeezed under the barrier and darted inside.

'Wait! Luke!'

He grinned impishly and waved through the glass.

'Luke!' Kate gasped again as a man wearing a battered brown leather jacket loomed behind the child, placed a large hand on his shoulder and said something, presumably in Dutch. Were they going to get thrown out before they had even got in? The little boy swung around in confusion. But perhaps the stranger switched to English because Luke suddenly nodded and pointed at his mother. Watching anxiously from her place on the steps, Kate found herself gazing straight into a pair of peculiarly piercing blue eyes which flickered over her with a mixture of warmth and amusement. Their owner was probably smiling but his expression amounted to a softening of his features rather than a widening of his lips, and his hair, more blond than brown, was pulled back into a pony tail.

No one ever tries that look in England, Kate thought, but here, somehow, it worked. Instantly Amsterdam began to seem different and exciting. The man seemed to be having quite a conversation with Luke who was responding eagerly. Kate scuffed her feet against the concrete, trying to hurry the queue forward so she could join in, but the two elderly Americans in front of her were not to be rushed.

Before she had made it inside, the stranger had given Luke a final pat on his shoulder and was pushing open the door to go out. He reached Kate just as she got to the ticket office.

'Rudy,' he said in fluent, accented English, stretching out a hand which she hesitantly took. 'Great kid, you have there.'

Well, I think so...' she stammered, confused by the candid, appraising and completely _un_British way he was looking at her.

'Enjoy your visit,' he added. 'It's a fantastic city.'

She opened her mouth to reply, then closed it again. He had already gone, bounding down the steps, vaulting onto the saddle of a battered pushbike and disappearing into the traffic.

Wow. Kate grinned. Maybe this was the kind of Dutch guy that Paula had envisaged. Well, he had certainly given her a buzz.

'Madam. Madam....' The woman behind the grill was waving an arthritic hand to attract her attention. She shook herself.

'Of course. Sorry. One adult and one child.' She bent towards Luke. 'What was he saying to you?'

'Who?'

'The man with the ponytail.'

'Oh. Him.' Luke frowned. 'He said he was a painter. I asked if he had done the paintings in here, but he said that was someone called Van Cough, but we won't be able to meet him because he's dead.' He paused, trying to remember. 'He also said it's a very good museum.'

'Really?'

'Yes,' Luke nodded emphatically. 'I told him I wanted to see the sunny flowers because it rains too much here. And he said I was right.'

'The sunny flowers it is then.'

Kate took her son's hand and together they climbed the steps to the first floor, dodging between the shuffling clusters of Japanese tourists and the wealthy Americans propelled ever onwards by the audio guides clamped firmly to their ears.

Entering the main gallery, Kate caught her breath. The walls were filled with paintings; one man's vision of the world. The effect was stunning. She walked across the room slowly, enthralled. There were Luke's Sunflowers and beside them Van Gogh's bedroom; the wooden bed, neat with its plumped-up pillows and brick red cover, the washstand with its jug and bowl, the looking glass that would reflect the artist back to himself. All of it was familiar from a million posters but now here was the real thing with the paint thick and still glistening on the canvas, as he had left it. She pictured how he would have been, sitting there in the corner, just off camera with his brushes and easels, his palette. He had obviously painted quickly, completely absorbed in his work.

To have this concentration, Kate thought, this passion infused into every single moment, no wonder he went mad.

'I can't see,' Luke complained, tugging her jacket, craning his neck upwards.

Kate crouched down beside the boy and together they stared up at the *Sunflowers*. The awkward angle spoilt the picture

'I could pick you up,' she offered.

'Na, it's okay.'

Kate imagined Van Gogh lifting his painting from the wall and standing it on the floor for Luke. She pictured him more at ease with this child than with the smartly-dressed adults who were admiring his masterpieces. But perhaps that was wrong. Perhaps he wasn't really comfortable with anyone.

Did he know how good he was? she wondered, looking round the hall. Did he know he was Van Gogh?

'Mummy, I'm thirsty,' said Luke after about fifteen minutes.

'Oh,' said Kate, nonplussed. She had been engrossed in the paintings. 'But look, Luke, Van Gogh went to Paris then to Arles. He painted lots of pictures in France. We went to France on our camping holiday.'

Luke pulled a face, refusing to be drawn by this tenuous connection.

'Don't you like the paintings?'

'I do, but I'm thirsty. Can we go to the café now?'

Kate looked at the price on the entrance tickets and nodded reluctantly. 'We'll have a drink then we'll come back for another look before we go home.'

'I think I'll get a museum pass,' Kate decided, as they stirred their hot chocolate. 'That way we can come whenever we like and it won't matter if we only stay ten minutes.'

'Can we go back on the tram?' Luke asked.

'Of course. But first I want to stop at the shop and buy some postcards.'

'Will you play football with me in the park when we get home?'

Kate sagged, glancing unenthusiastically out of the windows towards Museumplein where the trees shifted energetically in a gusting wind.

'Just a quick game, I suppose, if it's not too muddy.'

'Hurry up with your drink, then,' said Luke.

A gang of boys were already installed on the patch of scruffy turf when they walked past the park. Two or three women, presumably their mums, were sitting on the benches with their legs crossed inside their high-heeled boots, chatting. They didn't seem to be paying much attention to their sons. Kate moved across to stand near them and watched as Luke, so confident at his local park in England, hung around hopefully on the edge of the grass waiting to be noticed. At last, after a very long five minutes, an older boy beckoned to him. Luke hurried over, but his face creased in bewilderment as he was given instructions in Dutch. Kate's hands twitched inside her pockets but she managed to keep her feet glued firmly to the ground.

'Don't worry,' a tall thin woman, murmured, appearing at her side and exhaling clouds of smoke across Kate's air space. 'They are nice boys.'

Kate smiled and tried not to lean away, grateful at being addressed in her own language. To her relief, Luke seemed to have grasped which way he was shooting and who was on his team. He was sent to defend his goal which consisted of two, now very dirty, coats.

'I am Saskia,' the woman offered, extending her hand. Kate guessed she was a few years her senior and her ultra-tanned skin suggested she had recently returned from a skiing holiday. Her aura of robust good-health left Kate feeling puny and pale.

'Kate,' she replied. 'And that's Luke, my son. He doesn't really know anyone yet. We've only just moved here.'

'And he is going to go to the English school.' Saskia phrased it as a statement rather than a question.

'Oh no,' Kate corrected hurriedly. 'We want him to go to Dutch school with everyone else so he learns the language.'

'So he will soon be bi-lingual,' said Saskia, pulling deeply on her cigarette. 'And why not? There is a good one nearby. Heijn goes there.' She pointed to the tallest boy in the group. 'But I don't think they will be in the same class. Your son is quite small, no. Perhaps he will be in the nursery group?'

'He'll be five in the autumn.'

'Really? He looks younger.'

Kate blinked. Did he?

'So,' Saskia continued. 'He can start immediately in the reception class. Heijn is already six, but they will be together just for a couple of months until the summer.'

'Luke will be pleased about that,' said Kate, with feeling.

'The tram home was packed,' Kate grumbled to Sean that evening as she stirred a box of coconut milk into a pungent chicken curry. 'I could hardly keep hold of Luke.'

'I'm not surprised. At five o clock in a capital city what did you expect?'

'I don't know.' She had somehow forgotten about rush hours on public transport. 'Maybe I should get a bike and Luke can ride on the back like all the other kids do.'

'Probably makes sense. What did Luke make of the museum?'

'He liked it, for about quarter of an hour. Then he wanted to come back and play football over the road. Luckily some other boys let him join in so I didn't have to play with him. One of the mums came over and spoke to me. She lives round the corner in Apollolaan.'

'So you both made some friends today.' Sean's face brightened. He had been expecting scowls and recriminations for leaving Kate alone with the removal van so anything positive was a huge relief. 'Curry smells great, by the way.'

'Good. It's just about ready.' She passed him a piled-up plate. 'Friends? I wouldn't go that far. But at least I talked to someone and Luke got a game of football. Only for a few minutes though, because it was already late when we got back from the museum. And freezing cold.' She recalled the wind whipping through the climbing frame making the metal sing. 'If you'd been back a bit earlier,' she couldn't stop herself adding, 'Luke would have told you himself.'

Sean's mouth tightened and he reached across to the fridge for a beer. His first few weeks at work had gone well and he was quickly gaining a reputation for finding solutions to apparently impossible problems. He refused to let Kate's nagging drag his mood down.

'I keep trying to explain,' he said, enunciating slowly. 'It won't be forever. It's only until it's all set up.'

Kate pressed her forefinger firmly onto a grain of rice, squishing it onto the painted surface of the table.

'So you say... By the way,' she added. 'I think I'm going to invest in a museum card. The Van Gogh gallery is really amazing.'

'Good idea.' Her husband pushed away his now empty plate away and reached for his briefcase. He caught Kate's glance. 'Sorry. Just got a couple of bits to finish off.'

Go ahead, she thought, staring at the top of Sean's head over the lid of the laptop. I have hardly spoken to anyone all day, but just ignore me, that's fine. She recalled the painter-guy with his vivid blue stare. He had inspected her with obvious approval, made her feel she was worth looking at, that she might actually matter. She picked up the dirty plates and tried to remember, had Sean *ever* looked at her like that?

Chapter 4

'It doesn't look much like my school,' said Luke.

He sat on his saddle outside the gates and pushed the blue bike backwards and forward with the balls of his feet.

'Not like your school in England, no,' Kate conceded. Glossop Road Primary was a purpose-built Edwardian building with a large tarmacked playground containing a two-classroom port-a-cabin and markings for a netball court. Luke had been looking forward to starting there. Now, where once there had been red bricks and tall gothic windows, there was this strange, avant-garde construction. The gates were firmly shut but it was easy enough to see though the stems of wrought iron that the playground was very small indeed.

It's a city, Kate reminded herself. What did you expect?

More disconcertingly, the actual building resembled nothing she had ever seen before. In fact, it was more like a smart block of flats than a school; every floor had a balcony and wherever possible glass had been used in place of more solid materials. Vitamin D deficiency wouldn't be an issue, Kate thought wryly. If there was ever any sunshine the kids would get it. She pressed the bell.

Almost immediately the gate buzzed open and they were shown up to the headteacher's office by a motherly-looking secretary who smiled encouragingly at Luke. The principal, Rita Thijs, turned out to be much more formidable. She was a woman in her forties, impeccably dressed in patent leather court shoes and a navy skirt-suit which adhered snugly to her solid and substantial curves. Her hair, straight, thick and the colour of Devon butter, had been expertly clasped into a French pleat. She towered several centimetres above Kate and predictably, spoke excellent English.

'Fortunately, we can accommodate your son,' she said, settling herself behind her large desk and gesturing them to sit down. 'Luke can start in two weeks, after the Easter holidays.' She smiled briefly. 'In the reception class he will learn through play. We emphasise motor skills and socialisation.'

'Motor skills?' Kate repeated. 'What about reading?' She had been teaching Luke letters since he was two-and-a-half.

'It is not the policy in Holland. We don't find it beneficial when they are still so young. They learn to read in the next class which they enter at age six. Then, with all the techniques they have been practising, they learn very quickly.'

Kate looked doubtful.

'Why do you want him to attend Dutch school Mrs..er..Butter-worth?' Rita Thijs enquired. 'Do you know there is an English school very close by in Cliostraat?'

'Oh yes. Yes,' affirmed Kate, who didn't. 'But we would like him to integrate and learn the language.' English-speaking school had never been seriously considered. She and Sean had decided that as long as they were in Amsterdam they should make an effort to be part of the local community.

Mrs Thijs inclined her head graciously. 'Of course. So kindly complete these registration papers and we'll see your son after the Easter break.'

As they left the office the school bell rang and a river of jostling children came cascading down the narrow stairs. Luke eyed them with trepidation.

'Don't worry,' the head teacher reassured him from her doorway. 'The first classroom is all alone on the other side of the play area. And everyone is a bit excited because it's the last day before the holidays.'

He glanced at her gratefully.

'So when can I start school, Mummy? What did the lady say?' asked Luke tugging his mother's sleeve, as they slid open the gates and retrieved Luke's bike from the rack.

'She said you can start in two weeks, after Easter. You heard her, sweetheart.'

'Is she my teacher?'

'No, she's the head teacher. She's the boss, in charge of all the teachers.'

'What does my teacher look like?'

'I don't know, but I think she's quite young. That's what Mrs Thijs said. Apparently her name is Maud.'

'Not Mrs Jenkins?'

'No, sweetheart. She's the teacher at Glossop Road Primary in England. You know that, Luke. Two weeks isn't really very long and as soon as you get to school you can start to make some friends.' Kate smiled with deliberate enthusiasm.

'But Mummy,' whispered Luke, 'they all speak funny. I don't know if they understand English.'

'That's Dutch. You'll learn it very quickly. Don't worry, it'll be fine,' she squeezed his hand.

Mother and son stood together for a moment surveying the children charging round the cramped playground. Some older boys were kicking a tennis ball, others swarmed over a climbing frame.

'I can't see any grass,' said Luke.

'That's because we're in a big town,' Kate explained. 'There's not as much space as at home.'

Unimpressed, Luke climbed on to his bike and twizzled the pedals sulkily.

'Don't forget your helmet,' Kate reminded him.

'No one wears a helmet here. I'll look silly' He tossed his head and cycled off along the path before his mother could argue. Kate looked after him apprehensively. Perhaps they were asking a bit much.

'He can start almost straight away,' Kate reported later to Sean. 'It's a kind of preschool class between four and six. They do drawing and painting but he won't learn to read.'

'Well, there's no rush is there?' asked Sean, glancing up from his laptop.

'I don't know. Henry will be learning to read. Luke might feel left behind.'

'Henry won't be learning Dutch,' Sean countered. 'And you can teach him to read if he really wants to learn.'

'There's an English school quite near here, apparently. Maybe he should go to there?' Kate suggested, her hands twisting.

'Why?'

'Because he already speaks English.'

'But he'd miss out on an opportunity to become bi-lingual and we'd just end up as part of the ex-pat network. I thought we didn't want that. We discussed it, didn't we? Is that what you want now?'

They had indeed discussed it over several evenings in their Suffolk kitchen. Once Kate had actually come round to the idea of the move, Amsterdam had felt like something that should be experienced to the fullest; an opportunity for a genuine, exciting adventure.

'No,' she said, aloud. 'No, I want to see this city from the inside. But it's tempting. It would be so much easier for Luke, that's all.'

'Do you think he'll have problems?' Sean took off his glasses and rubbed them on a soft cotton handkerchief pulled from his trouser pocket. Kate always found this an oddly vulnerable gesture. It had been one of the first things she had liked about him, after his rather hesitant smile.

'Give the Dutch school a try for a few months, see how he gets on,' Sean suggested, wondering who Kate was actually trying to protect. He maintained that Luke was far more resilient than his mother would allow. Was she worried about him breaking away from her? Exploring a new language and finally being able to hold conversations she wouldn't understand?

Kate nodded reluctantly. 'See how he is when they break up for the summer, you mean?'

'Exactly.' Sean replaced his spectacles and returned to his laptop.

So that was it; she and Luke had two more weeks together before school started and he was sucked into wider society. It would be good for him, of course, Kate knew that, as long as he managed okay with the language. And really all the research – she had spent hours trawling the internet for articles related to bilingualism– suggested he would.

'Just me then,' she sighed, glancing across at Sean who was frowning over some spreadsheet. She picked up the biography of Van Gogh she had bought in the museum shop and curled up on the sofa. 'I had better get something out of this place.'

Chapter 5

'That's the Artis!' exclaimed Luke in excitement. 'Where the elephants are. I can read the letters on the gates.'

'I'll drop you off here and find somewhere to park,' Sean suggested, pulling up beside the kerb. 'It looks pretty busy.'

Kate and Luke hurriedly scrambled out.

'Daddy is coming back, isn't he?' Luke asked, as they waited on the pavement.

'Of course. He won't be a minute. He doesn't want you to have to walk too far. You might have a lot of walking to do inside.'

'To see all the animals do you mean?' said Luke, hopping from one foot to the other.

'That's exactly what I mean,' Kate agreed, ruffling his hair.

'There he is!' Luke slipped his mother's hand and charged through the throngs of people to launch himself at his father.

Sean laughed, catching him easily.

'Steady on! Okay, let's see about tickets shall we?'

For once it wasn't raining and Kate was hopeful that the sun might actually come out. She had felt able to dispense with some of the more constricting winter garments and without the crown of a woolly hat Luke's hair swung softly as he moved. She watched her men together and saw how little Sean fussed Luke, not seeming worried if he lost him briefly in the crowd, not expecting him to stay glued to his side as she did. And Luke's face, as he trotted towards her, bore no sign of the tiny thoughtful crease that hovered too often on his forehead. She had a brief image of her arms as wings encircling her son so protectively that he was unable to fight his way out from beneath them.

God, I need to move on, she thought, but where to?

Sean led the way through the gates and bought tickets. Luke darted through after him. Somehow Kate managed to get stuck a couple of people behind.

'Stay with Daddy, sweetheart,' she heard herself call. But of course he was going to, that was why he'd squeezed through in the first place.

'I've bought tickets for the year,' Sean said, grinning. 'I thought we'd probably be coming a few more times and that makes it much cheaper.'

'Yeeesss!' shouted Luke throwing his fist in the air. 'We could even come without Mummy,' he added, blushing crimson as he realised Kate had caught them up. Her smile faltered a fraction.

'Well, I don't want to spend every Sunday visiting elephants,' she agreed.

'Daddy says they're called *olifanten* in this country,' admonished Luke.

'*Olifanten*, then,' Kate sighed.

'I'm not sure I do either,' said Sean, reaching across to take her hand and pulling her gently to stand beside him.

'Come *on*,' said the small boy impatiently, tugging his father's coat.

'We're coming, Luke.'

In front of them stretched a large, paved avenue lined with trees. In the spring sunshine the leaves were beginning to unfurl, breaking up the black monotony of the winter branches.

'There's a petting zoo, Luke. You can stroke the animals in there,' said Kate, pointing to a fenced area full of little huts and small children.

'What kind of animals?' Luke demanded, torn between the desire to stroke the pigmy goats he could see eyeing him through the fence and his wish to see the more important animals as soon as possible.

'Well, not *olifanten*, obviously. But we have lots of time.'

'O-kay then,' he conceded. 'If you say so.'

Kate laughed, aware that the petting zoo would remain her idea, but also knowing that Luke was desperate to go in.

'I'd like to stroke those goats,' she said. 'Come on.'

'And you, Daddy,' said Luke sternly.

'I'm just going to stay here and watch you,' said Sean shaking his head. He leaned forward with his forearms on the fence. 'Look, I can see you from here. I might even take a photo for Facebook then Henry's Mummy will see it.' He slid his mobile out of his pocket and aimed the camera eye at his wife and son. 'There,' he said, snapping Kate and Luke bending over a miniature white and black goat. 'Perfect.'

'Let's stroke that little pig, now.' Luke rushed over and crouched beside a small, fat hog with a long pink snout, droopy ears and a classic curly tail.

'Another photo, Daddy,' he called, looking up. But Sean had turned away and was talking into his phone.

'Ohhh,' pouted Luke.

'Never mind,' said Kate. 'You stand there and I'll take one.'

'Can you put them on Facebook, too?'

No, sweetheart. Sorry.'

'No point taking it then, is there?'

'There is,' Kate replied. I can use it as my phone screen.' She tapped a few buttons and showed Luke the result.

'It's nice,' he conceded. 'But Henry can't see it there.'

'We'll make sure Daddy takes one of you with the elephants for Facebook,' consoled Kate.

'*Olifanten*,' said Luke. 'You forgot again. Okay, then. Can we go there now?'

'We can,' his mother assented. 'Let's go and tell your Dad to get off that silly phone.'

Side by side they marched through the gate and back to where Sean was standing.

'Sean...' Kate began.

'Dad-dy!' said Luke.

Sean pulled an apologetic face and lifted his hand to shoo them back.

'Just a minute,' he mouthed.

Kate folded her arms across her chest and stood staring at him. Luke copied her. Sean turned and took a couple of steps away from them. They waited.

'He's not s'posed to be at work now, is he, Mummy?'

'No, sweetheart, he's not.'

Eventually Sean lowered his mobile and put it back in the pocket of his jeans. He took a deep breath and released it slowly through pursed lips. Kate watched him unmoving. Luke, who had tired of the folded arms posture was hopping between the paving slabs trying not to tread on the lines.

'The bears might eat me,' he was muttering to himself. 'And there's prob'ly real bears here too. Better watch out.'

'So?' said Kate.

Sean took off his glasses, examined them against the light, extracted a handkerchief from somewhere deep inside his coat and rubbed the lenses gently.

'I need to call in at the office on the way home. One of the sales guys has been in working over the weekend and the system's playing up.'

'Can't it wait 'til tomorrow?'

'Not really.' He replaced his glasses and studied a sign about the giant anteater that apparently lived in the bamboo hut just behind the railings. 'I'm worried we're going to lose data.'

'You mean you actually want to go now.'

Sean turned to face his wife.

'No, Katie. That's not remotely what I want to do. I want to stay here at the zoo with you and Luke and have some fun with my family for a change.'

'But?' Kate's eyebrows lifted expectantly.

'First problem...' he pursed his lips and blew out noisily, '...my boss is American. He thinks – as they all seem to – that there is no life beyond corporate life. Work comes first and everything else is just an add-on. Second problem – as I explained, I'm the only techie who really knows the system. I'm supposed to be training up someone else but they haven't actually employed this person yet. *Ergo*, every time there's a hitch, they call me.'

'And how about if you couldn't go?'

Sean shrugged. 'Well, then I couldn't go. But I can go and Cassidy knows it.'

'Who's Cassidy?' asked Luke.

'My boss,' said Sean. 'He's the American.'

'Is he very fat with a big cowboy hat?' Luke enquired.

'Ha!' Sean burst out laughing. 'No, he's tall and very athletic-looking with a kind of pickled tan.'

'A bit like my new friend Saskia then,' said Kate.

'It's a local type,' said Sean, still grinning. 'Anyway...' He looked from his wife to his son in search of inspiration. 'The question is...'

'I know,' said Luke, helpfully. 'We'll all go to see the *olifanten*, then we'll all go to your office. I want to see it and I should think Mummy does too.'

'Does she?' Sean turned to Kate. 'Do you?'

'Why not,' she conceded. 'It wouldn't hurt just this once.'

'Good. I shouldn't be there long. Afterwards we could go and get a pizza or something. Save cooking.'

'Hurray!' cried Luke.'

Kate smiled. 'Okay. Let's do it.'

Sean studied the zoo map.

'It seems that, in accordance with sod's law, the elephant house is right over the other side.'

'Lead on,' said Kate.

'Yes, lead on,' echoed Luke, taking his father's hand.

'We can't stop for anything else though,' Sean warned, setting a pace that resembled a route march.

'Can we come back next weekend, then?' the boy puffed, jogging to keep up. 'You said you had tickets for a year,'

'I'm not promising. We'll have to see.'

'Come on, Mummy,' the boy cried, seeing Kate was lagging behind.

'I'm coming. I'm just a bit tired.'

Sean threw a sharp glance over his shoulder. Kate shrugged, adjusted her scarf and stopped deliberately in front of the chimpanzees.

'I'll catch you up,' she called after them.

The chimps swung across the bars of their enclosure, sleekly groomed and muscled, their pink bottoms grotesquely distended, ignoring their audience save for the occasional fleeting glance. A tiny baby clung resolutely to her mother's tummy fur.

You wouldn't want to fall from up there, thought Kate. The chimp stopped her random swinging and squatted on a wide branch stroking the back of her baby's neck with gentle fingers. Kate watched spellbound. The animal raised her head and just for a second their eyes locked. The chimp mother, one great hand resting on her infant, sent a look of supreme contentment across the void of a million years. Kate blinked hard and turned away. Her mobile was vibrating in her pocket. She knew it would be her husband.

'Hi, where are you?'

'Pretty much where you left me,' she admitted, turning back to the chimpanzee house for a last look, but the mother and her baby had disappeared into their den.

'We need to go now. Stay where you are, we're coming back that way.'

'But Mummy hasn't seen the *olifanten*.' Kate heard Luke protest.

'She'll have to see them another day,' said Sean. 'We have to go to the office. You're coming with me remember.'

'Borrring!' said Luke.

'Yep,' his father replied. 'Be there in two secs,' he added into the phone.

Kate stared up at the steel bars of the enclosure and wondered if female chimpanzees had trouble conceiving in captivity, if they somehow assimilated the hang ups and neuroses of their human captors. She thought she remembered reading something of the kind. It wouldn't be surprising.

'Mummy!' yelled Luke as he raced towards Kate, launching himself at her like a small explosive missile.

'Urgh!' She staggered backwards, not fully prepared for the force of the assault,

'Luke,' reproved Sean. 'You can do that to me, not your Mum. You'll knock her over.'

Sean reached out to take Kate's hand, but she pulled away. His lips compressed fractionally, one hand went up instinctively to rub the soft prickles of his scalp.

'It's a bit severe,' Kate had complained when he first came home with his 'barely there' haircut.

'It's falling out,' replied Sean bluntly. 'It's either this or a comb-over.'

'I thought it was alright before. Not a comb-over, just a bit longer.'

'Looks untidy. Looks like I haven't noticed it's thinning.'

The conversation had taken place one evening a last autumn. Sean had avoided her eyes, occupied himself by rooting through the medicine cupboard for an aspirin.

'Headache,' he explained.

Kate still wasn't sure that she liked it, though she could sympathise with Sean's reasoning. He was thirty-eight. It was an awkward time career-wise apparently. He had told her this, defending his long hours at the office. 'This is when you find out if you're destined for higher things – or not, basically,' was what he had said.

'Are you, then?' Kate asked.

'Borderline,' said Sean. 'That's why I have to work so hard.'

Kate frowned. 'Why only borderline. You're good aren't you?'

'Not good enough. You have to be good at your job and a good corporate player especially with all these Yank consultants around. You have to have the right politics in the company, make the right noises, you know?' He smiled bleakly. 'That's what I'm not so great at. Bit of a maverick sometimes. Don't really take it seriously.'

'Oh,' said Kate, feeling she should have known these things without being told. It was a long time since she had been part of a big office. 'Does it matter, then, if you don't get there?'

Sean paused, his face screwed up thoughtfully.

'It does because, it's more interesting to be in charge of the project than doing what someone else tells you to. And if you're not in charge there is almost certainly going to be some idiot who doesn't really know what he's doing ordering you around.'

'Oh,' said Kate again.

And Sean was still striving to make it to that elusive next level. That was what all this was all about, she supposed. That was why they were leaving the zoo early. She pulled her coat round her, pinned it in place with both arms and walked straight ahead towards the gates a pace or two behind Sean and Luke who was skipping beside him.

'Where's the car?' she asked.

'Just round the corner. We can easily walk there.'

'How long will it take us to get to your office, Daddy?'

'Only about 15 minutes.' There shouldn't be much traffic today.'

'It's just outside the city,' said Sean, as the Mercedes purred into life.

Chapter 6

The offices were in a tall, purpose built block on the edge of a large estate of similar buildings. The huge blue Ikea warehouse with the bright yellow logo was just visible on the other side of the industrial park. Luke got out of the car and looked around him, obviously unimpressed. Kate wondered what he had expected. Some exciting, workshop-type place, perhaps? Sean used a special code to open the door. That was more interesting, but Luke got annoyed because Sean refused to trust him with the number.

'Your memory is far too good,' explained his father, making it into a joke. 'You might give out the information under torture.'

Once inside, Sean called the lift and they rose smoothly to the eighth floor.

'There are three more,' said Luke, reading the lift board.

The eighth floor was full of desks and computers.

'This is where I come every day,' said Sean. 'I usually sit here.' He had a well-placed desk in a corner next to a window. On the desk was a photo of Kate and Luke on the beach in France the previous summer. They looked relaxed and happy. Their matching copper-brown hair had acquired matching blond highlights, bleached-in by the strong sunshine.

Kate picked up the photo and looked at Sean.

'I didn't know you had a picture of us,' she said.

Sean pulled out his wallet and extracted a different photo. It was Kate, just after they had met, on a day out in London. She was standing with her back to the river, a breeze lifting her hair.

'You probably didn't know I had this either,' he said.

Kate blinked. 'I look so young.'

'You were, I suppose. We were.' He folded the wallet and replaced it in his pocket.

'Coffee, maybe?'

She nodded.

'The machine's over here. I'll switch it on. You can help yourself once it's warmed up. There might be some juice in the fridge too. I'm just going to find Gert. He's usually next door.'

'I want to come,' said Luke immediately.

Sean threw a pleading glance at Kate.

'Stay here with me, sweetheart,' she said. 'Daddy won't be long. We'll have a drink and play noughts and crosses.'

'If I have to,' Luke sighed.

Half an hour passed without any sign of Sean returning. Kate contemplated another coffee but she had turned off the machine and decided she couldn't really be bothered to wait for it to warm up again. She looked longingly across the skyline towards Ikea, home of pale wood and bright objects. This office was so dull, grey and lifeless devoid of its staff. Luke had long abandoned their game and was crawling around on the floor pretending to shoot imaginary enemies.

'I'm just going to find your Dad,' Kate decided, 'to see what he's up to.'

'I'm coming,' shouted Luke, jumping up quickly and cracking his head on the corner of a desk. He burst instantly into fierce tears.

Kate rushed over to him and pulled him onto her lap, rubbing the bruise with the palm of her hand. Luke howled louder and Sean appeared beside them.

'Okay,' he said quietly. 'Not a very successful experiment. I think we'd better leave now. Let's go and find that pizza.'

Luke's wails subsided into hiccups.

'Did you sort it?' asked Kate, handing the little boy to her husband to carry out to the lift.

Sean put him on the ground.

'I think you can walk,' he murmured. 'No, I didn't really sort it, but I've made sure it won't do any damage. I'll need to get in early tomorrow though to fix it properly before anyone else arrives. It's not operational at the moment.'

'How early is that?' asked Kate

Sean pulled a face. 'As soon after six as possible.'

They arrived at *Le Quattro Stagioni* before the real start of the evening rush. Late on a Sunday afternoon it wasn't hard to find a place to park.

'This is where Gert always comes,' explained Sean. 'I think he actually lives in the next street. It's good because it's pretty central but too tucked away for the tourists to find easily. Our side of town too, so if we like it we could make it a regular stop.'

Kate looked up and down the road. This was a million miles from Suffolk; rows of narrow, elegant facades, filled with wide-windows beyond which Amsterdammers, she imagined, lived interesting, urban lives full of breakfasts in cafés and lunchtime walks in the park. Pushbikes were chained to lampposts, coloured pots containing stark winter foliage in clever shapes had been placed outside little shops selling things you wanted to touch and take home. Despite the chill of the air and the persistent pale grey of the sky it felt like a street she would like to live in herself.

'The Vondelpark's just round the corner,' Sean was saying. 'You and Luke could walk there if you wanted to. We're not really very far from home.'

Kate's eyebrows lifted. From the location angle, this move was definitely getting better.

On the inside the pizzeria was a wonderful mixture of contemporary practicality and period detail. Luke rushed over to a table by a window and the Italian waiter smiled indulgently.

Kate examined the menu, running a finger down the selection of pizzas. 'What are you having?'

'Not sure,' Sean replied, taking off his glasses and giving them a wipe. 'Let's have a look.'

He's still worried about work, Kate realised. She pushed the thought away and concentrated on choosing her meal. 'A glass of wine, I think, definitely.'

Sean ordered a carafe of the house red and an apple juice. Almost immediately the waiter returned with the drinks, a colouring sheet and a box of wax crayons.

'For the young man,' he explained, putting them down in front of Luke. Luke beamed and Kate felt some of the tension that had been bouncing between the three of them, begin to slide away.

'Wonderful pizza,' she enthused as they made their way back to the car. 'Really light and crispy like we had in Rome that time. Do you remember?'

Sean glanced at his wife. Of course he remembered Rome. A fantastic weekend snatched just before they were married. Sex, food and culture had proved the perfect antidotes to pre-wedding nerves – exactly the kind of feeling he had hoped they might be able to recapture here in Amsterdam. But with the job as it was at the moment and Kate so tense so much of the time, there didn't seem to be much chance of that. Still, the restaurant had been good, and importantly, on his current salary they could afford to come back – every week if they wanted.

The meal was a success, at least, thought Kate, later, sitting at the dressing table and brushing her hair with one of the silver-backed brushes she had brought from home. Stroking it, rather, Sean always teased, since the soft bristles hardly penetrated beyond the top layer. It had always tended to be fine, now in the dry static of the central heating, it took flight, hovering in bronzed strands before sinking slowly back onto Kate's shoulders where it shone the colour of toasted sugar in the lamplight. The heavy curtains had been drawn tightly across the French windows shutting out the cold of the night and the lights from the flats opposite. Sean was showering. Kate could hear him humming to himself. Until she met her husband Kate had never believed that some people really did sing in the shower. But there it was. She studied her reflection as she massaged a smear of night cream into the skin around her eyes. Definitely glowing, but then, it was probably prime baby time. Maybe tonight?

When Sean emerged wrapped in his bathrobe it was clear the water had washed off some of the ease acquired in the restaurant. He gave her shoulder an absent squeeze.

'Have I got a clean shirt for the morning, Babe?'

Kate's hand flew to her mouth. 'Oh, no! Sorry. I don't seem to have got into a proper routine.'

His lips tightened fractionally. 'Never mind, I'll do it.'

As she crawled in between the sheets Kate heard the crash of the ironing board in the room next door. It would only take him a couple of minutes. She waited, conscious of her anxiety mounting. At last he returned, hung his shirt on the back of the chair, removed his bathrobe and slid in beside her, naked as usual and as always, somehow, warm. She nestled into him, letting her hand drift across his chest.

'I have to get up in six hours' time,' Sean murmured, catching her wrist. 'I'm sorry.' He hugged her clumsily, already dozing. She turned over, her abdomen aching with expectancy, and fell asleep with her hand between her legs.

Chapter 7

At least the roads are empty this time in the morning, Sean reflected, plugging his IPod into the car stereo. The main advantage of the generous company car policy, he considered, was that he got a decent music system in his vehicle. He didn't much care about speed but he hated tinny music. The sound of Snow Patrol filled his brain: *Chasing Cars*. He swallowed hard as the familiar lyrics crawled into his gut. Great for snuggling in bed next to Kate, but definitely not what was ordered at 6.15 on a Monday morning when he had a stinker of a technical problem to deal with.

He had placed a cup of tea on his wife's bedside before leaving not because he thought she would actually wake up and drink it but because not to would be like ignoring her. He wanted Kate to know that he had thought of her, that he had touched the soft hair spread across the pillow. Her forehead had creased as he did so, a tiny line between her brows. She had grunted and nuzzled further under the duvet. Sean had watched her for a moment, pensive. So far the whole move thing definitely wasn't going as well as he had hoped. They had been in the country barely a week but already her isolation and his workload were squeezing a relationship that was already under strain. Now instead of just a vague dissatisfaction with their life together which might conceivably have been remedied by a pay rise and a couple of weeks on a Caribbean island, their problems were threatening to harden into something brittle, something that might actually snap. If they hadn't let their house in Suffolk, Sean suspected Kate might have turned around and gone straight back home.

He had known that she wanted to make love last night. Of course he had. But he had also known why and the whole thing was beginning to make him freeze. He wasn't a baby-making machine, for Christ's sake, but a man who needed to be desired for himself. To be the object of desire wasn't just the prerogative of women, surely? Although they sometimes behaved as though it was. He had also been tired, preoccupied and had probably drunk more than he should have done. Plus, he had to admit, he had been a bit miffed that she hadn't ironed him a shirt. She wasn't his slave, he knew that, but if he had to keep up with domestic stuff too that would leave even less time to spend with Luke. Why was another bloody baby so important anyway? They already had a great kid. Surely what Kate needed was a life, something to immerse herself in that wasn't her son. He pulled up in front of traffic lights and flicked the IPod onto something more invigorating. He would be at the office in ten minutes and he really didn't need to be thinking about this stuff right now.

Although there were one or two cars in the car park the building felt deserted when Sean stepped inside. Chances were he wouldn't see anyone else for at least an hour or so. To punish himself for some unspecified offence, he decided to skip the lift and take the stairs. The generous roll of surplus calories that had accumulated round his waist over the last couple of years wobbled disconcertingly and around the fourth floor he began to seriously regret the decision. By the time he reached the eighth he was puffing like Percy the Green Engine. He wondered how all his Dutch colleagues seemed to stay in such good shape. He pushed open the doors to his office and stood for a moment breathing heavily. Through the windows opposite the great blue carcass of Ikea with its yellow logo imposed itself on the landscape with remorseless jollity in the emerging light. He turned away, bleary eyed, swallowed a couple of paracetamol from the packet in his briefcase and switched on his computer.

'Hey Sean, how's it going?'

Christ! Where had she come from? Sean looked up, blinked and yawned. It was the girl from downstairs. The one he had been trying very hard to avoid. He had danced with her at the

Melkweg the evening he had gone out with the guys from downstairs, just before Kate and Luke had moved over. Lenni? No, Lena, that was it. He remembered hazily that he had fondled her bum rather more than was strictly called for and blushed at the memory. Since then he had bumped into her a couple of times at the coffee machine. Presumably she was as addicted to her morning caffeine shot as he was. Sean always found himself surprised by her smallness, barely up to his shoulder, and the fact that she always managed to convey exactly the same level of bubbliness regardless of weather or the time of day. An achievement he considered impressive but faintly suspect.

'What? Sorry,' he mumbled. 'Tired.'

'Here, you look like you could use this.' She placed a steaming styrofoam cup in front of him and Sean wondered how he could possibly have forgotten something so essential. That probably accounted for his headache. She stood over him like a nurse while he sipped his drink.

Lena's precise role in the company was a mystery to Sean. Her job appeared to involve something obscure concerning liaison between the two parties in the joint venture. But what exactly she was supposed to do and how she would know when she had done it, he really could not imagine. He had always thought he would hate a job like that. At least with the technical stuff you could see you were aiming for even if you struggled to get there.

'Er, great. Thanks. Probably just what I needed.' He glanced up at her, managing a small smile and noticing that her skin was the same shade of 'café crème' as they had used in their sitting room in Suffolk. How did she manage to look so composed and awake at this hour? Even when she worked in the West End Kate had always dashed out of the house with only half her make up on.

'Do you always get here at this time in the morning?' he asked.

'Not always,' Lena admitted, perching on his desk, 'but pretty often. In theory it means I can get away earlier.'

'And does that happen?' enquired Sean, with genuine interest.

'Ha! Not usually. All these Americans, they think we should sleep here.' She tucked a stray strand of black hair behind her ear. The remainder had been twisted into a chic coil on the back of her head. Sean had observed that she always wore it like that, just as she always wore a smart skirt and jacket with the sleeves pushed up – except at the Melkweg of course. Then she had been wearing some shimmery top-thing and satiny trousers with her hair looking, presumably deliberately, as though she had just got out of bed. He turned back to his screen. Lena didn't move from her position on his desk. Her neat rear end squashed into a very squeezable mound against the smooth surface. Sean wished he hadn't noticed.

'What's the crisis then?' she asked.

He shook his head.

'I have no idea but I need to find out fast. Gert seems to have accessed some program he should never have been able to get into and messed up some data. Bloody chaos, actually.' He tapped some keys and frowned.

She responded with a sympathetic smile.

'Well, since I don't suppose you had any breakfast, call me when you've solved the problem and we can go and get lunch. I need to talk to you about some of the stuff on my project too. You are in charge of IT aren't you?'

'For my sins,' Sean agreed, wondering what on earth that could have to do with inter-company liaison.

'Lunch then. Don't forget.'

'Okay, whatever – thanks again for the coffee.'

She turned and waved, but Sean was already immersed in his work.

Just before one-thirty she reappeared, sashaying across the now buzzing office floor straight to his desk.

'You didn't phone. Aren't you finished yet?'

Sean hesitated.

'Just about,' he admitted, glancing round. Chatting to Lena in an almost empty building was one thing – doing it when everyone was around was another. He made a stab at a relaxed smile.

'I've still got a few things to tie up. Why not just tell me the problem and I'll get back to you?'

Lena's eyes glinted with amusement. 'I could do that, but hey, it's only lunch and we're both hungry so how about we get out of this building for half an hour.'

It was tempting. God, was it tempting. Sean was sick to death of staring at his computer screen and his stomach was beginning to make some very disconcerting noises.

'Well,...' he began.

Lena broke in quickly. 'I'll take that as a yes.'

Sean shrugged. 'Okay, why not.' He could really use some food. Surely no one could object to a working lunch with a colleague. It would probably do him good to escape from the office for a little while, anyway.

He grabbed his jacket from the back of the chair. 'So, where to?'

'How about Ikea, just for fun. The restaurant's okay and there's never anyone there on a Monday.'

'Ikea? Are you a regular then?'

Lena tossed her head. 'I head over there from time to time.'

'Oh well. At least if you're inside you can't see that bloody yellow logo,' Sean said, with feeling.

She laughed. 'Come on, we'll take my car.

He folded his large frame into the front of the Volkswagen Golf and pushed the seat back to its limit.

'Do you only carry short passengers?' he asked.

'I don't usually carry any passengers at all,' she replied.

'I forgot you had to do a tour of the building to get to the restaurant,' Sean remarked, glancing helplessly about him at the cushions and sofas. Kate would have loved a trip like this, he realised guiltily. Stick Luke in the ball pond for an hour, browse bedlinen, wardrobes and kitchen gadgets uninterrupted by whingeing four-year-old, then extract said four-year-old from child-care facility and treat him to an Ikea lunch. What could be more perfect? Sean quelled the pang by resolving to bring his wife as soon as possible, although he really didn't see the appeal himself. If you wanted something you checked it out online, ordered it and picked it up from the bay downstairs. There was no need to trail round the shop. Lena, he noticed, wasn't distracted by the merchandise on offer but headed straight for her goal.

'I really don't want to waste my lunch hour examining kitchen units,' she said, laughing again.

It seemed to Sean that she laughed a lot and that it was something that seemed to have gone missing in his life lately. It was a nice sound. He took a tray and followed her into the queue. She picked salad, of course, and some fishy thing that was probably the 'healthy option.' Sean chose spaghetti and meatballs, though when it arrived on his plate he wondered why, as it was exactly the kind of thing he would be served at home. It amused and appalled him to discover that he was such a creature of habit. Of course, he should have gone for something more adventurous. He inhaled the steam from his dinner. On the other hand, who could care? They did smell good.

Lena chose a seat by the window. It was tucked behind a water fountain which gave the impression that they were sitting in a private booth. Sean wondered if somewhere more exposed might have been better; it looked like they were hiding. Admittedly, there was less chance of being spotted by any random work colleagues who might also decide to eat here. Sean had no idea how many of these there might be or whether it was better, or not, to be seen by them. His dining partner didn't seem to share his uncertainty. She was pouring water for them both from a jug that reminded Sean of school dinners. In fact, the whole experience resembled school dinners, he decided, on which grounds the meal could hardly be termed illicit, could it? 'Illicit' took place in candlelit restaurants, surely. Well, one thing was certain, he wouldn't be doing this again, it made him far too jumpy. Next time she wanted something they could have their discussions at the table beside the coffee machine, the same as everyone else did. He looked up. She was watching him closely through her large black eyes.

'I hear you brought your kid in yesterday,' she said.

'New travels fast.'

'And your wife. You sure know how to give her a good time.' The eyes widened mischievously.

'We went to *Quattro Stagioni* afterwards,' said Sean defensively.

'That was okay then, was it?'

'Sort of.'

'You said she wasn't that keen on the move. It must be hard for her, coming to a new country. It's different for you. You have work.'

Had he said that? Sean wondered what else he might have inadvertently let slip that night at the Melkweg.

'It's not that,' he blurted, suddenly weary. 'She wants another baby and it doesn't seem to be happening.'

His mouth closed abruptly and he rubbed a hand energetically across his head looking everywhere but at Lena. God, where had that come from? Butterworth, keep your trap shut, can't you?

'I mean,' he muttered, staring hard into his dinner, 'it's getting to her a bit, that's all.'

But his colleague wasn't going to let him off so lightly.

'I see,' she said carefully. 'I had a friend who went through that. Sex by timetable and stuff, hey?

'Sort of,' Sean mumbled, dissecting a meat ball. 'Uggh, what do they put in these things?' He peered, apprehensively at the differently shaded globules.

'Ha, better not to look!' Her beautifully white teeth clamped delicately around a piece of fish. Sean could see her tongue, pink and pointed, and wished he hadn't. He felt a faint blush rise to his cheeks and realised Lena was regarding him with frank amusement.

'You British!' she exclaimed.

Sean coughed uncomfortably and directed his gaze through the window and into the car park below. A line of Ikea vans were stationed in the bay directly opposite. Ready to rent out, he supposed.

Could be useful, he told himself, if ever we need to get anything big for the house. Although admittedly this was pretty unlikely as it was a furnished let. He forced himself to imagine driving a large van manfully through the congested Amsterdam streets. It was a distraction of sorts.

'How are the meatballs?'

'Yep, great,' said Sean, hurriedly turning back to his meal and twisting a wad of spaghetti round his fork. Somehow a strand of pasta loosened in transit between the plate and his mouth spraying a dollop of tomato sauce onto the front of his white shirt.

'That's all I need!' He lay down his cutlery and attacked the mark with a serviette. It remained a stubborn pink smudge. 'I'd better have a go at this in the gents.' He stood up and pushed back his chair, which fell over with a clatter alerting the entire café to their presence.

'Back in a minute,' Sean mumbled, and dashed towards the bathroom. For a couple of seconds he simply stood beside the urinal, staring at his reflection in the mirror. He looked exactly like Luke just before he dissolved into tears. Forcing himself to take a long, deep breath, he` tore off some toilet paper, wet it, added a squirt of green slimy soap from the dispenser and began rubbing hard at the mark. As he wiped, he rehearsed what he would say to Kate: 'A few of us went over to Ikea for a lunchtime meeting. We thought it would be a bit more civilised than sandwiches round the coffee machine.' (Short laugh) 'I should never have chosen the meatballs, though.' And Kate, seeing no reason not to believe, would smile and say: 'Oh well, I never did like that shirt much.' And he would hug her, for being there and for being Kate.

'Better?' asked Lena, when Sean finally sank back into his seat.

'I think so.' He felt more composed, more controlled. The deep breaths had helped. He had been rushed into this lunch, he decided. He hadn't had a moment all morning to think or relax. From the second he had leapt out of bed, a full twenty minutes after the alarm sounded, he had been on the back foot. No wonder he felt hassled and couldn't even manage to eat a dish of meatballs without throwing his food around like a toddler. He pushed the plate away. Enough of that.

'You haven't finished.'

'I'm not hungry.' He smiled tiredly and for the first time in five years wished that he still smoked. A cigarette was exactly what he wanted right now.

'I'll get coffee, then.'

'Really, don't bother. I should get back.'

'Sit still,' Lena instructed. 'They can live without us for another five minutes. Technically we have an hour to eat, you know. We're not paid for that. Anyway, we haven't talked about my computer problem.'

Sean leaned back in his chair and resigned himself to seeing the meal through to its bitter end.

The coffee wasn't bad, he decided, when she returned with two cups and it did almost the same job as a smoke.

'So what exactly is the technical problem?' he asked.

'It's not really so important.' Lena cocked her head on one side. 'Actually it's not really much at all. But you know, you work such long hours and you always look so worried, I thought maybe lunch would help.'

'You thought lunch with you would stop me worrying!' exclaimed Sean, incredulous. 'You've just given me a whole new bunch of things to stress over.'

'I thought maybe you needed to talk,' she picked up her bag from beneath the table and made a show of fiddling with the clasp. 'It's okay.'

'Now I've offended you.' He sighed. 'I didn't mean to. Fine, look, maybe lunch was a good idea. You're right, I never stop during the day. 'Sandwich at the desk' kind of guy. Heading for an early heart attack, no doubt.'

'And I think that when you change country home can be stressful too at first,' Lena prodded.

Sean's lips tightened. He really couldn't discuss his wife's moods with this far-too-attractive and terrifyingly persistent colleague, tempting though it was.

'It's not too bad, really.' He attempted a dismissive shrug. 'Kate's exploring the city. She seems to really like the Van Gogh museum. And Luke is starting Dutch school next week.'

'That's fine then,' Lena's tone implied this was probably a long way from the truth. She paused. 'You English guys, you know, I like you a lot. I find you more caring than the Dutch men. But the trouble is you care about everything; your jobs, your families, your football teams, the war in Syria, whether a coalition government is sustainable. You should just choose a couple of things to care about, and the rest of the time you must spend playing sport. That's what the Dutch guys do. It's healthier.'

'Really?' said Sean, bemused. 'You speak fantastic English, by the way.'

'Of course.'

'Us Brits don't seem to be much good at languages,' he added apologetically.

'So you say. But I think you can learn Dutch if you want to. It's really a simple language. But why bother when we are all bi-lingual after all?' She set her cup on the table in a business-like manner and stood up. 'Shall we go?'

Sean was only half way through his coffee. 'Eer, okay,' he agreed, tipping the last mouthfuls down his throat. Seconds later he found himself chasing the neatly clad bum, as it wove expertly through the browsing customers, this time towards the exit.

Chapter 8

Luke and Kate walked slowly through the Vondelpark, scarves wrapped tightly against the wind. They had been in Amsterdam for one week and six days but it seemed like much longer, as if the hours had been stretched like pictures on Photoshop – wider, taller, but less textured, less intense than the hours back home had been. Because each day started out empty instead of filled with work, playschool, errands, dentist appointments and play-dates, Luke and Kate had instinctively slowed their pace, drawing out each separate activity and savouring it, whether it was feeding ducks, looking at paintings or drinking hot chocolate in the Van Gogh museum café.

At the north end of the park, in front of the film museum, they stopped to watch the mad parrot lady. Luke loved the fact that there were real green parrots living in the trees in the middle of a city.

'They must have escaped from Africa.' His eyes widened.

'Perhaps, their ancestors did,' Kate agreed, 'but these ones were born here. They're naturalised.'

They had discovered that the parrot lady came every day to feed her birds. She stood beneath the branches of the trees, very still, very patient, and offered up fruit and nuts. Sometimes a parrot flew down and sat on her head.

'Why do you say she's mad, Mummy?' Luke asked. 'They need feeding because Africa is a long way to come.'

'I don't know.' It was a very reasonable question. To Luke nothing seemed more normal and sensible than coming every day to feed these special birds. 'Perhaps she's not, then.'

'Can you read to me now, Daddy?' Luke asked that evening. He was sitting in his pyjamas on his parents' big bed watching his father change out of his suit.

'In a minute I can,' said Sean, unknotting his tie. 'What have you and Mummy been doing today?'

'We went to the Vondelpark and saw the parrot lady. That's a lady who comes every day to feed the parrots and Mummy says she must be mad. But I would feed them every day too if I was allowed.'

'Me too, if I had time,' said Sean.

'But you wouldn't wear a long green skirt and a green knitted jacket,' said Kate with a gentle smile.

'Probably not,' Sean conceded.

'That's so she doesn't scare them,' Luke explained. 'They just think she's a big kind of parrot. Like a Mummy or Daddy parrot or something.'

'That seems completely reasonable,' Sean agreed, amused.

'I think you're wrong this time, Mummy,' Luke apologised. 'Daddy agrees with me.'

Kate gave an exasperated sigh and placed Luke's warm milk on the bedside table.

'Why don't you take him to the Zoo tomorrow, Sean, and you can do some of the explaining for a change.'

'Yeeehh!' whooped Luke and began to bounce wildly on the mattress. 'You said we could go again soon because last time you had to go to work.'

Sean raised his eyebrows. 'Thanks for that, Kate.'

'My pleasure.'

The following morning Kate waved Luke and Sean off in the car and took the tram to the centre of Amsterdam. It was odd, suddenly being alone, without the responsibility, the nuisance, the company, of a curious child. Kate felt exposed, and then exhilarated. She had spent two long weeks wandering through this town always looking for the child's angle, trying to find things that might keep Luke amused. Now she could please herself. She got off the tram at Prinsengracht excited by the hard paving slabs beneath her feet. As Sean had hoped, she was beginning to like being back in a proper city. For once the sky was blue rather than grey, though a pale shade that was more Wedgewood than Delft. The odd cloud skipped across it and was reflected in the canal. Tall, narrow houses lined the towpath regarding the world with their solemn glass eyes. They wobbled slightly in the liquid mirror as the water, with imperceptible slowness, continued its journey, barely rocking the boats that were moored at its edge. Someone had told Kate that the Amsterdam *grachten* were full of old bikes and were dredged once a year to clear them. She peered in but saw nothing but a quivering woman with a pale face and straight hair staring back at her. A flat-bottomed passenger boat chugged by with a tour guide explaining the passing sights in multiple languages. A boat trip was on her list but not today. It was something to be done with Sean and Luke when the weather warmed up. Just now, without having consciously taken the decision, Kate realised she was slowly heading back to the Van Gogh museum.

The museum cards had already proved a good investment. The gallery was the perfect refuge for a rainy afternoon. It was easy, just a short trip on the tram, which was always fun, priority entrance to the museum, so no queuing, half an hour with the pictures and a drink in the café. Sometimes they walked back across Museumplein for a bit of fresh air and caught the tram home a couple of stops further on. Luke liked it because there were no shops involved. He hated shopping. One afternoon they had tried out the Rijksmuseum, just to see what it looked like inside, but had come out again quite quickly without staying to sample the hot chocolate.

'A bit boring,' Luke decided.

Kate presumed that there would also be other things to do as they got to know the city better, but for now the Vondelpark and the Van Gogh museum were their destinations of choice. Every time they climbed the steps to the entrance Kate caught herself wondering if the guy with the ponytail would put in another appearance. She felt they hadn't quite finished their conversation. It would have been good to ask him about the museum, about painting, about Van Gogh. She hadn't met anyone else who might want to talk about these things. Certainly not Sean who spent every evening poring over some spreadsheet. The tormented artist was beginning get a hold on Kate. He had been so passionate, so single-minded – and so very lonely.

It was early afternoon when Kate reached the museum quarter, trailing the canals as they drifted through the city. She had stopped at a café for lunch on the way ordering a bowl of soup and a hunk of bread and butter, chasing it down with strong Dutch coffee. Sitting at a scrubbed pine table in the muggy warmth of the narrow, lamp-lit interior she felt like she had moved a step closer to belonging.

The Van Gogh museum came into view as she rounded the corner from Leidseplein. The queues were spilling right down the steps and onto the pavement. Thanks goodness for the magic card. It was Saturday, of course and therefore extra busy, but despite the crowds, standing in the main gallery for the first time without Luke she felt calmer, more able to concentrate on the paintings. The *Sunflowers* were beautiful, anyone could see that and it was easy to understand why her son liked them best. But they were simple, surely, intended to decorate. They told no story that Kate could find. She was more drawn to the hints of dissolution in the *Glass of Absinthe and a Carafe*, which seemed, to her untutored eye, to be a more complex work. But she loved the whole collection – loved the deliberate, anxious brush strokes, as though the painter was terrified his concentration might falter or the moment disappear before he had captured it on canvas. Biting her lip she realised that she might once have tried to tell Sean all this. She would have insisted he go with her to the gallery so she could measure his reaction against her own.

But these days there didn't seem to be much point. He was always too busy, too preoccupied, to give serious attention to anything beyond work.

'So, this is the one you prefer?' enquired a voice in lightly accented English.

Kate turned sharply. The tall man with the pony tail and light blue eyes had somehow materialised at her elbow.

'You are the woman with the young boy, I think? Or perhaps I am mistaken?' He raised his eyebrows in polite query.

'Er, yes, no,' she heard herself stammer. 'At least, I haven't got my son with me.'

'So I can see.' The eyes glinted amusement. 'You are perhaps staying a long time in our city so you can come often to this museum? You can come to know the artist well.'

'I hope so.' Kate surprised herself with the force of her words. 'I love these paintings.'

'Of course.' The man's expression stated clearly that anything less would be unreasonable.

He understood! Kate felt as though she had been given a shot of adrenalin.

'This work,' he indicated the *Glass of Absinthe*, 'this was painted in Paris. I expect the setting is familiar to you. The light is green-grey. It's a bit like London, perhaps? The *Sunflowers* on the other hand...' with a light touch he turned her towards them, '...you must go south to know these. You cannot really understand these paintings until you see the *zonnebloemen* in the fields.'

She twisted back to face him. 'You seem to know an awful lot about it all.'

'Sure.' He smiled. 'As I told your son, I'm a painter but I also teach Van Gogh, here in the museum. We have a class starting next week. Why don't you join us?'

Kate frowned. 'I'd love to but the language...'

He held up his hands to silence her. 'That would be no problem. You can start to learn Dutch and after the class we can take a coffee and go over everything in English.'

'But really..,' Kate stammered, 'I mean, that would be great but...isn't it a bit much to ask?'

'Did you ask? I didn't hear you. I thought I offered.' He shook his head. 'You don't understand. I am Dutch, I don't say things just to be polite.'

'Thanks. I'll think about it.' She smiled, doubtfully.

'I believe that's English for 'no'. Pity.' He gave small shrug, his eyes crinkled at the corners. Kate felt their gaze like the strokes of a brush on her cheeks, tinting them red.

'Anyway, I must leave,' he concluded. 'Enjoy your visit.'

She took a sharp breath as if to reply although she had no idea what she might have been about to say. It didn't matter anyway because he had gone and she was left standing, exposed, in the middle of the gallery, her back hot where he had touched it. She shook herself and took another look at the *Sunflowers*, trying to imagine them in the fields of southern France.

To postpone the moment when she must relinquish her solitude and return to the flat, Kate bought a book of Van Gogh's letters from the shop on the ground floor and thumbed through it over a cup of vanilla tea. When she finally caught the tram home the sky was grainy with dusk. Sean and Luke would probably be wondering where she was. The realisation was both gratifying and mildly irritating. She walked back from the main road feeling peculiarly elated. Maybe she would think about the Van Gogh course after all.

Sean was standing in the kitchen wearing his butcher's apron, chopping onions and wiping his eyes with the back of his hand when Kate finally reappeared.

'Didn't think you'd be so long,' he sniffed. 'Making spag bol.'

'My favourite,' she said, quickly shutting the front door to keep out the cold of the evening.

'I knew it must be from the number of times we have it.'

The kitchen was bathed in the cold neon of the strip light. Kate's nose wrinkled. The room was itself a museum piece. There was none of the subtle lighting they had installed at home here. Luke was kneeling on a chair at the table working on a large sheet of sugar paper with his poster paints.

'What are you painting?' Kate craned her head towards the picture. Luke put up a hand to stop her.

'No! It's a surprise. You can look at Daddy's one.' He waved towards the garden door where a second large sheet had been sellotaped to the glass.

Grey splodge with legs, thought Kate with a smile. Luke Butterworth, an early work.

'Elephants, I presume?' she said aloud.

'What else do you think?' muttered Luke, crossly.

'Luke!' reproved his father, throwing the onion into a pan.

'Well, Mummy was supposed to be home earlier.'

'Why?' Kate enquired, reasonably.

'Luke was getting worried about you. You don't usually stay out late,' said Sean, his voice deliberately level. Technically, of course, they both knew she had done nothing wrong. It was just that she normally came back sooner, or phoned to explain. He said this.

'Explain!' Kate gave an irritated laugh. 'Explain what? It's half past six.'

Sean shrugged. 'We couldn't get through to your mobile.'

'I always put it on silent in the museum. I must have forgotten to change it back.' She pulled the phone from her pocket and two missed calls flashed up. She sighed.

'But you two had a nice day at the zoo, I presume.'

'Magic!' shouted Luke, jumping down from the chair and barrelling across the room to fling his arms round his mother. 'It's finished! Yours is finished. Can I watch Tom Tank now?'

'One episode,' Sean agreed, 'then it'll be teatime.'

Kate stood with her head on one side and considered her gift; bright yellow smudges of colour and long green sticks rising from a brown rectangle. The paint flowed across the page in thick, rapturous sweeps.

'I couldn't quite do the vase,' Luke explained, reappearing in the archway.

'It's beautiful,' said Kate, meaning it.

'As good as Van Cough?'

'Almost.'

'I'd like to have a museum to myself when I'm grown up,' said Luke, throwing himself onto the sofa.

His parents exchanged an amused glance.

'He gets it from you,' laughed Kate.

'What?'

'Whatever it is.'

Sean reached out and squeezed her arm but it didn't tingle afterwards, she noticed.

'So, where did you go?' asked her husband. For once they were watching the television together; sitting on the black leather sofa, limbs entwined, without the distraction of Sean's laptop. 'What did you do all day long?'

'Wandered round, had lunch in a café and went to the Van Gogh museum. That's where I spent most of my time.'

'You're going there a lot.'

'I'm going to study him. I want to understand how he saw things.' Her jaw was set. She had made the decision on the way home, almost without realising.

'Good idea.'

Kate's eyes flashed. Was he patronising her?

'Why don't you come and have a look? You haven't even seen the pictures yet.'

'No, well... That's okay. It can be your thing. I've got loads to do.' He hugged her closer. 'I'm glad you've found something you can get passionate about.'

'So I won't get bored and nag to go back to England, you mean?'

He pulled back so he could look at her properly.

'It's not as bad as that, is it? I like this country and I want you to like it too. Work's good. Hardly any commute. Nice clean city. We weren't going anywhere much in the UK. I think we can have a good year here, maybe even stay longer, so if studying Van Gogh is what grabs you then go for it.'

Sean's right, Kate thought. They had been stagnating in Suffolk. They needed this change to shake them up a bit. The problem was that they both knew (but weren't saying) that Van Gogh was a substitute for the other thing that she was trying not to mention. She bit her lip. At least she had found a distraction – something other than Luke.

Chapter 9

'Sorry,' said Sean. 'I thought I would get back before this, but the boss wanted another one of his 'little chats'. I swear he sits by the lift door so he can grab people on their way out. I'm going to start using the stairs.'

'Never mind,' said Kate. She had made a pact with herself not to grumble, at least for a few weeks. It couldn't be much fun to come home and get moaned at every night. In fact, you probably wouldn't feel like coming home at all.

'Guess what,' she said, 'I bought a bike, today. Me and Luke rode home on it.'

'Really?' asked Sean, looking up and down the hall. 'Where is it? I didn't see it outside.'

'It's in the garden, of course. With a bike cover to protect it from this incessant rain.'

'Right. Good idea.'

'It'll make getting Luke to school much quicker.'

'It's only two streets away.'

Kate shook her head impatiently.

'The bike'll be good for other things too. It'll make it easier to get to the museum, for instance.'

'I thought you could get a tram to the museum'

'I can, but now I won't have to wait about. I've signed up for a course.'

Sean's eyebrows flew up. 'Wow, you are taking this Van Gogh thing seriously.'

'Of course,' Kate replied, eyes flashing dangerously. Didn't he understand her at all? 'There's no point otherwise.'

'Okay, well that's great.' Sean opened the back door and took several bottles of Amstel from a crate outside, opened one and put the others in the fridge.

She watched him impassively. He really didn't get it. He was just pleased she had something to keep her quiet.

'Anyway,' she continued doggedly, 'as I was going to say, buying the bike was a joke. Most of them were much too big for me and my feet didn't touch the ground. In the end the man found me a short bike.' She gave Sean a look that was half-amused, half-frustrated. 'I'm not used to being short.'

'What are you trying to tell me?'

Kate stopped midway between the sink and oven.

'That this isn't my home, maybe,' she said at last.

Sean took off his glasses and rubbed the lenses gently with his handkerchief.

'Guess what,' he said after a moment, 'I already know that, Kate.' He drained his beer and regarded his wife from the far end of the kitchen. She had moved to the back door and was standing in front of Luke's paintings in a roll-necked sweater and Levis, her hair had been pushed untidily back behind her ears. She was as pretty as ever, but it was the crease between her eyebrows that got him. Why did she always look so worried? They were okay, weren't they? It was still early days, surely? He wanted to hug her, tell her that, but it didn't seem to work anymore.

'I'm going for a quick shower before tea,' he said, finally. He set the empty bottle on the table, turned and went upstairs.

Kate sank onto a chair and pulled her laptop towards her. She wished she didn't feel like crying. What had people done without the internet to distract them? There was a message from Paula.

Hi,

Almost three weeks and I've hardly heard from you. Henry is dying for some news. Has Luke started school yet? Henry wants to know if he can speak Dutch. What's the apartment like?

It was true, Kate thought, guiltily, she hadn't been that great at keeping in touch. Before she left she had assumed she'd be writing to Paula all the time. They had seen each other almost every day, after all, communication would just continue electronically, surely? But somehow the things she was happy to discuss and dissect over coffee in Paula's cosy, untidy kitchen, where they were interrupted constantly by requests from the boys and shouts from baby Oliver, would not allow themselves to be typed. She had tried a few times but the words seemed to be so much more important when they didn't simply disappear into thin air. On the screen they could be examined, considered, referred to, as she was now studying Paula's message:

Our news is that Dom is thinking of having the snip. Ollie is still refusing to sleep through the night and we are both at our wits' end. He says he can't stand the thought of having another one like this. I'm trying to talk him out of it as I'd really like a little girl (can't just order them, I know!!) and I'm hoping I don't have to resort to getting pregnant 'accidentally'.

Kate grimaced. Of course some people, probably lots of people, got pregnant accidentally. She tugged a strand of her hair. It was just, well, how unfair was that?

But how are things in that most romantic of cities? Are you both a bit less stressed? Hoping things are good between you. We'd love to come over for the weekend sometime if you think you could put up with us. Henry is desperate to see Luke's new bedroom. Aren't kids weird! There are loads of cheap flights at this time of year and Mum has heroically offered to come and look after Ollie. But we haven't even been invited yet!!

Looking forward to an email from you,
Paula

Well, we've made love four times in the last three weeks, thought Kate, deeming it much safer to answer Paula's implied question in her head. That's how things are. He knows that when we do it that I am wondering if *it* will happen this time. I don't seem to be able to help it. Maybe our sex life will improve after the menopause when I've finally given up on this stuff.

In the email she wrote:

We'd love to see you. Come whenever you like but maybe leave it a few more weeks until the weather is better. It certainly knows how to rain over here. Luke is settling in alright, I think. Fundamentally not much has changed – I'm still a terrible cook and Sean's still getting home late and spending the weekends glued to his laptop.

The only new thing is I've decided to study art –Van Gogh specifically. It's a project. His paintings are amazing and (as I'm sure you know) there's an entire museum full of them here. I used to be a bit of a gallery freak in London.

She paused. That was it, all she could bring herself to write. Kate signed off and pressed send.

'I hope they come,' she muttered aloud. It wasn't only that she missed talking to Paula, she realised. She wanted someone to approve of this move, to tell her how lucky she was. Then, perhaps she might stop feeling so bloody lonely and start to appreciate it.

Sean reappeared at the kitchen door freshly showered, dressed in jeans and a sweatshirt and smelling of aftershave. He looked younger.

Quite sexy, actually, Kate judged. He seemed unaware of his wife's approbation but headed straight to the fridge for another bottle of Amstel.

'What's in the oven? I'm starving.'

'Lasagne,' said Kate. 'The star of my mince repertoire. And if you drink too much you'll spoil your dinner.'

'Unlikely.' Sean inhaled deeply. 'Smells good,' he said. 'I had a thought while I was in the shower.'

'Which was?'

He opened the bottle and settled himself at the table.

'Cutlery would be good,' remarked Kate, dishing up.

Sean stood up again and went to the drawer.

'This Van Gogh course that you've signed up for, won't it be taught in Dutch?'

'Mostly,' Kate agreed.

'Then it'll just be a waste of money, surely?'

'I've spoken to the lecturer. He says he'll help me with anything I don't understand.'

'But you won't understand any of it.'

'I might,' countered Kate. 'I've bought some CDs. I'm going to put them on my iPod. Anyway, he's promised to go through everything with me after the lesson.'

'He probably fancies you,' her husband teased.

'He probably doesn't,' she contradicted. 'He probably wants to help me learn about Van Gogh.' *Unfortunately*, she added silently.

'Both could be true.' Sean grinned, imagining an elderly art history professor painstakingly translating his lecture into ponderous English for the delightful young woman who had joined his class. The two of them would pour over the *Sunflowers*, or whatever, discussing brush strokes and use of colour. He pictured Kate leaning earnestly forward with her hair tucked behind her ears, while the old man's eyes, sharp behind his little oval glasses, strayed to her breasts. Sean decided he could probably cope with the scenario if it made his wife happy.

After supper, Sean returned inevitably to his laptop so Kate sat on the sofa with the book she had bought at the museum. Van Gogh seemed to have been as prolific a letter writer as he had been a painter. Kate realised she was absurdly excited about the course and astonished that she had found the courage to sign up. She probably never would have done if the guy with the ponytail hadn't appeared again to encourage her. He had materialised while she and Luke were admiring the *Sunflowers* for the umpteenth time, striding over just as Kate was explaining how Van Gogh had painted the picture for his friend Gauguin who he hoped would come and visit.

Luke was nodding, earnestly. 'Was Gauguin his best friend do you think?'

'Ah, the English lady who loves Van Gogh,' said a lightly accented voice. 'And her son of course,' he added, fixing his gaze on Luke. 'Actually, I think Vincent very much hoped that Gauguin would become his best friend. It's important to have a best friend. Do you have one?'

'I do,' said Luke, 'but he lives in England.'

'I see,' said the Dutchman thoughtfully. 'So you are like Van Gogh; waiting for your friend to visit.'

Luke regarded him with gratitude. It wasn't often that grown-ups made such intelligent comments.

'Since you are often in the museum it's time we introduced ourselves, I think.' The man turned back to Kate. 'Rudy.' He extended his hand. She took it. It was firm and dry.

'Kate.' She smiled uncertainly, trying to ignore her churning stomach.

'And you, young man?'

'I'm Luke.'

Rudy inclined his head solemnly.

'So, Kate, did you register for my course? Are you going to join us and learn about the best painter in the world?'

'Well, I'm not really sure...' she mumbled, bending to examine an imagined mark on Luke's hoody.

'Why not, Mummy? You could do that,' her son said helpfully, shaking off her fidgeting hands, 'but not me because I'm starting school soon, aren't I?'

Rudy's eyes crinkled in amusement. 'So now you will have to find a very good excuse not to come.'

'It's the language,' Kate protested. 'Surely that's a very good reason?'

'It's not as important as you imagine. I can't teach the course in English because there may be some people who don't understand, but as I said, we can go over the material afterwards.'

Kate vacillated. 'I couldn't...'

'It would be a pleasure.' He paused and Kate had the sense she was being examined. His gaze as it swept over her contained something hard and real, like a chunk of sapphire. 'And now I must go, but if you are interested, you can sign up at the information desk beside the shop. Tell them Rudy de Jong sent you.' With a brief smile he disappeared down the stairs. She wanted to shout after him, to ask what he had seen when he looked at her like that. Luke was tugging at her sleeve.

'There, Mummy,' he said. 'Now you can go to school too and you won't miss me as much because you'll be busy.'

Kate threw her son a sharp glance.

'I'd better go and sign up then,' she said.

Chapter 10

Luke padded across the bedroom carpet, along the landing and pushed open his parents' bedroom door. They were still fast asleep although it was light outside and there was a real racket coming from the street —shouting and quite a lot of crashing. The noise had woken him up. He supposed his Mum and Dad couldn't hear it as they were on the garden side. Sean was lying on one half of the enormous bed with his arms spread-eagled. Kate was on the other curled into a tight ball. In the middle was a big space that Luke was tempted to crawl into, except that he wasn't tired and he would probably only get told off. Instead he shook his mother's shoulder.

'What's up?' she mumbled.

'Are you going to wake up now? It's daytime and there's a lot of people outside.'

Kate opened her eyes and stretched out an arm towards the clock. 'It's only half past seven. Don't forget it's a holiday today, there's no work or school.'

'There's still a lot of people in the street.

'Are there?'

'Yes,' said Luke.

'I suppose I'd better come and have a look then,' she shuffled up onto an elbow. 'Pass me my dressing gown.' She glanced over at Sean who instantly began to snore loudly. Luke let out a peal of laughter. Kate grinned and put a finger to her lips.

'It's probably my turn to make the tea today. We'll wake him up gently.'

In the front bedroom she pulled back the heavy curtains while Luke stood on his bed trying to peer out over the balcony.

'See,' he said.

'I do indeed.' The normally quiet street had turned into what looked like a huge car boot sale. Orange flags hung from every street lamp and orange bunting had been strung across the road and was flapping in a brisk breeze.

'It's Queen's Day,' Kate remembered. 'The Dutch celebrate the Queen's official birthday on April 30th.'

'There's Heijn,' crowed Luke, bouncing up and down. 'I can see him. Can we go out now?'

'Careful up there,' said Kate automatically. 'We can go out after breakfast. First we need to wake Daddy.'

It was a good hour before Sean and Kate were dressed and ready to venture outside. At first Luke nagged them every five minutes:

'Have you drunk your tea yet? Do you really need a shower, Mummy,' but as the minutes wore on he became more subdued.

'What's up?' Kate asked. 'Don't you want to go now?'

'I dooo, but I was thinking. If today's Queen's Day then tomorrow's the weekend and then after that it's school. Is that right, Mummy?'

'That's right.' She picked up her bag and rummaged through her purse to check she had some cash. 'Are you looking forward to school?'

'Sort of,' said Luke cagily. 'I'm more looking forward to Henry coming. How long is it now?'

'Four weeks, you know that. I showed you on the calendar and you've been ticking off the days.'

'I s'pose.'

'And school will be fine,' said Kate with deliberate cheeriness.

'I s'pose,' Luke repeated, more doubtfully. It was alright for them, they didn't lie in bed thinking about being surrounded by lots of big boys and girls they couldn't understand. What if he couldn't do it? What if they laughed at him? What if Heijn didn't keep an eye on him like he had said he would? Heijn had lots of friends, Luke knew this from the park. At school he might be too busy to keep a look out for a boring little English boy. Then he wouldn't know anyone and he wouldn't understand. Luke had a nightmare where he was standing in the middle of a classroom in his underpants and all the children, including Heijn, were sitting at desks sniggering and pointing at him while the teacher kept shouting something in that funny-sounding Dutch. He'd had this dream twice now. He hadn't mentioned it to Kate because her eyes would go all frowny and worried and she would fuss lots. He really wanted to tell his Dad, but Sean hadn't got home early enough the last two nights. Now it was Queen's Day so perhaps he'd get a chance tonight. Since he wouldn't have been at work, Luke reasoned, he should be at home.

'Come on, Sean.' Kate called. 'Goodness, he takes longer getting ready than I do.'

'Not always,' countered Luke, loyally.

Sean finally came downstairs wearing a bright orange tee-shirt under his jacket.

'I was looking for this,' he explained.

'You're going native?'

'When in Rome and all that.' He took his son's hand and propelled him through the door onto the busy street. It seemed to Luke that every single person in Amsterdam must have a stall just outside their apartment. Entire cellars had been emptied out and the contents piled on the pavement. Luke saw furniture, discarded toys, baby equipment, clothes and a woman with a whole table piled high with ballet skirts in a rainbow of colours, cleverly made from sparkly netting. Kate longed to buy one, but couldn't think who would appreciate it. She needed a little girl, of course, but stamped quickly on the thought before it ruined her day again.

Luke rushed over to Heijn and stood in front of him grinning, school momentarily forgotten.

Heijn grinned back and the boys shook hands solemnly. Saskia was smoking, as usual, hugging her denim jacket round her. She was standing behind a mountain of jumpers and jackets which Kate was longing to sort through, but which she knew she would be too embarrassed to wear anyway.

'Hi,' puffed Saskia, raising a hand. She and Heijn had been joined by a tall, broad man with a face squashed like a prize fighter's and a completely bald head. Not at all what Kate had expected Saskia's husband to look like, although on close inspection he did bear some resemblance to his son. He was wearing an enormous bright orange sweat shirt. He extended his hand to Sean.

'Dennis.'

His voice was so deep Kate wanted to giggle.

'So this is Queen's Day,' said Saskia, gesturing the packed street. 'When Amsterdam sells its junk – and buys it of course. That's the problem; usually you just go home with a whole new pile of junk.'

'So many people,' said Kate feeling a bit swamped by the crowd.

'Mum, can I buy Heijn's train set? Look it's a real one and it's for sale.'

Saskia shrugged. 'I think it was really Dennis's toy.' She glanced at her husband in amusement. 'Heijn was never very interested.'

Sean made an offer which Saskia knocked a few euros off and the set was handed to Luke.

'Isn't it Monday you start school, Luke?' she asked.

'Yes,' muttered Luke, clutching the train set.

'So come and have pizza with us tonight. We already have some other guests. You can meet another boy in your class.'

'Great, we'd love to,' said Kate, gratefully. Wouldn't we, Luke?'

Luke grunted.

'We would,' Kate affirmed. 'See you later then. We're heading up to the Vondelpark now.'

'Good luck,' said Saskia. 'It'll be packed.'

It was, way beyond anything they had been expecting. Worse still, some of the gates were locked to channel the crowds. Kate's palms began to sweat and she hadn't got very far beyond the entrance when her breath started coming in gasps. She clutched Sean's arm.

'Hey, sorry but I need to get out of here,' she muttered, lurching sideways as a drunken orange giant barged into her unseeing. Suppressing the urge to cry out, she grabbed Luke and steeled herself against a mounting tidal wave of panic.

'Please take me home.' She threw a stricken glance at her husband. He nodded, ashen-faced.

'Hold my tee-shirt, Luke, and don't let go,' he instructed, grasping Kate by the elbow and steering her back through the ocean of people towards the exit. Kate forced herself to focus on putting one foot in front of the other and not for one second allowing her brain to flitter away from her intention to reach the iron gates. Magical gates, the path to salvation. And when they finally made it and had passed through them into the street she burst into gulping tears of relief.

All the cafés nearby were full but Sean managed to grab a table by jumping forward as a couple rose to leave. Kate sank gratefully into a chair. The sun had come out so as well as being crowded it was also getting very warm.

'I've never seen so many people,' she murmured, closing her eyes.

'Do we have to go home if Mummy's not well?' asked Luke, worriedly.

'I think we should,' said Sean.

'But me and you can come out again, after we've taken Mummy home, can't we?'

'I don't know.' Sean hesitated. 'We'll see if Mummy minds.'

'Yeehh,' Luke shouted. 'You don't mind, Mummy, do you?'

'No,' said Kate, who did, in fact, very much. Having planned to spend the day with her husband and son, she now seemed destined to be stuck at home by herself again.

'It's not surprising you feel a bit ropey, given the number of people,' said Sean.

Kate smiled wanly and sipped her cold beer.

'Who's that lady, Daddy?' said Luke suddenly.

Sean swivelled round. Lena was sitting just behind them in a vibrant orange shirt with a girl Sean thought might work in accounts. They were both drinking brightly coloured cocktails full of fruit and pink umbrellas.

'She winked at me,' Luke explained.

'Hi,' Lena gave a global wave that just about included Kate.

Sean introduced everyone.

'Too bad your wife's not feeling well.' Lena shrugged. 'They have loads of street performers on Leidseplein. It's great for kids.'

'Can we go there this afternoon, Daddy? When we've taken Mummy home?'

'Maybe, we'll see how Mummy is.'

'I might see you up there,' said Lena, getting up. 'I promised I'd take my niece.'

'Looks like you've got a date,' Kate remarked coldly as Sean's colleagues sashayed into the crowds.

He looked flustered.

'Well, we don't have to go. We'll stay at home if you're feeling…'

'You said we could,' Luke interrupted.

'I said...'

'Oh for goodness sake. Do you really think I mind if you spend half an hour with another woman in broad daylight accompanied by a pair of four year olds?' Kate grinned suddenly. 'She almost certainly fancies you though.'

Sean turned to the waiter to ask for the bill. He didn't trust himself to reply.

'So which bit of today did you like best?' Kate asked that evening as she pulled Luke's duvet over his skinny shoulders. 'Pizza at Heijn's, the carboot sale or the street theatre on Leidesplein?'

'I liked the street theatre but I didn't like Daddy's friend much. She put her arm round him,' Luke explained.

'Really?'

'Yes, but he didn't put his arm round her back, Mummy, so it's okay.'

'Of course.' Kate took a deep breath and forced herself to smile. 'Of course it is.'

'And I liked the pizza but I didn't like Diego.'

'Why?'

'He didn't like me,' said Luke simply. 'He kept telling me to go away.'

'Do you know how to say that in Dutch?'

'I do now.' Luke sounded philosophical. 'It's "*ga weg*". So the best bit was buying the train set. Oh, and Daddy reading me a story.'

'You funny old thing,' smiled Kate, ruffling his hair. 'See you in the morning.'

Luke lay in bed staring at the swirly patterns in the plaster on the ceiling. Talking to Daddy hadn't been quite as useful as he had hoped. Sean didn't seem to see the problem with school. He just kept saying that everything would be fine. Luke knew it probably would be, but the dreams had been scary, nevertheless, and meeting Diego hadn't helped much. Diego obviously didn't want Heijn to have another friend and especially not an English one who was only nearly five. Luke would have liked some practical advice from his father, but it was clear Sean didn't have any to give. He might have to speak to Mummy after all. Actually, Luke thought, Daddy had seemed like he wasn't really

listening. A bit like when he was thinking about work. Except that Sean hadn't been to work today so that couldn't have been the problem. Luke didn't get any further with this conundrum as his eyes closed and he drifted into sleep. It really had been an extremely
busy day.

Kate made herself a cup of tea and stood in the archway between kitchen and sitting room. Sean was sprawled on the sofa with a beer.

'Come and sit next to me,' he suggested, patting the cushion.

She shook her head; her mouth was drawn in a tight line.

'Please yourself. So what did you make of Dennis and Saskia?' he asked, pressing the shooter to turn the telly down.

'Saskia's nice. I knew that already, of course. And Dennis seemed fine. I didn't really talk to him much.'

'Very Dutch, I thought.'

'I suppose so. Whatever that means.'

'When we say it at work it means he's tall, speaks excellent English, leaves the office soon after five, doesn't always say thank you and isn't quite as good at his job as he imagines he is. It also means he'll tell you exactly what he thinks – which is a good thing.'

Kate managed a small smile.

'For Christ's sake, Kate! What is the matter with you? I've known hamsters who were better company. We had a nice evening didn't we? We got invited out!'

'Luke said she put her arm round you,' Kate blurted.

'Is that what this mood is about?' Sean's eyes darkened. 'Lena! Well maybe she does fancy me then, like you said. That's more than you do.' He took a swig of his beer and turned the volume back up.

Kate bit her lip hard. When had she turned into this shrew? Was it on the ferry across the North Sea or had it started before that? She perched on a chair as far away from the telly as possible and opened her book. Van Gogh's meditations on apricot blossom swam before her eyes. She glanced across at her husband. He seemed to be completely engrossed in whatever stupid programme he was watching. She dropped the book onto the coffee table next to her, enjoying the satisfying slapping sound as it hit the wood. Sean didn't react. She decided to take her laptop up to the bedroom and email Paula. It wasn't quite late enough to sleep.

Sitting at the dressing table beside the French windows, Kate found herself gazing across the darkened gardens into the softly lit room of a neighbouring apartment. A dress of some pale, shimmery material had been thrown over the back of a chair, a delicate china cup left on a table – chance objects, random markers of the lives that were lived there. Kate had never seen the people, though she had looked often enough. They moved in and out when she wasn't watching, strewing things about the apartment for her consideration. And in the evenings, before drawing the curtains, she would survey what they had left and imagine their lives, presuming a grace she couldn't find in her own.

She sighed, pulling the heavy curtains closed. Of course she wouldn't email Paula about this silly little episode. What had she been thinking? And really, what was there to write? Some girl at work had put an arm around Sean. Kate had probed quite hard and according to Luke, his father hadn't responded. What her own reaction really emphasised, Kate concluded, was just how old and inadequate she was feeling. She and Sean were probably just going through a 'bad patch'. All relationships had them. They had been under a lot of strain, after all. It didn't mean anything was fundamentally wrong, did it? Surely, in ten years' time they would look back on their few months in Holland and laugh about it all.

Kate undressed slowly, slipped into her nightdress and sat on the edge of the bed with her hands on her knees. She had a gut feeling that this problem went deeper than the woman at work. Something in her and Sean's marriage had shifted; they were no longer running in parallel. This move that was supposed to be bringing them closer together seemed only to be accentuating how far apart they had grown. In Suffolk Kate had at least had friends, and an (admittedly dull) job which gave her a purpose beyond taking Luke to playgroup and cooking dinner. Here in Amsterdam she felt she was disappearing, receding, thinning like Sean's hairline, failing to occupy a proper amount of space. Her very identity was being gradually wallpapered over; eventually she would be nothing but part of the background.

Yet, surely her choices were still her own? She sniffed, despising her own self-pity. Perhaps things would be better when the Van Gogh course started – three mornings a week from next Monday. Maybe it would give her back her sense of self. Or was that asking a bit much? Well, it would be a distraction from worrying about Luke at his new school, if nothing else.

Chapter 11

Luke walked slowly to the classroom. He knew Kate was watching every single step and that as soon as he turned round she would wave. But he wasn't going to turn around, he had decided that already. It might make him cry and Luke knew enough about making friends to realise that tears would not be a good start. How could Heijn introduce him to anyone if he was sitting there blubbing? Carefully he took off his coat and before hanging it on the peg the teacher had shown him, he unwound his scarf and stuffed it in the sleeve just they had done at playschool. Then he went steadily to his chair. He wasn't on the same table as Heijn, unfortunately – the class seemed to be split into age groups. But it was alright because he was sitting next to a boy he thought was called Tobias and opposite were two girls; one with yellow hair and one with black hair. The black-haired one had the friendliest smile, he decided. And Tobias looked okay. It wasn't lesson time that was really bothering him, anyway, it was break. It was easy to get on with stuff during lesson time. Today it looked like they were going to do some collage thing. Well, he had done those before. No, the worst time would be in the playground. And what kinds of games would there be? What did Dutch children do? These were the things he had tried to explain to his mother the previous evening.

'Some children must play on that log,' Kate had replied carefully, wanting to be helpful. 'Some others were having a game of football, I think.'

Luke nodded. He had seen those things too. But what he really wanted to know (and he was beginning to see that neither his mother, nor even his dad could answer the question) was – would anyone ask him to play with them?

'I don't know if anyone will ask you to play, Luke,' Kate said, trying not to frown. 'But maybe if they don't, you could ask to join in.'

'Hmmm.'

His mother didn't really understand much, Luke decided. It would be more sensible to hang about on the sides watching and throwing the ball back until someone *invited* him to join in. That might take several days but it was better than being told to '*ga weg*'. This was going to be his strategy.

Feeling something hard touch his arm, Luke looked round. Tobias was prodding him and nodding earnestly in the teacher's direction. She was calling Luke's name. Perhaps she had already said it a couple of times because the rest of the children were grinning broadly, or even laughing out loud. In panic, Luke glanced across at Heijn who gestured theatrically that Luke should go to the front. Slowly, he rose from his chair and walked towards the white board where the teacher was standing smiling. She was young and bouncy and curly-haired and Luke thought she seemed nice but she might speak to him in that Dutch talk and then he would look stupid. He swallowed and kept his eyes fixed on the floor tiles; square with brown swirly patterns. Maybe he could nod a bit and just pretend to understand. But it was okay. She put a warm hand on his shoulder, swivelled him gently round and introduced him to the class. Then she explained to Luke in his own language that she had told everyone that having him around gave them a fantastic opportunity to improve their English and they should consider themselves very lucky. Luke beamed gratefully.

The course on Van Gogh didn't start until ten so Kate had time to go home and grab a coffee after dropping Luke off at school. She had watched anxiously as he plodded through the door of his classroom and took off his coat. A small, stoical child with a pale face and hopeful eyes. She had willed him to look up, to smile and wave, but he had done neither, turning deliberately away from her and heading into the melee of jostling bodies, alone. Kate had swallowed hard and cycled quickly back to the apartment where she was now sitting, trying to focus on a book of Dutch verbs. She had spent the previous evening listening to her CDs and was now saturated with funny guttural sounds that she couldn't seem to join together. She had grasped at this class as a lifeline. She hoped it wasn't going to turn out to be a big mistake.

Rudy stood in front of his small group of students, most of them well into middle age, and nodded a welcome.

'Good morning,' he said in Dutch.

Got that, anyway! Kate thought, sucking her pen. Probably don't need to write it down, though.

'Over the next six weeks I will be introducing you to the life and work of Vincent Van Gogh. We will be looking at the influences on his work, especially his relationship with Gauguin; his use of colour and technique; his life – and sad death; and his family background, including of course his relationship with his brother, Theo Van Gogh...' He inclined his head fractionally towards Kate, who was by now completely lost. 'We do have an English-speaking student with us for this course so I may need to repeat some phrases in English. I hope this won't be a problem.'

Seven faces, five of them bespectacled, turned to examine Kate with expressions ranging from benign tolerance to barely concealed irritation. Kate smiled back bravely.

'We will start,' Rudy announced, 'with a tour of the permanent collection. I'm sure these paintings are familiar to you all. If you could just come this way...'

'So how did you find it? Did you manage to follow at all?'

Kate glanced down at her notebook which was almost empty. 'Bits here and there.'

Now she had had the chance to study him more closely, she realised that Rudy was older than she had at first thought, close to her own age, probably. This made it easier to tolerate his scrutiny – and everything seemed to be subjected to his intense blue gaze.

'Okay, well, I thought it might be like this. So now we can go to the café and I will go over everything with you. It really won't take long. I think you already understood more than you think.'

'But your time...?'

'In the afternoon I usually paint. I can spare half an hour.' His blue eyes creased attractively. 'The deal is that you buy the coffee.'

'But are you sure?'

He held up his hand. 'I am Dutch. If I wasn't sure I would not say it. But our meanness is legendary; this is why I do not buy the coffee.'

Kate grinned. They certainly knew how to make things simple in this country. How much easier to just say what you mean than try to unravel the endless nuances of English conversation.

'It is important,' said Rudy, stirring sugar into his coffee and leaning forward so a long strand of fairish hair fell across his face, 'that you understand a little of a painter's life, of where he has come from. You see, learning about painting is like getting to know a person, it takes time and energy. You have to invest a lot of yourself in your relationship with the painter. In return you get more from his paintings. A painter like Van Gogh – maybe all painters, I'm not sure – is not just aiming to paint something pretty. Sometimes, it is true, he needed to sell canvases in order to eat, so he thought about his eventual audience, but even then he was trying to capture the essence of what he saw.'

Kate's pen flew across the page, wide letters that looped and hiccupped.

'It's so long since I've tried to write anything.' She stretched out her hand and wiggled her fingers. 'We do everything on computers now.' She glanced up, hoping to meet his gaze but he was concentrating on unwrapping more sugar to add to his espresso. Long, brown fingers with strong, square tips, peeled back the purple paper and let the coffee soak into the cube before releasing it into the cup. He had taken off his jacket and it hung carelessly on the back of the chair. Kate noticed that his tee shirt was the same deep blue as his eyes.

The colour of the sky in the painting of the Yellow House, she thought, feeling her cheeks flush.

'Van Gogh was born into a very religious family,' Rudy continued. 'His father was a preacher in the Dutch Reformed Church. This means he had a very serious upbringing – without much fun, I think. In this kind of church there is a big emphasis on the relationship between God and Man. There are none of the bishops and priests that you find in Catholicism. For the first part of his life Vincent Van Gogh wrestled with his desire to serve God and also to be an artist. Later he concluded he could serve God through being an artist.' He paused and sipped the sweet, thick coffee while his student scribbled. Outside the café window the trees on Museumplein swayed in the wind.

At three-thirty Kate found herself back outside the school gates waiting nervously.

'I suppose this is where mothers spend a lot of their time,' she reflected, looking round. Dozens of faces, most of them several inches above her eyeline were all chatting in this language that seemed to have its register only just beyond the reach of her understanding, like some strong dialect of English that she couldn't quite grasp. Once or twice, in the museum, she had turned sharply, mistakenly thinking that the people behind her were Scottish, so close was this tongue to some variants of her own. And yet she could barely understand a word. She stood in silence trying to look pleasant and approachable, an English island in a European sea. A couple of women smiled at her but no one came across to speak. Kate felt a pang of longing for the British school in Cliostraat where she surely wouldn't have hesitated to go up to the other parents and introduce herself. She swallowed guiltily. How many similar pangs must Luke have felt today?

At last Saskia came to her rescue, scattering dogs and small children as she bumped her bike onto the pavement.

'Hi, how are you? They aren't out yet? I thought I might be late. Luke's first day at school, isn't it. Amazing. I hope Heijn has looked after him.'

Kate smiled. 'I'm sure he did.'

'I've been into the Bijenkorf, you know it? It's a big shop in the middle of the city like your Selfridges.'

'Really?' said Kate, doubting this.

'Ah good. Here they come.' Saskia tossed her short, blonde hair, lit a cigarette and took a sharp pull.

Heijn emerged first, followed by a dark-haired boy Kate didn't recognise. Saskia enlightened her:

'That's Diego. But Heijn is a naughty boy he has forgotten Luke.'

Kate watched anxiously as the children emerged in twos and threes. Luke had better hurry up as the bigger ones would be out in a few minutes and he would be crushed in the stampede. At last he appeared clutching a large piece of sugar paper, his scarf trailing out of the end of his sleeve. She felt a wash of relief; he was grinning.

'There, he's fine,' said Saskia, robustly. 'No need to worry.' She turned to her son. 'And did you let Luke play football with you today?'

Heijn looked shifty. 'I promised him he could play tomorrow.'

Luke spotted them and came charging forward launching himself at his mother, complete with painting. His eyes were ringed with black smudges.

'You're exhausted,' Kate murmured, hugging him.

'I learnt a new word,' he shouted. 'Look,' he held up the picture. '*Zonnebloemen*.'

'Sunflowers.'

'You told me Van Cough painted lots of them for his friend. I'm painting lots of them for you, Mummy.'

Kate smiled. 'I'll put them all round my room. Did you paint a picture too, Heijn?' She asked, trying out her new language skills.

Heijn threw her a sulky look and said something to his mother that Luke and Kate couldn't understand.

Saskia pressed her lips together and barked a reply in Dutch.

'I've told him that it doesn't matter that Luke is a bit younger than him, they can still be friends.'

'It's okay,' Luke said, squaring his jaw stubbornly. 'Tobias is going to be my friend in school.'

Saskia shook her head. 'Come along Heijn, you have football training this evening.'

The older boy climbed sullenly onto the bike behind his mother.

'It's a very good club,' she called over her shoulder. 'Maybe Luke could join next season, nee, Heijn?'

Heijn gave a small shrug and said something that was probably the Dutch equivalent of 'whatever' as they pedalled off.

Luke clambered onto the identical seat on Kate's bicycle and settled his feet on the footrests.

'So was it okay?' Kate asked.

'Yeah, it was okay, but Heijn doesn't talk to me much and Diego doesn't like me playing football with them.'

'I hope you weren't too disappointed.'

'Nah,' said Luke sounding very grown-up. 'Me and Tobias went on the log.'

Kate swallowed the lump that had risen in her throat. He really was alright without her.

'School seems to have gone well,' Sean remarked, coming downstairs after reading Luke a story. He had arrived home unexpectedly around five thirty. So early that at first Kate had assumed something was wrong.

'No, I just thought I would get home in time to ask Luke how his day went.'

'And what did he say?'

He was chuntering happily about someone called Tobias, so I assume it was okay.'

Kate looked up sharply. Did Sean sound odd somehow?

'Yes,' she replied, searching his face and finding nothing. 'So far, so good. No thanks to Heijn though. It seems he's okay at the park but if anyone else is around then Luke's not really cool enough to hang out with.'

'Well, that doesn't matter if he's making other friends, does it? How did the Van Gogh thing go, by the way?'

'I didn't think you'd remember.' Kate looked pleased. 'There are eight of us and as you might imagine the other seven are retired.'

'To be expected, I suppose.'

'Of course I don't understand much of the Dutch yet, but the tutor is great. He went over it with me afterwards like he promised. It's going to be really interesting.' Kate felt her face grow hot and she turned hastily to stir the risotto. She needn't have bothered. Sean didn't notice. He was fiddling with the settings on his laptop.

'Is that risotto?' he asked, glancing at the bubbling pan.

'Yes, why?'

'Dunno. Bit dull, that's all.'

Kate swung round, eyebrows raised.

'But fine,' he added, hurriedly. Or it would have been if he hadn't already had it once today. He had lunched with Lena again. It hadn't been premeditated – at least not by him. She had suggested it casually when they came out of a meeting around one o clock. She had read him well. He was starving and his sandwich was up several flights of stairs on the other side of the building.

'Ikea,' she suggested brightly, slinging her smart red jacket across her arm. The colour, Sean couldn't help noticing, really set off her shiny, almost-black hair.

'Um well,' he mumbled, 'really I...'

'Is that how you English say "great I'd love to?" Lena's eyes narrowed with amusement.

Sean looked uncomfortable. 'Er, well, that wasn't...'

'You didn't say no, so I'll assume you said yes. Come on. Let's get out of here for half an hour.'

Her car was parked what Sean now thought of as 'strategically close' to the door with a clear line for the exit. He followed her as if on autopilot, wondering helplessly if his hand would fit right over her left buttock and how firm it would be if he squeezed it.

Fortunately the restaurant had been almost empty so they were able to pick up their trays and go straight to 'their table'. Lena actually called it that, jolting Sean out of the 'Fuck, it was only risotto and I was hungry,' argument he was having in his head with an imaginary Kate.

'Look, our table's free.'

'We have a table?'

'Sure we do. In the corner by the water fountain. Don't you remember?'

Of course he remembered. Sean wondered vaguely how he was going to extricate himself from this –whatever it was – and if, indeed, he had sufficient willpower to do so. All the attention was really very seductive.

But in the event, he reflected, picking up a forkful of his second risotto of the day, it had been a perfectly pleasant forty minute break involving nothing remotely incriminating and certainly nothing that would impact on his marriage. They had talked almost exclusively about work, which was a relief as there were some personnel issues Sean wanted a second opinion on. Gert, in fact, who was becoming a pain in the butt. He thought he should be head of IT because he was Dutch and Sean wasn't. Though quite what this had to do with doing the job Sean confessed he had no idea. He was pleased and not a little relieved to hear that Lena agreed with him. Speaking Dutch in this multi-national company was surely not a prerequisite, she argued. Anyway, as Sean pointed out, it was Gert who caused most of the IT problems so how could he possibly be in charge? Lena nodded sympathetically. At least she was interested, he told himself, which was more than Kate was. So there was no reason to feel guilty about talking it over with her, was there?

Chapter 12

Luke sat on the edge of his bed with his legs dangling down the slide. He didn't feel like launching himself down it just for a minute. His skinny shoulders hunched over as he ran Percy up and down his thigh. It was two weeks since he started school and things didn't seem to be going to plan. He didn't know how to tell his Mum. She always seemed so worried, meeting him at the school gates, her eyes all crinkly at the corners as she bent over him.'

'How was it, Luke? Do you think you'll like it? Did you make any friends?'

Well, of course he hadn't made any friends. Not real friends. He couldn't understand anything anyone said for a start. The teacher could speak English, but she spoke mostly in Dutch, even to him and only repeated it if he asked her. He didn't like to keep asking. Surely she should realise he couldn't understand. Like when she told him to get his shorts out because they were going to do gym. He only knew what she meant by copying the others. He always had to look at them to check he was doing the same. Tobias had seemed quite promising at first and he really was pretty friendly, staying with Luke most break times. But he lived a long way away so they couldn't really be proper mates and meet up after school too.

Heijn was okay, as well, and he had helped him quite a bit after Saskia said he had to, but he was obviously pretty important in the class and he had made it clear he wouldn't be spending all his time looking after a little English boy. Still, it was useful, Luke supposed, having him on his side, and their mums kind of knowing each other. Heijn's friend Diego didn't like it much though. Luckily Luke only saw him in the playground because he was in the class above. But he was always grumpy and would never let Luke join in the football game. Luke wondered if maybe Diego was miserable because he didn't have a dad around anymore. Everyone knew Diego's dad had left because he had gone to Spain in the holidays to visit him. Luke wasn't sure how he had understood this, but he had. He thought he would feel very odd if his own dad didn't come home in the evening and hadn't much liked those few weeks just before they moved when Sean was only around at the weekend. He didn't see him most nights, of course, because he was at work until quite late, but he was there in the mornings. Anyway, Diego obviously didn't think much of Luke and called him the *'Englese'*, or something like that. Luke knew it meant the English kid. It was one word that he had come to understand pretty quickly.

What Luke was really looking forward to was Henry's visit, which was going to be in fourteen days, according to his calendar. He was ticking them off one by one. Sometimes he was tempted to tick off an extra day and see if that made the time go faster. If he ticked off Tuesday on Monday, for instance, would he wake up the next morning and find that it was Wednesday? He thought probably not, but he didn't dare try without being sure in case there were things his mum wanted to do on Tuesday. Kate was being a bit vague at the moment. When they played Junior Monopoly she spent half her time staring out of the window and kept missing her turn. It was very annoying and it meant there wasn't much point asking her about anything. Everything would just have to wait until he saw his Dad in the evening and could ask him.

It was the new art history lessons that were absorbing most of Kate's attention and Sean and Luke were feeling the effect. As far as paintings went, Van Gogh's sketchy style didn't really do it for Sean. He preferred a proper picture, something with more form and detail. Canaletto, maybe. But he was pleased she was enjoying the course. It had given her a focus apart from Luke and she had stopped mentioning the baby they weren't having – not that it was remotely likely to appear now anyway, as their sex life had dried up completely. Apart from the lack of sex he thought they were rubbing along alright. The last couple of weekends they had all been to the Artis to visit the elephants. Sean had hoped to branch out, extend Luke's interest to the penguins and giraffes, but his son remained stubbornly attached to the great, grey beasts. One elephant in particular attracted his interested and affection, a huge male he had nicknamed Colonel Hathi after the chief elephant in Jungle Book.

'That's the daddy elephant, isn't it?' Luke asked, on each visit.

'Probably a granddad,' said Sean.

'Really?'

'I shouldn't be surprised.'

'He must be quite old then.' Luke regarded the stately beast with considerable awe.

The downside to Kate's new interest was that she had become distant somehow. Preoccupied, Sean supposed, by some question of colour or form in post-Impressionist art. He couldn't bring himself to ask in case the answer was long and boring. There were also tangible drawbacks: she forgot to buy bread and toilet paper, for instance. And Luke had mentioned a couple of times that she had been late picking him up from school. The time she didn't spend at the gallery she spent reading round her subject. There were several books on –isms, as Sean termed them, lying around the house full of bookmarks, together with a fat biography of Van Gogh. She had even started sketching, for goodness sake! Sean had no idea where that had come from. It wasn't as if she had ever been particularly artistic.

'She's gone nuts over a dead painter,' Sean told Lena during one of their increasingly regular Ikea lunches.

'Displacement, I expect,' Lena suggested.

'What's that supposed to mean?'

'Simple, she's displaced her fixation with having another child onto Van Gogh. Now she's fixated on him instead.'

'Well, I suppose broadly speaking that was the idea of it,' Sean agreed. 'Though I wish she wasn't quite so intense about everything.'

'According to Freud she'll be as intense about the displacement object as she was about the original.'

Sean rubbed his prickly scalp and looked perplexed.

'At least I can talk to you about it. All this mooning about is giving me the willies. I'm glad she's happier, but I could kind of understand the baby-thing. This – not a clue!'

Lena smiled sympathetically. 'I expect it'll burn itself out.'

If it doesn't burn us out first, thought Sean, taking off his glasses and polishing them gently with the serviette.

Lena watched him.

'You really have very sexy eyes. Did you ever consider getting contacts?'

'I did once but I didn't get on with them. Couldn't be bothered with all the cleaning and soaking.'

'There's lots of new materials on the market. These days you can get lenses that you can leave in for a month.'

'Really? Maybe I'll think about it.'

Lena nodded. 'You should.'

Sean blushed, and hurriedly replaced his spectacles.

*****

Kate sat in the café of the Van Gogh museum opposite Rudy, his espresso cup and a pile of sugar wrappers. He had paint on his fingers and he smelt of turpentine. It had taken Kate a while to identify the scent but eventually she had tracked it down in their cellar amidst some paint-encrusted brushes and half-empty pots of gloss. It was exciting, she thought, to imagine him going back to his studio after their coffee and working intently on some painting that might one day be as famous as the *Sunflowers*. Rudy glanced across the table at her folder which was rapidly filling up with notes all carefully cross-referenced.

'You've been working hard,' he commented, watching her carefully.

Her mouth twitched and she felt her colour rise. It really was an enormous file.

'Not especially,' she murmured, hoping to sound nonchalant. 'I've got time, that's all.'

She grimaced. That was worse. Now she looked like Katie no-mates and she guessed Rudy was too astute to be brushed off easily. This was their eighth session in the café and so far they had stuck pretty strictly to discussing Van Gogh and related subjects. Inevitably however, Kate had speculated. Was there a permanent someone in his life? He wore no wedding ring, but that meant very little. His clothes were clean and fashionable, but rarely ironed. Could he be gay? She didn't think so; wrong vibe. But perhaps he lived alone. His hair, tied back simply into that pony tail, was casually unconventional, but less so than it would have been in England. And those cobalt blue eyes had a depth of colour, a shifting quality. She glanced up and finding them fixed on her, quickly looked away. Vincent had identified the same chameleonic trait in the sea at Les-Saintes-Maries-de-la-Mer;

the Mediterranean — has a colour like mackerel, in other words, changing — you don't always know if it's green or purple — you don't always know if it's blue...' [1]

That's how Rudy's eyes were, as if the base colour was purple or green and the blue was an overlay. Kate understood that she was thinking differently, more visually, since starting to learn about painting. She had begun to see how artists built up colour in layers to give depth, like flavours in a meal. How Van Gogh had experimented with green and red to give his flesh the right tones in his self-portraits. She now saw that shades contrasted with each other, creating light, shadow and atmosphere rather than simply filling in the space between outlines. As someone who had always thought mostly in words she was being immersed in an unsuspected world of colour and form. She had bought pastels and was modestly trying them out –sketching birds, leaves, majestic canal houses, Luke from different angles, and once, even Sean. She had drawn him in the evening, bent over his laptop, a picture in three-quarter face. When she had finished she was disturbed to find that the sketch looked a lot like the man in front of her, but she didn't recognise him.

'So,' Rudy pressed her, 'why are you working so hard? What do you need to prove?' The blue eyes hovered between amusement and concern. 'What are you looking for? What is it that you have lost?'

Kate drew a sharp breath.

'Everything,' she mumbled. 'And nothing.' She smiled bleakly. 'Can I ask you something?'

'Of course, I am Dutch. You can ask questions and if I don't like to, I won't answer. You forget how easy it is with us, Kate.'

There was no mystery, then. Was this what he was saying? Just a regular guy?

'You're a painter?'

'Of course. But I cannot make my living from painting, and unlike Vincent, I have no brother to send me money. So I teach.'

Kate tapped the table with her pen and scribbled some circles in the margins of her notepad.

'You're not married?'

'No, I'm not married. And I'm not gay either. It's difficult when you work like I do.' His eyes narrowed with amusement. 'You should spend more time with Dutch people. You are becoming freer.'

Kate felt her colour rise again and cursed her pale English skin.

'English women have fine skin,' Rudy observed, as if reading her thoughts, 'like porcelain.' He hesitated. 'In fact, I would like to paint you.'

'Me!'

'Yes, you see, it's the colours. You don't see it too often here. Many Dutch women are too bright, too bold; hair the colour of brass; coarse, tanned skin. It is striking, of course, but it isn't subtle. It reflects their character, perhaps.'

'Okay,' said Kate doubtfully, 'and the English?'

'Paler, of course. More pinks, whites, creams and a little gold. The colour is inferred, suggested, you have to look for it. It is far less obvious.'

Kate's jaw tightened. 'So if you paint me, do I have to take my clothes off?'

'You don't have to do anything you don't want to, but really there is no other way to paint a woman.' Rudy shrugged. 'You can think about it. At the moment I am working on a painting for the council to be hung in the Amsterdam city hall. For me, this is very good; it shows my work is becoming known.'

Kate's head was spinning as she cycled home. It was a long time since she had stripped for anyone. Sex with Sean, if it happened at all, usually began with a familiar fumble under the bedclothes. Once, at the beginning of their relationship, in the tiny flat he had rented above a betting shop in Belsize Park, they had lit a fire in the little Victorian fireplace in the sitting room, put on some music and she had taken her clothes off item by item while he sat and watched. Afterwards the sex had been amazing, but none of it had come easily. She remembered several shots of vodka and coke had been necessary to get her in the mood. But this wasn't about sex, was it? It was about art. Rudy thought she was worth painting, studying, spending time and trouble over.

The idea was way beyond flattering. Sure, Kate knew she was in reasonable shape, but this was something else. She wondered what he saw when he looked at her. Not the rather sad and intense wife-and-mother-approaching-middle-age that Sean seemed to see. Someone trapped by her inhibitions, perhaps? It might be liberating to be painted naked. Nude, that was a better word. Soft flesh and – a horn sounded and Kate braked sharply inches from the passenger door of a car pulling out of a junction. Her large bike wobbled and she almost fell. The driver yelled something in Dutch. Kate was about to protest just as loudly in English, until she remembered the 'priority to the right' rule. Breathlessly she scrambled back into the saddle and peddled off.

It was his hands she couldn't stop thinking about, she realised five minutes later when she had reached home safely and was tugging the bike across the parquet floor and through the kitchen to the back garden. Those large brown hands with the square fingertips. She pictured them guiding the paintbrush. She imagined them gently caressing her skin. There, she had admitted it. Now she could wrap up the thought and lock it away deep inside her brain. It was neither appropriate nor helpful.

Chapter 13

Paula heard Ollie shouting as soon as she stepped out of the shower. Where was Dom for goodness sake? Saturday morning was supposed to be her time; a couple of child-free hours to pamper herself a bit. She needed to pluck her eyebrows, wax her legs and generally turn herself back into some semblance of a desirable woman after her week at home with the boys. She and Kate had used to laugh about how easy it would be to just let yourself slide into a hairy, lardy heap when there was no one much to look at you anyway. Husbands seemed to stop noticing and all the fanciable blokes kept themselves hidden away in offices during daylight hours. Kate always said that one good reason for going to work was that it forced you to change out of your pyjamas. She had a point. Paula wrinkled her nose. She was surprised how much she missed Kate. And Henry missed Luke. He had been much quieter since they left and grumpier with Ollie. She was even beginning to look forward to him starting school in the autumn.

September, only a few months away. It didn't seem possible that her first baby was going to be joining the big wide world so soon. The years since his birth had rushed by in a blur of broken nights, Pampers and hugs. Good years, really, despite the odd patches of total exhaustion. Paula didn't feel quite ready to let them go yet. Like Kate she was keen to have another child – and this time preferably a girl. That was what she had always wanted. She and her mum were so close it seemed inconceivable she wouldn't enjoy that same relationship with a daughter of her own. Her friend's experience had shown her that things don't always go to plan, but Paula felt she was more likely simply to conceive another boy than not to conceive at all. It was definitely worth a try – there was just Dom to talk round. The poor guy was still feeling a bit shell-shocked from the arrival of Ollie.

Their second son was by no stretch of the imagination an easy-going child.

She listened. Ollie seemed to have shut up so either Dom had picked him up or he had fallen back to sleep.

Reassured, Paula tipped some scented oil into her palm and began to moisturize. She was pleased to note that she still had some of the colour from last year's holiday. She tanned easily – unlike poor Kate who tended to go from white to cream. It would be great to see her friend again. She could hardly wait for the weekend.

Suddenly her hand jerked away. Something solid was lurking beneath the spongy, post-baby flesh of her left breast. She swallowed, forcing her unwilling fingers back to the spot. They prodded cautiously, exploring the size, the texture of this new object. A hard, bean-like thing was growing inside her body.

'A lump,' she whispered. 'Oh my God, a lump...' She lurched dizzily sideways, clutching at the basin for support and sat down heavily on the edge of the bath cradling her chest.

'Breathe slowly, Paula,' she told herself, her head hanging low over her knees. 'No need to panic. Eighty per cent of breast lumps in women under forty are benign. You're thirty-five. There's probably nothing to worry about.'

'Paula!'

She raised herself slowly. Dom was shouting up the stairs.

'Paula, your mum's on the phone shall I tell her you'll call back?'

She gulped, forcing down the bile that had filled her throat.

'Yep, just give me five minutes.' Hurriedly she pulled on her jeans and ran a comb through her wet hair. *Now then, Paula, no hysterics. It's probably nothing.* She glanced in the mirror and practised a smile. Did she look normal? And if she didn't would anyone notice? She pulled back her shoulders and unlocked the bathroom door.

Chapter 14

Late on Friday evening, Sean drove to Schiphol to pick up Paula, Dom and Henry. Dom looked exhausted, Sean thought. His complexion was the colour of a dirty puddle – presumably the result of long hours spent commuting. It occurred to him that he was no longer used to seeing faces with this pallor although there had been enough of them amongst his colleagues on the 7.15am to Liverpool Street.

'It's not just work,' Paula explained. 'It's Ollie. We don't seem to be able to get him to sleep through the night. And of course, if there's a toddler yelling then everyone wakes up.'

'Except me,' Henry piped up.

'Except you, thank goodness,' his mother agreed, nudging him into the backseat of the car.

Sean, loading their bags into the boot, nodded sympathetically. That was the problem with babies, you could never be quite sure what you were going to get. According to assorted female relations, Luke hadn't been too bad. Sean remembered being worried by this; he had seemed quite demanding enough, thank you.

By the time the car drew up outside the apartment Luke had been sitting on the bottom stair facing the door for forty-six minutes and thirty-two seconds, but now the visitors were actually there in front of him he was crippled with shyness.

'Say hello to Henry,' said Kate, giving him a prod.

'Hello, Henry,' he said in an odd voice, holding out his hand.

'Hello,' said Henry,' shaking it solemnly. The two boys stood taking stock of each other until Luke finally blurted:

'Guess what, Henry, I've got a train set. And I've got a real slide.'

'Can we go down it backwards?' Henry asked.

'You can if you want, but I might not.'

'I will though.'

'Come on, then,' said Luke, grabbing his old friend by the sleeve and half-dragging him up the stairs.

'We probably won't see them again until Sunday evening,' Paula laughed.

Sean opened beers for himself and Dom while in the kitchen Kate stirred the soup she had made earlier and chatted to Paula.

'I thought you might need something hot. I didn't know if you'd have had time to eat.'

'Dom came straight from work,' Paula admitted. 'He caught the train to Stansted.' She grinned. 'I'm impressed at all this cooking.'

'Only for special occasions.' Kate grinned. She hadn't realised how good it would feel to have a proper girlfriend around again. She felt as if she was being pulled out of a deep lake and back up into the air. Had she been drowning in Van Gogh? If she had she   hadn't known it.

'You look great, by the way,' said Paula.

'I thought I'd better tidy up a bit, they're all so smart round here.'

'Well, it suits you.'

On the other hand, Kate didn't think Paula looked great at all, although she didn't like to say so. There were deep smudges beneath her eyes that seemed to have been drawn with a marker pen. It could just be Ollie, of course, but he had been around for a while now and she didn't remember them being there before. She put down the wooden spoon and turned so she could examine her friend more closely.

'And so, how are you?' she asked. 'Apart from a serious lack of sleep, of course.'

Paula's face suddenly crumpled and Kate thought she might be about to cry, but she recovered herself and breathed in deeply.

'Fine,' she said, smoothing an imaginary crease from her skirt. 'Fine.' But she still looked sad. 'How's your course going? It must feel good to be using your brain again. Mine has turned to jelly I think, with all the nappies and talk of bottles and potty training.'

'It is good.' Kate said, realising that this was true. 'And the tutor is amazing. The course is in Dutch, but he goes through everything with me afterwards to make sure I've understood.'

'Wow,' said Paula. 'He must fancy you. Is he about ninety?'

'No, he's about thirty-five.'

'Thirty-five?' She threw her friend a sideways glance.

'Yes.'

'Right.'

'It's fine. He's just a tutor.' Kate tossed her hair.

Paula shrugged. 'Sure.'

Kate's face set. 'Call the boys would you, the soup's ready.'

At breakfast the following morning it was quickly agreed that they would split up with Sean and Dom taking the boys to the Artis to visit the elephants and the girls heading for the shops and possibly the Van Gogh museum. Luke had been adamant that the first thing Henry must do was meet Colonel Hathi. Dom confessed that this was fine with him as he wasn't really a museum kind of guy.

'That makes two of us,' said Sean.

'Three,' said Henry.

'Four,' said Luke.

Kate looked offended. 'Luke, I thought you liked the Van Gogh museum.

Luke gave an ostentatious sigh. 'I like the sunflower picture and the hot chocolate, Mummy. You know that.'

Kate had to concede that this was probably true. Perhaps she had forced the gallery on him just a tad.

'That's great,' said Paula, grinning broadly. 'Shopping it is for us, then.'

'But I must take you to see the paintings too,' Kate insisted as they set off towards the tram. 'I want you to see a couple that I really like. Maybe we should go there first.'

'Is your enigmatic tutor likely to be there?'

'It's possible. Sometimes he does personal tours for rich foreigners. It's very lucrative apparently, keeps him in canvas.'

'Okay then, it's a deal.'

'So best of all, you like the picture of the chair?' laughed Paula as they stood half an hour later in the main gallery. 'Why choose the chair?'

Kate shuffled her feet. 'It's the colour,' she said. 'That amazing turquoise-blue. And because it's Gauguin's chair. You can see in the painting how pleased Vincent was that Gauguin had come to stay. It's a friendly picture.'

'They fell out later, didn't they?' Paula remembered. 'Wasn't that connected somehow with the ear?'

Kate nodded.

'They spent nine weeks together in the yellow house in Arles but they argued about art. Gauguin was moving further away from impressionism and becoming interested in primitive stuff. Van Gogh didn't really get it. But neither of them were very stable people.'

'It seems funny to fall out over painting,' Paula mused.

'That was what mattered most to them.'

'That's what seems funny.' Paula glanced round the gallery. 'No sign of this Rudy guy, then.'

'Apparently not. Shall we have coffee here, anyway?'

They sat with their croissants and cappuccinos savouring the chocolate-sprinkled froth and the pleasure of being out in a big city without small children.

'So where do you recommend for shopping?' Paula asked. 'It's so long since I was here. I expect most of my old haunts have disappeared.'

'We can start with Cornelis Schuytstraat, there're lots of boutiquey-type places down there. If it's too expensive we can go to the shops in town.'

'Sounds good to me,' said Paula, dunking the tip of her croissant into her drink and nibbling it daintily. 'Funny how these things never taste quite as nice in England.' She surveyed the café with satisfaction.

'Hey, there he is.' Kate spluttered, her colour rising. Rudy had just come in accompanied by a lady with lavender-coloured hair and an elderly man who had teamed his brown-checked suit with a baseball cap. The couple leaned into each other, whilst keeping their eyes fixed firmly on their guide.

'Who?'

'My art-history teacher.'

Paula swivelled round. 'The guy at the counter with the pony tail? What's he doing?'

'I think he's just introducing those people to the waiter. He doesn't seem to be buying anything.'

'Is he going to sit down?'

'He probably hasn't got any money.'

'A penniless painter.' Paula raised her eyebrows meaningfully. 'Bad idea, Kate.'

'I'm not planning to...' Kate broke off. Rudy had turned and was looking in their direction. Perhaps he had caught their English voices through the low babble of the café. His cobalt blue stare moved slowly from Paula to Kate and his face creased into a smile of recognition. He nodded politely to the elderly couple and came towards them. Kate's blush deepened.

'*Dag*, Kate.' He bent forward to plant the obligatory three kisses on her cheeks and extended his hand to Paula. 'You must be Kate's friend from England.'

Paula smiled slowly. 'I am.'

'I've been showing some Americans around the museum.' He shook his head. 'They have this tick list of major works. From here they'll go to straight the Rijksmuseum and I expect they'll be in Paris by tomorrow. But for a change they seemed genuinely interested. And they pay well, as always.' He glanced around to make sure they weren't in earshot, but the couple in question were shuffling across the café to a seat at the far end.

'Would you like to join us for a coffee?' Kate asked.

Rudy looked slowly from one to the other. Paula felt his eyes delving into her, peeling back her skin, revealing her skull. He shook his head.

'Thanks, but you two look far too comfortable together. I don't want to interrupt. Anyway, I have to get back to work or I will never be the second greatest painter in the world. Have a good weekend in Amsterdam, Paula.'

'God!' Paula exclaimed, her gaze following his retreating back. 'Well, I would!'

'Shush, you're being silly.' Kate found her hands were shaking and quickly put them under the table.

'Am I?'

'Yes,' said Kate, as firmly as she could manage. 'Of course.'

Hours later Kate and Paula struggled out of the crowded tram with their brimming carrier bags.

'Shall we have one more coffee?' Kate suggested, 'before we go home.'

'Why not make it a beer?'

'Good idea. The boys will probably be watching football or something anyway.'

The café next to the Albert Heijn supermarket was closest. They installed themselves at a table by the window. The plush seats sank tiredly under their weight.

'That's better,' Paula sighed. 'My feet are killing me.'

'I think we're going out for Chinese tonight,' said Kate, 'so I don't have to cook, thank goodness.'

'Henry will like that. He loves Chinese.'

Kate ordered two bottles of Hoegaarden, sweeter and stronger than the *Amstel* Sean always drank. Paula took a large mouthful and held it for a second, savouring the taste.

'It's good.' She closed her eyes and the shadow Kate had noticed the previous evening flitted back across her face, settling on her features, obscuring them as the dark branches of a tree outside a window shroud the shapes in a room.

'Are you sure everything's okay?'

'Why wouldn't it be?'

'No reason, I just thought–' Kate was beginning to suspect something was very wrong, but if her friend didn't want to talk about it there wasn't much she could do.

Paula turned her head aside and examined the shelves behind the counter with their rows of dusty, coloured bottles.

'I found a lump,' she said, her voice monotone.

'What?' Kate stopped dead, her glass half-way to her mouth. A slow chill like an injection of ice, crept through her bowels and stomach and into her fingers. 'Where?'

'Usual place.'

'Which side?' Kate heard herself say. Although actually, what did it matter which bloody side? The world had shifted. She remembered a large metal globe she had owned as a teenager, a thirteenth birthday present from an uncle. When the light was switched on the world showed in relief. She had dropped it once and the two halves had fallen apart. It had never gone it back together properly. North and south just wouldn't line up.

'Left,' said Paula.

'When did you find it, have you… ?'

'I haven't done anything, yet. I only found it Thursday evening. I don't know how long it's been there. I don't check very often. I know you're supposed to.' Paula's voice dropped to a whisper. 'I'm shit scared.'

'Have you told Dom?'

'I didn't want to spoil the weekend. I thought four more days wouldn't make much difference. I'll tell him when we get home.'

'Go straight to the doctors.'

'Of course.' Paula waved a hand at the overflowing carrier bags. 'I don't know what I've bought all this stuff for. It's going to look a bit crap with no hair and only one boob.' Her hands flew to her face.

'Oh fuck,' said Kate, moving closer so she could put an arm round her. 'You know it might not be. It could be benign.'

'It's not,' said Paula with conviction. 'My aunt had it, my mum's sister. And my grandmother. My aunt died. She was thirty-nine. She left three children'

Kate squeezed her tighter. 'No wonder you look tired.'

'Yes, well, it wasn't just Ollie that kept me awake the last few days.' Paula admitted, wiping her eyes.

Kate caught the waiter's eye. 'Two more, please.'

'Even worse than telling Dom,' Paula went on, 'will be telling Mum. She's been through it all twice already.'

'I can imagine. But it's you that you really have to think about.'

'That's not obvious.' Paula smiled bleakly. 'We won't mention it again this weekend, okay?'

'But you'll let me know?'

'Of course. I'll tell you when I start the chemo.' She bit her thumb hard and swallowed. 'Look, I just wanted to say…'

'What?'

'I was joking earlier about your art teacher. Don't throw it away, that's all.'

'Meaning?'

'Well, you and Sean have been through a lot with all this stuff about the baby and I know it hasn't been easy.'

Now it was Kate's turn to look away. She studied the still-busy street through the window. A tram stopped on the main road. An elderly woman got out and walked slowly across to the costume jewellery shop opposite, leaning heavily on her stick. She paused outside to admire the sparkling paste jewels before pushing the door and venturing in. Fleetingly, Kate pictured her buying something pretty, for no reason, except that she wanted it. Then she thought about Sean; about the late evenings at work which, after an initial effort on his part, were slowly creeping back; about sex, which had once been fun and even after that a mundane pleasure, but was now so loaded and spoilt that both of them had lost interest; and about the girl with the orange tee-shirt that had put her arm around him.

'Maybe,' she said, through pressed lips, 'maybe it's not only me that's doing the throwing.'

It was a slow walk back to the apartment. Kate felt exhausted, weighed down by carrier bags and by their conversation. She could see Paula felt the same. Neither spoke much. On the doorstep, Kate glanced at her friend. Paula took a deep breath, composed her expression and nodded. Luke had obviously been listening for the key because the click of the opening door was instantly followed by the thud of feet on the wooden floor. As the women entered, their sons launched themselves towards them like friendly missiles. Paula staggered backwards but managed to smile. Kate caught Luke and, bending down, buried her face in his shoulder and squeezed him hard.

'You'll never guess what we saw,' he said, struggling free and looking expectantly at his mother.

'Erm, don't tell me,' Kate laughed. 'Elephants?'

'Yes, obviously. But what *kind* of elephants?'

'An *oliphant*-elephant?'

'Mu-um, you're being silly.'

'So, what kind then?'

'A baby elephant,' Henry shouted, unable to contain himself.

'Henry!' Luke yelled, his face contorted, 'I was supposed to say that.'

Henry hopped from one foot to the other and gave a little shrug.

'It doesn't matter,' Kate consoled. 'It's still exciting. Was it very sweet?'

'Quite sweet,' Luke admitted. 'It's called Mumba and it sucked milk from its mummy-elephant.' He turned to his friend, recent treachery already forgotten; 'But Henry liked the giraffes best, didn't you, Henry?'

Henry nodded placidly. 'I like their long necks,' he explained.

'I can see why you would,' said Paula. 'I like them too. And their faces always seem to be smiling.'

Sean appeared in the hallway, looking, Kate thought, more relaxed than he had for weeks.

'Would you girls like a glass of wine or something before we go out? You've got about half an hour. The table's booked for seven.'

Kate looked sheepish. 'No thanks. We stopped on the main road for a beer. The opportunity was too good to resist.'

Luke gave an elaborate sigh. 'No wonder you took so long.'

'Have I got time for a quick shower?' Paula asked.

'I should think so. Towels are in the cupboard in your bedroom.'

Paula climbed the steep grey stairs, slowly, using the banister, as though everything was already different. She will take off her clothes, Kate thought, and stand naked in front of the mirror. She will try to fix her body in her mind, knowing that it must soon be altered. She will stand in the shower and the water that runs over her will mix with her tears.

She realised Sean was watching her. Had her face given something away? Her mouth twitched into a semblance of a smile. The boys had disappeared into the living room and were pestering Dom. It sounded like he was wrestling with them. Kate kept her fingers crossed for the leather sofa. Sean opened his mouth as if to speak, then closed it again like a fish. Kate jumped in quickly.

'Did you have a good day?' she said brightly.

'Yep. Kids loved it as usual. Dom and I managed a quiet beer in the café while they tormented the goats and piglets in the children's zoo. Did Paula like the museum?'

'She did.' Kate averted her gaze, picking up her handbag to search for some imaginary object.

'Is everything okay?'

'Yes,' she said. 'Of course.'

'If you say so.' Her husband rubbed his hand across the soft prickles of his scalp.

'I do.' She looked up full into his face. It occurred to Sean that she had been crying. 'Just for the moment, anyway.'

Dom appeared in the living room doorway with a small boy under each arm. He was shorter than Sean but much stockier. In his youth he had been an excellent scrum half for the school rugby team. The boys were wriggling with fierce delight and pummelling his chest.

'Do you want these anywhere in particular,' he grinned. The grin faded as he looked from Sean to Kate. 'Er sorry,' he mumbled and backed into the kitchen still holding Luke and Henry. 'Now, you two, I need another beer so I'll have to drop you here.' He lowered them to the floor amidst squeals of protest. Beyond the kitchen door the twilight gardens descended into night.

Twenty minutes later, Paula came down the stairs, her short, dark hair fluffed up by the drier and her eyes oddly bright as if propped open with invisible matchsticks. Kate's gaze flicked from her to Dom in the kitchen, to Sean and lastly to Luke and Henry. The moment hung, as if the pause button had been pressed; it slowed and stretched, seeming, as Kate watched, to develop the graininess of history, to fill with the passionate intensity of a Van Gogh painting, colour and form flung onto canvas with deliberate, focussed intent. Beneath the chandelier Paula stood and waited, light bouncing off her soft hair, the dip of her mouth uncertain, the green of her dress vibrant. Around her the two boys played, scrambling on the floor like puppies, firing imaginary guns. Kate swallowed.

'Let's go then, shall we?' she suggested, cheerily. 'You must all be starving. Get your coat, Luke.'

Paula clutched Dom's arm and Kate saw him look down at her, thrown by her sudden vulnerability. The worrying had begun.

Chapter 15

Sean blinked hard. The lenses didn't feel as bad as he had expected and now they had been successfully inserted they could apparently stay in for up to twenty-eight days – although he wasn't sure he fancied leaving them there as long as that. Kate had spotted them the night before, of course, when he had spread the little case and cleaning products along the bathroom shelf.

'Contact lenses?' she looked at him curiously. 'I thought you were dead against them.'

'I was,' he mumbled in reply. 'But I heard about these new ones that you can wear for a month.'

'Did you? Who told you about them?'

'Just somebody at work.'

'Really?' She had stared at him even harder. 'Do you talk about things like that, then? I thought you only discussed the joint venture, computer programmes and who was having it off with whom.'

She had pronounced the 'm' on whom quite deliberately which had irritated Sean. Had she always been this pedantic?

He had consciously avoided saying that the lenses were Lena's suggestion. The less he mentioned her the better, he felt. She didn't appear to bring a very positive vibe into the household – even though there was absolutely nothing between them apart from friendship. And just at the moment Sean felt very much in need of a friend. His wife seemed to have gone off on some art tangent of her own, which hadn't really been what he meant when he had suggested she found a hobby. He should have known that whatever she did Kate would have to throw herself into it or it wouldn't mean anything to her. At least the baby-stuff was shelved and that was a relief – but unfortunately so was the sex that went with it. Sean's stomach felt increasingly like a tightly coiled spring and he was getting thoroughly fed up with DIY quickies in the bathroom. They weren't a patch on the real thing.

Lena was standing by the coffee machine when he arrived at work. It crossed Sean's mind that perhaps she was waiting for him. These days she always seemed to be there at around this time. Consequently he found himself saving up things to say to her, anticipating her presence, just as once he had used to with Kate. Yet he knew he didn't feel the same way about her as he felt about his wife. This thing – whatever it was – was more exciting, but much less substantial. Lena was pretty, sexy, smart and she had made it clear that she fancied him. It was an intoxicating mixture and definitely made Sean feel high. But that was all it was. He was married and this was just a harmless flirtation with a colleague.

'Hey,' she grinned as he stepped out of the lift, 'at last we can see the real Sean Butterworth.'

She slurred the double 't', Sean noticed, as an American would, and couldn't quite manage the 'th'. Once the trans-Atlantic twang would have annoyed him; now, he simply found it cute. He smiled shyly, hoping the feeling that he had a fly in his eye would soon go away.

'I'm glad you approve.'

'Do they feel strange?'

'A bit.'

'You'll get used to them real quickly.'

'Good.' He blinked again. 'Are we doing lunch?'

Lena allowed herself a tiny smile of triumph. They had eaten together four times so far, always at Ikea and always at the same table, but this was the first time he had suggested it. She handed him a cup of sweet, black coffee.

'Sure. I presume you'll be at Cassidy's leaving party on Friday.'

'Absolutely. That's a cause for a celebration if ever there was one!'

'I just wonder what the new boss will be like.'

'Well, he's Dutch, so he'll almost certainly be taller.'

'Ha, ha.'

It had always been a bit of a joke in the building that their American managing director was a head shorter than most of the Dutch women and about half the size of the men. Hence his Attila the Hun complex, Sean maintained.

'Anyway, I must go and do some work,' Lena announced, strutting across to the door. 'See you later.'

*****

'So how are you finding it?' Rudy asked as he and Kate settled themselves at their usual table in the museum café.

'I'm understanding a bit more, I think,' said Kate, 'but there's something I'd like to mention. That is, I'm not sure the other, err, students approve of these extra lessons.'

At the end of the last session a very thin woman with a back like a ramrod who Kate thought might be called Rita had peered down her nose and declared:

'I presume you and Mr de Jong will be going over it all again now. How nice to benefit from private tuition. I wish we all had your charm.'

Kate had blushed scarlet and mumbled something about not really understanding Dutch.

'Perhaps you shouldn't have joined the course then,' Rita had snottily remarked.

'I don't really seem to have gelled with the other students,' Kate confessed, 'except perhaps Wim.'

'Ha,' Rudy laughed. 'It would be impossible not to gel with Wim. He's everyone's friend.'

Kate pictured the jovial old man who earlier had pulled a tube of Droste's chocolate pastilles from his pocket and offered her one.

'I wish they were all like him.'

'Don't let them intimidate you,' said Rudy firmly. 'They have paid for a course on Van Gogh and that is what they're getting. For me this teaching, this is to make some money. I tell bored housewives and pensioners about the greatest painter in the world and maybe the time is not wasted. Maybe they really want to know and they see the world a bit differently afterwards. I am teaching them well.' His voice softened and his eyes crinkled in the way that always made Kate's toes curl. 'You simply get a bit more. Surely this is my choice.'

'I suppose it is,' she said, frowning. 'Am I a bored housewife, then?'

'You tell me. Maybe you are a little bored, but mostly I think you are sad.'

Kate bit her lip and dunked a cinnamon biscuit into her coffee. 'When I leave Holland,' she said, deliberately changing the subject, 'I might have to arrange for these to be sent over.'

Rudy gave her an odd look. 'Maybe you don't leave as soon as you think. Anyway, I will send you cinnamon *speculaas* once a week. You won't have to worry. Now,' he ran down his notes with a brown, square-tipped finger, 'today I was talking about madness. *Krankzinnigheid* we say in Dutch, or more colloquially, *gekheid*. I have read Van Gogh's letters extensively and it is quite clear that he was not nearly as interested in his madness as his critics have subsequently been. Of course, he understood the parallels that were being drawn at that time between genius and insanity. You may already know that the second half of the nineteenth century was a major period for the development of psychiatry and all illnesses of the mind. Vincent was not an ignorant man, he too knew of these things. But he did not want to be known for insanity; he wanted to be known as a first class painter. He almost never wrote letters during periods of mental crisis, just as he didn't paint at these times. It seems likely that he didn't want this instability to dilute and encroach upon his art.'

'Surely it must have done,' Kate protested, looking up from her notebook where she had been scribbling hard. 'If it was a part of him, it must have been a part of his work.'

'I think Van Gogh wanted to keep control of his art,' Rudy explained. 'When he was in crisis he was maybe not in control. Realising this, he didn't paint and he didn't really write. It's as if he went into his cave, like an injured animal that finds a quiet solitary place, and waits for the storm to pass. You see,' his frown deepened as he tried to find the best English words to explain his ideas, 'his letters, like his paintings, show that he was a man possessed, obsessed, enraged perhaps, passionate certainly, but ultimately Vincent is still there guiding the pen and the brush. When he was in crisis Vincent was no longer in control of his tools, he was subsumed by his illness. That is why he did not paint or write; it would not have been his work.'

Kate put down her pen and folded her arms. 'But you're saying that the madness wasn't him. How can that be? Perhaps without the madness he wouldn't have had the genius.'

'Of course.' Rudy shrugged. 'That's completely possible. But I imagine he wanted his conscious self to be the pilot, the captain of his art. In times of madness it is perhaps the unconscious that takes over.'

'I see what you mean.' Kate chewed the end of her pen. 'I'll think I'll go back up to the gallery and have another look before I go home.'

'Good idea,' Rudy agreed. 'I think there you will find genius, but not madness.' He closed his notebook. 'By the way, Kate...'

'Yes,' she said, tucking a stray strand of amber hair behind her ear.

'I wanted to ask, all this studying Vincent Van Gogh, are you beginning to see the world in a new way?'

'I am starting to see shape and colour where before there were just things,' she admitted. 'The world has become more broken up, but also more connected.' She paused. 'You know, I would really like to go south, to Arles, to see the sunflowers and the Yellow House, to understand where these pictures came from.'

Rudy nodded. 'Everyone who studies Vincent's work must go to Provence, eventually. But Kate,' he said, frowning as he caught sight of the café clock, 'did you forget it's Wednesday?'

'Oh my God, Luke! I've got three minutes to get there.' She crammed her books into her bag and pushed back the chair. 'See you Friday.'

How could she possibly have forgotten that Wednesday was half day?

She arrived at the school hot and breathless to find Saskia and Heijn standing outside the gates with Luke. Luke looked very small and brown beside the tall, blonde Dutch people. His cheeks were smudged and puffy.

'*Hoi*, what happened to you?' Saskia asked. 'I was just thinking about adopting him.'

'I'm really sorry,' Kate gasped. 'I got held up at the museum.'

'Don't worry, that's cool. I just thought you had maybe fallen off your bike or something.' She swung a leg over her own enormous machine, a great black beast with drum brakes and a child seat that resembled an arm chair. 'Come on Heijn, jump on. We have to hurry,' she explained, 'he has football again this afternoon.'

'Of course. Thanks ever so much for waiting with Luke.'

'You forgot, didn't you, Mummy,' said Luke accusingly, as soon as they were left alone.

'Yes,' Kate admitted. 'But then I remembered.'

Luke's eyes filled with tears. 'I don't like it when you forget.'

'No, I'm not surprised. I won't forget again.'

'Is that a promise?'

Kate swallowed. 'The trouble with forgetting is that you forget, so it's hard to promise.'

'I want you to promise.'

'Okay, then, I promise,' Kate reluctantly agreed. 'Was school okay?'

'Yep, apart from Diego. But Tobias asked me to play this afternoon. Can I go to his house?'

'I don't know where he lives, sweetheart. Let's arrange it for next week when I've had a chance to talk to his mother.'

'Hmmp. If you'd have been here you could have talked to her today,' Luke pointed out, climbing crossly onto the bike seat.

'You're right,' Kate acknowledged miserably. Pedalling off along the quiet street she reflected how easy it had been to lose track of time.

'Mummy,' Luke shouted throwing off his coat and dashing into the sitting room while Kate put the bike away. 'There's a message on the phone.'

'Coming.' Kate pressed the button and Paula's voice filled the apartment.

'That's Henry's Mummy. She sounds funny.'

'Shush, listen.'

'Hi Kate,' said the recording. 'It's just like I said. I need to talk. Call me back as soon as you can.'

'What's does she mean?' Luke demanded.

'I don't know,' Kate lied. 'Would you like to have lunch in front of the telly while I phone her?'

'Hey, yeah!' This was an unsought treat. 'Can I have pasta?'

'Why not!' In fact, Kate thought bitterly, why not give them everything they want? You never know when stuff like this is going to happen. Who wants to be remembered as the mother who wouldn't do pasta lunches in front of the telly?

Once Luke was settled with Percy, penne, tomato sauce, babybel and CBeebies, Kate took the phone up to the bedroom and sat cross-legged against the pillows. From the bed she could see the buildings that made up this grand square of apartment blocks and the patch of blue sky above them. For once, the sun was shining and in the gardens below, the trees were clothed in the bridesmaid green of spring. A flowering cherry, prolonging its annual moment of glory, still wore clusters of the palest pink flowers, delicate against its black boughs like a Japanese print. It reminded Kate of Van Gogh's almond blossom paintings. Was she now destined to see everything as a reflection of his work? She dropped the phone into her lap wondering what she should say to Paula. There was nothing, she concluded, nothing she could say that would help at all. Her job was simply to listen. She pictured the tumour as a throbbing, octopus-like organism, sending out tentacles which burrowed deep into tissue, spreading rot where it touched. She hastily blocked out the image and pressed the speed dial. The phone rang four times and clicked onto the answering machine. Kate hesitated but then decided to speak.

'Hi, this is...'

There was a rustling sound. 'Hi!' breathed Paula's voice. 'I'm sorry I didn't pick it up straight away. There aren't many people I want to talk to.'

'That's okay. I do that sometimes,' Kate admitted, 'usually to avoid all those cold callers trying to sell me solar panels or frozen meals. How are you?'

'Awful,' she said simply. 'A mess. I can't handle it at all. I'm not the slightest bit brave. I keep bursting into tears.'

'Oh God,' murmured Kate, not knowing what else to say. 'So you found out for sure. I mean, you've had the results of the biopsy.'

'I got them yesterday, but I wanted to tell Dom first.'

'Of course. And what were the results?'

Paula sniffed hard and Kate could hear a nose being blown.

'There's no secondary cancer, but it's not nothing either. It's spread into the lymph nodes and that's not good. I'll have to have a mastectomy, and after that chemotherapy. If I get through all that I'll still have to take medication for the rest of my life.'

'But did they sound optimistic? I've been reading up a bit on the net and it looks like more and more women are coming through it,' said Kate, trying to sound upbeat.

'All they would say was that if the cancer doesn't come back within five years, there's a good chance I'll live 'til I'm seventy. And if it does, as far as I can see, I've pretty much had it.'

'Okay, but it's not going to come back within five years. Think positively.'

'They have to get rid of it this time first,' Paula reminded her. 'And they tell me this tumour is already quite big. With my family history I should have been going for regular mammograms, apparently.'

'Did you know that?'

Paula gave a choked laugh. 'Kind of. I didn't want them to find anything so it seemed better if they didn't look.'

'Oh Paula!'

'That's exactly what Dom said. It doesn't make me feel any better. I'm just a coward, Kate. And now I feel it's all my fault I've got this stupid lump.'

'Of course it's not your fault. It's rotten bad luck. How did Dom take it generally?'

'He was amazingly fantastic.' For the first time Kate heard a smile in Paula's voice. 'He said he would love me regardless of how many bits were cut off or reconstructed. He's much more optimistic than me. He spent last night researching treatments while I sat in a heap and watched *Eastenders*.'

'That's great, then. At least you're in it together.'

'I suppose so.'

'So do you know when you have the operation?'

'They've booked me in for next Tuesday.'

'No hanging about then. That's good, anyway.'

'Is it?' Paula asked. 'Doesn't it just mean it's really serious? It's the National Health remember. Nothing happens fast unless you're dying.'

Kate bit her lip. 'It's happening fast to stop you dying.' She tried to sound encouraging. 'That's the point.'

'Hmm.'

There was a crash in the background.

'Oh dear,' said Paula, 'I'd better go. It sounds like Ollie's woken up and is throwing his toys out of his cot.'

'Let me know, won't you. About everything. We'll talk again soon.'

Kate found she was clutching the phone very tightly as she went back downstairs.

'Breast cancer,' said Sean, sitting down at the kitchen table and opening his first beer of the evening. He ran his hand across his scalp. 'Christ, that's really crap. The only person I knew with breast cancer was the tea lady at our office in London but she was a lot older than Paula. Probably about fifty I should think.' His brow furrowed as he tried to remember. 'She died, actually. There was a collection for flowers. Poor Paula.' He took a swig of his beer. 'And poor old Dom. He's in for a hard time.'

'Poor old Dom!' cried Kate, slamming the chopping board onto the counter and scattering the onions. 'Why 'poor old Dom'? It's Paula who might die, for goodness sake!'

'Eh?' A hunted expression swept across Sean's face. 'Of course, but I mean, it's Dom who'll have to take all the flack, look after the kids and stuff if she... well even if she doesn't. She'll still be ill, won't she?'

Kate stared at her husband. 'Yes, she will,' she said more quietly. 'She'll be very ill indeed.'

'Right. That's what I meant. Well, I think I'll take a quick shower before tea,' murmured Sean escaping to the stairs.

As the water pummelled him he thought about what Kate had said. This life they promised you, it was far from guaranteed, it seemed. It could mess up even if you didn't do anything wrong. He had always known that in theory – it might be a car accident, plane crash, you could have a heart attack or you could get breast cancer – they all amounted to the same thing. One little bolt of lightning, someone up there marking your card and that was it. It made everything else a bit pointless didn't it? Why would you bother to play by the rules with that hanging over you? He stepped out of the shower and rubbed himself vigorously. All these thoughts of mortality were getting to him. He needed to feel alive. He really hoped Kate would feel like a shag tonight.

But it was late when she finally came to bed. So late that Sean wondered if she was banking on him being asleep, but sleep wasn't really an option for him just now. Through half-closed eyes he watched her get undressed in the soft light from the hallway. Her face was sad and still as she pulled off her tee-shirt and slipped on the silky nightie she liked to feel against her skin. He wanted to hold her against him, comfort her with his warmth. She slid under the duvet without glancing in his direction and turned automatically towards the window, away from him. He wriggled closer, spooning her so she would feel how much he wanted her. She didn't move. Sean hesitated. Perhaps, if he was really gentle... He edged his hand along the curve of her hip and tummy until it cupped her breast. Now she reacted, pushing it sharply away.

'Come on, Katie, let me at least see if I can get you in the mood.'

'No.' It was a short, sharp uncompromising syllable.

'Why not?'

'Because my best friend has cancer and weirdly enough that means I don't feel like it.'

'Doesn't it make you want to live while you can?'

'Not tonight. It just makes me feel sad and numb.'

'Christ,' muttered Sean, rolling over, 'I can't stay here like this, we never make love anymore. I'm going in the spare room.'

'Bed's not made up,' said Kate flatly, still lying motionless, her face turned from him.

'It's not that cold. I'll find a blanket.' The bed rocked as Sean swung himself into a sitting position and reached for his dressing gown. His erection was rapidly subsiding but the irritation remained.

He locked his fingers behind his head and flexed them until they clicked loudly.

'What the fuck's the matter with you? You never used to be like this.'

Kate did not reply. Sean pulled the robe round him and strode across to the door, shutting it firmly behind him. With the light from the hallway gone the room was pitch black. Kate heard the floorboards creak in the spare room and when she was sure he wasn't coming back she pushed herself up on her elbow, reached for a tissue from the bedside cupboard and blotted her face.

Chapter 16

It wasn't until he was already half-way to work that Sean realised he had forgotten to tell Kate about Cassidy's leaving party that evening. This wasn't particularly surprising as they had hardly spoken for the last two days, ever since the news about Paula's breast cancer and the complete breakdown – well, that was how it felt – of any relations at all on the sexual front. This illness thing had made them both feel a bit weird, he decided. Vulnerable, that was it. Kate had reacted by switching off completely, withdrawing into herself, while conversely the news had made him want to grab what he could while he could because it seemed you never knew what was coming next. There you are having kids, paying your mortgage and generally minding your own business when *wham*, someone above picks you out for target practice. It was crap, basically.

Nevertheless, he found himself humming as he filed onto the Amsterdam ring road and a little self-analysis revealed that this was based on the anticipation of having drinks later with Lena. The usual format for leaving parties was a quick gathering with the presentation of a gift, cake and some cheap bubbly in the office followed by everyone adjourning to the nearest bar for more drinks. The hardcore often stayed on for food and made an evening of it. Sean thought he might do this if Lena was interested. He could easily get the tram home if he needed to and it would be good to talk to her somewhere other than Ikea. The place everyone usually went to, *Het Witte Paardje*, had a great ambiance and apparently served an excellent hamburger and salad. He decided to text Kate and tell her what he was doing rather than phone and risk any recriminations that might ensue. It wasn't that he was bothered about her worrying, he told himself, but rather that he didn't like the idea of Luke waiting up for him and then being disappointed. The text was short and factual, deliberately without any hint of apology.

Forgot to mention Cassidy's leaving do tonight. Will probably be late. Don't let Luke wait up, will see him tomorrow.

Kate would take it in the spirit it was intended, he surmised. Their marriage had hit a rough patch, that was for sure. They didn't seem to be on the same wavelength any more – if Kate was actually on a wavelength, sometimes she seemed to have fallen completely off the bandwidth. He wondered, as he entered the lift and pressed the button for the eighth floor, if they should see a counsellor or something, but this thought evaporated as the doors opened and he caught sight of Lena's buttocks covered with some silky stuff waiting for him beside the coffee machine. *Waiting for him!*

'Hey, great shirt,' she said as he approached.

'Really? Thanks,' Sean replied, trying to look as if he had put on his best Ted Baker-lucky-buy-at-Bicester-Village completely by chance that morning.

'I love the colours, especially with that tie.'

His grin widened, though a part of him did wonder if she was going maybe a tiny bit over the top.

'So, you can make it to the leaving party?'

'Of course.' Sean sipped the coffee she handed him.

'We'll probably be heading to the bar afterwards. It should be a good night – or do you have to get home?' Her black eyes flashed.

'Not especially.'

'Great, see you later then.'

He watched appreciatively as she walked away, ignoring the small, insistent voice that played over in his head; *That one's trouble, Sean mate, trouble.*

Kate picked up the text as she sat at the kitchen table with her coffee waiting for Luke to finish his Rice Krispies. There had been a time not very long ago, she thought, when he would have phoned, or failing that covered the text with kisses and claimed the whole thing was a pain and he would rather come home, even if it wasn't actually the truth. Now he apparently didn't feel the need. Presumably – and she felt she had to presume this – because he would not rather come home. In fact, he would rather go out boozing with his work mates, who might or might not include that coffee-coloured girl with the tight orange tee-shirt and boob job that they had bumped into by the Vondelpark. Kate tried to work out how much this bothered her and discovered that she was weary of Sean's empty promises to come home earlier. She was fed up at the way he had transplanted them all to this city with talk of improved family life. It wasn't happening; instead he used the time he gained on the commute to stay later at work. She was upset by his lack of understanding about the absence of a baby; what a failure she felt and how much it mattered. And most recently, she was dismayed at his evident inability to discuss Paula's illness. She had broached the subject a couple of times but he had brushed it aside. He claimed to have emailed Dom and she could just imagine what he might have said:

Just heard about Paula. Bad luck, mate, that's really terrible news. Let us know if we can do anything to help. By the way, what do you think of Harry Kane? Or something like that. So perhaps in the end she wasn't all that bothered that Sean would be late home this evening. Maybe she had got tired of caring.

Unfortunately the same couldn't be said about his son. Luke was furious, banging his glass on the table so the apple juice splashed over his sweatshirt.

'Why isn't he coming home 'til late? I wanted to tell him about Tobias's birthday.'

'You can tell him tomorrow,' Kate had soothed. 'It doesn't make much difference, does it?'

'It does to me.'

'His boss is leaving and they all have a little party to say goodbye.'

'Well, they should have it in the day time. Evening is for coming home.'

Kate sighed. 'Never mind. Look, pop upstairs and change your jumper, it's nearly time for school.'

What, after all, was she supposed to say? She was sick of making excuses for her husband. He would just have to come back and make his own.

After dropping Luke at the school gates Kate cycled slowly to the Van Gogh Museum for her class. The morning was sweet; a poached-egg sun, hung hazily in the delft-blue sky and the air was filled with the honey scent of early summer. She felt a surge of love for this calm, tolerant city, followed by a shaft of guilt. It felt somehow disloyal to enjoy herself when her friend was so ill. She supposed this must be a normal reaction but it was uncomfortable nevertheless. The image of the burrowing cancer refused to leave her. It seemed to have taken root in her mind just as it had in Paula's body. Kate bit her lip. She was grateful she had Rudy and his lectures; they gave her something else to think about.

'Maybe,' Rudy suggested, as they settled themselves in the café, 'if you are free after we have talked about Vincent, then you might come with me to my apartment so I could start to paint you? I will also make photographs so I can continue in the summer when I am no longer in Amsterdam.'

'Where are you going in the summer?' Kate asked. The words came out more quickly than she had intended.

'I am going to France. In the summer I do lectures at the Musée d'Orsay in Paris. This is very good work for me and I can tell many people about the greatest painter the world has ever known.'

'Do you believe that? I mean, I know he was good, of course, but do you really think Van Gogh was that great?'

Rudy's light blue eyes studied her seriously.

'That is what I really think, Kaatje.' He leant back in his chair. 'Of course, not everyone thinks this. There are many who would disagree.' He threw her a challenging look. 'It is for you to make up your own mind. But first you must inform yourself. Now, shall we take a look at the lesson?'

'Today the Amsterdam summer has begun,' Rudy announced as they cycled side-by-side along the Prinsengracht towards this studio in the Jordaan.

'I've never been to this area before,' said Kate looking round. It seemed more eclectic, more interesting, than central Amsterdam, full of tiny little shops selling junk which spilled onto the street and boutiques crammed with rails of vintage clothes. She wished she had known about it before, she could have brought Paula here. They would have had a great time exploring the secret little shops and galleries hidden down the side streets.

'It's an area that is becoming more known, unfortunately,' Rudy explained. 'Just a few years ago I bought this apartment with some inheritance from my grandmother. Now it is worth quite a lot of money.'

'Why unfortunately? Surely that's good for you,' said Kate.

'*Nee*, you are thinking like an English woman.' He grinned at her. 'This is no surprise, of course. But you see, I just wanted a place to live. I liked the area. The value wasn't important. Now it becomes important because the people that used to live here, they are moving out and I like the new people less. Here we are.' He braked abruptly in front of a tall thin building with peeling casement windows, one for each storey like a child's painting. He vaulted from the saddle and locked his bike to the rack. Kate copied him, though more hesitantly, and followed him inside. A bare wooden staircase rose in front of them exuding an odour of baked wood and dust. Blurred sunlight shone through the grimy glass and Kate felt her skin desiccating in the heat. The windows probably hadn't been opened for years. She climbed slowly and with each turn of the staircase found herself gazing out from a platform a couple of metres higher than the one before. Below the canal drifted, green-brown and flat as glass, lined with boats, reflecting the tall houses with their painted-white woodwork and the summer-green trees which wobbled almost imperceptibly in the breath of breeze. At last they reached the very top floor and Rudy pulled a key from his pocket.

'An artist must live in a garret, don't you think? After you.'

Kate stepped through the open door and her hand flew to cover her mouth. The air was stifling, heavy with the competing smells of warm paint, linseed oil, dirty underwear and the remains of a take away.

'Sorry. It's always hot here in the summer. I'll open a window.'

There were plenty to choose from. The apartment had been built into the attic space and extended across the entire top floor of the house. One small pane of glass looked out onto the world but the roof was lined with huge skylights through which light poured. Rudy wrestled with one of these and a gust of fresh warm air rushed in. Kate breathed deeply and looked about her.

The flat was half artist's studio – paints, canvases finished and unfinished, an easel, brushes and jars of oils; and half student bedsit – futon unmade under the eaves, pillows still dented from a sleeping head – just one, she thought – cloud-balls of dust unswept in corners and a cheap Ikea rug on the wooden floorboards. In one corner, below the little window was a tiny kitchen with sink, two electric rings and a microwave. The worktop was stained and dirty and a plate covered in breadcrumbs lay forgotten on a battered pine table. It was a long time since Kate had been in a room like this. Rudy caught her glance.

'I have no wife,' he said with a shrug.

'That doesn't mean…' Kate blustered, but stopped abruptly when she saw the amusement in his eyes. 'Alright then,' she said, 'we haven't got long, so what do you want me to do?' She hadn't meant to sound so terse but suddenly this man, this flat, this whole idea….

'Are you comfortable with this? If you are not comfortable we can just take a coffee and you can go home,' Rudy suggested quietly.

'I don't want to go home. It's just…' Her gaze dropped. How could she say that she felt like she had stepped outside her settled self and even as she stood there she was being remoulded like a piece of plasticine under strong, shrewd fingers. And the experience wasn't entirely unproblematic.

For some moments Rudy regarded her intently.

'Yes,' he said at last, 'I see that you want to stay. Now, before we start I want to show you something. Come over here.' He led the way to a corner of the flat where an elderly wooden ladder leaned against what looked like a loft hatch. 'My garden, he explained, climbing the wobbly steps with careless confidence.

At the top, he pushed open the trapdoor, stepped through and disappeared from sight. Kate found herself staring at a square of blue sky. She followed more slowly, poking her head up and looking round tentatively like an animal checking for predators. Rudy waited. His face had resettled into its usual expression of wry amusement. As she mounted the last few steps he held out his hand and helped her out on to a square patio with brightly coloured pots overflowing with trailing foliage and a rickety iron table on which sat jars of half burnt candles. Beyond the railings that encircled the terrace, a patchwork of roofs stretched to the horizon. Some, steeply gabled, sat like pompous hats on top of the canal houses; others like this one, had been cut away to make an outside space in a crowded city; a garden room of rusty furniture, plants and sky.

'A world above a world,' Kate exclaimed, sensing that here she was being shown a glimpse of a different Amsterdam, a city perhaps closer to the one Vincent might have known. She turned to Rudy to find him studying her with open curiosity, through serious blue eyes.

'So,' he said, when she had finished marvelling at the view of the Westerkerk and he had persuaded her back inside. 'I would like you to lie over there.'

Kate blinked. She had been so busy disapproving of the general mess in the studio that she hadn't noticed the daybed in the corner.

'Then the light falls on you,' Rudy explained. 'This light from the north is good; indirect light. You see, the southern light is too strong for English skin. Everything must be subtle.'

Kate stared at the sofa and then at Rudy.

'You can undress behind the screen. There is a robe. I will put silk on this couch. I have a piece of green silk. Like emeralds. That is right for you, I think. You don't need to worry, it is clean, I promise.'

Kate swallowed but did not move. The studio was warm despite the open window but her skin prickled. What was Luke's mother, Scan's wife, doing in this place with this attractive man? Was she really going to take off her clothes and lie on the couch as he had said? Normally, she struggled to go topless even on a beach. Her thoughts bounced back to a holiday in Rimini with Paula and Dom when she and Paula had giggled and agreed 'I will if you will'. There were plenty of younger, firmer breasts to ogle and the boys had barely noticed. She remembered feeling slightly insulted that Sean hadn't complimented her on figure or mentioned her boobs at all, not then or later in the hotel bedroom, despite the fact they had turned a pleasant golden colour during the course of the week.

Paula wouldn't be doing that again, Kate realised with a jolt. It was terrifying how things that you took for granted, small things that made up the sum of what you did or might do, could just be sliced randomly out of your life.

So perhaps, she decided, someone should appreciate me before it's too late. Someone should look.

Rudy was watching her.

'You're worried,' he observed. 'You shouldn't be worried. I am a painter. I am interested in your body, of course, but I want to capture it on canvas, not in my arms.' He looked straight at Kate and she thought she caught a darker flicker of sapphire in the topaz blue of his eyes. 'Are you happy with this, Kaatje?'

'Kaatje?' she enquired lightly, deflecting the question.

'It is the Dutch diminutive. It makes Kate softer. If you don't like it I will stop.'

Kate shook her head. 'No, don't stop.' She forced herself to hold his gaze. 'I'm happy.'

Hidden by the screen she slipped quickly out of her clothes and into the robe Rudy had left for her. The material felt cool and slippery as she drew it over her arms and wrapped it loosely round her waist. On a shelf just above her eye level was an assortment of objects; a chipped china egg cup; two half-finished tubes of acrylic paint, cadmium yellow and sap green (sunflower colours, Kate supposed); a cowrie shell for listening to the sea and a cream plaster frame containing a photograph. All except the photo were cloaked in a fine film of grey dust. She frowned, taking down the picture to examine it more closely, running a finger across the glass and along the serrated edge of the frame. The plaster had the grubby feel of something that is handled too often. The image was striking; a raven-haired woman with black eyes, olive skin and a high, straight nose that made Kate think of Roman statues. She was looking, not at the camera, but at a child – barely more than a baby – that she held at head height. Its face was turned towards hers in a study of mutual adoration.

'Are you alright?' Kate heard Rudy ask.

'I'm coming.' She hurriedly put the photo back on the shelf, but the image stayed with her as she emerged into the room. 'There's a picture behind the screen,' she said. 'A woman with a small boy.'

Rudy's mouth twisted.

'She's beautiful.'

'Yes,' he agreed shortly, his glance slipping away from her. 'She was.'

Kate gave him a searching look but his face had hardened. He concentrated on mixing his paint. Clearly the Madonna and child were not to be discussed.

'Lie down, Kaatje,' he instructed. 'Maybe you can look,' he hesitated, '*weemodig* – that's the word? Wistful.'

Kate felt she spent most of her existence yearning for some or other unspecified thing, so it shouldn't prove too difficult. But as she lowered herself onto the couch her thoughts returned to the photo and her mind whirled. Who was the unknown woman with the baby and how were they significant in Rudy's life?

'Move your hand slightly, just there. Good.' Rudy stood back and let his gaze sweep over every inch of her with an oddly detached expression, as if she were already a painting. A flame of desire licked through Kate, chasing the path of his eyes. She squeezed her lids together tightly.

'Not like that. This is use to me.'

She tried to quieten her face, to meditate on the clouds scudding across the skylight and ignore the melting longing that had come from nowhere and flooded her.

'That is good.' Rudy moved back behind the easel and she heard the scratch of a brush and a soft murmuring in Dutch as he prepared his materials.

'Oil,' he explained, with a wry smile. 'For my masterpiece.'

She was stiff with stillness when she made her way back down the narrow stairs towards her bike.

'See you on Monday,' Rudy said, lightly touching her hand. As the door closed behind her she wondered what he would do next. Would he continue to paint based on the photos he had taken? Or put the brushes down, perhaps, light his oven and heat up a pizza for lunch? Or meet up with a crowd of friends at a nearby restaurant and make them laugh with stories about bored ex-pat housewives? Or would he maybe, just for a few moments, do as she was doing and stand staring into space thinking about Van Gogh, about madness, about beauty and passion. A web was being spun that contained the three of them, but Kate wasn't sure who the weaver was.

Chapter 17

Luke generally enjoyed the trip home from school on the back of his mother's bike. It gave him a chance to think about things. In England he might have felt a bit daft perched up in the air being pedalled like a baby, as if he didn't know how to do it himself (which he did), but here it was normal. About half the kids in his class went home like this, even Tobias and he had quite a long way to go. Admittedly, if it was raining his mum came to fetch him in the car. But the rain had stopped at last and the sky that Luke had thought would stay grey forever was now a beautiful shade of blue. He had tried to paint it today at school. He had drawn a picture of the parrots in the Vondelpark against a background of trees and sky. He was quite pleased with it, except that it had been difficult to get the right shade for the sky. He thought perhaps he needed different paints and wondered what kind Van Cough had used to get all his different colours. It was harder than it looked being a painter.

One thing Luke often pondered – mostly because people kept asking him – was if he was learning Dutch. In truth he really didn't know. He supposed he must be. Although he couldn't really say anything except *nee* and *ja*, he could understand a bit. And the thing about understanding – as he had tried unsuccessfully to explain to his Dad – was that you didn't really notice what language it was in. You either got it or you didn't.

School was much better now than it had been at first. Another boy, Jimmy, had started so he wasn't the newest any more. Jimmy wasn't from Holland either, though he spoke Dutch. The teacher had shown them a map so they could see where Jimmy was from. It was a place in South America called Sooninam, or something like that. Anyway, it was a long way away, much further away than England and Luke could see that Jimmy wouldn't be going back to visit his friends very often. He was a brown boy with smooth black hair. He smelt a bit funny but he was very, very good at football and Luke quite liked him. Diego didn't like him at all because he was better at football than him. Heijn was even trying to get Jimmy to join their team on Wednesday afternoons which made Diego mad. But then, Luke had noticed that it was pretty easy to make Diego mad and a lot of the other kids weren't really friends with him, they were just scared. Luke usually managed to keep out of his way.

Yesterday had been Tobias's fifth birthday and his Mum had brought the most gi-normous cake into school and a balloon for everybody. They had sung a kind of happy birthday in Dutch and then sung it again in English to make Luke feel at home. Tobias's Mum was taking Tobias and three friends to the Efteling amusement park on Sunday and Luke had been invited. He was so excited he couldn't stop jumping up and down. Luke had already decided that he wanted to go to the Artis for his birthday and introduce his friends to Colonel Hathi. He thought he would take Tobias, Heijn and maybe Jimmy. That would fill up the car if his mum and his dad came too, which they should. These were all things he wanted to tell his Dad, but Sean never seemed to come home early enough. However, tomorrow was Saturday, so he should have a chance to talk to him then.

One thing he had learnt from Tobias was that birthdays were a big deal in Amsterdam and it was important that Luke made Kate understand this.

'When it's my birthday, Mummy, you have to take stuff into school.'

'What do you mean stuff?' Kate enquired over her shoulder.

'Well, something for the whole class.'

'Like a cake?'

'Well, probably more than that. Like a cake and sweets or a present.'

'We'll see Luke. There are 24 children in your class, that could work out a bit expensive.'

'But everyone does it,' Luke insisted. There had been the balloons from Tobias yesterday, and before that Lien had brought everyone a little tiny soap – blue footballs for the boys and pink heart shapes for the girls. It was true that Fenna's mum had only brought sweets and everyone had seemed pleased with these, but Luke was very anxious not to lag behind in the generosity stakes.

'Sweets would probably be okay,' he conceded, 'as long as they were good ones.'

'Hmm, we'll see,' said Kate, refusing to commit herself. 'We've got a few months before we have to worry about that. Your birthday is after the summer holidays, remember.'

'I know,' said Luke, his face creased with concern, 'but you will get something, won't you?'

'I'll get something,' Kate assured him, bumping onto the pavement and swerving toward their front door. 'And you can help me choose.'

Luke nodded, satisfied.

*****

Grant Cassidy wasn't particularly well-liked amongst his staff but it was accepted that a leaving party for one of the bosses would be a generously funded affair and this one was no exception. The cake and champagne were quickly demolished and those who were obliged to pick up children left soon afterwards. Everyone else, probably a couple of dozen people, adjourned to *Het Witte Paardje* where enough euros had been put behind the bar to cover several drinks each. Anyone who thought to analyse it would have doubted that this cash had come from Cassidy's personal finances, but pretty much no one would have cared. Sean certainly wasn't interested in how the evening had been paid for. His only concern was whether he could manage to spend it with Lena without his colleagues noticing. Lena obviously had the same idea as she stayed with the group from his floor, joining in the general conversation but making a point of standing beside him. Sean hoped that this would look accidental to any casual observer. He felt it was important not to break away and become a 'couple' – that would be instantly remarked upon. The crowded bar meant that being next to Lena inevitably meant touching her occasionally, brushing against her arm or thigh, contact which was rapidly rendering Sean incapable of rational thought. From time to time, just to make sure he was really hooked – a fact which he grasped in one isolated moment of cynical clarity whilst raising his fifth bottle of Amstel to his lips – she would flash him a look with those large black eyes.

Around seven-thirty Cassidy gave another goodbye speech on how great they had all been to work with and people started to drift away.

'I'm starving,' Lena declared. 'I'm going to see if they're still serving food. Want to join me?'

Sean felt like a puppy with his tongue hanging out. 'Absolutely. Definitely. I'm starving too.'

Lena winked at him. 'Let's eat, then.'

'Hey Sean,' Gert called across the bar. 'You got a late pass or something?'

'Yeah, huh, fun-ny,' Sean responded. 'Luke's at a sleepover and Kate's gone to a concert with a friend. No point dashing home.'

'None at all,' Gert laughed, nodding pointedly at Lena.

'I think we're allowed to eat, Bakker.'

'Sure you are, Butterworth. Sure you are.' Gert knocked back the remains of his drink and leered at the two of them.

'Maybe you should go steady on that bourbon,' Sean suggested, getting irritated.

'Maybe you should go steady with that *meisje*,' Gert retorted.

'We don't have to eat here,' said Lena loudly. 'It could be that the company is better somewhere else.'

'Suits me,' said Sean. 'I'll get your coat.'

'I hope Gert wasn't insulting you,' Sean murmured as they stepped out into the summer evening.

'No, no,' Lena assured him. 'He wouldn't dare. *Meisje* just means girl. He had an affair a couple of years ago and his wife walked out. Since then he does nothing but drink.'

'Really?' Sean ran his finger under his collar. It was really pretty warm.

'Sure. Now, I live pretty near here and my local bar serves an excellent steak. How about we head over there? Do you want to pick up your car?'

'I don't think I should be driving,' muttered Sean, beginning to feel distinctly less comfortable than he had done an hour before.

'No, me neither, but it's not a problem. We just go a couple of stops by metro then we get a tram.'

'I thought you said it was near.'

'Well, it is. *Het Witte Paardje* is the only bar on this estate. It's mostly offices round here. You have to travel to go anywhere else.' She turned towards him, one eyebrow raised. 'Do you think I'm going to eat you or something?'

Sean shuddered. 'No, no, of course not. Let's go.'

They hardly spoke on the train. Lena was busy sending emails with her iPhone so Sean got out his laptop and pretended to be engrossed in a document he was supposed to have read by Monday. Every now and then an image of Kate flashed through his mind rapidly followed by the memory of his last attempt to make love to her. She was linking everything back to Paula's illness when, really, it had nothing to do with them and if anything it should surely make her want to jump in to bed with

141

him and fuck like rabbits while they could. That was how it made him feel anyway. It just drove home the message that you never knew when your time was up and it would surely be a crime to go to your grave feeling this horny. Christ, he might get run over on the way home tonight, or stabbed on the metro and never have sex again. He looked at Lena's legs, smooth, brown and exposed, demurely crossed beneath her mini skirt. Waxed, no doubt. He wondered idly how far up the waxing went.

He was still wondering when she slipped her phone into her bag and stood up.

'Are you coming? If you want to go straight home you just have to stay on this train another couple of stops and then take the number five tram.'

'Er, no,' said Sean, leaping to his feet. 'Not at all. No point,' he added, keeping up the lie he had told earlier. 'No one there just now.'

A few minutes later he found himself following Lena into a concrete building near the Oosterpark which seemed to resemble flats rather than the bar he had been expecting.

'I hope you don't mind,' she said, 'I just need to get out of these work clothes first.' She slotted a key into one of the doors and it swung open to reveal a small living area combining kitchen, dining room and lounge.

'Not big but *heel gezellig, nee?*'

'Eh?' Sean swallowed hard. Christ, how had he let himself end up here?

Lena made a tinkly noise which was oddly unlike her usual laugh.

'It just means cosy. You really should learn some Dutch if you're going to live here.'

'But I'm not,' blurted Sean. 'Not permanently, at least.'

Again, the eyebrow lifted questioningly. Lena opened the fridge and poured two generous glasses of Chablis from an already open bottle.

'Do you always have full, open bottles in your fridge?' asked Sean.

'Not always,' Lena replied vaguely. 'Now, make yourself comfortable. I won't be a minute.' She disappeared through one of the two doors leading off the living room. Bedroom, Sean presumed, which made the other the bathroom. He decided to avail himself of its facilities. It wasn't until he was confronted with the toilet bowl that he realised just how much he needed a slash. Drying his hands he caught sight of a pale man with panicked eyes in the mirror above the basin.

'Christ,' he muttered. The sight of his slightly swaying image brought home to him at last what he had fallen into. 'Butterworth, you so need to get out of here.' Okay, well, no problem. He would simply walk out of the bathroom and straight out of the flat before Lena had finished changing. Great in theory, except that when he opened the door she was standing there in a pink floaty dress with the dark hair that she normally kept wound up in a tight bun loose across her shoulders.

'Hey,' she said, lifting her glass. 'Cheers.'

As if in a dream, Sean retrieved his drink from the shelf where he had left it and downed it in one. There was no chance of anesthetising his prick but if his memories were hazy he hoped he might feel less guilty. Lena linked her arms round his neck and pulled his head towards her. Her lips were warm and firm against his own and her tongue pressed insistently at his teeth, forcing them apart. It was a very long time since he had eaten and the wine chased the beers into his veins unimpeded. Then Sean did something he had been wanting to do for a long time – he reached down and spread his hands over her buttocks pulling her towards him. He heard himself groan and somehow, without being aware of movement, found himself sprawled on her soft red sofa where she was unbuttoning his trousers and her head with that beautiful, tumbling black hair was bent over his cock. Christ!

It was almost ten o clock when Sean finally left the flat, dishevelled and hoping that he didn't smell too much of Lena's strangely pungent perfume. It was completely different to the more classical scents that Kate usually wore and which Sean (he had to admit) actually preferred. Worryingly, his wife had a nose like a police sniffer dog and would detect it immediately. But fragrance apart, Kate would probably guess something was up simply from the enormous grin he was unable to wipe from his face. The sex had been undeniably fantastic, although a little voice wondered if this could have been simply due to recent deprivation in that quarter. Hadn't sex with Kate once been just as good? He thought so, a very long time ago. However, he had never in his life felt so *pursued* by a woman, especially not one as attractive
as Lena.

It was only when he changed from the train to the tram that Sean remembered he still hadn't eaten. Lena, in her intensely focussed and ultimately successful attempt to seduce him, had ignored the needs of his stomach. This was a disappointing oversight, Sean wryly concluded, but picking up a kebab on the way home would conveniently solve two pressing problems. Firstly it would stop him being hungry and secondly (and possibly more importantly), five minutes in a take away would leave his suit reeking of fried food and spicy sauces, hopefully smothering all vestiges of Lena's *Eau d'Harem*.

The big question, he told himself as he walked back to the apartment trying not to dribble kebab-grease down his best shirt, was whether this evening was a one off event – a hiccup in an otherwise strong marriage – or whether it was the start of a real love affair. If he had to choose between Kate ten years ago and Lena, Sean knew he would choose Kate every time. She was much more obviously long term material and he had loved her – more accurately, they had been madly in love. Deep down, he had no doubt, he loved her still. But lately, during the five years since Luke's arrival, she had changed; slowly distilled into something narrower and more anxious than the woman he had married, like a sauce that has boiled for too long and become viscous. He didn't know how to dilute her, plump her up, to pour the sunshine back in – and it made him miserable. With Lena, for a couple of hours on that red settee, he had been able to stop worrying about whether his lovemaking would have any issue, whether he was giving out the wrong vibe or being insufficiently sensitive; he had simply enjoyed himself. The frissons of guilt had assailed him both before and afterwards, but at the time, frankly, it had been great, easy. Fun! So, if she wanted more and was happy with a no-strings arrangement which no one but them needed to know about, then he reckoned he was up for it. For a while anyway.

'Is that you, Sean?' Kate called as he pushed open the front door. The voice came from upstairs. He breathed a relieved sigh. She must be in bed.

'Yep.'

'You're very late.'

She sounded sad, he thought, rather than angry. This was disconcerting.

'It went on for a bit longer than I thought. Just going to have a cup of tea and a quick look at the telly, then I'll be up.'

'Well, I'll be asleep so you might as well go in the spare room again.'

'Okay,' Sean agreed, with what he hoped sounded like friendly acceptance. 'See you in the morning.' It was odd how much more affectionate he felt towards his wife now he wasn't sexually frustrated. In the long term this little affair might be good for his marriage as well as for him. It might just help them over a bad patch.

Chapter 18

'Judging from the time you got in I presume it was a pretty good leaving do,' said Kate placing a cup of tea on the table beside her husband's spare-room bed. She kept her tone carefully neutral.

'It was,' Sean agreed, amazed at how relaxed he sounded. 'Except there was too much booze and not enough food so I ended up getting a kebab on the way home.'

'So I see.' Kate examined the Ted Baker shirt. 'Most of it is on here, I think. Ugh, it smells like a brothel.' She pulled back the heavy blue curtains and regarded her husband dispassionately. He looked younger somehow, she thought, more like he had when they lived in London. Perhaps his night out had done him good. Maybe he actually needed a bit more down time with the boys. Had she been pushing him too far into his role of husband and father?

'Well,' she said, trying to sound casual. 'I'm pleased you enjoyed it.'

Sean decided to change the subject. 'What time is it?'

'About eight-thirty. Luke is dying to tell you about Tobias's birthday so you'll have to wake up.'

'Shush, Mummy,' said Luke, coming up behind Kate and head-butting her without any real force. 'You're spoiling it.' He glared with a determined ferocity that sat incongruously with his Thomas the Tank Engine pyjamas and blue dressing gown. His fringe had grown again and the fine, golden-brown hair rested on his eyebrows in a neat, straight line. With an automatic gesture Kate pushed it aside. Luke immediately shook his head and it fell back across his forehead.

'Yes, well, there you are,' she said. 'He's all yours, but I think I'll open the window or the pair of you risk suffocation.'

'Thanks,' said Sean.

Kate shot him a curious look. 'Well, don't lie there too long. I need you to take me to Albert Heijn later for a big shop. We're out of all kinds of basics.'

'Looking forward to it already.'

'You're in an odd mood, Sean Butterworth,' Kate muttered as she turned and left the room.

'Why aren't you sleeping in the big bed with Mummy?' Luke wanted to know as he launched himself on his father.

'Okay. Ooff! Steady on, Luke! You're getting a bit big to jump on me like that without any warning.'

'Serves you right,' said Luke. 'You should have been watching. Anyway, you stink.'

Children get much less pleasant, Sean decided, when they start school. Presumably this was what they called socialisation.

'I didn't sleep there last night because I got home too late from a work party and I didn't want to wake your mum up.'

'Was it someone's birthday?'

'No, it was someone's leaving party. The boss's, actually.'

'I remember, Mummy told me. I think you were too smelly to sleep with Mummy, anyway,' Luke concluded.

'Probably,' Sean agreed propping himself up on the pillow and pulling his son up beside him. 'Now, what's this about your friend Tobias?'

Luke grinned and pushed the floppy hair out of his eyes. Kate kept talking about getting it cut but Luke hoped she would forget. There was a good chance this might happen as she was forgetting quite a lot of things at the moment.

'Well, Dad,' he began. 'Have you ever heard of the Efteling?'

'Nope,' said Sean. 'Never. So you can tell me about it now.'

'It's a great big park not very far away with lots of rides. And there's even a water slide. Tobias's mum is taking us for his birthday and it's tomorrow.'

'Sounds great,' said Sean, wondering vaguely what Luke would request for his own special day and hoping it wouldn't require too much in the way of organisation. Luke chattered on and Sean quickly discovered that he could listen to his son's babble and at the same time treat himself to a leisurely mental rerun of the previous evening's events. What exactly was it that Lena had been murmuring? He would really have to brush up his Dutch.

A couple of hours later Sean was standing beside the trolley in Albert Heijn staring blankly at the huge cheeses on the deli counter when Lena messaged him:

Hi, I'm in the shower, where are you? Last night was great. Hope we can do it again soon.

He frowned and glanced around surreptitiously hoping he didn't look too furtive. Just moments before Kate and Luke had been arguing about chocolate yogurts nearby – Luke requesting them and Kate insisting they weren't healthy. Now they had both momentarily disappeared. This was disconcerting; it meant they could be hiding behind any one of these immensely tall shelves and might re-materialise any second.

Calm down, Sean, he told himself. He got messages all the time, didn't he? Why would Kate be suspicious? He applied himself to composing a reply. It didn't seem quite right to admit that he was in the supermarket helping his wife with the weekly shop, so he skipped that part and concentrated on the important bit. Of course, they could do it again soon – the sooner the better, frankly. But there had to be some kind of understanding that a) it was a short term thing; and b) there were absolutely no strings attached.

You were amazing, he tapped, *but we need to talk. Lunch Monday?*

The reply came back immediately. Presumably she was out of the shower then or did they make waterproof iPhones?

Not in Monday. Tuesday is good.

Not in Monday? Sean was perplexed. Where was she going then? He didn't feel he could ask her, especially considering the 'no strings' stipulation he was about to make. Alarmingly, mistresses seemed to be far more mysterious and independent than wives.

'Are you alright?' asked Kate arriving with an armful of pasta packets which she dumped in the trolley. Luke trailed behind her. 'Why are you staring like that? Do you want some cheese? The lady is asking you.'

Sean snapped out of his reverie.

'Just a rumour that the new boss is gay,' he said, waving his mobile ostentatiously.

'Does it matter, then?'

'Not at all, but it gives people something to gossip about.' He managed to focus on the cheese. 'I really wanted to try some of that Old Gouda.'

'Fine,' Kate nodded, giving him another odd look, 'we'll ask for 200grams.'

That night Sean slipped back into bed beside his wife. He had stayed up pretending to watch a film after she had gone upstairs, hoping that she would be asleep. But she was not. She was awake. Not exactly waiting for him, just restless, lying tensely on her half of the cool, white sheets, staring through a crack in the curtains at the black shadows of the buildings and the slice of velvet above them. There was no starry night. A few splodges pricked the darkness but the city sky had been glazed with an impenetrable varnish of light pollution. She was remembering Rudy's studio, his gentle, enigmatic smile, the way he had looked at her as he painted, and she was swamped, once again, with an unexpected wash of desire. So much so that when Sean climbed in to bed beside her and his hand reached out as a peace offering, she turned to him half-choked with tears and they made love in an oddly apologetic way, with neither of them fully present.

Luke found them in bed on Sunday morning and stood for a moment surveying his sleeping parents with some satisfaction before drawing their attention to his presence.

'It's better,' he announced, loudly, 'when you're both in the big bed. But you have to get up now. The little hand's on the eight.'

'Eh?' said Sean, groping for his glasses and then remembering that thanks to the new contact lenses he could now see without them.

'I have to be at Tobias's house at nine o clock, remember? I told you, I'm going to the Efteling.'

Sean swung his legs over the edge of the bed.

'So you did.' He looked across at his wife. 'Stay there. I'll go.'

Kate smiled gratefully. Her cheeks felt sticky and her pillow was oddly damp as if she had been crying again in her sleep. She heaved herself out of bed and peered in the bathroom mirror. Her eyes blotchily returned her stare. Was it Paula's illness that was making her feel like this? If so, then Paula herself seemed to be dealing with it a good deal better than Kate was. She had spoken to her only yesterday and now that she had come through the operation she was sounding much more positive.

Sean returned with tea and Kate sipped it while she watched him get dressed. He was humming. Why? He hadn't hummed for ages.

'What's that song?'

'*Chasing Cars.*'

'Why that one?'

'No idea.' There was a muffled grunt as he pulled a tee shirt over his head. 'IPod was on random. It came up.'

'Do you know where Tobias lives?'

No, but I hope you're going to tell me. I'm also going to pop into work and pick up a couple of files.'

'I thought everything was accessible on the internet now.'

Sean sat down on the edge of the bed to put his socks on. His face was turned away from her.

'Most things are. These aren't. Unfortunately.'

'You didn't fancy going out somewhere, then, just the two of us? Delft maybe? Have lunch in a café or something?'

As she spoke Kate wondered if this was what she really wanted to or if she was just saying it to test him.

'I wish you'd thought of it before. I would have done this report last night.'

'So that's a no?'

'I'm sorry.'

Having decided he couldn't wait until Tuesday to see her Sean had messaged Lena the previous evening just before climbing into bed and making love to Kate. It was the kind of double-think he supposed he would have to get used to. But the two situations, he argued, fed into each other. This seemed some kind of justification.

Can't stop thinking about you. I'll have an hour free tomorrow morning. How does a quick breakfast sound?

Even as he was writing it Sean had known that this wasn't completely true. It wasn't exactly Lena that he couldn't stop thinking about. More accurately, it was her neat little arse and clouds of dark hair.

Pancakes, my place, around nine o clock?

Absolutely. See you then.

'Well, if you're busy,' Kate declared, finishing her tea. 'I'm going to go and study the *Sunflowers*. I have an essay to write.'

'You always have work, Daddy,' Luke observed. 'And Mummy always has the museum. Can we go now?'

'Yup. Just about.'

Sean dropped a kiss on Kate's hair. It smelt faintly, familiarly, of Chanel's *Allure* and he briefly regretted his breakfast arrangement. It would have been so much simpler just to get back into bed with his wife. Their eyes met briefly and he thought he saw a challenge in hers, a question mark, and his regret was instantly replaced with irritation. What did she expect? She had made him feel like a baby factory these last couple of years and a pretty third rate one at that. Now, suddenly, he felt like the most desirable man on the planet. Hey, and maybe Lena actually thought he was!

The Van Gogh Museum was already packed when Kate arrived. She chained her bike to the rack and as usual, pushed to the front of the queue with her museum card. Disappointingly, the main gallery was so busy she had to practically fight to see the paintings. It must always be like this at weekends, she supposed, and she pitied the throngs of people nudging each other for a better view; they would never have the privilege of knowing the pictures like she knew them. Looking round she realised that she had been half-hoping to see Rudy, escorting some of his elderly Americans on a personal museum tour perhaps. For some reason they always imagined Gogh was pronounced 'Go'. A misguided attempt at a 'European' accent, Kate presumed, as if they thought all foreign languages were basically the same and Dutch was simply a lesser known dialect of French. Rudy made jokes about them, but Kate had watched him patiently explaining the rudiments of the paintings to more than one nodding couple. He wanted everyone to see Vincent's genius.

Kate didn't stay very long at the museum. It was difficult to concentrate when people kept wandering in front of her. She retrieved her bike and wondered what she could usefully do with her free morning. There wasn't much point in going home yet. Sean almost certainly wouldn't be there and it wasn't as if she had gardening or decorating to do. It was strangely liberating, this renting business, and yet, also peculiarly dislocating. She was missing the sense of rootedness that actually owning the house she lived in had given her. She felt as if she had been cut loose and suspected that Sean felt something similar. He was certainly behaving strangely. Did it have something to do with that woman at work? Kate considered this. Her husband might flirt but she didn't really think he would be unfaithful and anyway, surely Lena wasn't his type? Questions of fidelity apart, however, she did feel that they hadn't been able to gel as a proper family in their Amsterdam apartment. Without the fertile East Anglian soil holding them fast they seemed to be spiralling outwards, away from one another. Even Luke was less dependent on the unit than he had been; he had school and now his own language – Dutch. It was a gradual process, but Kate had the alarming impression that slowly, inexorably, they had begun to spin apart.

She cycled desultorily along the Stadhouderskade in what she told herself was an arbitrary direction. Nevertheless, she wasn't remotely surprised when she found herself outside Rudy's flat in the Jordaan. She stopped and stood for a minute beside the canal observing the tiny ripples in the duck-green water and listening to the bursts of Dutch that she caught on the breeze. She was beginning to understand some of what was said and with the understanding came a nascent sense of belonging. There was a café on the corner of the block and she decided to have a coffee before heading home. Pencil and sketch pad were always in her bag these days so as she sipped she tried to capture the narrow buildings with their tall, thin windows. Was Rudy up there, she wondered, painting in his garret? Or still asleep, maybe. And if so, had he slept alone? She shook herself. She was pitiable, she decided. A stereo-typical lonely housewife looking for attention. It could probably have been anyone – ski instructor, gardener, even the young guy at the Albert Heijn checkout. She should be making use of her time by focussing on Van Gogh, wasn't he interesting enough?

'Sure,' Kate could hear Paula's voice gently mocking her, 'but dead, sadly. And maybe a bit too loopy to fall in love with, anyway.'

Kate had read about Vincent's doomed love affairs and was forced to agree. But there, she wasn't about to have a love affair. What nonsense. She stood up abruptly and paid the waiter. This was a phase, a bad patch for her and Sean which they would get through. And tempting though it was, sleeping with Rudy wouldn't help, even if he suggested it, which – Kate reminded herself – he hadn't.

There were two weeks of the Van Gogh course left, she reflected as she pedalled slowly in the direction of home. Two more weeks of seeing Rudy regularly, of being painted. Her stomach contracted. Only fourteen days, then he would be leaving Amsterdam for the summer. He had said so. And Kate would be left with two months of long, empty days alone with Luke. What on earth would she do? She pulled up at a red light and waited as a tram crossed the road in front of her heading for Central Station. As it pulled away the Van Gogh museum loomed into view once again and beyond it the expanse of Museumplein with its sprinkling of students and tourists dozing, picnicking or playing frisbee on the grass. The scene was mellow, pleasant, but, she suddenly felt, ultimately unsatisfactory. This wasn't where Vincent had wanted to be, imprisoned in the pale tolerance of northern Europe.

In that moment, Kate decided that she must go south, to Arles. She wanted to see the Yellow House where Van Gogh had waited for Gauguin, and the fields of sunflowers – the acres of yellow blooms turning, in silent worship, to face their namesake. She wanted to experience proper, intense heat that scorched the earth and shimmered in the air from the early morning until late at night. Above all, she wanted to feel what Vincent had felt when he looked at colour in the relentless sunlight and was *driven* to capture its ferocity on his canvas. She was beginning to see that what Rudy admired was not only the artist's work, but also the desperate capacity for concentrated experience which he revealed in his paintings. Kate wanted to look where Van Gogh had looked and to see if she could perhaps live, for a moment or two, in his turbulent reality.

'I want to go to Arles for a couple of days when term ends,' Kate announced that afternoon when both she and Sean had returned from their separate jaunts. 'I've decided I have to see the sunflowers for myself.'

'Just yellow blobs in a field, surely? Plenty of pictures on the internet.' Sean looked up from his laptop, his forehead wrinkled. 'Why don't we go to Barcelona or maybe Disneyland Paris?'

'*I'm* going to Arles,' Kate insisted, 'the first weekend of the holidays. A few of people from the group are heading down there. I'm tagging along. Flights to Marseille are pretty reasonable apparently, then we hire a car. Everyone's leaving on the Thursday evening so could you book the Friday off to mind Luke? You two could spend some quality time together. I'll be back late on the Sunday.' She smiled brightly, impressed at how easily she had managed to lie. The invention of companions was to stop Sean suggesting they should all go. That would just ruin it. She had to be alone to commune with Vincent. She had a strong feeling that she needed to understand his paintings before she could move on. Though move on to where she had no idea.

'I suppose so,' Sean shrugged. He was in a benign mood, breakfast had gone well, although, as seemed to be customary at Lena's, they hadn't actually eaten. He recalled coffee and half an hour on the red sofa with a tangle of black hair and silky stockings. Given those things he had felt he could skip the Weetabix course. Even more amazingly she had agreed to his suggestion of an uncomplicated shagfest type arrangement. In fact, it had been pretty much her idea. Sean presumed this kind of thing must be more common in cities like Amsterdam where everything was known to be much freer and everyone drifted in and out of sexual encounters in a much more relaxed and easy-going way than they had ever seemed to in London. Actually, he

155

was feeling that the city really suited him. He liked its vibe. The only difficult thing might be keeping their little thing a secret at work.

'If we stop having lunch together people will get suspicious,' Lena maintained. 'We must carry on as before and when you are free you can come over to my place for supper.' Her eyebrows had lifted tellingly when she said supper and Sean imagined he might be about to lose some weight.

'Sure, sounds wonderful.'

'We can do it for as long as it suits as both. Just great sex. We're compatible, I think, in that way. Don't you? Then if it gets difficult or we want to move on, that's okay too.'

Sean's head nodded vigorously. 'Compatible. Yes, we certainly are.'

And he had pushed her back down on the red sofa just to prove it.

'Thanks for dropping him off,' Kate called, as Tobias' car pulled away. She turned to her son.

'And how was your day? What's the Efteling like?'

'It's really cool,' said Luke. 'And guess what.'

'What?' Kate bent down and opened her eyes wide to show she was giving him her whole attention.

'The rubbish bins really talk.'

'Really?'

'Yep. They say *Dank U Wel* when you put something in them.'

'Amazing.'

'Yep. And we went on a water chute. I've got a picture. Tobias's mum bought one each for us.'

He carefully extracted a photo of five grinning people zooming over a small waterfall in a capsule-type boat.

'It looks brilliant,' said Kate. 'We'll stick it on the fridge.'

'Is it tea-time?' Luke yawned.

'It is if you just want pizza.'

'Pasta.'

'Fine.'

Once Luke had been fed, bathed and tucked into bed where he barely managed to kiss his mother goodnight before his eyes closed, Sean went out to pick up a Chinese takeaway and Kate was able to hurriedly book her trip to France; return flights to Marseille, a cheap two-star hotel in Arles and a very small car. She was all set. Her insides fluttered nervously. She hadn't been anywhere by herself since she was single and she very much hoped her school French was still retrievable. Did she really have the courage to spend a weekend in a strange country on her own? In three weeks' time, she would find out.

Chapter 19

The following morning, Sean stepped out of the lift on the eighth floor brooding over the fantasy football team he had put together the night before. If it won tonight he should go top of the league but had he been bold enough? He was playing it safe with four - four – two. He looked up and clocked Lena beside the coffee machine as usual. What was she doing there?

'I thought you weren't in today,' he said, blinking hard.

'Change of plan.' She smiled brightly and handed him a styrofoam cup.

He took it automatically, wondering whether he was actually pleased to see her. Parts of him certainly were, he registered, but she did seem to need an awful lot of attention and his work was slipping a bit. He had been banking on spending the whole day without female distraction. There was a glitch in one of the accounting programs that would need some serious concentration in order to sort it out. Plus, the last time they went over to the Ikea restaurant they had been a bit late back and he had missed the start of a meeting. Sean had not failed to notice Gert's sly smirk as he blustered his apology and quickly took his seat. It would be unwise to forget that the Dutchman wanted his job.

Lena picked up her own coffee and made as if to move away.

'Things to do. Better get on,' she said airily.

Now Sean was instantly on alert. What was this all about then? Presumably she had been waiting for him so why was she now dashing off? Had he done something wrong? Just because he was reflecting on the wisdom of the relationship didn't mean he was ready to end it. Especially when the interesting part had barely got under way.

'Hang on,' he spluttered, immediately forgetting his resolution to get on with some work. 'As you're here after all, how about that lunch?' He realised too late that he sounded far too eager. But she had confused him. Why was she in the office at all when she had said that she wouldn't be? He didn't get it. He felt like he had signed up for a new game and no one had told him the rules. He even wondered fleetingly whether he might not be a bit out of his depth but dismissed the thought at once. They were at work, for Christ's sake, she was hardly going to throw her arms around him was she? Anyway, they had fully discussed their situation only yesterday morning at her place and they were both totally cool with it. This was just a pleasant interlude while his marriage was going through a rocky patch and in a few weeks or months – however long it took – Lena would find somebody more permanent to share her red sofa and he would return, rejuvenated, to Kate and they would all get on with the rest of their lives.

'Sure,' flung Lena over her shoulder, as if lunch was a totally new idea. 'Why not?'

'See you in the car park about one o clock, then?'

Sean found himself trailing her across the office as he spoke. Realising suddenly how this must look, he cleared his throat and announced loudly:

'We really need to discuss those merger files as soon as possible.' Before turning on his heel and walking with slow deliberation towards his own desk.

Lunch turned out to be brief and, if he was honest, disappointing. The selection of main courses in the Ikea café was not, Sean felt, up to the usual standard and was he imagining it or was Lena just a tiny bit distant? It was hard to tell, frankly. After the steamy sofa sessions over the weekend she would have seemed distant if she was sitting on his lap. The real low point, however, had been spotting that woman from their block swishing past with a sack full of velvet cushions. Sean couldn't remember her name although it might have been Natasha.

159

Something Eastern European-sounding anyway. Whatever, she had sure as hell remembered his:

'Hi Sean,' she waved, approaching his table with her bulging blue bag and forcing him to stand up and offer his hand. He had mumbled Lena's name by way of introduction and fervently hoped that this intrusion of his domestic life into their exclusive little bubble wouldn't put her off sleeping with him again. But Lena rose sublimely to the challenge, shaking hands politely, her eyes a studied expression of cool indifference, while Sean blushed and bumbled.

'She has gone to report this to your wife.' Lena announced when Saskia had left. Sean noted uncomfortably that she seemed amused by this.

'No. Do you think? Why would she –?'

'Yes,' said Lena with certainty. 'I *know*. But there, we were eating pasta salad, not even holding hands.'

Unfortunately, a part of Sean thought. He almost wanted to be caught to show Kate what happened when she ignored him. What was a bloke supposed to do, for goodness sake?

Nevertheless, he made a point of heading off early that evening. Not that there was any reason to stay on late anyway. Lena left around four o clock with a couple of guys from the acquisitions department. On some work-related mission, Sean forced himself to assume. They were hardly off for a gang-bang now were they? All the same he felt hot and irritated and played *Blink 182* very loudly all the way home.

Chapter 20

Once Sean had left for work and Luke had been deposited at school, tired and a bit grumpy from his busy Sunday at the Efteling, Kate sat in the kitchen sipping the strong Dutch coffee to which she had been converted and revising Van Gogh's letters before her class:

'I'm painting with the gusto of a man from Marseille eating bouillabaisse, which won't surprise you when it's a question of painting large Sunflowers.'[2]

Van Gogh was waiting for Gauguin. Rudy had explained this to the class when they worked on the sequence of sunflower paintings. He had been planning 'a dozen or so panels.....a symphony in blue and yellow' to decorate the studio he hoped to share with his fellow artist. Kate pictured the anxious Vincent rising before dawn to capture the very essence of the blooms before they wilted in the fierce Provençal heat; waiting for news of his friend; longing to discuss his ideas.

It was very hard not to feel sympathy for Van Gogh, Kate thought. His eagerness reminded her of Luke but it was an unequal friendship. Gauguin's replies to Vincent's excited overtures were sporadic and casual. Eventually, however, he did travel to Arles, but after only a few short weeks winter set in and the weather worsened. The little yellow house proved too small to contain the two intense and powerful personalities cooped up inside it. Gauguin began to talk of a voyage to the tropics and, like a possessive lover, Vincent became more demanding as his friend's departure loomed. On December 23rd 1888 their fraught relationship exploded resulting in Gauguin's flight to Paris and the severance of Van Gogh's ear.

Was Vincent just too needy? Kate wondered. Did he push his new friend too far with his febrile passions and dogged enthusiasms? A man like that could not have been easy to live with. What must it be like to exist in such constant turmoil? Kate glanced up from her book and her eye caught Luke's sunflower picture. The sugar paper was creased and the thick poster paint cracked in places, but there were the blooms, huge unmistakeable splashes yellow swaying drunkenly in their vase.

Painted by a boy who needed a friend, she thought. Now he seemed to have several. In just a few short weeks things had moved on and it was only she, Kate, who still seemed to be adrift in this city.

After the morning lecture Rudy suggested they skip the café session and go straight to his flat.

'There was nothing complicated today, I don't think. You understood what I was saying about Vincent's intentions during his stay in the asylum at St Rémy? With discipline imposed from without, he was able to find calm within.'

Kate nodded.

'Then perhaps we can carry on with the painting? I have been working from the photos but it is so much more satisfying to work from life.'

Kate scanned his face for hints of a hidden agenda, but found none. He looked at her questioningly. A strand of yellow hair had escaped onto his forehead making him appear younger somehow.

'What is it, Kate? If there is something, you know you can ask. Questions are only words.' His eyes crinkled. 'I can always choose not to reply.'

Kate turned abruptly away. 'There's nothing,' she lied. 'I was just wondering about the picture.'

The studio was cooler this time. Rudy had left a window open and a breeze had freshened the air.

'Must I close it? You will be cold, perhaps?'

'No, don't worry. But could I have a coffee or something before we start?'

'Sure, of course, sit down.'

Kate seated herself at the scrubbed pine table and traced the sunlight on the wood with her fingertip.

'I should have offered coffee. I am like any artist, thinking only of my canvas, not of its subject.' Rudy laughed. 'This is okay if I paint apples, but the *Engelse* dame I must take more care of.'

He placed a cup of strong coffee in front of her together with a packet of *speculaas*. Kate smiled shyly and dunked one in her drink, savouring the combination of sweet spicy biscuit with the kick of the Douwe Egberts. She scanned the room. It was pretty much the same as before except that the washing up in the sink was a slightly different collection of cups and plates and three new canvases were now leaning against the low walls of the attic; copies of Van Gogh's sunflowers.

Rudy followed her gaze.

'They sell,' he explained. 'I have a friend who will put these in his gallery for me and the tourists will buy them. I get a good price, he gets commission and we both eat.'

Kate's eyebrows lifted soundlessly.

'You're disappointed, I can see. You think this is cynical.' Rudy sighed. 'Kaatje, I am no cynic, but I have to be realistic. As I told you, I have no brother like Theo van Gogh to indulge me.' His cobalt eyes were teasing, but there was a spark of challenge nevertheless. 'If I could choose I would not do these paintings and I would not teach art history, but I am not as pure as Vincent, and sadly, not as talented either.' His arm swept round the room. 'But these paintings are good copies and people know what they buy, so I think it doesn't matter. This is not a bad way to earn money and my mind is still free for my real work.'

Kate's glance strayed to the couch spread ready with the green silk.

'Exactly,' Rudy grinned. 'Today, you are my real work. Perhaps you will be my masterpiece. Who can say?'

It was a seductive idea. Kate rose and with a final slanting look at her painter, disappeared behind the screen. She could hear him assembling his materials as she peeled off her clothes; the easel, brushes, palette, paints and finally the unfinished picture. Her stomach churned. How did he perceive her? She tried not to think of it but slipped on the robe and reached up to the shelf to re-examine the photo of the beautiful young mother and her child. What clues might it give to Rudy's past? He presented himself as a regular guy, simple and straightforward, but in fact, he never gave much away. Kate drew a sharp breath; the photograph had gone. Now in the greasy dust, there was only the china eggcup, the shell, the tubes of paint and a mark where the picture had stood. Her hand fell back empty and her eyes darkened with disappointment. He didn't want her to look at it. They weren't friends, there was no relationship. She was his student and his model. Nothing more.

Reclining undressed on the couch was much easier the second time than it had been the first, Kate discovered. She positioned herself on the low cushions with barely a thought for her nudity.

'You are more comfortable today, Kaatje,' Rudy noticed. 'Maybe you could earn a living like this. We artists, we always need models.' His eyes flicked across her, intent, amused. Kate felt their trace like a finger skimming her skin. Once more that laser burn of desire. She turned her face hurriedly away.

'Kaatje,' he said more gently, 'Kaatje, look out there at the sky, as before. Can you see the sun?'

She complied. The sounds of summer drifted through the open window – birds, shouts, laughter from the café below – while she lay naked in this long, narrow attic, her hair carefully arranged to fall across her breasts. She listened to the scratching of the brush on the canvas and when the noise stopped she felt Rudy's gaze upon her as he paused to contemplate the secret shadows of her body, considering every curve, every nuance in a way her husband had never done and would never think to do.

She lay for two hours immobile, drowsily meditating on the clouds. Each time she crossed into sleep and her hand tumbled loosely from its position on her thigh, Rudy called her, with soft, hissing Dutch syllables:

'Kaatje.' and she snapped instantly awake. Surely this Kaatje (pronounced 'Katya' like some enigmatic heroine in a Russian film), this mellow, mysterious interpretation of the too-harsh 'Kate' or the more childish 'Katie', was who she really was, who she had always been? Rudy had baptised her, revealed her true being with his long, whispering vowels as a sculptor reveals the form in a lump of stone. In this attic studio, she reflected dreamily, she had stumbled upon her quintessential self.

*****

'Hey, Kate, how are you?' Saskia saluted later that afternoon as they waited outside the school for their sons.

'Pretty good,' Kate replied, feeling, for once the equal of this confident Dutch woman. There was nothing like being admired for improving one's temper, she decided.

Saskia grinned. 'Great.' There was an infinitesimal pause, her voice dropped conspiratorially. 'I saw Sean today,'

'Huh? Where?'

'I called in to Ikea to pick up some pillows – is that the right word?'

'Cushions?' Kate suggested.

'Sure, cushions. He was there, in the restaurant, having lunch with a woman.'

'Really?' Why was Saskia telling her this? Still, she couldn't stop herself asking. 'What did she look like?'

'Dark hair in a ponytail, around thirty, a lot of make up.'

'Right,' said Kate slowly, feeling her stomach knot.

Saskia gave her a level look. 'If it was my man, I would want to know. It helps if you keep one step ahead.'

'Sure, but it's probably just a work colleague.' Kate made a sweeping gesture. 'In fact, I think he mentioned her.'

Saskia shrugged, her eyes narrowing indulgently. 'But I forget, you English do things differently. Maybe you like to keep things hidden? Then, in that case, I'm sorry.'

'No, no. I'm glad you told me.' Kate managed an unconvincing smile. 'Keep one step ahead. Yes, I see what you mean.'

There was a rush of noise inside the gates. The women braced themselves for the flood of children that were about to come tumbling out. Saskia turned one more time and winked.

'Really, it's best like this. Now you are the boss. You have the cards.' She nodded with a certainty that Kate was unable to match. Fortunately, before she could say anymore, Heijn charged over and greeted his mother by kicking the wheel of her bike. Saskia ignored this. 'Hop on Heijn,' she said. 'And Kate,' she murmured over her shoulder. 'Don't forget you can always call me.'

'Er, great. Thanks.' She swallowed hard.

'What is it, Mummy?' asked Luke, pushing his fringe out of his eyes. 'Why are you going to call her?'

'I don't suppose I am,' said Kate vaguely, shaking herself.

'Then why did she say...'

'Just get on the bike, Luke.'

Luke's face hardened where once, not so long ago, it would have crumpled.

'I *am* getting on,' he muttered. 'And I only asked.'

The sky, which had been bright with warm sunshine for most of the day, clouded over as Luke lounged on the leather sofa watching CBBC and munching Oreos. In a few minutes, Kate knew, his school-induced tiredness would melt away and he would bounce into the kitchen demanding to be taken across the road to the park. She glanced out of the window hoping it wouldn't actually rain as she would still be required to sit there in the drizzle until he had burnt off at least some of his recharged energy. The theme tune to *Roar* jingled in the sitting room and Kate concluded she was safe for another few minutes at least. Luke could be relied on not to move until it had finished. There was probably enough time to call Paula. She pressed the speed dial.

The phone rang several times with no response and Kate was beginning to think that she should have sent a text first. Paula was probably asleep. Now she didn't know whether it was better to hang on in case someone was almost there, or to quickly cut the line and call back later. She decided to hang on.

'Hello,' a small and distant voice eventually whispered. A fragile voice, Kate thought.

'Hi, it's me, Kate.' How are you?'

'I'm grotty. I think that's the best word.' There was slightest trace of a smile.

'I'm really sorry. Did I wake you up?'

'Not exactly. I'm just lying on the bed dozing and feeling sick. The phone in here is on silent and it's hard to hear the other one. Dom's Mum is looking after the boys but she's taken Ollie to pick up Henry from school.'

'Is it the chemo that's making you feel so awful?'

Paula shuddered. 'It's horrible. Really, I can't tell you....'

'I should let you rest.'

'No, talking's good. I've spent the last two days resting. It's deadly dull and Mary's driving me mad, although the boys love her. She insists on ironing everything, even underpants. I'm looking forward to seeing *my* mum and dad again. They're coming next week. In fact, when this is over, I think we might move closer to them.'

'Really?' Kate had a sudden unpleasant image of returning to a Suffolk that no longer contained her best friend.

'You can't grumble.' Paula managed a short laugh. 'You're not even here.'

'I wish I was.' Even as she said it Kate knew this wasn't strictly true. She wasn't ready to leave Amsterdam just yet. In the last couple of weeks she had transformed from being just plain Kate into Kaatje, a mysterious woman who sat for painters in garrets in the Jordaan. It was too soon to give that up. But she did genuinely wish she was able to offer more help to her friend. She hadn't expected Paula to sound quite so shaky. It had seemed a good idea to phone her up, get an update on her progress and have a moan about Sean. But now, hearing her voice, fractured and hesitant, Kate wondered. Perhaps she shouldn't worry her with details of Sean's dubious behaviour.

She had failed to appreciate the profundity of her friend's boredom, however. Paula's days were currently circumscribed by the walls of her house and an assortment of hospital treatment rooms. Whatever the topic, she was keen to gossip.

'How's your sexy art-history teacher?' she began, eagerly.

'Attractive and elusive as ever. He's painting me, did I tell you?' Even to herself Kate sounded unpleasantly smug.

'Wow.' Paula was instantly alert. 'Nude?'

'Erm, mostly.'

'Mostly!' she laughed out loud. 'You mean "yes". Does Sean know?'

'Okay, yes. And, not exactly.'

'What's that supposed to mean?'

'I think I mentioned it.'

'But not the nude bit?'

'Perhaps not.' There was a pause while the women digested this. Kate had never actually discussed being a nude model with anyone until now. Paula knowing somehow made it much more real.

'So is it... does he....? How exactly does it work?'

Kate could clearly picture the little crease between her friend's eyebrows as Paula tried to visualise this new situation.

'Well, I cycle to his studio in another part of Amsterdam, go behind a screen and take my clothes off and then I lie on a chaise-longue thing. Rudy scratches his brushes about a bit and after a minute or two, he starts painting.'

'Have you seen the picture yet?'

'No, I've still got a couple more sittings. I'm waiting until it's finished.'

'That's really exciting.'

'Yes,' Kate agreed, realising that it was. This time, this city, these choices were never going to be offered again. She felt as if she had grasped her fate, chosen a path, agreed to change. Now she was waiting to see how it was all going to turn out.

'And have you shagged him yet?'

'No! It's not about that!' she protested, managing to sound mildly scandalised whilst silently acknowledging the perspicacity of the question.

'Just wondered. How about Sean?'

'I'm not shagging him much either!'

'Ha!'

Kate heard a rattly laugh and followed by a burst of coughing.

'That's you and me both then,' Paula gasped. 'What's really rubbish is that I can't even pig-out on chocolate as a substitute.' There was a silence while she caught her breath. 'But you know,' she continued in a quieter voice, 'sometimes it's better just to do these things and get them out of your system.'

'Really? Are you speaking from experience, then?'

'Kind of. I thought afterwards that it was probably what I should have done. I would have realised then it was nothing.'

Kate's antennae wobbled doubtfully.

'It might not have been nothing. What if it wasn't?'

'I think it would. And sometimes if you don't, then you get kind of fixated on it. That's what happened to me anyway.' She paused. 'It was a long time ago. Dom was working away a lot.'

'I would never have imagined.... Hang on, I thought you said it was Dom who…'

'It was a bad patch for both of us.'

On the other end of the phone, Kate imagined Paula waving the conversation away with a sweep of her hand.

'Well anyway,' Kate pointed out, 'he hasn't suggested it.'

'But he probably will.'

'You think so?'

'I'm sure of it. Maybe you should decide in advance how you're going to react?'

This was a new idea, but Paula had a point. It moved the whole experience up a notch. Of course she had thought about sleeping with Rudy. Whilst lying on the couch she didn't think about much else. But actually doing it, that was a different matter. Perhaps that would complete the transformation and she would really become Kaatje, someone who follows her impulses, a woman Kate still didn't quite know.

'Are you still there?' called Paula's disembodied voice. Behind the voice a door slammed. 'Kate? That's Mary and the boys back. I'll have to go, sorry.'

'Okay. Hope you feel better before too long. Speak again soon.' As she lowered the phone to its cradle Kate heard Henry yelling in the background: 'Mummy! Guess what?' and she swallowed a pang of homesickness.

Outside, hard, cold rain had begun to fall, shot through with a tricky shaft of sunlight. It was sufficiently persistent that Kate felt she could veto any requests for a trip to the park. But when she returned to the sitting room Luke was still curled on the sofa, long lashes half-closed over his hazel eyes.

'Budge up, sleepy head. *Blue Peter's* my favourite too you know.'

'Not sleepy,' he protested, shuffling his legs sideways.

Kate settled herself in the empty corner and allowed her son's socked feet to creep across her knees. With half an ear tuned to the presenter's skydiving exploits and the success of the latest charity appeal, she reflected on what Paula had said. Would sleeping with Rudy really 'get it out her system'? It didn't sound like standard marriage-guidance advice, but perhaps this was Sean's current approach to their faltering relationship. It would certainly explain his clandestine lunch with that tee-shirt totty. Kate swallowed. She wasn't the only one that had changed. Paula, Sean and Luke had all shifted away from the people they had been just a couple of months earlier. In the high-ceilinged sitting room with the grey rain splashing outside, far away from Suffolk and the home she had created for them all, Kate felt she didn't know very much about anyone anymore.

Unusually, Sean was home by six o clock that evening. Kate didn't mention her conversation with their Dutch neighbour or the lunch immediately so he decided to earn some brownie points by offering to bath Luke. It was only after he had made the suggestion that he realised it was the thing most likely to make her suspicious. Stories, zoo, manly chats and football were what he and Luke did, not baths. Kate watched him twitching through supper and finally decided to put him out of his misery. She was curious, anyway. Would he lie? Was there anything to lie about?

'Saskia said she bumped into you today.'

'Hmm, yes, in Ikea,' Sean agreed, head pumping rapidly.

'Oh?' Kate looked interested. 'Ikea? Did you buy anything?'

'Eh?' She was asking the wrong question. Sean was momentarily thrown.

'In Ikea?' Kate repeated, her eyes wide. 'Did you buy anything?'

'Only pasta. I was having lunch.'

'I thought that sandwich company came round to your office.'

'It does, but Lena and I had some stuff to discuss.' Sean waved his hand airily to indicate that it was all pretty inconsequential.

'Oh. You were there with Lena? That's the girl we met on Queen's Day, isn't it?' Kate stood up and began to stack the plates in the dishwasher. 'I suppose the food's pretty good – and cheap?' Her voice was light. Sean declined to hear its gentle irony.

'Exactly. We usually go over there a couple of times a week.' Owning up to the lunches was a good plan, he decided. It made him look honest and headed off any future awkward encounters.

'Makes a change, I expect, when you're stuck in the same building all day,' offered Kate.

'Indeed,' Sean agreed happily. He should have realised she would see it like that. Kate wasn't the suspicious type. That was why their marriage had always been so good. He grinned at her.

Kate almost felt sorry for him. His disingenuousness was so typical, she felt, of a man who sees only what he wants to see. Had he always been this stupid? She thought not. Infatuation had dumbed him down, distilled him, and the resulting substance, unsurprisingly – though nevertheless disappointingly – had turned out to be fifty per cent testosterone and fifty per cent ego. Two questions remained unanswered, however. Firstly, had he slept with her? And secondly – assuming he hadn't – could she be bothered to fight for him? Right now she wasn't sure about the answer to either one.

Chapter 21

Kate spent most of the Wednesday morning Van Gogh lecture trying to analyse what she felt about the man standing beside the projector while simultaneously trying to follow his careful Dutch, without much success on either count. At the end of the lesson he approached her as usual and suggested they go back to his flat to continue the portrait. Kate hesitated, their time together was running out.

'I'd like to go to the café first, like we did before.'

He eyed her curiously.

'If you don't want to do the sitting, you must tell me.'

'Of course.' She could hardly ask him if he was planning to seduce her. Surely even Dutch women weren't normally that direct. Instead she said, quite truthfully:

'It's not that. The café's a kind of treat for me, you see, and I've been missing it. We lonely housewives don't get out much.'

Rudy shrugged, his eyes crinkled.

'Of course, if you are paying, it's not a problem!'

'That was always the deal.'

His contribution was his time, hers was the coffee. She was the ex-pat with the well-paid husband; he was the poor artist looking for patronage. The relationship was clear – had always been clear – but Kate suddenly felt less comfortable with it. Something more equal would have been much better.

'Will you perhaps have a little time afterwards to continue with the sitting?' he enquired.

Kate nodded and reminded herself not to be tempted by the wonderful pastries on display behind the counter or her tummy would bulge unappealingly when she stripped off.

A couple of hours later she descended the steep wooden stairs that led from Rudy's studio to the canal-side pavement. The scents of hot wood, dust, paint and turpentine trailed after her, clinging to her thin summer clothes until they dispersed in the breeze of cycling. Once again, nothing had happened. If he fancied her then it wasn't obvious. He had been as usual – polite, friendly but always just a bit distant. He had chatted a little about his parents who lived in Utrecht – which was a nice city, he said, she should visit it – and he had talked about Van Gogh, about painting and how difficult it was to make a living even if you were really good. But mostly he had been silent and except for the sound of the brush and the cries that drifted through the velux windows, the studio was quiet. Kate had almost confided her plans to go to Arles, but decided against it. It made her sound a bit sad and lonely, wandering off like that by herself and he might think she was asking him to go with her although he had already said he was spending the summer in Paris. She imagined him lecturing beneath the ornate ceilings of the Musée d'Orsay – wasn't that where lots of Van Goghs had ended up? She planned to see them herself one day, but first she wanted to visit his landscapes and feel the searing southern heat. She had begun to wonder, as she lay on the green silk in the attic studio, if perhaps, like Vincent, she was going a little bit mad.

Luke waited impatiently outside the school. Kate always seemed to be among the last to arrive and then she would dash up cycling hard and looking very pink. It was annoying because Tobias's mum always came first and Kate was never there to discuss possible playdates. Luke was looking forward to being grown up so that he could sort out his own social life. Having to rely on his parents – whose movements seemed to be increasingly unpredictable – was frustrating. All Kate talked about at the moment was some holiday she was planning. She said she was going as soon as school broke up for the summer and that Luke would be staying with his Dad for the weekend. Normally Luke would have thought this was an excellent plan, but Sean never seemed to be paying attention these days and

Luke was worried that he would be left alone watching the telly while Sean went out. He had tried to explain this to his mum, but she had scoffed at such an idea.

'Of course he won't go out, sweetheart. Not when he knows he's looking after you.'

Luke had to conclude that she just hadn't noticed how weirdly Sean was acting lately and he wondered if he would be able to survive if he was left by himself. He thought he probably would, as long as there was stuff in the fridge.

'How long are you going for?' he enquired in a small voice.

'Only three days,' said Kate reassuringly. 'Friday, Saturday and Sunday – not really long.'

'When are you coming back then?'

'Sunday evening. I'll probably be back in time to read you a story.'

'Okay, then I s'pose.'

'You would be bored stiff if you came.'

'I don't want to come, it's just that...'

'What?'

Luke sighed. 'Nothing.'

How was he supposed to tell her that he would like it a lot better if they all did things together like they used to instead of keep going off in different directions. She would only look vague and concerned and suggest a trip somewhere that wouldn't happen. Luke just hoped his Dad was up to the job of this weekend in charge, because he was definitely feeling in need of attention and there were things he had been waiting to discuss with him. He wanted to explain, for instance, that he was worried about learning Dutch. It didn't seem to be going as quickly as he'd hoped and every break-time Diego came over and kicked him on the shins because of it. He said he would only stop when Luke could understand him. He said England was crap and it was time Luke was a proper Amsterdammer. Luke already had to say he supported Ajax and was asking for a home shirt for his birthday. But that was okay, because he told himself he could support Ipswich Town when he was in England and Ajax Amsterdam when he was in Holland, that way he didn't feel like he was being disloyal to Henry and Dom who had taken him with them to watch Ipswich play a couple of times. Dom was mad about football. He said that was because he came from Newcastle and everyone was mad about football up there. Luke still missed Henry although he had Tobias now. He hoped friends were like football teams: you could have different ones in each county without being a traitor. If he was honest though, he still liked the English ones best and sometimes the longing to sit next to Henry on their sofa watching *The Simpsons* and munching Oreos while Ollie shouted was almost overwhelming.

He was hoping that when this weekend without his Mum happened – and it must be coming up quite shortly because school was breaking up soon – his Dad would take him to the zoo. It seemed ages since he had seen Colonel Hathi and the baby elephant. In fact, not since Henry was here. When they first came Sean had said they could go every weekend. Luke made a mental note to remind his Dad about this. He was beginning to realise that just because parents said something it didn't always mean it was definitely going to happen. You had to watch and see what they actually did. They tended to forget, or sometimes simply decide that the thing they had promised was no longer relevant for some reason. Basically, Luke concluded, they mainly did what *they* wanted to do.

His eyes were glued to the corner of the street as his mother finally came hurtling round it, cycling like a crazy woman and bumping up onto the pavement. He glowered from beneath his fringe. It was embarrassing to be left outside the school looking stupid. He had considered going home by himself and waiting on the step. He could easily do it. He knew the way.

'Sorry, sweetheart,' Kate gasped, leaping breathlessly from her bike. Her son eyed her testily.

'Next time you're late I'm walking home,' he threatened. 'Why don't you give me a key? I'm big enough. I'm almost five.'

Kate bit her lip guiltily.

'Almost five probably isn't quite old enough for a key.'

'So I'll wait outside then. I don't care. It's better than standing here.'

'I promise I won't be late again,' said his mother. It was horrible to find him there practically alone and on the verge of tears. What had she been thinking? She was shocked at herself. Yet, it had been so easy to stay five more minutes cocooned in that warm nest above the Eglantiersgracht with the soporific painting smells, basking in Rudy's gaze. Disturbingly easy. She held the bike so Luke could climb onto his seat.

'You promised before,' he said sullenly.

'I didn't promise before. I distinctly remember not promising.'

'You didn't want to, but in the end you did,' Luke insisted.

He's right, thought Kate, reddening, ashamed at discovering she was less than she had believed she was.

'I'm sorry. It won't happen again, really.' She could tell from his look he was no longer sure. But the picture was almost finished. There was to be just one more sitting tomorrow and then on Friday after the last class Rudy and Kate were to view the painting together. Conscious of her own mounting apprehension as the day approached, she turned and planted a kiss on Luke's little-boy smelling hair, inhaling its faint bovrilly scent, before settling herself on the saddle for the short ride home.

*****

Sean was sitting in a dishevelled heap on Lena's red sofa wondering how he had allowed himself to be talked into this again. The quick 'coffee' at her place after work had somehow turned into a major session. He knew he must leave. The flat was like one of those fairy tale dens; once you enter you can't ever get out.

'I need to get back. Luke'll be waiting for me and Kate might be worried.'

'So, does that matter to you?' Lena demanded, her dark eyes flashing. 'Is it important that she cares about you?'

'Well, it would be nice if someone cared,' said Sean, wearily.

'How about if I told you I cared?'

She saw him recoil.

'That *you* cared,' he repeated slowly. 'I didn't think that was what this was about.'

Lena burst out laughing. 'It's not,' she said. 'Of course I don't care. I'm only interested in you for sex. That's all, it's quite simple.'

Sean's face flooded with relief.

'Come here now and give me what I want.'

'I haven't got much time,' Sean protested. 'I said I'd be back in time to read a story.'

'Okay, in ten minutes you can leave. Look, he is ready,' she ran a finger along the waistband of his shorts. 'Such a shame to disappoint him.'

Sean cursed his overactive member and resigned himself to satisfying its apparently insatiable appetite. He hadn't felt this horny since his student days and he had forgotten how damned *inconvenient* it was.

Ten minutes, of course, wasn't long enough and it was nearly half an hour before he managed to escape from Lena's apartment and make his way back to the company Mercedes – parked a couple of streets away as a precaution. He had told himself at the beginning of this – this what? Relationship? Liaison? – that he specifically wouldn't do this. He wouldn't let this 'whatever' eat into the little time he had with his son. And yet, here he was on a Wednesday evening sneaking off early for a shag. Sean was alternately disgusted and excited by the new self-image which this conjured up. While he was lounging in Lena's flat or driving down the motorway in his smart, new car, he felt had become a man of the world, someone desirable and experienced in matters of women and sex – practically James Bond. He joked with himself that he would be getting a gun next. But when he arrived home, 007 disappeared. Instead, there stood a very ordinary guy, fast approaching middle-age, indulging in a bit of illicit pussy on the side. This was a much less appealing persona, especially when the same guy climbed the stairs to his son's room too late, as usual, to read a story, and was confronted with the boy's reproachful gaze. Luke was not yet five and already his dad was a tarnished hero. Of all the possible versions of himself, Sean liked this one least.

During the drive home Sean sharpened up enough to realise that Lena's comment about caring had not been entirely facetious. Was she hinting that she was falling in love with him? Was it possible that a woman like Lena might fall in love? She really didn't seem the type. He wondered if he had trivialised her feelings partly because it had suited him and partly because she herself had refused to include them in the equation. All he knew for sure was that he wasn't falling in love with her. Still his penis, twitching once again at the memory of her tight little bum smiling at him invitingly from the sofa, wasn't quite ready to give her up. Especially as there was no suggestion that full relations with his wife might be about to resume. However, he had been given a way out should he need one: a job offer back in England. David Knight, his old London boss, had been moved to a new site in Cambridge was looking for someone to run the IT department. Sean had a good record and the job was his if he wanted it. No expat benefits of course, but a relocation package to Cambridge and a very competitive salary. Sean had received the email that morning and had spent the day mulling over what it might mean. He should discuss it with Kate, of course, but he suspected she would jump at the chance to go back. Or maybe she wouldn't, which was perhaps a scarier thought. He had been given a couple of weeks to think it over as the premises were not quite ready and there was no start date yet. The only certainty was that it would all kick off before school resumed in September. David had mentioned this specifically, knowing about Luke.

Chapter 22

'For the last two months of his life,' explained Rudy, standing beside a large pull-down screen onto which the painting *Wheatfield with Crows* had been projected from his laptop, 'Van Gogh returned to Paris to be nearer his brother Theo. However, he found the noise of the city too much for his sensitive temperament and soon retired to the countryside, finding lodgings in Auvers-sur-Oise...'

Kate had read all this already but she dutifully made notes, translating haphazardly from the Dutch as she transcribed the words onto her page. She had seen the painting many times in the gallery and had always found the canvas disturbing: a dead-end track through fields of wheat towards a half-obscured orb in a cloud-dark sky. And then the flock of crows; heavy, angular strokes of black.

How difficult it is to be simple, [3] Van Gogh had written. What sense of foreboding, of impending fate.

It feels like a death scene, Kate concluded. The paintings from Auvers were Vincent's requiem, whether he had known it or not.

'Many scholars think that this was Van Gogh's last work,' said Rudy. 'It is seductive to introduce the idea of prophecy, of portent. To see it almost as a statement of intent, a suicide note. But this is simply romanticism and the truth is that we cannot know. There are no letters from the last days of Vincent's life. We cannot say if the bullet that killed him was premeditated or simply the impetuous act of a man whose madness sent him suddenly toppling over the edge.'

Kate imagined Van Gogh's coffin processing to its interment as Rudy described it, completely covered in yellow flowers.

At the end of the lecture Kate's fellow students surged forward surrounding their teacher with their goodbyes and good wishes. Would he be teaching next year? Could they perhaps take their studies further? A trip to Paris, maybe? Rudy shrugged. His blue eyes were light and tired. He shook hands with everyone but answered the questions evasively. He wasn't sure; he really felt he needed to apply himself to his own work, he would certainly consider the idea.

He doesn't want to, Kate surmised. He is bored with this teaching even if he is passionate about his subject. She waited quietly on the edge of the group and his gaze met hers briefly through the bustle. A look that said clearly; *Wait for me. I'm coming.* And of course, she would wait. Today was the last time that they would see each other for two months, perhaps forever. This mattered very much. And yet, they were hardly even friends. Whether Rudy returned to teach in September or not, Kate was beginning to feel that she wouldn't be here in the autumn; that one way or another this period was drawing to a close. Now she was going to see the portrait Rudy had painted of her. It was finished. Was today to be to be some kind of apogee, a summation of her time in Amsterdam? The moment in which she found out who she was and what she was destined to become? Her gaze switched back to the image of the *Wheatfield with Crows,* but the screen had been rolled up. Rudy materialised beside her.

'They've gone,' he said, quietly. 'Shall we go and view the portrait, or would you like coffee first?'

She chose coffee.

'I'm going to have one of those pastries, since I don't have to take my clothes off today.' She attempted a smile.

'Good idea. And today is my treat, to say thank you. Did it bother you, taking off your clothes?'

'At first, but then it got easier.'

'You are very beautiful naked.' He nodded seriously. 'This is something you must remember.'

Kate felt a rush of heat to her cheeks.

'No need to blush,' Rudy explained. 'I am simply telling you what I think. I have studied you, after all.'

Thank you, then,' she said, returning his smile.

'When you have finished your cake you will see for yourself.'

He led the way out of the museum and into a light drizzle. Kate pulled off the precautionary plastic bag she had learned always to put over her saddle and pedalled out onto Paulus Potterstraat. A number five tram rattled past reminding her of Luke and the first time they had come to the museum together just a few short months ago. She tried to fix in her mind the image of Rudy's worn cotton jacket flapping in the breeze as he cycled, the shoulders darkening with the gentle, but determined rain.

'Just as well I'm not sitting today,' she shouted, 'my hair's in rats' tails.'

He glanced across at her and shook his head.

'It wouldn't matter.'

They seemed to arrive at the apartment very quickly. Raindrops splatting on the canal disturbed the reflection of the buildings and sent out rippling pools of light and dark. Rudy secured their bikes in the rack. In the stairwell the damp seemed to have permeated the dust making the air soupy and hard to inhale. Kate climbed slowly, one heavy foot in front of the other. By the time she reached the top he was already inside the flat opening a window.

'Usually not too much rain comes in if there's no wind,' he explained. 'And I think we need air.'

Kate stood in the doorway her chest rising and falling visibly.

'Do you have asthma?' He was clearly concerned.

She shook her head. She was panicking. How could she tell him that?

'No, I'm fine. Or at least, I'll be fine in a minute.'

He gave her a considered look.

'It's difficult, perhaps, to see the picture. Too much anticipation. How is it that someone sees you? I think I understand.'

She took a deep, slow breath.

'I'm okay.' A small smile.

'So perhaps we should do this quickly, as if it happens every day?'

She hesitated. Part of her wanted ceremony, a speech, something *significant*. But then, this must be much less important for him. He painted all the time and of course, he already knew what it looked like, what he had made of her. Perhaps he guessed was she was thinking because he grinned suddenly and picked up a scarf from one of the pine chairs.

'I'll blindfold you and lead you towards it. Is that right?'

'Yes,' she agreed, laughing now. That was what she wanted.

'Is that okay? Can you see?' he asked tying the scarf securely behind her head. 'Stand there while I position it correctly on the easel... Now, come with me.'

He took her hot, damp hand in his warm dry one and she felt the gentle pressure of his fingers on her palm as he led her across the studio.

'Okay,' he said. 'Are you ready? We are here.'

Carefully, Kate pushed up the blindfold.

'Oh!' she swallowed hard, goosebumps prickled her arms. 'Oh!' she repeated. 'Oh my God.'

Rudy stood back, biting his lip, watching.

This was a portrait of a woman she didn't know, yet, that was exactly her. Was that really how her hair fell across her shoulder? Did her skin truly shine as if lit from inside? But despite the model's loveliness, Kate sensed hesitancy, poignancy even; something holding her back. Rudy had made Kaatje both beautiful and desirable, but she grasped the world uncertainly. She was a woman waiting to live.

'In the style of Van Gogh, you see?'

Kate nodded. She did see. He had done his job well.

'Will anyone buy it?' she whispered. Could she somehow buy it herself?

'It is my masterpiece and it is not for sale. In the autumn it will hang in an exhibition.'

'Exhibition?'

'It's okay. It's not here in Amsterdam, but in Brussels. I have been asked to send something. It's very prestigious for me. Perhaps you will become as famous as Augustine Roulin, *La Berceuse*. When I am as famous as Vincent that is.' His smile was teasing.

'Except that my identity will remain a mystery like the Mona Lisa.' Kate giggled. 'I quite like that idea. And what will you call it?' she asked, intrigued.

'Well, if Augustine Roulin is a lullaby, I think you can be a sonnet. Shall I compare thee to a summer's day...?' He was laughing now, then he stopped and became suddenly serious. 'But yes, *The Sonnet*. Why not?... Ah, I almost forgot. This is for you. Maybe you will want to remember someday.' He handed her a small paper bag. Inside was a photograph of the portrait in a black velvet frame.

Kate shook her head not quite believing. 'I must go,' she said. There was Luke to pick up. She paused. Somehow she must prise herself from this moment, turn and walk out of the door. A lump rose in her throat. Was there anything left to say?

'Thanks,' she murmured, at last. 'Thanks for everything.'

'For what exactly?'

She reached up to peck him on the cheek but instead he took her face in his hands.

'I will miss you,' he said lightly, bending to place a quick, brushing kiss on her lips. 'There are not often such beautiful women in my Van Gogh class.'

And I will miss you, she thought, blinking hard as she descended the stairs, disappointment crystallizing in her gut. It hadn't happened. He had remained polite and (almost) correct until the end. Perhaps this way was best. She would go back to her apartment, the school holidays, to Luke and to Sean. Except that she had one last thing to think about; her trip next weekend to see the sunflowers. A solitary holiday. It made her feel like a bit of a Billy-no-friends but she didn't care, she wanted to see them. She wanted the challenge of travelling alone. She wanted somehow, to see who she was outside the cocoon of her family, to find out if Kaatje was real.

Chapter 23

'So what's happening this weekend?' asked Lena who had somehow appeared in the car park just as Sean was unlocking his car. He couldn't prevent a puzzled frown. He hadn't seen her in the lift. Had she dashed down the stairs to intercept him? She seemed as usual, completely cool, without a trace of having hurried anywhere in her entire life.

'Well, er...'

She waited, eyebrows raised expectantly.

'I think I'd better spend some quality time with Kate,' he said. 'She's going to be away next weekend on some trip with the Van Gogh museum.'

'Okay,' Lena said slowly, 'so who do I spend quality time with then?'

'Eh?' Sean wondered at what point he had become responsible for keeping her entertained. 'Just do whatever you used to do before our – er –thing. See a movie, maybe, with a girlfriend?'

Lena's eyes narrowed. 'And you said Kate's away next weekend?'

Shit, thought Sean, Tactical error.

'That's right, but I'm in charge of Luke. He wants me to take him to the Zoo.'

'The Artis?'

'Of course. He likes the elephants.' He gave up trying to get into his car and instead leaned back against it, blinking hard. The contact lenses were suddenly irritating him.

'So in the evening you could get a sitter for a couple of hours and come over to my place. How about Friday night? We could watch a movie together. I have quite a collection.'

'I don't doubt it,' Sean wished she would stop looking at him like that. Despite his best intentions he was starting to tingle inconveniently. 'Look I'll see. It's supposed to be quality time with my son.'

Lena sighed. 'So much quality time with everyone except me. And he'll be asleep, anyway.'

She had a point, Sean thought, feeling his resolve weakening. Maybe one evening wouldn't matter. And he could do stuff with Luke during the day after all.

'I'll get back to you on that,' he said, making a show of opening the car door.

'You do that,' said Lena. 'In the meantime, I'll see you around.'

Half an hour later, snarled up in the Amsterdam rush hour, Sean reviewed the scene and thought she might actually have been tapping her foot, although he couldn't swear to it. Mistresses were surely supposed to wait for you patiently in secret boudoirs wearing lacy underwear, not confront you noisily in the car park after work. He rubbed a hand over his scalp. What on earth had he got himself into?

Luke, as usual, was in his pyjamas by the time his father got home. Normally he would have been in bed but they had now switched to 'holiday timetable', which meant later nights and hopefully correspondingly later mornings. Though it was only Kate that would really benefit, Sean reflected glumly. She was on the computer looking at pictures of Arles.

'He painted so much while he was there,' she said, by way of greeting. 'It was a really prolific time. You know that famous picture of the yellow café at night?'

Sean said he thought he did.

'Well, that's in Arles.'

He peered over her shoulder.

'Surely you wouldn't have all those stars in a town,' he grumbled.

'Might have done. It was more than a century ago, remember. Much less light pollution.'

'Hmmp.' Sean got himself a cold beer from the fridge and sat down on the sofa next to Luke.

'What's on?'

'*Misty Island Rescue*. It's nearly finished.'

'Don't you know it by heart?'

Watching the engines dash around the screen Sean thought that *he* probably did.

'So what if I do?' Luke clutched Percy the Green Engine more tightly and Kate shook her head warningly. Sean sighed. He supposed it didn't really matter.

'How does it feel to have broken up from school, then?'

'Okay. At least I don't have to see Diego.'

'Is he still being a pain?'

'Yep.'

'But I thought you only saw him at break time, anyway.'

'Yep,' agreed Luke, thinking how he and Tobias spent quite a lot of time keeping out of Diego's way and sometimes that meant not playing football with the others. 'Can we take Tobias to the Artis next Friday?'

'Sure,' said Sean. 'We'll pick him up on the way. Anything anyone wants to do this weekend?'

'I want to go to the Hoge Veluwe,' said Kate. 'It's a national park about an hour from here. You can cycle and walk round it but there's also a museum with loads of really important Van Goghs.'

'Kate!' Sean groaned.

'No, really, I've just found it on the internet. You two don't have to come into the museum if you don't want to, but we can also do a bike tour. The bikes are free and there're places to picnic.'

'Picnic?' The Thomas the Tank Engine DVD drew to a close and Luke turned round excitedly. 'It sounds okay as long as we don't have to go to the museum. Don't you think, Dad?' He looked earnestly at Sean.

'Alright, then. It does sound pretty good.' Cycling and paintings weren't really what he'd had in mind but he didn't have a better suggestion.

'I thought the Van Gogh course had finished now,' said Sean an hour or so later when Luke was in bed and the dinner plates had been cleared away. 'So how come you need to look at more pictures?'

'It has,' Kate agreed. 'We had the last lecture today. But that doesn't mean I've stopped being interested.'

'No, of course not,' said Sean, hastily. 'Anyway, I've just googled it myself. This Hoge Veluwe place looks perfect for Luke to let off steam and it might be good for us all to get out of the city for a few hours.'

Kate gave him a searching look. 'Yes,' she said at last, 'I'm sure it will.'

*****

'So we can just take them?' asked Luke, disbelieving. They had arrived at the Hoge Veluwe, dropped off Kate at the museum and parked up in front of one of the racks of white bicycles.

'Seems like it,' said Sean, reading the notices that had helpfully been written in English as well as Dutch.

'How long will Mummy be?'

'Just an hour, I should think. Here, this one looks about your size.'

'Where are we meeting her?'

'At the café in the middle of the park, but I can always phone.'

Luke nodded, reassured. A bike ride was a good idea but he would have preferred his mum to have come too. On the other hand, she wanted to see pictures and he definitely didn't, especially not now that the sun was shining. So perhaps this was the best solution.

Sean grinned, which made Luke think that he thought so too. His Dad was wearing shorts and a tee shirt instead of a boring suit. It really felt like the holidays.

'Right,' said Sean, making a show of checking his back pack. 'Water, biscuits, bananas. I think that's everything. Ready, Luke? Let's go.'

Sean set off at a steady pace and Luke followed, pedalling hard.

I'm going to ask Mum if I can cycle to school next year, he decided. This is much better than sitting in that stupid seat.

'Don't get distracted,' Kate told herself, walking through the museum entrance. 'Just Vincent's paintings and most importantly, the ones he painted at Arles.' She forced herself to ignore the Mondriaans without too much trouble, but had to pause before Renoir's *In the Café*; the softly curving forms of the women, the light reflecting off the top hat... how had she never been interested in art before? And then there were the unmissable Van Goghs; his signature rapid strokes, bright colours and the deep sense that the artist had captured not just the form of a thing, but its essence. All of it now felt intensely familiar and Kate smiled at how far she had come in a few short weeks. She instantly recognised the *Langlois Bridge*, the strange tombs of *les Alyscamps* and finally the *Café Terrace at Night*. After the *Sunflowers* the *Café Terrace* was perhaps the picture that most epitomized Vincent's work and here it was in front of her; the striking blue and yellow canvas, the luminous white of the waiter's apron echoed in the moon-round tops of the bistro tables, the black silhouette of a church tower against the indigo sky and of course, the huge splashes of stars. Next week she would visit the Place du Forum, the actual square in Arles where it had been painted. She shivered expectantly.

As the end of the hour approached, Kate tore herself away from the gallery and bought a few postcards in the museum shop. Agreeing to see Sean and Luke at the café meant that she too was obliged to take one of the white bikes and cycle over to meet them. There were several parked in the racks outside the building but to simply pick one felt uncomfortably like stealing. Presumably someone had left the bike there and was now inside examining a Seurat or whatever. She couldn't help wondering if this bike distribution method really worked. Was anyone ever stranded without wheels?

She took one anyway and to her surprise, found the café easily enough. Unusually she was even a little bit early. She ordered a coffee and settled herself to wait. The boys turned up a few minutes later, pedalling along side-by-side, Sean with his hand on Luke's back to help propel him forwards. She spotted them before they saw her and was able to watch them dismount and park the bikes in the stands. They were chatting as they did so and Kate felt a pang as she noted how relaxed they seemed. Luke was flushed with the exercise and looked radiantly happy.

In the same moment both father and son glanced up, caught sight of her and beamed broadly. It was like being caught in a shaft of sunlight. She had never thought that Luke particularly resembled Sean but in that second he undoubtedly did. With this sudden likeness and their evident ease in each other's company, Kate sensed the possibility of them regrouping, reforming themselves as a family in a way they had failed to manage back in, Amsterdam. All she had to do was stand up and walk towards them. She pushed back her chair and stepped forward, raising her arm in a wave.

Chapter 24

Sean was beginning to feel he had been exceptionally stupid. After the trip to the Hoge Veluwe on Saturday the family had stopped at *Le Quattro Stagioni* for the first time since their very first weeks in the city. It really was a great little restaurant and they did unquestionably excellent seafood pasta. Luke had been impeccably well-behaved, soaking up the attention of the Italian waitress. Sean couldn't think why they hadn't been there more often. Kate simply shrugged when he mentioned this.

'We don't seem to have done many of the things we meant to do,' she said, raising her eyes very deliberately from her forkful of *penne* and treating him to an uncomfortably searching look. Sean felt himself redden and decided it was high time to extricate himself from the 'thing' with Lena. It had made him feel so great at first, as if he could conquer the world. And he couldn't deny that he fancied her. But he fancied his wife too and together they had so much more than he ever could with a slightly dodgy work colleague – however inviting her sofa.

That night, mellow with fresh pasta and Pinot Grigio, he and Kate made love properly for the first time in weeks. Initially it was a little bit awkward and tentative, an inquiring finger gently running along a thigh. But Sean quickly found he could take pleasure in just holding his wife, feeling her skin against his own, inhaling her subtle, familiar perfume and letting everything else take its course. And it was good, like the meal they had just shared. Yet later, as they lay still touching, he sensed through his drowsiness that Kate was weeping, quietly. He had no idea why.

Sean managed to avoid Lena for most of the following week. At first he attributed this to his own evasive tactics which basically meant foregoing coffee, but then he learnt she was out of the office until Wednesday afternoon anyway. He wondered if she was playing hard to get, in which case it wasn't working. But he had a strong feeling it was going to be very difficult to fob her off come the weekend.

Since Saturday he and Kate were definitely getting along better and had repeated the love-making – this time without the subsequent tears. Kate had even snuggled up to him whispering:

'It doesn't matter anymore, about the baby I mean.'

Sean felt himself tense, but she said it again, more firmly:

'No, it really doesn't matter. It's just one of those things. What matters is what we do have.'

He squeezed her tightly by way of reply.

It helped that the holidays had started and Luke was staying up a bit later so there was none of the bubbling resentment when Sean failed, once again, to get home in time to read to him. The whole story thing had suddenly become a whole lot more challenging, anyway. Instead of Thomas the Tank Engine adventures, Luke was now insisting on hearing chapters from factual books about elephants. Kate had been persuaded to order a selection from Amazon.

'It's research for when we go to the Artis,' Luke explained. 'Like Mummy does about the sunflower man, you know, Van Cough.'

Sean agreed he did know.

'Well, I'm finding out all about elephants for when we visit Colonel Hathi and the others. Then I can understand them better instead of just looking at them. That's what Mummy says anyway.'

Sean nodded, bemused. With his wife and son conducting all this in-depth research into diverse subjects he was beginning to feel a bit left behind.

During those first school-free days, Kate could almost believe she had been transported back to their initial weeks in

Amsterdam. A time before Rudy, when Van Gogh was simply the artist who painted sunflowers and went mad. It was just her and Luke once again, wandering hand in hand through a foreign country. They slowly crossed the Vondelpark on their way to the Melkhuis for an ice cream, stopping to watch the parrots and even spotting the parrot lady with her flowing dress. Yet when Kate turned to look at the boy at her side, it was obvious that he had grown, and that he was much more at ease with the city and the language than he had been at first. So then it became clear that things were not the same and that in fact, everything had changed.

There was her marriage, for example. Both she and Sean were acting as if all the problems had disappeared overnight, mended by a nice meal and some decent sex, but really the rift ran much deeper than that. Luke knew it. He was twitchy when his parents were together, liking to see open displays of affection and quickly jumping in to negotiate if there was the slightest disagreement. She had meant what she said about the baby and them mattering, but Kate still caught herself looking out for Rudy as she sat sipping coffee on the Melkhuis terrace. In fact, she realised she had automatically positioned herself so she could keep half an eye on Luke in the play park, and still watch the gate.

I am being silly, she told herself. He has gone to Paris. And even if he hadn't, whatever was between us was entirely my fantasy. He was an artist and he wanted a model. That was all.

But regardless of how resolutely she repeated this, a little voice in her brain murmured over and over; there are not often such beautiful women in my Van Gogh class.

It was the first time anyone had called her beautiful. Sean had called her 'gorgeous' and 'sexy' plenty of times when they were younger but 'beautiful' in that quiet, serious way Rudy had that made you instantly believe what he said, her husband could never manage that.

'Hey Mummy, wake up,' Luke was shaking her arm vigorously, jolting her out of her daydream. 'Tobias is here. That's his mum over there. Why don't you go and talk to her, then maybe Tobias could come home with us.'

Kate followed Luke's eagerly pointing finger.

'The lady with the red bag?'

'Yes, you met her before remember?'

'Of course,' said Kate, giving herself a little shake. 'I don't mind if your friend comes back for the afternoon.' She closed her book and stood up. The boys had run back to the swings and a tall, dark woman with a scarlet holdall was looking in her direction. She smiled and waved. Kate waved back and picked up her coffee cup. She would go over and join her. This was territory she understood. For an hour or so she would simply be a parent again.

'Tobias seems a very nice boy,' said Kate to Luke who was sitting in the bath.

'Of course he is,' said Luke, frowning as if she had said something completely idiotic. 'He's my friend. Is his mummy nice, too?'

'She seemed very pleasant. She makes pots, apparently.'

Luke shrugged. 'Hmm.'

In fact, Kate had found her very easy company, gentler than many of the women she had met in this city.

'Maybe she could be your friend,' Luke suggested. 'Then we'd be like with Henry and Henry's mum and we'd just have to get Daddy to like Tobias's dad.'

Kate laughed and ruffled his hair. 'It's a nice idea, but I'm not sure it works quite like that.'

'Why not?'

Kate confessed she wasn't sure why not. It just didn't.

'Well, it should,' said Luke.

The conversation reminded Kate that it was time to give Paula another ring. It was scarily easy to get caught up in your own life and not notice how quickly the days were slipping by. As soon as Luke was in bed talking elephants with Sean she picked up the phone. Dom answered. His voice echoed distractedly down the line.

'Yeah, hi. Who is it?'

'It's Kate. Is this a bad time? I can always phone back tomorrow.' She could hear herself babbling, thrown by Dom's curt tone.

'Paula's not here. She didn't respond very well to her treatment today. Her blood pressure shot up and her heart beat started jumping about a bit. They've decided to keep her in for a night or two.'

'A night or two!' If Paula was occupying precious NHS bed space it must be because she needed it.

'Yeah, look, sorry Kate, but Paula's Mum and Dad should be here any time now. I'm just trying to sort out Ollie.' Dom was clearly in no mood to talk.

'Goodness'. Kate bit her lip. 'Right. I'll ring back in a couple of days, then. Give her our love.'

'Sure.'

The phone went dead and she sank onto a chair. Setbacks hadn't been in the script. Her friend was supposed to have the surgery, the chemo, the radiotherapy and then be back to normal, pretty much within six months, a year, max. Except – it was now dawning on Kate – you were probably never completely back to normal, if normal was defined as the person you had been before the cancer. How much younger and more innocent must that old you suddenly seem from the new post-illness perspective? Stuff changes people, second by second, hour by hour. When Paula recovered, assuming, of course, that she did – Kate faltered, the alternative now suddenly seemed possible – she would never again blithely take for granted the fact that she would live to watch her boys grow up. Instead, she would count every single day as a blessing.

'Luke's almost asleep,' said Sean coming into the sitting room. 'Are you okay?'

Kate nodded.

'Well, you don't look it.' He squeezed her shoulder. 'How was Paula?'

'Back in hospital. She's had a few problems. Dom didn't say much. It sounded like he had his hands full.'

'It's probably only a hiccup. She'll be fine.'

'She might be. She probably will be. But just at the moment she isn't.'

Sean's frown deepened. It could so easily have been Kate. Then Luke would have been scuttling around worriedly as Henry must now be, playing up and demanding attention. Out of his usual routine Ollie would be screaming even more than usual. Dom would be trying to pull the household together, reassure everybody. Maybe he was busy at work too. And all the time all he would be longing to be with Paula. Nightmare scenario.

'I'll make you a cup of tea,' said Sean, decidedly. He wanted to hold his wife to make absolutely sure she was still there. She seemed to have shrunk, almost disappeared, into the huge leather armchair.

She looked up at him, face pale.

'Tea,' she said, 'is exactly what I need.'

Kate had left the curtains half-open and was staring at the dense black shape of the huge magnolia against the navy sky when her husband climbed into bed beside her.

'I thought you were reading,' he said. 'I only stayed downstairs to watch the end of the film.'

'I couldn't really concentrate.'

Sean grunted sympathetically.

'The worst is being so far away,' said Kate. 'I feel I should have been able to help more.'

'Your life changed,' said Sean. 'That's all. Lives do. It could have been the other way round.'

'Dom sounded like he wanted me to go away.'

'He was busy, Katie, worried. He didn't have time to talk.'

When had Sean last called her Katie? Kate found she couldn't remember. It had been a while. She let him snuggle up to her chastely, absorbing his warmth. Within minutes his breathing relaxed and she knew he was asleep. Much easier to let him think that was all that was bothering her. Tomorrow she was going to Arles. A woman travelling alone. She would stand where Vincent had stood and try to see what he had seen. But was it Vincent van Gogh or Rudy de Jong that she wanted to feel closer to? Truthfully, she really didn't know.

Chapter 25

The plane began its descent, sweeping the bay before it touched down. Through the window Kate could see Marseille spread out below her; docks, oil refineries and the Mediterranean, azure blue under a blistering sun. She clutched her bag, straining to make out as much as possible. Was that a field of yellow in the distance? Impossible to be sure.

Stepping out of the cabin onto the steps was like walking into an oven. Kate took off her cardigan and stuffed it into her suitcase. Aéroport Marseille Provence. This was what she had come for. She was smiling as she trundled her bag towards passport control, her head spinning with the heat and the exhilaration of being alone; no Sean striding off ahead, no turning round to check on Luke. Just her. And she had a strong feeling that here, where Vincent had found the colour and sunshine he craved, she too, would find what she was looking for.

Marseille airport was smaller than Schiphol, thank goodness, and the people waiting for their luggage were no longer extraordinarily tall and fair but rather small and olive-skinned. There were a good sprinkling of Arabs too, waiting for flights to Jeddah or Algiers. Would Van Gogh have felt as she now did when he arrived in the south, as if she had crossed a continent instead of just a country? But there were no planes in those days of course, and Vincent would have taken a steam train from the Gare de Lyon in Paris, probably third class, sitting on a rattling wooden seat as it clattered through the interminable fields of northern France towards the sun. His luggage, mostly paints, canvases and an easel, would have been stashed overhead on a wooden rack where he could eye it anxiously from time to time. And it would have been far colder. The painter had made the trip in February, hunched up in his great coat, no doubt, collar turned up around his ears. Kate shook herself. The girl at the car hire centre was addressing her, pushing across papers to sign. The cold weight of the key in her hand made Kate instantly wish that she followed Van Gogh's example and chosen to go by rail. Driving in France would take some nerve but how else would she get to see the sunflowers?

In fact, once she had negotiated the airport car park and managed to get herself out of Marseille and onto the *Autoroute du Soleil*, she discovered that Arles wasn't actually a difficult drive. And she found the Hotel Régence easily enough, arriving just as night was falling. She had chosen it deliberately because it wasn't buried in the old city centre which was bound to be full of narrow streets and complicated one way systems. Instead it looked out over the Rhone and there was even parking in the street outside – definitely a good omen. Kate pushed open the car door and gasped at the strong, warm wind which caught her hair as it gusted southwards. Of course, the mistral. She tugged her little suitcase out of the boot and, with a quick glance up to reassure herself that she had found the right place, trundled up to the quay to have a look at the river. The wind scudded along the dark ribbon of water, rippling the layers of black and causing the chime of lights, reflections from the bank, to wobble uncertainly. The night was compelling. It seemed to be including her, pulling her into it. She leant for a few moments on the parapet with the Rhone lapping below, breathing in the wind and allowing the warm darkness to seep inside her before reluctantly turning back to the hotel. There would be plenty of time to explore in the morning

Perhaps they weren't used to people arriving late because no one appeared immediately at the reception desk. Kate examined her surroundings; tiled floor, wooden staircase with strips of carpet on the treads to deaden the noise, a stained glass window decorating the door to the back office. It seemed clean but smelt slightly stale, as if the door was never open long enough to clear the air. She thought fleetingly of the Amsterdam apartment and wondered if Luke was in bed. He should be, it was almost 10 o'clock, but Sean might have let him stay up. On the odd occasions he and Luke were left alone together the child's usual bedtime tended to be ignored.

'You worry too much, Kate,' Sean would say. 'Staying up an extra hour or two in the holidays is really no big deal. And she would bite her lip and wonder if she was trying just a bit too hard.

'*Madame?*' A young man was asking her name, addressing her in polite, Gallic-flavoured English. She smiled. Perhaps tomorrow she might try out her rusty French but tonight she was just too tired. He showed her to a small room on the second floor with a river aspect. She had chosen this, even paid ten euros extra for it, because she knew it would do her good to look out over the expanse of water. For all its architectural charm, Amsterdam was flat and enclosed. There were no views except from the roof terraces. The only hills were the bumps of the bridges over the canals. Kate was missing space; missing the wide Suffolk fields and the huge bowl of the sky. She was surprised that this had become possible. She threw open the window to let in the night air. It was good to be so far away in a completely new place. Provence. She soaked up the word and all it implied; shimmering heat, fields of lavender, carafes of red wine and of course, sunflowers. Staring out across the Rhone, breathing the in the scent of the river, she had become simply an anonymous woman with amber hair, waiting. For the first time she acknowledged that this weekend might be about more than Van Gogh and Rudy. It might also be about her own life and how she planned to spend what remained of it. The mistral squalled violently; the window banged against the frame. Reluctantly, Kate pulled it closed.

It could send you mad, this wind, she reflected.

Switching on the lamp, she noticed her mobile had tumbled out of her bag and was lying mute on the rose-coloured bed cover. She hadn't given it a thought since she landed. She had forgotten to text home, forgotten to text her safe arrival. Had she already stopped being Kate Butterworth, then? Could it happen so quickly? She turned it on hurriedly, guiltily. There were two messages from Sean.

Hope you've arrived safely. What's the hotel like? xx

Getting a bit worried. Please let me know you're ok. xx

There were kisses, she noticed.

I'm fine. In Arles. Hotel seems perfect. View over river. Very tired so now going to bed. Hope all well at home. Love to you both xx

She hit send and turned off the phone. She would only switch it on periodically, she decided, maybe twice a day. She wanted to be in charge of her time and how it was used. This trip was about her, a kind of retreat.

During a solitary breakfast of brioche, orange juice and coffee, Kate discovered that she was not the only person in the hotel, although she might be the only *Anglaise*. Disappointingly, the other guests all seemed to be the tall, fair Netherlanders that she thought she had left behind; people with suitcases on wheels and holiday wardrobes just like her own.

Come on, Kate, she scoffed silently. Did you expect to wake up in some nineteenth century boarding house full of artists? She took a deep breath, drained her coffee and decided that she would go to the tourist office first. It would be heartbreaking to have come all this way and later find out she had neglected something essential. The Yellow House, of course, was the most important, totally unmissable thing to visit.

Kate resolved to try out her French on the polite receptionist who had been reinvented this morning as waiter.

'Excusez-moi de vous déranger, Monsieur, mais où se trouve l'office de tourisme?'

The young man grinned broadly.

'*Vous parlez très bon français, Madame,*' he began. But this compliment on her linguistic skills was all Kate managed to understand because the rest of the sentence was delivered in an impenetrable Marseille accent. She smiled uncertainly and concluded she would find it herself. In a city like Arles the tourist office must surely be fairly well signposted.

She had dressed carefully, conscious of the heat, knotting her flyaway hair firmly at the nape of her neck and choosing a cream dress with yellow flowers that she thought Vincent might have admired. As an afterthought she added a lacy shawl to protect her shoulders in case the sun became too strong. She blended in well; the city was full of yellow, she discovered, as she began her walk through its streets. Many of the buildings had been painted in a yellow distemper with blue shutters set against them.

Like the blue in Vincent's cobalt sky, thought Kate. Everywhere she looked the colours were thrown into sharp contrast by the clear southern light.

It was early and Arles was still waking up; cafés were pulling out their awnings, council vans sprayed water onto the pavements to dampen down the dust and elderly dogs hobbled about their business. Kate picked her way carefully through the cobbled streets until she came to the Place de la République with its beautifully understated twelfth century church and Lego-like town hall. Just opposite the church, in the window of a tall, narrow house above a *tabac,* was a sign advertising an apartment to let. She gazed up at the slatted shutters and wrought iron railings with an odd smile. What if she didn't go back? What if she walked out of her life and into the *tabac* and asked to rent the rooms? Women did that sometimes, she had read. When their lives became too much, too confusing, they simply exchanged them for another, as if they were dresses. What would that new dress feel like? And how long before it came as complicated and demanding as the old one? She shrugged and turned deliberately away.

The *Office de Tourisme* was prominently placed on the main road and it had only just rolled up its shutters when Kate entered. She browsed distractedly among the postcards and tourist guides in myriad languages, allowing the woman at the desk time to settle herself, before approaching.

'*Madame?*' Deftly drawn brows rose enquiringly above a pair of calm, brown eyes.

Kate explained her mission but the lady shook her head emphatically.

'*Mais, non, Madame.* The Yellow House was bombed in 1944.'

'Bombed! 'It can't have been!'

'I am afraid so.'

Kate hoped she wasn't about to cry. What an idiot she must seem. It had gone, the studio where he painted with Gauguin, the bedroom with the wooden chair. It had been turned to rubble and swept away. Why hadn't Rudy told them that?

'So what can I see? Is anything left? The Café Terrace? Or was that bombed too?'

'The café terrace is still there,' the lady assured her kindly. 'And there are many things you can visit. Take this map and you can do a walking tour of the city. You will see all the places where Van Gogh' – she pronounced it Gog – 'painted. There is a *panneau* at each one.'

'*Panneau?*'

'A copy of the picture.'

'Thank you!' Kate felt somewhat compensated. She took the map out into the sunlight and squinted at it hopefully. It seemed that Vincent had done most of his paintings within the city walls. One or two were a bit further away. The tour would easily take all day. It was oddly reassuring to discover that people came looking for Van Gogh all the time; she was doing nothing strange. In theory the *Café Terrace at Night* – the painting she had seen in the Kröller Müller museum just the weekend before – should be the first stop, but it was so important she wanted to save it until the end. Instead, she decided to head back up to the river and look for the site of *Starry Night over the Rhone*.

The location proved easy enough to find but at first glance the view hardly resembled Van Gogh's masterpiece.

'And why should it?' Kate muttered, swallowing her disappointment. 'It's broad daylight, for a start.'

On closer inspection, however, the shape of the river was clear, as were the buildings that should, when darkness fell, provide the lights in the painting. There would be no couple, however. No husband and wife to stroll obligingly across the foreground, taking the evening air, their clothes turned to navy shadows by the dusk. The man with his battered hat and his spouse in her woollen shawl were as long dead as Vincent himself and had probably never known how they had been immortalised by an artist's brush. Kate took a photo of the Rhone with the *panneau* beside it, taking care to get the same angle as Van Gogh had done.

Next on her agenda was the site of the Yellow House. This proved harder to find because of the absence of the house itself. However, the building behind it was intact, its shape clearly recognizable from the original painting. This time the *panneau* had been placed unceremoniously in the Place Lamartine between a plane tree and a blue Renault. Kate tried to conjure the square house with the arched doorway on the empty patch of pavement, but it failed to appear.

Perhaps, she thought, I'm trying too hard as usual.

The sun was rising rapidly. She decided to sit for a moment on a bench in the shade of the tree and caught herself chatting to an imaginary Luke, explaining to him about bombing and how a house can disappear. Suddenly, the trip was seeming a bit pointless. The reality of being a solitary tourist was dissolving the optimism she had felt on setting out from the hotel that morning.

Maybe you didn't actually find out much about yourself when you were on your own, she reflected. Perhaps you needed other people to mirror back to you. She sipped a bottle of water and set herself to picture the city in 1888 when Vincent would have been sitting quite close to where she was now; painting the house that no longer existed. But the thrill of history revisited that she had been hoping for continued to evade her and eventually, defeated by the persistent traffic noise, she gave up and checked her phone instead.

Hi, Sean had written. *All ok here. Just going to pick up Tobias and then we're off to the Artis. Hope Arles is good and the Dutch wrinklies aren't too irritating. Miss you. xxx*

The message had come in about half an hour before. Perhaps Sean really was missing her. She pictured him in the kitchen with Luke, excessive jollity hiding the faint panic that bubbled just under the surface. It took a moment to remember that the Dutch wrinklies he referred to were her fictitious companions. Kate decided not to mention them. Perhaps she would own up when she got back and admit she had gone alone.

All fine. Enjoying myself, but Yellow House bombed. Very hot. Hug Luke for me.

She tried to work out if she was missing Sean but couldn't decide. She sent kisses anyway: *xxx*

It would have made sense to go from the Place Lamartine to the Arena but, drawn by the wide stretch of water and the persistent breeze, Kate decided she would prefer to stroll along beside the river. Pulling the shawl across her shoulders, she walked slowly, admiring the buildings and letting the heat saturate her bones, her pace mirroring the sleepy, languid feel of the ancient town. Centuries of daily life – Roman, Medieval, Renaissance – were assembled here in a jigsaw of history. Each new era using, adapting, never quite demolishing, what had stood before.

The next stop was the Trinquetaille Bridge and this, it turned out, wasn't far from her hotel. But the original bridge had been replaced and the new one was disappointing. Gone too was the cobbled street that should have led up to it, and the sweep of the stone steps had been spoilt by parked cars. All that really remained of Van Gogh's original picture was the plane tree. Still a sapling in the painting, it had flourished as the rest of the scene had not and grown to a substantial size. She could hardly stretch her arms around its trunk. Kate stood for a moment in its shade, contemplating how Vincent had also stood in that very same spot and looked upon a different scene. Shifting layers of time, each moment coating the one before, seconds and minutes falling like dust.

She climbed up the steps onto the bridge and leant over the railings, studying the multiple shades of turquoise that shifted in the water. Several strands of hair had been tugged loose by the wind and were flying wispily about her temples. Periodically she captured them and attempted to secure them behind her ears.

How to paint a river? she wondered. She lifted her head and looked down the Rhone's length, willing herself to see the sea. Lost in her daydream she failed to notice a familiar figure pausing at the top of the steps then making his way towards her.

'I did not expect to see you here,' he said, conversationally.

She swung round and there was the Dutchman, fair-hair roughly attached in a band, a faded blue tee-shirt pinned back against his ribs by the breeze.

'Rudy!' Her face suffused instantly with pink. Rudy smiled, stooping for the obligatory three kisses greeting.

'Why are you not in Amsterdam?' he asked, puzzled.

Kate's hands fluttered around her face as she tried vainly to tidy her hair.

'I just wanted to see Arles, to see the sunflowers, to try and understand Vincent better, so I thought I would come here, just for a couple of days, alone. But you, you're in Paris!' She blinked in bewilderment.

'Apparently not,' Rudy laughed. 'It seems that I too am here alone, just for a couple of days.' He rested his forearms on the bridge next to hers, brown and lean with a coating of golden hair. 'So we are both here at the same time. Is this good or bad luck, Kaatje?' He threw her a sideways look and she saw that today his eyes were the same colour as the Provençal sky.

Kate swallowed hard, unable to match his lightness. 'I don't know,' she whispered. 'Why have you come?'

He shrugged. 'My lectures don't start properly until next week. I have a few friends down here and I like to be in the south. It's good to see the sunshine. Arles is important, I think, for understanding Vincent. I find it refreshes my outlook. Every time I come, I discover something new. It is easy to feel close to Van Gogh because this city is very small. His footsteps are everywhere.'

Kate nodded. She had felt this too.

'Also, there is an exhibition of Cezanne at Aix. This is too important to miss. Normally, I will go there tomorrow evening and stay until Sunday.'

'Tomorrow. ' Kate repeated. 'I catch a plane back to Holland on Sunday afternoon.'

'Then we are both free today, so perhaps, if you have time in between your exploring, we could have lunch together.' Rudy glanced up at the sky. 'It is almost noon. You must know that the French are very serious about their *déjeuner* and if we leave it for too long they won't serve us.'

'Lunch?' said Kate, as though she had never heard the word.

Rudy grinned. 'English, I believe, for *middag eten*.'

'Of course,' she smiled suddenly. She was being silly. 'Just lunch.'

'*Ja*. And if you want, afterwards, I will show you Arles. There is much to see and explain. Especially *les Alyscamps*, it can be difficult to find.'

'What I would really like,' said Kate, turning to look straight at him, 'is for you to come with me to see the sunflower fields. I hate driving through this mad French traffic on my own and I'm not sure where to go.'

'Of course,' said Rudy.' There are fields just outside the town, I saw them from the train. We can go this evening. Come, I know where we can eat.'

He steered her to a tiny restaurant just inside the old city walls.

'The food here is good. Never go to the big cafés in the main squares, the menu will be over-priced and third rate. There are too many tourists who will never come back. This place, this is for the local people, those who work in the town. It has to be excellent every single day. The French will demand that, at least.'

Kate nodded. Alone she would have chosen one of those large, brash bistros hoping for anonymity, hiding among the families and middle-aged couples. And no doubt she would have been fobbed off with second rate food. With Rudy she was freer.

How did they look together? she wondered. Friends, or more than that? Could a man and a woman ever be just friends? Walking beside him, keeping to the shade of the buildings, listening to him chatting about Vincent as if he were a personal acquaintance, this had been easier than she imagined. But sitting opposite him at the round table with the green tablecloth and the wineglass placed so casually – because *déjeuner* was unimaginable without at least one small carafe of house red – this was much more difficult and imposed a complicated intimacy. Or perhaps it had existed already. Something had been shared in that Amsterdam garret above the Eglantiersgracht, something that she had tried to push away. And now here, in Provence, it had come to find her.

Chapter 26

'When did you say Mummy would be back?' asked Luke.

'Sunday evening,' Sean replied, patiently. 'I've told you lots of times already.'

'I was just checking.'

Luke was sitting in his Thomas the Tank Engine dressing gown on the leather sofa with Percy the Green Engine rolling backwards and forwards on a brushed-cotton knee. He was watching *The Voyage of the Dawn Treader*. He had chosen it earlier from the DVD library because there was a boat on the cover but actually wasn't enjoying it as much as he had expected to. Sean sat beside him fiddling with his laptop. Luke peered across at the screen.

'Who's that?' he asked, nodding towards a photo in the corner. 'Is it your friend from the office?'

'Er, that's right.'

'Why is she on there now?'

'I had to ask her something about work.'

'Mummy says you work too much.'

'Does she?' asked Sean. 'She could well be right.'

'You should stop then,' advised Luke, whizzing Percy the length of his thigh before returning his attention to the television screen.

'What are they doing now, Dad?'

Slowly, Sean closed the lid of his computer and ran a hand across the close-cropped hair of his scalp. It felt familiar, prickly and oddly reassuring.

'Okay, let's see if we can work out what's going on.' He pulled Luke closer so the boy nestled onto his chest.

'It's not too bad without Mum, is it?' Luke consoled. 'As long as she comes back on Sunday.'

'No, not too bad,' Sean agreed, giving him a squeeze. 'As long as we know she's coming back,' he added.

Sean had been ambivalent about Kate's trip right from the start. Of course, he wanted her to follow her interests and he couldn't pretend that he would enjoy a Van Gogh pilgrimage, so in principle it was fine that she had the chance to go with these people from the art-history course. He couldn't help feeling, however, that there might be a bit more to it than that, stuff she wasn't telling him, but he had his hands too full with Lena to analyse his wife's actions too deeply. His *mistress* – he was sure Kate would see it like that – was becoming difficult. So much for casual sex – did it actually exist? Sean was rapidly coming to the conclusion that he wasn't really cut out for it. Maybe he was just too obviously husband material. Plus he had discovered he was missing his wife. Despite their brief reconnection at the weekend after the trip to that park place, Kate seemed in many ways more remote and distant than ever. All things considered, Sean felt it was definitely time the Lena-thing came to an end. It was just that he wasn't quite sure how to finish it.

'So we're definitely going to the Artis tomorrow?' asked Luke as Sean was shooing him up to bed.

'Of course. It's all arranged. We're picking up Tobias at 10 o clock.'

'And you know where he lives because you took me there to go to the Efteling.'

'Exactly. And then we're driving to the Zoo and we're having tiger burgers at the café.'

'And we're going to see Colonel Hathi.'

'That's the most important bit,' Sean agreed. 'We're going to visit the elephants.'

'Is that your favourite bit too, Dad?'

'Do you know, I think it might be,' said Sean, who was actually fairly indifferent towards zoos in general and would have probably preferred all the animals to be back in the jungle or wherever, rather than peering at him from too-small enclosures making him feel guilty. However, he wasn't about to share this opinion with his son and out of all the beasts he had to admit that the elephants were unquestionably among the most interesting and intelligent-looking. Maybe one day he would take Luke and Kate on a proper African safari and they could see elephants where they were supposed to be. That would be much better.

He had only just finished Luke's story when his mobile rang. Lena. His heart thumped uncomfortably.

'Hey, how are you doing?' She sounded disconcertingly upbeat. Was it an act? Sean speculated. He could never tell with her what was real and what wasn't. At first this uncertainty had been quite exciting, but as the weeks wore on it had become much less so.

'Not much. Just got my son to bed, you know.'

'He's a great kid,' Lena enthused.

'I think so,' agreed Sean, somewhat perplexed. As far as he had been able to tell Lena didn't much like children. And if she was trying to portray herself as stepmother material she could think again. That had never been on the cards.

'Since you're all alone there I could come over and keep you company,' she suggested, in a deliberately silky voice. 'That's what we agreed wasn't it?'

'Did we? When?' Sean fought down a rising sense of panic.

'Last week in the car park when you told me Kate wasn't going to be around,' Lena persisted.

'Eer, I'm not sure we actually made a decision,' spluttered Sean nervously. He gave a noisy yawn. 'Wouldn't be any point tonight, anyway. I'm deadbeat and I've still got a few emails to reply to. Luke has a full-on day mapped out for me tomorrow at the Artis.'

'Hey, that's right. You're going to the zoo! Wow, maybe I'll join you. I'm free tomorrow afternoon. I haven't been to the Artis since I was a kid.'

'Really?' That was probably the most he had ever found out about her childhood, Sean reflected cynically, which just showed what a deep and meaningful relationship they had. Out loud he said:

'That wouldn't work, I don't think. You see, Luke's little friend's coming too.'

'All the more reason for your little friend to come along then, otherwise you'll just be following them around like, what is it? A lame duck? I'll see what I can do.'

And without giving him a chance to protest further, she hung up. He texted her immediately.

Not sure Luke will be very comfortable with you being there. Sorry.

And she immediately replied:

Why not? He knows I'm just a work colleague. Stop panicking.

At which point Sean gave up. She wouldn't arrive until after lunch, anyway. Maybe he could get the boys away by then. Take them to the park or something. He imagined the text he would write; *Sorry we missed you, it was probably for the best.* And then he would tell her kindly and firmly that their 'thing' was over. Which as far as he was concerned, it now definitely was.

'Dad, wake up, we've got to go.' Luke said, shaking him urgently.

Sean opened his eyes and blinked hard.

'God, why? What's up?'

'It's the Artis today, remember?' He said 'remember' in an exasperated tone of voice that Sean usually associated with teenagers. Luke was growing up fast.

'Okay, okay. What time is it?'

'Day time,' said Luke helpfully, pulling back the curtain. A very pale, early kind of daylight streamed in. Sean checked his watch.

'For Christ's Sake, Luke, it's only half-past six.' He lifted his head to get a better look at his son. 'And you're dressed already! I told you to never to wake me in the holidays until the small hand's on the eight.'

'It's not holi-days,' Luke protested, his lower lip beginning to wobble. 'It's the Artis day.'

'Hey, look,' said Sean, more gently, 'I know you can't wait to get there but it's hours before we pick up Tobias so there's really no point in me getting up yet. Come and wake me in an hour. Meanwhile, just play quietly with your train set or something.'

'Hmmph.' Luke slunk obediently out of the room and Sean closed his eyes again. He would never recapture the wonderfully deep sleep he had been enjoying but maybe he could doze a bit. He tried breathing slowly and clearing his mind in the way he'd learnt at a mediation class Kate had once dragged him to in Camden Town. He smiled at the memory. How sceptical he had been, but in fact the relaxation techniques had proved pretty useful. They had probably pushed back the executive heart-attack by a year or two. Right now, however, they weren't working at all. All he could see when he closed his eyes was a variety of nightmarish scenarios and all of them involved Lena. After a few fruitless minutes of trying to focus on his breathing, he gave up, got out of bed and switched on breakfast television. He might as well catch up on the cricket scores.

By the time they reached the zoo, Luke and Tobias were practically bouncing up and down on the back seat of the Mercedes, singing in Dutch at the tops of their voices. Sean didn't understand much of it but caught the word *olifant* several times. He vowed that if they stayed in Amsterdam he would make a proper effort to learn the language. This seemed to be another sphere in which his wife and son were way ahead of him.

If they stayed. Sean had been giving the Cambridge job some serious thought. Career-wise it was a sideways move rather than a promotion, but it was definitely a position he wouldn't have been offered if he hadn't taken the initiative to apply for the Dutch posting. He liked Amsterdam well enough but the things he had hoped for when they first showed up at the apartment in March didn't seem to have materialised; more time with Luke, family trips out at weekends, some quality time with Kate without the whole baby issue hanging over them... But perhaps he had been naive. How could a new country ever really have solved their marriage problems? In fact, without the familiar distractions of life in Suffolk all the issues between them had simply been thrown into sharp relief. What's more, the job itself was turning out to be less interesting than he had expected and the difficulties involved in trying to integrate two completely different computer networks were compounded by his boss's repeated and unhelpful interference.

Then there was Lena. Returning to England would crack that one forever and he couldn't deny that would be a major relief. But how would Kate and Luke feel about returning to the UK? He had uprooted them, insisted that a new life in a different country would offer them all endless benefits, forced them to adapt. Would they want to just turn around and go back, especially to a different town? The more he thought about it the less he knew. As soon as Kate came back from Arles he planned to discuss it with her. He only had one more week in which to make his decision.

Chapter 27

In the hot Provençal sunshine, the lunch date quickly extended into a long, sultry afternoon. Rudy and Kate wandered through the golden streets of Arles, dipping in and out of the shade. Kate was acutely aware of Rudy's presence and felt as if she had been fine-tuned to pick up every nuance that flowed between them. At first she thought he seemed every bit as self-assured as usual, relaxed in his role of Van Gogh guide. But then, in the garden of the asylum where the artist had once been incarcerated, she realised that he too, had been disturbed by their chance meeting. They were standing very close together as he pointed up to the balcony to show her where Vincent would have painted. She leaned forward to catch his words above the hum of conversation around them and a loose strand of her hair fell across his arm. She sensed rather than saw the tremor that ran through him and hurriedly turned away, somehow brushing against his tee-shirt in her haste. It was then, in the veiled blue of his eyes she saw that this wasn't just a lecture after all. In that moment they became more equal. She stepped back, making space between them, tucking the wayward wisp of hair behind her ear.

'This building,' she said, brightly, 'it's like a fortress. Imagine having to stay here.'

Rudy swallowed. 'I think it was Vincent's own choice,' he said quietly. 'And it is only like a fortress on the outside. Here in this inner garden it is beautiful. They created a safe place, you see. A place the world couldn't penetrate. Perhaps some people need that.'

'Like your studio?'

'You think my studio is safe, Kaatje? It's good that you think that. It's important to create a peaceful environment, I think.' He was studying her again with those disconcertingly piercing eyes. She made a small, dismissive gesture, as if brushing away the conversation, and indicated a little shop that was doing a brisk trade at the asylum entrance.

'I'm going to buy some postcards.'

'Then we can have a drink at the yellow café,' suggested Rudy. 'This is the hottest part of the day and we still need to see *les Alyscamps*.'

Kate's face fell. 'But what about the sunflowers?'

'I thought perhaps we could meet up again tomorrow morning. On Friday night the traffic around the city will be difficult.'

She nodded, not relishing the idea of being stuck in a French traffic jam. In the shop she bought a sunflower fridge magnet for Luke and postcards of all Vincent's Arles pictures, imagining them pinned to a wall where she would look at them and remember. But in that same instant she realised that her walls in Amsterdam were temporary and that she had nowhere to put them up. These mementoes would probably stay in their paper bag indefinitely, tucked into a drawer next to the photograph of Kaatje, *The Sonnet*. Kate bit her lip hard. She would just have to make sure she got them out from time to time. Before they left the asylum courtyard, she stopped to take a photo of the *panneau*, as she had done at every other point on the artist's trail, taking care not to include Rudy in the frame.

'These have to be the most expensive cokes in the entire world,' Kate laughed.

They were sitting on the terrace of the yellow café surrounded by plane trees, grown enormous over the previous century and providing slightly claustrophobic shade. They had split the lunch bill but Rudy insisted on buying the drinks.

'I think it's time for me to treat you even though I'm Dutch and theoretically it should be completely against my principles.' His face spread in a rare grin.

It made him look younger, Kate thought, and she suddenly saw beyond the facade of the artist-teacher – a person she had probably invented anyway – to the fair-haired boy who had kicked a football about in an Amsterdam park. Rudy was becoming much more than a focus for her lonely projections. He was turning into a real man. Suddenly she remembered the switched-off phone in her bag and along with it her other life. She swallowed her coke with a gulp. Just as soon as the drinks were finished, she really should go. This was no place for Kate Butterworth to be.

'So next we visit *les Alyscamps*?' Her companion leaned forward resting his forearms on the table. 'Actually Vincent's picture is not so interesting and I almost prefer Gauguin's, but the place itself, the tombs and the church...' He regarded her intently. 'You have to see it.'

She took a breath. 'I thought perhaps I should go back to the hotel, freshen up or something, maybe phone my son,' she mumbled, fiddling with the clasp on her bag.

'Really?' Rudy seemed genuinely puzzled. 'Did you really think that? Why?'

For goodness sake. Kate chewed her lip in exasperation. No English guy would respond like this. Sean would shrug politely and try unsuccessfully to hide his disappointment. She looked away, wishing she hadn't remembered Sean.

Rudy persisted: 'You told me Luke was at the zoo with his father. It's four o clock. Do you think he will be home already?'

'Yes. No. I don't know...'

'Look, come with me to *les Alyscamps* because it is difficult to find and also because I would like to be there when you see it. Then afterwards you can go back to your hotel and perhaps we can meet tomorrow to visit the sunflowers. Or perhaps not. It's up to you.'

This sounded reasonable. He wasn't expecting anything, she told herself. There was no pressure, she was just being silly.

'Okay. Good idea.'

As they walked along the main road, past the tourist office and the arena, Kate was very careful to maintain a distance between Rudy and herself. There was to be no more accidental touching of fingers or arms. They didn't speak much, concentrating on putting one foot in front of the other in the afternoon heat.

'Are we almost there?' She could feel the beginnings of a blister forming.

'Just across this road. In ancient times the world of the dead was separated from the world of the living so the necropolis was built outside the town.'

'Really? It's not very well signposted, presumably the dead knew the way. And you're right, I would never have found it on my own.'

A sign at the gate advised them of a negligible entrance fee. Rudy felt in his pocket for his wallet.

'No,' Kate almost elbowed him aside. 'My turn, you bought the drinks.'

Somehow without appearing to move Rudy placed his body between Kate and the ticket kiosk.

'Deux adultes s'il vous plait.' He took the tickets and handed her one. 'This weekend,' he said quietly, 'it's my turn to pay.'

Kate frowned, pressing her lips together and almost imperceptibly inclining her head. He responded with a small smile.

'Come on.'

She followed him into the cemetery, acutely conscious of a droplet of sweat trickling steadily down her spine. The place was deserted.

'Everyone's gone to the bull running,' Rudy explained. Kate pulled a face.

'Thank goodness we haven't.'

In the dappled shade of the tree-lined walkway two rows of ancient sarcophagi rested, warm and peaceful in the sunshine.

'So these are basically stone coffins?'

'Very old coffins; Roman.'

Kate tried to imagine the men and women who would once have lain in them. Men mostly, she presumed. Short men, in fact.

'So where are the bodies?'

Rudy shrugged. 'I don't know. A lot of the marble and carving is in a museum, I think. And some of the coffins were taken away to be used as water troughs for animals. They were very pragmatic, the French peasants.'

'All peasants,' said Kate. 'Probably a criteria for their survival.' The tombs and their long departed occupants were truly relics from another time. A world much further from their own than the past Van Gogh had inhabited. She speculated, perhaps for once the artist might have felt as she did, over-awed by the history, the sheer ancientness of this place.

'Here's the *panneau*,' Rudy said. 'It's a study of autumn leaves rather than the burial ground.'

Kate examined the picture. It wasn't a painting of history. Vincent seemed to have lived quite spectacularly in the present; autumn trees, the long alley, the cold blue-grey stone of the tombs, figures – people moving across the canvas. A transiting moment captured and stilled, a slither of time under a microscope.

'It's typical of him. He's painted almost nothing and seen everything,' she said at length.

'Now you begin to understand,' Rudy approved. To hide her pleasure, Kate tossed her head and walked faster towards the half-ruined church that awaited them at the end of the path.

'I don't know anything about architecture,' Rudy admitted, 'so please don't ask.'

'It doesn't matter. I can see all I need to know and there's an information board over there. Apparently it was an abbey rather than a church,' she read aloud. 'For years there were monks living here. They tried to restore some of the site.' She craned her neck to get a better view of the roof. 'You can see all the different styles from the differently shaped vaults in the ceiling. Teams of workmen kept coming back and adding new bits on.'

'There's a crypt, too' said Rudy, leading the way down some steps.

'It smells of damp,' Kate announced, adding more quietly; 'Damp and decay, like death.' Inadvertently she remembered Paula and wished she hadn't. With her friend's illness the whole mortality question had crept uncomfortably close. She pushed the thought away and made herself concentrate on the mysterious ill-lit chambers. The coffins in the crypt were still closed and so, perhaps, still occupied. Kate shivered and turned to check Rudy was still there.

'It remains an enigma, this death,' he murmured. 'Which is strange given how many of us have done it.'

'A curtain,' Kate murmured. 'Heavy, black velvet. Maybe a bit frayed in places.' She tried to smile.

Rudy touched her arm.

'Enough,' he said. 'We have come to find Van Gogh, not dead Romans.'

Back in the daylight, Kate blinked hard.

'They are difficult, these tombs? They remind us of our own transience, maybe.'

'It's my friend, the one you met at the museum. She's ill.'

'Ah. But she might get well again?'

'Yes, yes, she probably will. It's just that she's so young. Well, not really, I suppose, my age. But I feel young.'

They walked slowly back along the tomb-lined alley in silence. At the gate Rudy said:

'So now you would like to go back to your hotel to shower and make phone calls and perhaps we can meet up again tomorrow morning?'

'Yes. Yes, that's right.'

'But you have no one to eat with tonight, and neither do I. So I would like to invite you to have dinner with me. If you prefer not to, I will understand. But I will be at the yellow café at seven thirty, anyway.'

Kate regarded him uncertainly.

'I'll be there this evening and again tomorrow morning at ten o clock for the sunflowers. Come when you want, Kaatje.' He gave a small shrug. 'It's for you to decide. My time and my life are my own. Now, if you can find your way back, I would like to stay here a little bit longer. I'm going to take some photos to sketch later.'

He took a small Nikon from his pocket and began to examine the shutter. Although he hadn't moved at all, Kate had the impression that he had retreated somehow, shrank back out of her reach. Something inside her cried out at his withdrawal. She took a step backwards as if to create the same effect on the physical plane, to make better sense of it. In that moment she made a decision.

'Of course, it would be nice to have dinner together,' she said in an almost jolly voice. 'The evening will seem very long and dull otherwise.'

Rudy glanced up.

'It would be nice,' he agreed.

'See you later then.'

'At the café.' He lifted a hand in a brief wave.

Chapter 28

Freshly showered, Kate sat on the bed in her bra and pants with the window open to the wind and switched on her phone. There was nothing; absolutely no messages at all. She didn't know whether to be relieved or concerned. Presumably Sean and Luke had spent the day at the zoo with Tobias as planned and were now home. It must be tea time, or maybe bath time – hard to say which as Sean never kept to much of a timetable. They might even have gone to the Pizza Hut if he didn't feel like cooking. Kate contemplated phoning but decided she would leave it until the morning. If there had been a problem he would have tried to get in touch. She sent a text instead;

Had fantastic day. This place is wonderful. Going out to find some dinner soon. Hope zoo was good. Will call in morning. Love you both xxx

She waited a couple of minutes to see if there was any response but the phone remained silent. Well, she would talk to them tomorrow. Now, what should she wear? She flicked through the couple of dresses she had hung up in the hotel wardrobe and chose a simple shift dress almost the same green as the silk on Rudy's chaise long. It was comfortable in the heat and, importantly, wouldn't look like she was trying to impress him. It was to be a relaxed meal with an acquaintance. That was all.

Months later, she related an account of the evening to Paula and her friend laughed aloud.

'So you went on a date, but you refused to admit it.'

'That's basically it,' Kate agreed, looking sheepish. 'Yes.'

'And you didn't once ask yourself why you had put on your best underwear and smothered yourself in Chanel's *Allure*?'

She reddened slightly. 'Not really, no.'

Paula gave her a hug and Kate caught the scent of her skin, still slightly sickly beneath her perfume.

'Probably just as well,' she whispered, 'or none of it would ever have happened.'

On the way to the yellow café Kate took a wrong turning and suddenly found herself on the hill behind the arena, nowhere near the Place du Forum where Rudy would be waiting. She glanced at her watch, minutes were ticking away. She had hung back uncertainly in the hotel room not wanting to be early and not even completely sure until she left the building, that she was actually going at all. Now it was just after half past seven and she was lost. Panicking, she accosted a fellow tourist, a large-bellied American who was talking loudly to his equally plump wife in a soft mid-western drawl.

'Sure, I can help,' he said pleasantly, taking a map from his satchel and unfolding it carefully.

Kate's fingers twitched as he traced the roads ponderously with his finger.

'Now, I think the lady would need to go back in that direction, wouldn't you say, honey?' he said, passing the folded paper to his wife. The woman fished in her bag for her reading glasses and placed them carefully on her nose.

'You think so?'

'Well, maybe not...' Her husband retrieved the map with a slow frown.

'Please,' Kate squeaked, her hand hovering anxiously, 'could I have a look?' The seconds were ticking away. How long would he wait?

'Sure you can.' The American nodded genially and passed it into her twitching fingers.

Now she could see where she was; she had picked up the wrong road coming out of the hotel. What an idiot!

'Thanks so much.' Pushing the map back into the man's hands she hurried away.

'You're very welcome, Mam,' he called after her.

It was ten to eight when she finally reached the café. Rudy had managed to get hold of a copy of *De Volkskrant* and was sitting reading on the terrace. He was barely halfway through his beer.

'I thought I might have missed you,' Kate blurted, her forehead glistening with perspiration. She felt stupid now for having run.

He looked up in surprise.

'I'm not in a rush. And anyway, you were always late for class. I didn't expect you to be on time.' He put the paper aside and stood up, touching her arm lightly. The strong, dry fingers quietened her.

'Would you like an *apéritif*? This is France, after all.'

'Good idea. A glass of red wine, please.'

After a couple of sips she felt calmer.

'Did you make your phone call?' he asked.

'Not exactly. I decided to do it in the morning. Luke and Sean are probably enjoying their boys' time without me fussing. I sent a text.' She gave a brief smile and smoothed her skirt. 'Where should we have dinner, do you think?'

'I know a great little Italian place a couple of streets from here. How does that sound?'

'Great.' Or surreal. Kate wasn't sure which. The summer night was as warm as a bath. How had she come to be in this French town, sitting in a café that Vincent had painted, with this man?

'Us both turning up here at the same time, it's such a weird coincidence.'

'Coincidence? You think so?' Rudy's eyes crinkled reflectively. 'Come.' He set down his empty glass. 'Let's go and eat.'

He led her to a bistro tucked away down a quiet street near the Roman baths.

'*Gabrielli's*,' he said, spreading his arms with a theatrical flourish.

From the outside it was nothing much to look at and it certainly didn't compare to the *Le Quattro Stagioni* in Amsterdam. Instead of smooth wood furniture and immaculately papered walls there were printed blue tablecloths and posies of plastic flowers. Kate tried unsuccessfully to hide her disappointment.

'Perhaps it's not what you're used to?' Rudy lifted an eyebrow, at once ironic and amused.

She reddened. There were just four tables outside on the footpath with several more inside. A couple and a family group were already eating. Kate realised the family were actually speaking Italian and judged this to be a good sign. The light was just beginning to fade and heady smells of tomato and garlic clustered enticingly around the little *trattoria*.

Rudy watched her, thoughtfully.

'It's possible that Gabrielli serves the best Italian food in Provence but we can go somewhere else if you prefer.'

Kate shook her head, embarrassed.

'You have been spoilt, Kaatje,' His voice was gentle but she sensed his disapproval and worse, his disappointment. 'Life for a penniless artist is not so simple.'

He was right. Without realising it she had become the wife of a prosperous man.

The waiter showed them to a quiet table in a corner, holding out the chair for Kate and lighting the candle with a professional flourish. The flame sprang up, flickering between them through the orange glass jar.

'Do you often come here, then?' Kate enquired, more sharply than she had intended. She still knew almost nothing about his life.

'I come here when I'm in Arles. It's cheap and the food is good, you'll see. The waiter is surprised because I have a companion. Usually, I am alone.' He smiled and the harmony between them was restored.

'So where do you stay, when you come?'

'I have an old friend who lends me his apartment for a night or two and I do the same when he comes to Amsterdam. This weekend he has gone to Montpellier for a festival.'

Kate was silent, assimilating this information.

'It's a pretty basic apartment, just a bedroom and living room, but it's central. In fact, not so far from your hotel. I can also see the river from my window.' He said this conversationally, as if it might be a fact of mild interest, but Kate was aware of the sea-blue eyes searching her face. She turned her attention hastily to the menu.

'Fettuccine with Gorgonzola sauce, I think,' she said. 'Just because I love the word 'Gorgonzola.'

'I'm going to take the linguine with clams. And I think we need a bottle of the Verdicchio.'

'Do you? Are you a wine connoisseur as well as an artist?'

'Not at all, but I know that white wine goes with seafood and this one is usually good.' Rudy grinned.

Sean always orders Pinot Noir... Kate began to think, but quickly pushed the comparison away. This evening was so far from her life with Sean and Luke that she could easily have shifted to some parallel existence. In that moment she made up her mind that these worlds would stay parallel, must never collide.

The waiter returned and uncorked the bottle. Rudy shook out his napkin, took a mouthful of the wine and nodded.

'It's good, try it, Kaatje.'

He was right, it was good; dry and fruity. Instantly, Kate knew that the evening was going to be perfect. It had happened; she had slewed off her old skin and transmuted into the enigmatic Kaatje, whose life was so much more interesting, more intense than her own. It was Kaatje, naturally, who was obsessed with

Van Gogh; Kaatje who had lain on the green silk in the studio above the Amsterdam canal; Kaatje who, through a chance encounter, was sitting in a *trattoria* in Arles with a painter named Rudy – the very man who had, in fact, conjured this exciting *alter ego* into being. Of Kate, the woman who had often lain curled on a sofa in Suffolk weeping because once again there would be no baby, she refused to think.

Chapter 29

'So where to first, boys? You're in charge of the programme today,' said Sean as they arrived at the familiar gates of the Artis.

'First we're going to the petting zoo to stroke the goats, then to see the monkeys because Tobias likes those, then to the reptile house. After that we might be hungry so can we have tiger burgers like you promised? Then after lunch we're going to visit the elephants.'

'Well, you've certainly go that worked out,' said Sean, amused. 'Are you sure you want to leave the elephants until this afternoon?'

'Yes, because then we can spend more time there.'

'You mean the whole afternoon at the elephant house?'

'Not the whole afternoon, that would be boring.'

'Obviously,' Sean interjected. 'Silly me.'

Luke frowned. 'But most of it. And Tobias wants to go the climbing frame too.'

Sean nodded enthusiastically. He particularly liked the climbing frame. There were no sad, reproachful animals to stare at him and he wasn't required to show an interest. All he had to do, in fact, was sit on a bench and read the paper.

By the time they reached the *Twee Cheetahs Café*, Sean was beginning to congratulate himself on how well the day was panning out. The sun was shining, but only intermittently so it wasn't too hot (just as well as he had forgotten to bring suncream), the monkeys had proved reasonably entertaining, and he had actually got quite interested in the crocodiles, especially when one very obligingly opened its enormous mouth. Crocodiles looked evil and prehistoric anyway, so he didn't suffer quite the same guilt about them being caged up as he did with the mammals. And Luke had chattered incessantly to Tobias in a mixture of Dutch and English which his friend somehow seemed to understand, leaving Sean free to think about the job offer. Best of all, there was no sign of Lena so Sean was tempted to think she had got the message after all.

'Fin-ished!' sung Luke, dipping his last french fry into his tomato sauce and patting his stomach contentedly. 'Was it really tiger meat in the burgers, Dad?'

Sean hesitated. Another version of the Father Christmas dilemma. Should he stick to facts or tell Luke what he wanted to hear? He had promised Kate he would go with the Santa Claus story until Luke was at least seven, but today he thought it might be safer to stick to facts.

'Not sure,' he said. 'Tigers are an endangered species aren't they? So perhaps it isn't.'

Luke nodded sagely. 'You're not allowed to kill endangered species.'

'Ice cream?' Sean suggested, hurriedly changing the subject.

Luke translated the offer into Dutch for Tobias who shook his head.

'Not just now thanks, Dad. We're a bit full up.'

'Right then, elephant house.' He consulted the map. 'That way I think.'

Luke stood up and brushed the crumbs off his tee-shirt.

'Hang on, Dad,' he said, pointing at woman in a red dress standing by the café gates. 'Isn't that your friend from work?'

Sean froze. He didn't need to turn round to know exactly who Luke was referring to. Taking a deep breath he glanced, as casually as he could, across the tables towards the exit. What the fuck was she doing here, hadn't he told her to stay away? He was rapidly discovering that what was said between himself and Lena and didn't necessarily reflect any kind of reality.

'Did you say she could come, Dad?'

'No,' Sean replied firmly. 'No I didn't.'

Luke said something to Tobias in Dutch and twisted round anxiously to face the approaching figure.

'Can you make her go then?'

'She's not very easy to get rid of,' said Sean apologetically.

'You have to tell her it's just us, Dad,' Luke instructed, firmly.

'Yes, thanks for that.'

'I don't want her here.' Luke kicked hard at a stone which accidentally flew off at an angle and scudded towards Lena, glancing off her toe, exposed in open sandals.

'Luke!'

The boy scowled and hoped he wasn't going to cry with his friend standing next to him. Tobias was watching Sean carefully.

'Hi,' said Lena brightly when she got near enough. 'Oh and *dag*,' she added bending towards Tobias.

'*Dag*,' muttered Tobias with a small smile, reassured at being addressed in his own language in the midst of these angry English people.

Luke ignored her. He saw that the red stuff she had put on her toenails was chipped and smirked inwardly.

'I thought we agreed this wasn't a good idea.' Sean said pointedly.

'Well, you know... Like I told you, I haven't been to the Artis for years.' Lena flicked back her hair and regarded him steadily through sultry brown-black eyes. Sean felt himself getting hotter. Shit. Shit. Shit.

'We're going to the elephant house,' he managed to say, keeping his voice carefully devoid of expression.

'I love elephants,' enthused Lena. 'They're my favourite animal.'

Luke eyed her suspiciously, unsure whether he should like her for this or not.

'Have you seen the baby?' she asked, turning to him. 'I saw a picture of it in the paper a while back.'

'Yes,' he replied, in a deliberately bored voice. 'We saw it when Henry was here.'

Well, you're very lucky,' she went on. 'Because I haven't seen it yet.'

Perhaps she really did like elephants. Luke was uncertain.

'Dad, can I whisper something?'

'Um, quick then, while Lena's talking to Tobias.'

'Well,' he hissed as Sean bent down. 'I don't mind if she stays for a bit.' He nodded indiscreetly towards Lena. 'She could come and see Colonel Hathi with us.'

'Could she?' Sean sensed defeat.

'I don't suppose Mummy would mind as she's on holiday in Arles anyway.'

Don't you? thought Sean. Well, I bloody well do. But unless he wanted to make a huge fuss and insist that Lena leave immediately – which would seem even odder than letting her stay – it looked like he was stuck with the situation.

'Come on then.' Reluctantly, he led the party out of the café garden, past some lofty, pot-bellied giraffes who seemed to be eternally smiling down on their dwarf audience, and on to the elephant enclosure.

'She's bigger than last time,' Luke beamed, staring wide-eyed at baby Mumba across the pit that separated them. Even Sean had stopped looking cross. He had adopted a tone with Lena that he hoped was civil, but distant and she seemed to be following his lead. The idea was to imply that their 'relationship' was now over but that he was happy to be 'friends'.

'Elephants really live in hot countries,' Luke explained. 'We found it in a book. Their big ears help them keep cool.'

'Really? I didn't know that.' Lena treated him to a one of her dazzling smiles and Luke blushed.

Christ! thought Sean, miserably. She's got him too. He tried to think about Kate; her soft golden-red hair, intelligent hazel eyes, the way his arms wrapped around her, engulfing her, as though he was some enormous bear... Luke was prodding his arm.

'Hey Dad, where's Colonel Hathi?'

Sean glanced up. 'I don't know. Isn't that him over there?'

'No, silly. Colonel Hathi is bigger than that. He's huge.'

'Is this your special elephant?' asked Lena.

'Yes. He's the daddy. I want to adopt him. You can adopt them, you know, but they don't go home with you, it's just for visits.'

'That seems like a great idea.'

'It is,' said Luke, 'but he's not in there.'

'Shall I ask for you?' Lena offered. 'There's a guy over by that tree that looks like he works here.'

'Yes, please,' said Luke. 'You can do it better than me in Dutch.'

He watched as Lena made her way over to the keeper. She was smiling at him, Luke noticed. It seemed like she smiled a lot. And she did look nice in that red dress, but he felt guilty about liking her because he knew his Mummy didn't. It was all very confusing. She spoke for a quite a few moments to the guy by the tree and they were both waving their hands about. Eventually she turned round and that was when Luke knew something was wrong. Lena's face wasn't right. The smiling had gone and she looked very serious. Instinctively, Luke reached for his father's hand.

'I'm really sorry, Luke,' she said, coming back to them, 'but the big elephant died a couple of days ago. He was old, almost forty years, the keeper said.'

The colour drained from Luke's face.

'No!' he yelled, hating her in that moment. 'He can't die. He's the daddy elephant.' He swung his leg back and kicked her hard in the shin. Lena cried out in pain. In a flash, her hand shot out and slapped the boy's face. Luke howled. Tobias watched in confusion. Sean snatched up Luke and took Tobias's hand. He stared hard at Lena.

'On no account does anyone ever assault my son,' he said in a voice of pressed steel. 'I suggest you leave now.'

Lena was rubbing her leg which was slowly suffusing with purple.

'Jesus, Sean! Aren't you going to tell him off? What kind of kid have you got? Do you just let him kick people?'

The crowd that had been leaning over the rail watching Mumba rotated as one and regarded their small party with interest. Sean suddenly felt incredibly calm.

'You weren't invited to join us. If you hadn't barged your way in you wouldn't have got hurt.'

Lena's voice dropped to a menacing hiss.

'If you think you can fuck me about, take what you want and then walk away, Sean Butterworth, you are very, very wrong.'

'Just leave us, please. Put some arnica on your leg and it'll be fine.'

Lena turned on her heel and stormed off in the direction of the giraffes. Sean realised he was trembling.

'She's going the wrong way,' Luke observed, wriggling to get down.

'Oh well,' his father shrugged, setting him on the ground beside his friend. 'She'll find her way out.' He took a deep breath. 'Come on, boys, let's have an ice cream and a play on the climbing frame before we head home.'

'Now, Luke,' Sean began as they sat at the kitchen table that evening, empty plates of cheesy pasta in front of them. 'We need to have a little chat.'

Luke's gaze followed Percy the Green Engine as he trundled him across the table top.

'Put Percy in the shed and look at me,' Sean instructed firmly.

One by one Luke's fingers unclasped the model train and he raised his eyes to meet his father's.

'I understand that you were upset today about the elephant, and that Lena butted in to our outing without being invited, but

235

that is absolutely no excuse for your behaviour. Do you understand?'

Luke's chin dropped to his chest. Sean sensed, but could not see, his fingers working the fabric of his tee-shirt under the table.

'If Tobias hadn't been with us we would have gone straight home and you would have gone to bed but I didn't want to spoil his day more than it already had been. It wasn't Lena's fault the elephant died. He was old, almost forty, that's what the keeper said.'

'Forty's not old,' protested Luke. 'Elephants can live to seventy in the wild. It's the stupid zoo's fault.'

Sean sighed.

'I understand that but you're still not to kick people. Look, maybe one day we'll go on safari to see the elephants in Africa.'

Luke eyed him doubtfully.

'Mummy doesn't like her,' he said.

Sean's lips tightened. 'Did she say that?'

'Not really.'

'Well then.' He raised a hand to clean his glasses, then remembered that he no longer wore any. The hand dropped to the table. 'Time for bed, I think.'

'You said we could watch a DVD.'

'Now I say 'bed'.'

Luke's bottom lip trembled. He picked up Percy and climbed slowly off the chair.

'What about my bath?'

'I don't think you really need a bath every night.'

'Mummy says – '

Mummy's not here,' interrupted Sean, irritably. 'Just go to bed. I'll come and say good night in a minute.'

Luke sloped past him towards the stairs.

'I want Mummy, not you,' he muttered tearfully.

'Tough. Man up,' his father responded.

When the child had gone he put his elbows on the table and let his head sink into his hands.

Once he had checked Luke was in bed as he was supposed to be, Sean grabbed a couple of beers from the fridge and threw himself onto the sofa. What a bloody awful mess! Lena had sounded furious enough to storm round to the apartment as soon as Kate got back and tell her what a stupid prick her husband was. What the fuck was he going to do? And how on earth was he going to explain it all to his wife? Sean bit his lip and reached for the TV remote.

Chapter 30

'Even the coffee's amazing,' said Kate, draining her tiny cup of espresso.

The other diners had left half an hour before, moving out into the dimly lit street with calls and waves in romantic-sounding languages. In the restaurant only Kate and Rudy remained, leaning towards each other, their arms resting on the table, the tealight still fluttering between them. Beyond the glow of the *trattoria,* the buildings of Arles rose mysteriously on either side of the cobbled path, doorways and angles drenched in multiple layers of shadow. Rudy finished his Armagnac and paid the bill, silencing Kate with a gesture as she moved to protest.

'Thank you,' she said. 'That was a wonderful meal. And I meant to ask, what is happening to the painting?'

'Don't worry,' Rudy insisted, 'at the moment it's in Brussels, waiting to be hung in the exhibition, but it stays with me. It is not for sale, I told you already, it's my sonnet, my best work.' He placed his crumpled napkin on the table and held out his hand. 'Come, let's go and see the Rhone.'

Kate's fingers slipped easily into his as if they had been waiting all evening to do exactly this and as his hand closed around her own, she ceased to think, but simply existed, living each separate second, feeling only the touch of the palm that lay against hers and the brush of the wind on her cheek.

On the quayside the mistral blew stronger, whipping her hair. She leaned over the wall and stared down into the inky water, Rudy's arm slipped round her shoulder and she was conscious of the weight of it, the warmth of it, on her back. Across the river, lights glittered. Kate watched them, aware of her chest rising and falling, of each separate breath. Gently, Rudy turned her to face him, his fingers burrowing into the tangle of her hair.

Her gaze slipped away. The Armagnac was sweet and sharp on his breath.

'Your hotel is along there. If you like, I will take you.' He searched her face. She had read the question in his eyes. Nothing had been decided. Not yet.

'Or you can come with me.'

Kate was silent, listening to the river, passing, flowing, moving on. At length she said:

'Your friend, the one who owns the apartment, will he mind?'

Rudy looked puzzled. 'He won't mind. Why would he mind?'

Kate thought about all the people who might mind; Paula, Dom, Luke and of course, Sean. None of them were here. She was in this town a thousand miles away from everything and everyone she knew.

'It doesn't matter,' she said, finally looking up at him.

He gave a brief nod and his eyes darkened to navy. He tilted her chin with his finger, pressing his lips against hers. She breathed in the musky smell of his skin and returned his kiss.

They were only yards from his friend's place. He led the way up two flights of stone steps. She followed, noting with an odd, amused detachment, that stairs and apartments seemed to be a part of it all, whatever it was. They came to a door with peeling green paint and Rudy led the way into a high-ceilinged room with scuffed walls and huge windows that looked out over the river. It was sparsely furnished, as if just trying to make-believe it was lived in, like a stage set in a Pinter play; a sofa, a table with two chairs and a dirty sink. The shutters were open and the moonlight flooded in at an acute angle so it seemed as if half the room had been dipped silver while the other half remained in shadow. Slanting moon-rays slid from the sofa to the floor. It had the ethereal, strangely familiar quality of a dream.

'Shutters but no curtains,' Rudy explained. 'I think we don't need the light. The bulb's very bright. There are no lamps.' His voice sounded normal. Its foreign accent was known and reassuring in this room that seemed to have been plated with a film of night.

'I can offer you some wine, but first I must wash some glasses.' He gave an ironic shrug. 'You see, we are very alike, this friend and me, not very good at housekeeping.'

Kate stood dumbly in the middle of the floor, eyes blinking.

'I didn't bring my toothbrush,' she said.

Rudy stopped, turned. 'Your toothbrush?'

'Yes, I never thought.' she heard herself blustering. There was a moment of complete silence inside the flat. Out in the street someone shouted. Words neither Rudy nor Kate could understand.

Eventually, Rudy said quietly: 'Then perhaps you should go back to your hotel where you have your toothbrush.'

'Do you think so?' She looked at him wildly. 'I don't know.'

He placed the glass carefully on the draining board, wiped his wet hands and took hers.

'Kaatje. You must know.'

She said nothing. She was limp with confusion and desire. On the wall behind them their shadows played like puppets, moving as they moved, man and woman, the same old story.

'Even if you know nothing else you must know this one thing,' Rudy insisted.

'I thought,' she began, her voice hovering between a whisper and a whimper, 'I thought when you painted me that you didn't want me, you weren't interested.' She gave a strange, high laugh. 'Hah. Paula even thought you might be gay.'

'Paula?'

'My friend. The one who's ill.'

'Not wanted you...' Rudy said, incredulous. Behind him the shadow puppet shook its great shaggy head.

'You didn't seem to. I lay there naked. You never said.'

'Said? What was I supposed to say? You are beautiful, Kaatje. I wanted to paint you, to capture something that seemed to me

240

to be fragile and true. I would have been mad if I hadn't wanted to make love to you.' His hands fell to his sides and his eyes, sapphire-dark, bore into her. 'And,' he added hoarsely. 'I am not mad.'

'So why didn't you?' she demanded, accusing. 'Why didn't you? I didn't know.'

He spread his hands.

'Even we Dutch have some sense of honour. You are married, you have a child. And also, you are English. How could I tell what you wanted behind this porcelain skin? I had nothing to offer you, Kaatje. I have nothing to offer you now, except perhaps tonight.'

Kate scanned his face. He was telling the truth. He had always told her the truth. He promised her nothing. But they had met through a chance so finely tuned in this hot Provençal town where the shutters were closed tightly against the summer heat and the fields around were yellow with sunflowers, that it felt like fate. They had shared a meal on the terrace of a little Italian restaurant. They had this one night.

'I believe you,' she said, reaching up and pulling the clip from her hair so it fell loose over her shoulders. Rudy touched it gently.

'I knew it would feel like this,' he said. 'It is silk.'

As the large, impassive face of the moon spun into view outside the window spreading the silver light into the secret corners of the room, the man-puppet bent his head towards the woman-puppet and kissed her very slowly, very deliberately, as if breathing life into each separate particle of her being. Because he knew instinctively that these moments must count for everything, that this was their forever; that they were doomed to remain as shadows on that wall in Arles, for all eternity.

He lifted her easily, carried her to the bedroom and set her beside the rough pine bed. The moonlight was dimmer in here, filtered by the half-closed shutters. He slid down the zip of her dress, unwrapping her slowly like a favourite sweet. She stood very still and pale, watching him through half-closed lids as he shrugged off his tee shirt and stepped easily out of his jeans, acutely conscious of her own mounting desire. His eyes ran the length of her. He shook his head and peeled away her underwear so she stood naked before him.

'Lie down,' he instructed, quietly. 'Lie down, like you did in the studio.'

She obeyed. The untidy sheets were worn but smelled clean. Had he changed them? Had he known?

'Now,' he said, his eyes heavy, 'now can you see how much I want you?'

She looked and caught her breath. He came closer, squatted beside the bed and ran his finger over the mound of her belly. Her legs eased apart, an unconscious, involuntary movement. He watched his hand as it played on her skin, slipping between her thighs then pulling back, teasing, concentrated.

'Every single time as you lay down on the green silk I thought of doing this,' he whispered, telling her at last what she had been aching to hear. 'But really, you know this already, I could see it in your face as you lay there. Don't ask me why I didn't want you. You already knew that I did.'

Kate woke early, roused by the noise of the street through the half-open window. It took her a few moments to register where she was; a crack in the ceiling, a small table with a shadeless lamp, pale ribbons of light across the wall, the twanging accents of southern France. And Rudy beside her lying still, loose-limbed, the soapy-blonde strands of his hair spread across the pillow. She rested her cheek against his back and absorbed his warmth. He was beautiful.

A collector's piece, she thought in amusement, wriggling onto her elbow to admire him. She waited for the remorse, the guilt to assail her but none came, only an incredible, Zen-like calm, as if all the baggage of her life had been emptied out and neatly sorted. Where there should have been shame she was conscious only of a bizarre joy and the sense of something having been completed. There was only one other time when she remembered feeling something like this. She smiled to herself. Today, after breakfast, she and Rudy would visit the sunflowers, and then they would part. There was to be no second chapter, no later, no tomorrow. And that was okay.

She eased herself out of bed, taking care not to wake him. Outside the cocoon of the covers the air was unexpectedly chilly and the tiled floor felt cold beneath her feet. She pulled on Rudy's teeshirt and padded through to the living room. At the sink she paused to wash to cups and fill the kettle. There was a cafetière on the worktop so she hoped there might somewhere be some coffee. She felt weird, time-warped; she was wandering about a strange flat wearing last night's crusty make up and a top that barely grazed her thighs. It was like spinning back fifteen, even twenty years to a time before Sean had come on the scene, before Luke. She felt light. The blankness of the space made her want to stretch and move and dance around the room. She had become invisible. She had disappeared. No one except Rudy knew she was here so she didn't exist. Kaatje. Enigmatic as the Mona Lisa, she lived only on canvas and in this oddly empty flat in Arles. She pirouetted to the fridge and opened it. There was the coffee just as she had guessed. Also brie and chocolate biscuits. She assembled them all on a chopping board which could serve as a tray. But she had better just check the time before waking Rudy.

Somehow, in the cinematic unreality of last night her handbag had still ended up sitting in a perfectly orderly way on the sofa. She rummaged inside it and found her mobile. It was switched off, of course, but obediently chimed into life at the touch of a button. 07.18. It didn't seem too impossibly early to offer breakfast in bed. She placed the phone next to the cups

243

and picked up the loaded board. Almost instantly it erupted into life, shrieking like a siren as texts tumbled in one after another. Kate's eyebrows knitted in alarm. Six new messages and two missed calls. Her stomach contracted. Christ, that was a lot. That was a hell of a lot. She pressed 'read' and the most recent came though first. It was from Sean.

Saturday 06.33: *Longest night of my life. For God's sake, where are you??? Why don't you call?*

In a flash of panic, Kate wondered if she had left him the name of the hotel but thought probably not. It hadn't seemed necessary when they both owned mobiles. Her heart began to beat faster as she clicked through to the next message, then the one after that and the one after that. It was Luke. Oh God! Kate turned to the sink and retched, bringing up the acid residue of last night's wine. Her throat burned. She opened the tap and took great gulps of water, letting it spill over her face in a cascade. After a few moments she was able to force herself to read through the texts again, more slowly.

Saturday 00.08: *Waiting in A&E with a load of drunks but hospital taking this seriously. Meningitis? Expect you're asleep now. Phone asap.*

The noises from the outside the window disappeared. The walls of the room closed in on Kate like a trap. She skipped through the messages once more.

Friday, 23.28: *Fuck knows where you are. Calling ambulance.*

She had been exactly here. Here and invisible. At half past eleven she had been in this flat, waiting for Rudy to make love to her.

Friday, 23.13: Missed call.

Friday, 22.58: *Dosed him with Calpol but he seems floppy and not with it. Kate, phone me. I really need advice.*

Friday, 21.45: Missed call.

Friday, 21.42: *Babe, Luke woke up seems to have high temp. Where's Calpol?*

Friday, 20.03: *Sorry I missed your call, was putting Luke to bed. Had crap day at zoo – big elephant dead. Love you. xx*

The elephant was dead and Luke was ill and had been rushed to hospital. That was how things were. Kate realised she was shaking. She had to go home, to get out of this invented life and back to the real place. And she had to go now. She glanced at the makeshift breakfast assembled on the board. She had been playing houses. It was all pretend. Her eyes sharpened into focus and the years returned quickly, piling themselves onto her like lumps of mud. She was heavy, normal. The flat was dirty and uncared for. She was scared. She poured coffee and drank it as she pulled on her dress and rinsed her face in the grubby bathroom. She should leave a note. Rudy mustn't come after her. He understood how it was. She pulled an old receipt from her bag and scribbled on the back of it:

My son is ill. Going straight to Marseille for flight home. Thanks for everything. Kate/Kaatje xx

She took one last look at the guy in the bedroom; her painter, her co-star in some celluloid world. His eyelids flickered but did not open. She swallowed the heaviness in her throat and wiped her eyes.

In just a couple of minutes she was standing outside the Hotel Régence. The wind was stronger today and the Rhone as choppy as the sea, splashing up against the piers of the bridge. She called Sean; he answered immediately.

'Wait, I can't talk in here, mobiles aren't allowed. Call you back in a minute.'

Clutching the phone, Kate pushed open the door and ran up the stairs to her room, reassembling her life in her head. Her clothes were all still there in a jumble of indecision on the bed, half-hoping to be chosen. She began throwing them into the case, every nerve taut and ready for the ring tone, the first bars of the Chilli Peppers Zephyr song which she loved, but knew she would never be able to listen to again. When they came she

245

found she wasn't ready after all, but jumped, knocking the phone from the bedside table onto the floor. She sank down next to it, legs folding beneath her.

'Sean! How's Luke?' Her voice came out as an ugly squeak as though she hadn't practiced talking for a long time.

'Katie!' Sean sounded exhausted, worried, frightened, relieved and so far from pissed off with her that she cringed shamefully. 'Where are you? For Christ's sake. Did you turn your phone off?'

'Yes,' she admitted. 'I was in a restaurant. I forgot to turn it back on. But Luke?' She tried to rub her eyes but found she was shaking too much. 'How's Luke?'

'He's okay. At least...' She could picture Sean running his hand across his scalp, could almost feel the soft prickles of his hair under her own fingers. And she wanted to feel them. She wanted to feel the reassuring bulk of her husband in her arms.

'At least what?'

'At least, it's not meningitis, apparently. But he's not okay. Not really. He's ill. There're tubes in him and stuff.' His voice cracked. Kate heard him swallow hard. A siren shrilled in the background.

'But he's not...' he took a breath. 'He's not in danger or anything. At least, not now.'

'Not now?' she repeated blankly. 'He was, then? He was in danger?'

'Yes, no, I don't know.' Sean sighed and she heard how tired and scared he was. 'No one really knew, Kate. He just kind of – collapsed.'

'Look, I'm going to try and get back soon as possible. I'll just go to Marseille and demand to be put on a plane.' Kate was nodding as she said it, picturing herself rushing from desk to desk insisting she be allowed on a flight.

'Do that,' Sean agreed eagerly. 'Do it now. The others will understand.'

'What others?' asked Kate, forgetting.

'The Dutch wrinklies.' There was a pause. 'No Dutch wrinklies?'

'No,' said Kate in a very small voice.

'Fucking hell, Katie, just come home.'

'I'm coming,' said Kate quietly. 'Tell him, Sean. Tell Luke Mummy's coming. And give him my love.'

'I'll do that. I'm going back up to him now. Let me know when you have a flight time and whatever you do don't switch off that bloody phone.'

'No,' agreed Kate, wiping away the tears. 'No, I won't.'

Chapter 31

Outside the hospital entrance Sean stood and stared ambivalently at his mobile, his eyes blurred. He must look pretty pathetic, he realised, standing all alone, crying. Not that it mattered. The night had been bad but the broken grey of the Amsterdam daylight was definitely worse. What had Kate been playing at, going to Arles by herself? Didn't she know he would have gone with her? She only had to ask. Or would he? Sean shuffled his feet. Had she mentioned it maybe and he'd said no? Fuck, could be. All the stuff with Lena had grid-locked his brain for the last few weeks. Quite honestly he didn't have much idea what Kate had been doing. But equally, he hadn't had the impression that this had bothered her much. Their marriage was a mess; he could feel the shreds of it in his hands. For the first time it occurred to him to wonder if she had really gone on this trip alone. Maybe they weren't all quite as wrinkly in that art-history class as she had made out. Then there was the lecturer guy...

Sean swallowed hard. He wished he still smoked. A couple of people had come outside to do just that and it looked like it might help. A middle-aged woman with eyes smudged with yesterday's make-up had lit a Marlboro while he was talking to Kate, smoked it very quickly and immediately lit up another from the tab end. She inhaled urgently, never taking the cigarette far from her mouth, using her left hand to support her right elbow as she puffed. On the other side of him a grey-faced man with strings of hair that reached his ear lobes was slouching against the wall. Thin and unshaven in a scruffy black jacket, he had taken out a tin of rolling tobacco and was looking in his direction.

The human contact was encouraging, Sean decided, and moved his mouth in a kind of prototype smile. The man nodded and said something in Dutch. Presumably it was nothing too complicated, the type of thing people say outside hospitals everywhere. Except that he had no clue what that might be. This was the first time he had stood, alone and anxious, outside a brightly lit reception watching the purposeful comings and goings of the ambulances. Despite everything, part of his brain couldn't help but be impressed by the way the crews were able to focus completely on their tasks, and then in the next moment, when the patient had been trollied inside, detach from whatever human trauma they had just witnessed and joke amongst themselves. Unable to answer his new friend with the roll-up, Sean shrugged sheepishly.

'English,' he muttered.

'I speak little English,' said the lank-haired man. The creases in his skin moved like fault lines as he spoke, changing the geography of his face.

Of course, thought Sean, ashamed.

'My wife not good,' he went on. 'Problem with...' he patted his chest.

Was that lungs? Breasts? Sean didn't care but tried to look sympathetic.

The man's expression was sombre, but there was also the sense of an underlying satisfaction with the way things had turned out. As if this was what it had all come to and he had never expected any different. He lit his roll-up and inhaled deeply.

Sean realised he was supposed to offer reciprocal details on his own circumstances.

'My son,' he said, nodding towards the entrance that gaped behind them like a bright, sucking mouth.

Immediately, the man moved closer, frowning. He flicked the ash from his cigarette onto the tarmac.

'Your son? He is how old, this boy?'

'Nearly five,' said Sean. A sudden image of Luke lying in that white, impersonal bed upstairs connected to machines and tubes flashed into his brain. Christ, what was he doing standing around out here feeling sorry for himself? Nearly five was no age at all. He ran an anguished hand over his head.

The furrows on his companion's face deepened.

'Only five? His mother is with him?'

'No, no. I have to get back.' Sean turned abruptly.

'Hope he's okay.' The croaky shout followed him into the building.

Hope! Sean thought, choosing to run up the three flights of stairs rather than waste important seconds waiting for the lift. Hope wasn't enough. They had to *make* him okay.

Breathing hard he rounded a corner and almost collided with a sensibly trouser-suited nurse. At first Sean had thought these workers must be orderlies or something, but no, it turned out that the little skirts and starched aprons were a thing of the past and uniforms were all very pragmatic these days. Which was how you wanted your health service, really, he supposed. The woman lifted an authoritative arm and prevented him from barging into Luke's room.

'He's sleeping.'

'I'm his father.'

'I'm sure, but you must still be silent.'

Sean nodded miserably. 'I'll be really quiet.'

He pushed open the door. There was no noticeable change. Luke lay very still, covered by a sheet and one of those honeycomb blankets that reminded Sean of his grandparents' house. The boy's hazel eyes were closed against the world, his chest rising and falling in a gentle rhythm that was a little too fast for complacency. Sean knew this peace was mostly drug-induced, but it was reassuring anyway. When they arrived at the hospital last night Luke had been very far from calm; breathing rapidly and flailing his arms about like something possessed.

'He's distressed,' the duty nurse explained.

Even Sean could see that much.

'We're going to sedate him.'

It was a terrifying idea, but he had to admit it looked like the most sensible solution. He wondered if perhaps Luke was having some sort of fit but the tests proved negative. As the night went on, there were several more things that Luke was apparently not suffering from – meningitis among them – but no indication of what the problem actually was. He was running a very high temperature and his blood pressure was up but without obvious underlying cause. Sedation worked like a dream. So well, in fact, that Sean begun to wonder if the crisis wasn't psychological rather than physical in origin. Mentally he began to list all the stuff Luke had been asked to deal with during the last few months starting with moving to a different country and ending – he felt his insides curl up like a salted slug – with the crumbling of his parents' marriage. And on top of all that had come the death of his favourite elephant. Perhaps it was no real surprise, then, that the kid wasn't exactly coping.

Sean closed his eyes and tried to ignore the blip of the heartbeat monitor. It had been a truly awful night and he seriously needed some sleep. Not knowing what to do had been the worst. He was used to having Kate's instincts to rely on but this time he had been forced to take the responsibility himself. And thankfully he had called the ambulance instead of prevaricating as he knew he had a tendency to do. But it was okay. In the end he had been there, he had made the right decision. Although that didn't change the fact that he was more miserable than he had ever been in his entire life before. He really, *really* wanted his wife. The phone call had only served to accentuate how much he needed her; the extent to which they were in this together, for better or for worse. He glanced at the clock. It was just before eight. He was hungry and badly needed to wash and brush his teeth. The Twix he had picked up from the machine in the foyer around 5am had coated his mouth with a sweet slime that the hospital coffee could not penetrate. It would be hours before Kate could reasonably be expected but he couldn't leave Luke again until she got here. He calculated that even if she managed to get a flight from Marseille immediately she wouldn't be back before lunchtime. He closed his eyes. Maybe if he could just doze a bit...

Chapter 32

Kate checked out of the Hotel Régence on autopilot, hardly seeing the young man who had charmed her the day before. She didn't bother to try her French again, either. What was the point when he spoke perfectly good English? There was no space in her brain for complicated verb conjugations when her son was ill. Opening the door into the gusting wind she vaguely hoped she had been polite, but didn't much care if she hadn't. She wouldn't be coming back, that much was clear. This trip, this place, this night, had been a step outside her usual self. A fault line in her psyche had opened up and would now close again, leaving perhaps a little scar tissue. She would go back to Luke and to Sean and resume the life that she had left. She felt like a pilot who has veered off course. She had to find her way back before it was too late.

She lifted her case into the boot of the hire car and slammed it shut, pausing for one second to look out across the Rhone. Further along the quay was Rudy's borrowed apartment. She wondered, briefly, if he was awake, if he knew she had gone. And if he did, would he care? He wouldn't, she was sure. Care was not the word. But he wouldn't forget her either. Their meeting had been pivotal for him too. *The Sonnet*, the unidentified portrait of Kate (Kaatje) Butterworth, was his best work, a turning point in his painting. He had said so. And perhaps for him she had represented something he would never have, a window on a different, more settled life. The kind of life he had rejected in order to give himself space for his art.

She dropped off the rented Clio and trundled her suitcase blindly into the departures hall. Marseille airport was bustling but she saw no one as she moved anxiously from desk to desk waving her credit card. Five or five hundred pounds, it didn't really matter. She just had to get back to Amsterdam. Eventually KLM promised her a flight that was leaving in just under an hour. Barely time to check in. Fortunately she only carried hand luggage.

The plane was full. On one side of her a fat man in a suit claimed both armrests and encouraged his bulk to spill unpleasantly into her space. On the other, a middle-aged woman with heavy gold jewellery was reading a biography of Van Gogh in Dutch. Kate wondered if she had ever attended Rudy's art-history classes but found she couldn't be bothered to ask and probably didn't even want to know. She closed her eyes and debated whether Sean might be persuaded to quit his job and return to their house in England. Surely he would easily be able to find other work. Companies were always looking for IT people, weren't they? She imagined suggesting this and him nodding understandingly by way of reply. It wasn't working, this Dutch thing. He would see that, wouldn't he? And as for herself, well she had had her adventure and in the process had risked everything, including her beloved child.

I'm going back to save my son and my marriage, Kate concluded, and with that thought some of the peace she had felt on first waking returned. Luke would be okay. Everything would be sorted out. She took a deep breath and waited to land at Schiphol.

*****

Sean woke up a couple of hours later and rubbed his neck which had worked itself into a painful crick. It took him a moment to remember where he was and what was going on. Rising stiffly from the chair he leant across to check on Luke. No change. His son still lay just as pale and peaceful as before, the yellow liquid dripping steadily into his arm, his chest rising and falling with each breath. Gingerly testing his aching muscles, Sean moved across to the window hoping to spot Kate, but there was only the busy main road and the hospital forecourt with its clinical trees and tidy grass.

There was a sharp knock at the door and a nurse poked her head round.

'Mr Butterworth?'

He swung round, his hand lifting involuntarily, passing over his head as if testing the texture of the bristles.

'Yes?'

'Your wife.'

Kate stepped in, trailing her suitcase. Relief flooded over him. She had caught the sun, he noticed, and it suited her. He blinked and the pleasure in his eyes was amplified by the lenses of his spectacles.

'Hi,' she said. Her voice was very normal and made him think instantly of a cup of tea. He decided not to tell her that.

'Hi,' Sean replied, shaking his head in an attempt to clear it. The world felt frayed, still edged with sleep. He took off his glasses and cleaned them methodically with a tissue from his pocket, holding them up to the window every couple of seconds to gauge their clarity. He had abandoned his contacts. For some reason he didn't seem to be able to see quite as well.

'It was a long night,' he said, at last.

Kate wasn't sure she trusted herself to speak. She bent over Luke and lightly kissed his cheek. The child's eyelids fluttered but he didn't wake up.

'What's the matter with him? Is he just asleep?' She looked helplessly at her husband.

'He's sedated. But apparently he's responding well.' Sean replaced his glasses. 'Good trip?' he asked, lifting his hands hopefully, then letting them drop.

'It was until this morning. Arles is beautiful.' She glanced towards the window and the grey sky beyond it. 'The sun was shining, at least.'

Sean nodded. He longed to embrace her but wasn't sure he dared. She was worried, of course, but she was also something else. 'Complete' was the word that came to mind. He pushed it away. She didn't seem to need him, anyway.

'They're pretty sure he'll be okay. There doesn't seem to be anything really wrong. It was more like some sort of crisis.' He paused, trying to find some words to say what he was thinking. 'It's been a bit of a mess, this whole Amsterdam adventure, hasn't it?'

Kate swallowed hard and let go of her case which fell backwards onto the floor. Her hands flew to cover her face.

This was better, Sean thought. Now he knew what to do. With something close to gratitude, he collected her up in the circle of his arms and they clung to each other. Eventually Kate pulled back and wiped her eyes.

'So what happened?'

'Luke went to bed, woke up about an hour later with a searing temperature. I gave him Calpol – once I managed to find it – but his temperature only came down slightly. He started to get delirious and flail about. I didn't know what to do so I called the ambulance. I thought maybe he was having a fit. The hospital sedated him and he's been like this ever since. He's still running a bit of a temperature but his blood pressure has come down. He's obviously much less distressed. We just don't know how he'll react when he wakes up. They were keen to leave him asleep until you got here if possible.'

'They think it was because I went away?' Kate wailed.

'No, not really. But they think maybe he's been stressed and we haven't noticed. You going and the elephant dying were like the last straws.'

'Colonel Hathi died?'

Sean nodded.

'God, poor Luke.'

Kate and Sean stared at their son, motionless but for the shallow rise and fall of his chest. The boy was deathly pale, his long, dark lashes barely flickered. The soft, brown hair had fallen back and without its frame his cheeks looked bony and exposed. Kate sat down heavily on the chair beside the bed and clutched his fingers. She registered the dark smudges beneath his eyes, the awkward thinness of his face and bit her lip hard.

This has been much harder for him than I realised, she thought. He's been struggling and I've been so immersed in myself that I've hardly noticed.

The image of Rudy passed before her eyes like a ghost. He had been right, he had offered her nothing. *Kaatje* was a picture, not a person. She did not exist. Yet like some mythic siren she had lured Kate away from the son who needed her.

Sean watched, his fingers twitching. Several times his hand passed across his scalp. Eventually he said;

'I've been a fucking idiot, Katie.'

Something in his tone made Kate's eyes narrow. What was that supposed to mean?

'Lena...' He broke off as she waved an angry hand.

'I don't want to hear that woman's name in here.' It was true then. There had been something.

'Kate, I'm so sorry. I never meant....'

She swivelled round, glaring at him.

'Christ, Sean! You're sorry? Just shut up. Shut up.' She flung the words like javelins, low, hissing syllables.

He ploughed on. 'It was a huge, stupid mistake. I never stopped loving you. But you seemed,' he hesitated, searching, 'so remote. So uninterested in me except as a sperm donor.'

Ah yes. There had been all that. Kate had almost forgotten. It seemed so long ago. Her fury drained from her and she turned back to Luke. She didn't know what to think. People said he was

257

like her, but she had never thought so. Something about the set of the eyes always reminded her of Sean. She unpeeled one hand from her son's and poked her husband with a peremptory finger.

'Please' she said, 'just get me a coffee.'

When Sean returned a few minutes later a nurse was gently trying to rouse Luke. Slowly, sleepily as if the lids were incredibly heavy, his eyes half-opened. He registered his mother's presence, smiled and let them close again.

'You can talk to him now,' the nurse suggested. 'Wake him up gently. His temperature is still a bit high but everything else is back to normal. Perhaps you can take him home this afternoon.'

Kate glanced at Sean.

'Home,' she repeated. For her the word had not meant Amsterdam. 'Maybe we *should* take him home.'

Sean sipped his drink and pulled a face.

'Worst coffee in Holland. It's a fact.'

'Did you hear me?' asked Kate. 'I said perhaps we should take him home. I mean to our home. To Suffolk.'

Her husband turned slowly.

'Actually, I've been offered a job. I've been waiting for a good moment to tell you about it.'

'Now's a good moment,' said Kate.

'It's in Cambridge, not Suffolk, so it would mean a new start for us all.'

'I thought we just had one of those,' Kate observed. 'We didn't seem to cope too well.'

Sean shrugged dismissively.

'This would be different, wouldn't it?'

'Why would it, exactly?'

'Because now we know what we've got to lose.' Sean nodded towards Luke who was beginning to stir. 'And it's not that far away from where we used to live. You could still see Paula and your other friends. You could get into London easily for days out. There would be more interesting work around, too.'

Kate thought back to the self that had used to go out to work and decided she had quite liked it.

'Work might be good,' she agreed.

'It's a good job and a nice town,' Sean encouraged.

Kate imagined herself cycling through the streets of Cambridge. Perhaps she could do a course in something, retrain. She pictured Luke settling in to one of the primary schools; a bright little boy amongst other bright little boys. There were bound to be lots, surely, and most of them would speak English.

'Yes,' she whispered. 'Go for it. Tell them you accept.'

Sean reached across and squeezed her hand hard.

'Thank you,' he said. 'Thank you for everything.'

That evening, back at the Amsterdam apartment, Sean volunteered to walk up to the Chinese takeaway to save cooking while Kate helped Luke eat a large bowl of Rice Krispies. The boy couldn't stop yawning but the nurse had warned that he might be sleepy so Kate was able to deal with it without panicking. Mother and son sat comfortably at the small, round table in the kitchen. Luke's face was pinched and pale under the harsh light.

'The elephant died,' he said, picking up his bowl to drink the last dregs of sweet milk.

'I know,' said Kate. 'I think he was quite old.'

'He wasn't really,' Luke countered. 'He was only forty. Elephants can live to seventy you know. They shouldn't have kept him locked up.'

'At least he didn't get hunted.'

'He would rather have been hunted than kept in a cage.'

Kate reached across to brush the soft fringe from Luke's eyes.

'Maybe,' she said.

'Definitely.' The child paused, considering. Raising his large, serious eyes to meet his mother's he asked: 'Are you staying here now?'

'Yes. Of course.'

'But Lena's not, is she?'

'No. Why?' Kate's stomach contracted. 'What do you know about Lena?'

'She was at the zoo. I didn't want her to be there but she seemed alright at first.'

'Did Daddy invite her?'

'I don't think so,' said Luke shaking his head. 'She turned up when we were in the café. Daddy didn't look very pleased.' Luke studied his empty bowl fiercely. 'I thought she might come home with us instead of you.'

'Sweetheart...' said Kate, biting back a rush of tears. 'Come and sit on my lap.'

Luke clambered down from his chair and nestled himself against his mother's chest, breathing in her familiar scent.

'You smell much nicer than Lena.'

'Do I? Thanks. Listen, I'm not going to stay away anywhere without you again, okay. Not until you're grown up.'

'Promise?'

'I promise.'

'Is that a real promise?' Luke demanded, shuffling round to look at her. 'Not like last time.'

'It's difficult to really promise,' Kate explained, 'because sometimes things happen like snow or floods and people can't get home. But I promise that if it's possible to get home the same day, I will.'

Luke grunted, apparently satisfied.

An hour later with the remains of the take away and an empty bottle of Pinot Noir on the table, and their son asleep upstairs, Sean said:

'So did you really go alone?'

'Yes,' said Kate, because this much was true. 'I wanted an adventure, I suppose. You were never around. I felt stuck. Nothing seemed to be happening to me. I needed a kind of lightning bolt to bring me back to life.' She pulled a face. 'Like Frankenstein's monster or something.'

Sean nodded, up-ending the dregs of the wine into his glass. 'Shall I open another?'

'Better not, in case we have to dash to the hospital again.'

'No. He'll be okay now. Whatever it was is over.'

'You think so?'

'Yes,' said Sean. He sounded very sure.

'What was it then, do you think?'

'Everything, probably.' He took a second bottle from the rack and pulled the cork. 'We need this tonight. Well, I do anyway.'

Kate waited. He was keeping his back to her, busying himself with the wine. Something else was coming, she sensed it.

'Lena turned up at the zoo, you see.'

Kate's eyes flashed dangerously. 'Luke told me. Did you invite her then?'

'No, of course not. I mentioned I was going and she just arrived. I was trying to tell her it was over, that our marriage, our family was too important to jeopardise.'

'You realised that a bit late,' Kate remarked acidly.

Her husband's face twisted but he carried on: 'She was there when Luke found out about Colonel Hathi. And of course, he got really upset about everything.' Sean refilled the glasses and sat down again at the table, waiting for this information to settle between them before adding:

'He kicked her on the shin.'

'Really? Luke did?' Kate's face brightened. 'He kicks pretty hard.'

'He did.' Sean permitted himself a smile. Lena had been so creepy with the boys, turning up like that and insinuating herself

261

into their good books by talking Dutch and asking questions about the animals, it had almost served her right. 'He said he hated her.'

'Well,' observed Kate drily, 'he has good taste at least. But tell me, Sean, explain please; why exactly did you sleep with her?'

Sean took off his glasses and started polishing hard.

'She wanted me to,' he said simply, not looking at his wife. 'And you didn't. Not really. You hadn't done for a long time. You just wanted another child. So, my ego, I suppose.'

Kate lowered her eyes and examined the backs of her hands with their single gold band. Middle-aged hands, she thought. Aloud she said:

'It hasn't gone, you know, all that. Not really.'

'No,' said Sean, replacing his spectacles. 'I didn't suppose it would have done. But I have been thinking that once we get settled in Cambridge maybe we could talk about adoption. Perhaps one of those Chinese babies that get abandoned or something.'

'Really?' Kate's face lit up. 'I thought you weren't interested in anything like that.'

'Yeah, well. I've realised it would be good for Luke to have someone else around. Maybe for all of us.'

Kate sipped her wine and flicked her eyes round the kitchen. She had never liked it much but she would be kind of sorry to leave it.

'You don't think it would feel like we'd failed, if we left here?' she said. 'Sort of chickened out?'

'No,' said Sean. 'We've been given an escape route. That makes it okay.'

'So you'll accept the job then?'

'I'll email David Knight first thing Monday morning.'

Kate pushed her hair back from her face and leaned back in her chair. She found she was incredibly calm – just as she had been at the beginning of this very long day.

'I'm whacked,' she said.

Sean nodded. 'Me too.' He took her hand. 'Let's go to bed.'

They lay, side by side, with just the tips of their fingers touching. Sean told Kate that he loved her, that he always had and that he wanted to make it good for them all again. She squeezed his hand hard. He mustn't know, she decided. He must never, ever know about Rudy.

Chapter 33

Kate opened her eyes just in time to see Sean's back retreating through the bedroom door clad in the crimson towelling of his dressing gown. She stood up, pulled back the curtains and staggered across to the next room to reassure herself that Luke was still there and still breathing then retreated back to bed where she lay staring out at the magnolia tree and the fractured clouds. It was already after ten. She couldn't remember when she had last slept so soundly. Partly this was due to Luke not waking them up for the first time in almost five years, but it was also because yesterday had been unquestionably the longest day of her entire life.

Snuggled under the duvet, she identified the distant clink of a spoon against cups and smelled something she hoped might be toast. Moments later she heard the familiar creak of Sean's tread on the stairs and noted that the sound made her smile. A couple of seconds later the door was nudged open and her husband entered wearing an expression of intense concentration.

'Tea, toast, jam, orange juice.' He beamed shyly. 'I didn't think there was any point in getting up yet.'

That was true enough, Kate supposed. Somehow, after everything, it was still only Sunday. They had nothing planned. Luke showed no sign of waking. However, the more immediate issue was whether she was ready for what this tray of goodies implied. Sean must have plucked her thought from mid-air because he said:

'I'm not trying to seduce you – unless you'd like to be seduced – but I just thought that since Luke's asleep for once, you might fancy breakfast in bed.'

'Well, why not?' she agreed, sitting up. 'And you know,' she flashed him an amused glance, 'I find there's nothing quite like a plate of toast and jam to inspire erotic thoughts.'

'That was exactly what I was thinking when I got up this morning,' Sean agreed. 'Roses have their place, I accept that, but toast is up there.'

She had half-wondered when they would make love again and now she had the answer. Sooner was better, much better, than later.

A couple of hours later Sean was working on his laptop trying to tie up a few loose ends, Luke was lying on the sofa watching a DVD through still-sleepy eyes and Kate was sitting at the kitchen table with her coffee and the phone, gazing out across the tiny garden. A narrow shaft of tree-filtered sunlight squeezed through the back door gilding Luke's wobbly copy of Van Gogh's *Sunflowers*. Kate dialled Paula's number. Her friend answered almost at once.

'Thank goodness you're home!' She was surprised at how relieved she felt to hear the familiar voice.

Paula laughed – a tired laugh, but a laugh nevertheless.

'Thanks for worrying.'

'Is it all okay now?'

'Maybe not quite okay. I still haven't got any hair and I'm missing a boob, but it's better than it was.'

Kate swallowed. 'Your blood pressure and heart and everything are back to normal though?'

'Yes, that's all much better. Apparently it was an infection of some sort. Luckily they caught it before it really took hold.'

'Thank God for that.'

'Yes,' Paula agreed. 'I've heard a few stories of people picking up these things and not being strong enough to shake them off.'

'Don't think about it,' Kate advised, hurriedly. 'It's better now.'

'Did you hear the news this morning?'

'No, what?'

'Your painter, Van Gogh, there's a new book out claiming that he didn't commit suicide at all but was shot by a couple of boys playing with a hunting rifle.'

'Really?'

'It's just a theory, I suppose.'

Kate frowned. So, no requiem. Just madness and a couple of careless kids. It made sense. She had never understood why he had chosen to shoot himself in the chest. It wouldn't have been particularly easy and nor was it guaranteed to be quick.

'It makes his death seem a bit pathetic and pointless,' she said, twizzling a strand of hair round her finger.

'I suspect,' Paula observed, 'that deaths often are.'

'Rudy will have to rewrite his last lecture.' Rudy. Kate's throat tightened as she fought down the wave of desire and regret that had bubbled up at the memory of him. 'Actually,' she managed to say, 'I phoned to tell you that we're moving back to England.'

'Great!' Paula sounded pleased, then added more doubtfully; 'But is that what you want? I thought things were going okay over there now.'

'Not really,' said Kate. 'I went to Arles,' she stopped, aware of Sean's solid, trusting back bent over the computer in the next room.

'Arles in France?'

'I'll tell you all about it one day. Luke got ill and I had to come back. It was awful, he ended up in hospital. That was yesterday. He's home now.'

'Poor Luke. What was it?'

'They don't really know. His favourite elephant died, you remember the one? And he kind of lost the plot apparently. Anyway... he seems okay. He's just really tired.'

'Poor Luke,' repeated Paula with feeling. 'He's found it all quite hard, hasn't he?'

'Harder than we realised,' agreed Kate with a rush of guilt. 'Anyway, the bad news is that we're not coming back to Suffolk. Sean's been offered a job in Cambridge.'

'Awww,' Paula wailed. 'Oh well, Cambridge isn't too far. It could have been much worse.'

'Yes,' said Kate. 'It could all have been much worse. I really think it'll be okay.'

*****

A few weeks later, Sean closed the door of the Amsterdam apartment behind them for the last time and took Kate's hand.

'Will we come back, do you think?' she asked.

'Luke wants to visit Tobias so maybe we could come for a weekend.' He had a vision of them strolling along the canals just like ordinary tourists, not caring that they couldn't understand the harsh, twittering language. He felt as if their world was a jigsaw that had been thrown into the air and shattered. Now they were carefully replacing the pieces but the picture wasn't quite the same.

During this last month he had studiously avoided seeing Lena unless work matters absolutely required him to. And apart from one small incident on the first morning in front of the coffee machine when he could have sworn she actually spat at him, he had been reasonably successful. Since relations with Kate had resumed he found he could easily shrug off any temptation that seeing her strutting about the office might trigger. Even the memories of her red sofa had putrefied in his brain so the whole episode now seemed seedy rather than sexy. On her part, she had very quickly transferred her attentions to a much younger guy who was on some exchange from the Tunis branch. Comparing himself with his replacement Sean couldn't help but be astonished and somewhat flattered that she had picked him out in the first place. Was he really in the same league? He had expected to feel guilty about Lena – he had, after all, screwed her over – but he noted with slight unease that he didn't. Rather he was furious at her cynical attempt to wreck his marriage. He left it there. Sean maintained it didn't always pay to analyse too deeply.

Kate had spent most of her Amsterdam summer with Luke in the Vondelpark, sitting on a bench reading while he splashed in the open air pool or clambered on the climbing frame. A few times they had met up with Tobias and his mother in the Melkhuis café and the women chatted while the boys played. Once he knew for sure that none of it was going to be forever, Luke had been much more relaxed. Occasionally he would ask about Cambridge and Kate always replied that they had found a nice school and would very quickly find an equally nice house.

'They speak English there, don't they?' he invariably enquired.

'Yes,' Kate replied.

'And it's not too far from Henry?'

'Much closer than here. We can see him sometimes at weekends.'

'And Ollie and Dom and Paula?'

'Of course.'

'And Daddy's coming isn't he?'

'Definitely.'

Reassured, Luke would run off and resume whatever activity he had been involved in. Lena was never mentioned by any of them.

It seemed important to visit the Van Gogh museum for one last time before they left forever and Kate had her chance the Thursday before they moved. Luke had been invited to spend the day with Tobias so she took the number five tram to Museumplein. In the warm sunshine the queue stretched half-way to the Stedelijk but she pushed to the front as usual and flashed her museum card. She was quickly shunted through and without hesitation mounted the stairs to the first gallery where, ignoring the throngs of tourists, she stood in front of the *Sunflowers*. The *Sunflowers* and *La Berceuse*, the lullaby, side-by-side as Vincent had intended them. The two paintings had been as inseparable in Van Gogh's mind as they would always now be in Kate's. Madame Roulin, wife of an Arles postman, symbol of motherhood, of nurture, an acknowledgment the role his own mother had played in his life; and beside her, the *Sunflowers* to illuminate, almost to deify her image. He had considered these flowers his best pictures. Yellow on yellow, subtle and magnificent; Vincent's sunflower paintings were the ones Gauguin admired the most. And in the consciousness of the world Van Gogh would forever be Sunflower Man. Kate thought the epithet would have pleased him.

Inevitably, the museum made her think of Rudy and his portrait of Kaatje; boldly coloured with quick, deliberate brush strokes in the style of Van Gogh. *The Sonnet*, an emblem of romantic love with its undercurrent of unfulfilled desire. Kate found a seat on one of the benches and gave herself permission to reflect on her brief relationship with her Dutch art history teacher. She had never been in love with him, she admitted that. She knew almost nothing about him; could barely have told his age or whether his parents still lived. She was ignorant of almost all the details of his life, including how the mysterious woman and child in the photo might fit in. For her he was part man, part avatar, an image conjured by her own loneliness and longing; as much a part of her own subconscious as he was a separate person. But something in her, some genuine need, had called this archetype into being. And in that crowded gallery, surrounded by the works of a mad genius, she thought she grasped why. Rudy with his close, impersonal observation had identified something in her and captured it on canvas. He had shown her another version of herself and in so doing, had enabled her to claim it as her own.

Luke had found a piece of chalk and was drawing elephants on the paving slabs beside the car. The neighbours wouldn't like it but Sean didn't feel he had to care. It was right to be leaving. He put an arm round his wife, marvelling that she was somehow still beside him, despite everything.

'I wanted to tell you something before we left,' said Kate, looking up at him. 'Because it's about here really, and now I'm sure.'

'What's that?' asked Sean, distractedly. His mind had moved ahead to the sea-crossing and how long the journey was likely to take.

'We're going to have another child.'

'What?' He spun her round so they faced each other, his hands on her shoulders. 'What did you say?'

'A baby. I'm expecting a baby. It's very early days yet, but....'

He cut her short. 'Really?'

Kate thought she had never seen anyone look so happy.

'Yes, really.' She reached up a hand and gently touched his cheek. 'Don't cry,' she said. 'Come on. We should be getting home.'

Chapter 34

Cambridge

'Will they be here soon, do you think?' asked Luke, hopping excitedly from one foot to the other.

'I'm sure they will. Paula said she was going to get an early lunch and come straight afterwards.'

Kate was standing at the butler sink in a large, comfortable kitchen that she and Sean planned, at some point, to update. Through the window a garden was visible. Rain fell steadily, dripping off the overgrown shrubs and the new football net.

'You'll have to play inside, I think.'

'That's okay,' replied Luke cheerfully. 'We don't mind. Henry's still my best friend, you know, even though I don't see him at school every day like Ben.'

'I know,' said Kate. 'You've been friends with Henry since you were very small. Perhaps you'll stay friends forever.'

Luke considered this. 'I should think we will. He hasn't seen the baby yet, has he?'

'No, well, she's only two weeks old, after all.'

Kate looked at her son and reflected that she had been incredibly lucky; Cambridge suited them. After several months of house-hunting she and Sean had finally bought a pleasant Victorian mid-terrace not too far from the city centre with a bay window and a leafy garden. Luke's school was nearby and Sean could usually get to work in twenty minutes, even when the traffic was bad. A sturdy pushchair had been Kate's first investment and she fully intended to spend the summer going for long walks along the river with the baby. This life that she had decided to stay with was turning out well.

'I like Cambridge better than Amsterdam, Mum,' Luke was saying, as if to confirm what Kate had been thinking.

'I expect that's because everyone speaks English, isn't it?'

'Yes, but it's also because Dad comes home earlier and because Diego isn't here.'

Kate frowned. 'I never realised he was such a problem.'

Luke sighed. 'He was always kicking me,'

'Did he kick Tobias too?'

'No, only me, because I couldn't speak Dutch and I was friends with Heijn.'

'I wish you'd told me.'

'You couldn't do anything,' said Luke philosophically. 'And you were very busy with Van Cough.'

Yes, I was, thought Kate, ruffling his hair. And now she had applied to do an art history course at the university in the autumn. It made sense to use this time while the children were young, she thought. Studying was flexible. She could to go back to work soon enough. So she would continue to be busy with Van Gogh in a sense. And probably with Picasso and Gauguin too, but not with Rudy de Jong, of that she was quite certain. Rudy she had left behind in Arles and there he would stay, sleeping for all eternity in that empty, sunlit apartment on the Rhone. Occasionally she thought of the portrait. Sean had asked about it once:

'Wasn't that art history guy painting you?'

'Yes. I expect it's in his cellar somewhere,' she had replied, deliberately vague. And perhaps it was. Or perhaps it was even now being exhibited in Antwerp or Brussels. It amused Kate to think that this might be the case. Like Dorian Gray's portrait, Kaatje would take on a life of her own, separate from her subject, a shadow detached from its owner. She swallowed hard. None of it mattered now she had her longed-for daughter; a warm, flaxen-haired bundle with a face like a cherub. Kate's lips twisted in a Mona-Lisa smile and she bent to take a tray of chocolate chip cookies from the oven.

'I think the biscuits are ready, Luke. It certainly smells like it.'

Luke rubbed his tummy. 'Can I ...?'

'When Henry arrives.'

Just at that moment the doorbell rang and Kate jumped.

'They're here,' Luke yelled.

Disturbed by the sudden commotion the baby opened its eyes and let out a cry.

'I'll see to her, Luke. You get the door.'

Luke was already there, standing on tiptoes to reach the lock.

'Kate, you look wonderful, really radiant,' Paula enthused, kissing her friend on both cheeks. 'But where is she? Where's Anna?'

Kate grinned. 'Thanks. You don't look so bad yourself. She's in there.'

Paula bent over the cradle. Her hair had grown back curlier than ever and cavorted in mad whorls over her head, only now there were white streaks along with the black. She still moved quite carefully, as if something intangible had been taken away with her breast; a bounce, an elasticity maybe. Or perhaps it was simply the last vestiges of her youth. Kate suspected that only she saw this. It is not the kind of thing people, especially husbands, choose to notice.

'Hello,' she cooed to the infant. The baby girl with her fluff of blonde hair, translucent skin and light eyes gazed quizzically back at her. 'She's beautiful. You're very lucky.'

'I am,' agreed Kate. 'Probably far luckier than I deserve to be.'

Paula's hand travelled automatically to touch the space where her breast had once been.

'She's very fair,' she murmured.

'Sean's mother is tall and fair with very odd-coloured eyes. Her father was Scandinavian.'

'That's who she must take after, then.'

'That's right,' said Kate, brightly. 'That's why we named Anna after her, because of the resemblance.'

The women's eyes locked. There was a pause, a heartbeat.

'I knew,' Kate rushed on, more quietly. 'I knew straight away. It was just like it was with Luke. Nothing else mattered after that.'

Paula nodded slowly. 'Yes.'

'Come and see my new sister, Henry,' Luke could be heard shouting from the next room. The boys burst in closely followed by Ollie who was remarkably stable considering he wasn't yet two.

'She very pretty,' boasted Luke, 'but she's a bit boring at the moment.'

'Ollie's not boring,' said Henry. 'He's a pest, though.'

'How's school going, Luke?' Paula enquired.

'Fine,' Luke replied.

'He's doing very well,' Kate confirmed. 'And he's made a few friends. Haven't you, Luke?'

'What? Yes.' Luke glanced up briefly from prodding his sister. 'She likes this, Henry. See, she looks at me.'

Henry decided to try prodding too but Anna's face crumpled. Paula scooped her up and rocked her slowly, relishing the feel of the small, trusting animal against her body.

'Early menopause is one of the common side-effects of breast cancer,' she whispered.

Kate's gaze flicked from her friend to the baby.

'I didn't know.' Her forehead creased. 'That's tough.'

Luke and Henry were pulling at Paula's arm, still competing for Anna's attention.

'That's enough boys. Go and play in the other room,' Kate instructed.

'Can we have a biscuit, Mum?' asked Luke.

'Two each, no more.' The boys charged out followed, inevitably, by the shrieking toddler.

'He's got so much taller since you've been back,' said Paula, not taking her eyes from the infant. 'He used to be one of the smallest in the class.'

'Dutch fertilizer,' Kate grinned. 'He's changed too. He's more confident but also more wary somehow.'

'Sounds like he's growing up, then. You used to molly him a bit you know.'

'Did I?'

'Yes,' said Paula, firmly. 'And how is Sean?'

'Brilliant,' Kate's face softened. 'Coming home from work early to help with Anna and Luke, getting up in the night from time to time. He's great.'

'Good. It's all worked out then.'

'I think so. Look, do you mind holding her for a minute longer while I make us both a cup of tea? She seems to have settled with you.'

'We've both settled,' replied Paula. Still cuddling Anna she moved across to the French windows. The baby regarded her intently through her strange, sapphire eyes as Paula considered the rain. It wouldn't do to leave too late, she decided. The roads might be slippery in this weather.

The sound of the boys' noisy playing floated through from the next room:

'You can be Spiderman, Luke. I'm Batman.'

Okay, these are my webs.'

Paula almost managed a smile. In one sense she had been lucky too. Of course, she had; she wasn't going to die, not just yet. There was even a good chance she would live to see her boys grow up. She looked down at the babe in her arms. Anna's eyelids had begun to droop sleepily. Paula placed her reluctantly back in the cradle. Yes, she was lucky, she realised that. She bit her lip hard.

'Another cup?' Kate asked, as the two women came to the end of their conversation at about the same moment as they finished their tea.

Paula shook her head. 'No thanks. I'm going to get off home now, before the traffic builds up on the Orwell Bridge. You'll be over next weekend for Henry's birthday won't you?'

'Of course, we wouldn't miss it. I'll probably leave Anna with Sean. It's important for me to spend some time with Luke by himself, I think.'

'And it gives Dad a chance to bond with the baby.' Paula grinned.

'That too....Luke,' Kate called. 'Henry has to go now.'

'Awww,' Luke wailed.

'But we'll see him on Saturday.'

'Ohhhkaay.'

'You know,' Luke said, waving madly as the car pulled away. 'Henry still is my bestest friend.'

'Is he?' said Kate, hugging him. 'And Paula is mine.'

Chapter 35

Nine-thirty on a Thursday morning and Sean had loads to do. It was his first full week back at work following Anna's birth and there were two or three problems that needed some urgent attention. He didn't mind being busy. In fact, usually he positively relished it, but just now he was feeling a bit sleep deprived and he would have preferred to simply skulk behind his computer screen and have a quiet nap. He swigged a mouthful of coffee and pulled a face. Uggh. It wasn't a patch on the Douwe Egberts they had provided in Holland. You could clean toilets with this stuff. But never mind, it usually did the trick. He swallowed purposefully. A couple of cups and a doze would be completely off the agenda.

'Morning, Sean.' The company postie was coming across the office towards him. Even in his less than alert state Sean managed to interpret the wrinkle of curiosity furrowing Pete's forehead.

'This arrived for you this morning.' The old man handed over a white, handwritten envelope. Definitely one of the least likely pieces of correspondence ever to turn up in a busy IT department.

'Cheers.' Sean turned it over. Amsterdam postmark. He ran a hand across his scalp. Pete watched him with interest.

'Don't usually get personal letters here,' he suggested, looking at it pointedly.

'No,' Sean agreed, feeling himself begin to sweat. He knew that writing.

'Might even be the first time.'

'Really?' Sean managed to splutter. 'Well, I think I'll open it later. I'm pretty busy just now.' He very deliberately folded the envelope, put it in his trouser pocket and turned back to the screen. 'Thanks for that, though, Pete.'

'No problem,' the postman grunted, his voice heavy with disapproval.

Sean realised that by lunchtime most of the building would have been heard about his mysterious correspondence but at least they wouldn't know its contents. He had a pretty good idea who it was from. But what on earth could she want?

After a delay he judged to be reasonable, Sean slipped off to the gents where he sat down heavily on the lid of the toilet, pulled out the letter and turned it over several times hoping the outside might afford some clue that would lead him in gently. It was definitely from her. It even smelt of her! Thank God he had told Kate the whole thing – with a few details left out, of course. Life was good just now if a bit exhausting and he really didn't want to mess it all up. Kate was cooing over Anna like a cat who's got the cream and he had just started taking Luke to football training every Sunday morning. Boys' time, they called it. Luke seemed to be benefitting from the fresh air and the couple of hours they spent together. He was looking really relaxed and happy. The family was working again.

He fingered the envelope. It was quite thick, as though there might be something more inside than a sheet of paper. A piccy of Lena lying naked on that red sofa, maybe? He snorted; not a hope. But there was no way of knowing without actually opening it. His stomach churned unpleasantly.

Go for it, Butterworth, he told himself, slipping his finger into the corner of the envelope and ripping it quickly along the top. Yep, a piece of note paper – he unfolded the sheet – and, as he had guessed, a photo. Sean stared. The red sofa was there, unmistakably, but there was no sign of Lena, nude or otherwise. Instead, gazing at the camera and now at straight at him, was a baby girl about the same age as Anna, with a shock of dark hair and huge dark eyes, dressed in a pink sleepsuit. A phone number had been scrawled across the top of the paper together with a brief note.

Hi,

This is Sophia. It was taken a few days ago. I wasn't going to tell you, but I thought, in the end, that you should know. Give me a call. She's looking forward to meeting her father.

Best wishes,

Lena

Sean's fist curled around the paper and his eyes squeezed tight. He could feel his heart pounding like it did during a gym session. Sophia. Pretty name. But... Fucking hell! He jumped off the toilet, lifted the lid and emptied his breakfast into the bowl. This had never been part of the deal. Silly cow should have been using something. He had always assumed... But – an iceberg of pure fear pierced his gut –he should have known better, should have taken care of things himself. Oldest trick in the book. Still, he had to admit, he wiped his mouth on some tissue paper and looked again at the photo, she was a very cute kid and she looked a lot more like him than Anna did. But this news would crucify Kate and, even more than that, he could picture Luke's panic and confusion:

'But I've already got a baby sister, Daddy. Why is Mummy crying?'

What a bloody mess. What on earth was he supposed to do?

Sheer willpower and a useful ability to completely the focus on the task in hand was what got Sean through the day. It was a talent which had always infuriated his wife.

How can you possibly not have heard Luke screaming/noticed the overflowing rubbish bin/thought to get the washing in before it got soaked???

And such was his level of concentration after receiving the letter that he got to the bottom of the computer problems in record time. It was only once he turned the key in car ignition that evening that his thoughts returned to the baby. Lena's child. His child.

Perhaps it would be better not to tell Kate? He could probably find some pretext for making a work trip to Amsterdam every couple of months. He could stay in some cheap hotel – absolutely not with Lena – transfer a decent sum of money... Yes, he would have to do that. It was his baby and he should definitely contribute something. He could be a part of Sophia's life without Kate and Luke ever knowing. It was the only possible solution. Or perhaps he could just send the money and not see the child? Sean's mouth twisted as he considered this. Imagine growing up not knowing who your father was, believing he didn't care about you. Sean couldn't. He would have to see her, however infrequently. So did that mean he was about to turn into one of these men who have a secret family in another town? He had never understood how that could happen. But, as he was beginning to realise, there were lots of things he hadn't understood before they moved to Amsterdam.

He slammed on the brakes. Roundabout. He had almost driven straight onto it. He seriously needed to get a grip or there would be three kids without a father and his funeral would not be a good time for Kate to find out about his other daughter. He drove on, forcing himself to pay more attention to the road, although inevitably part of his mind continued to mull over his options. On balance, he wondered, would he have preferred not to have known? Would he have rather stumbled through life blissfully unaware of Sophia's existence? If he had been presented with the scenario hypothetically Sean thought he might have said yes. But now he had seen the photo he couldn't want to un-know. How could he want to disown something so cute and vulnerable?

He sighed. She had been okay, actually, Lena, and he probably hadn't treated her very well. It was quite flattering that she had actually decided to give birth to his child. It wasn't the only option, after all. So maybe now, to be some semblance of a father to this baby girl was the least that both of them deserved.

He turned the corner into their road. Nearly home. But the big question was still whether to tell Kate. He needed to sleep on it and probably more than once. He would make a decision in a day or two – whether to tell Kate, what to tell Kate, how to tell Kate. He pulled into their drive and glanced up at the house. Luke's bedroom light was on and it was about the right time for his bedtime story. With his hand in his trouser pocket fingering the folded envelope, Sean walked slowly towards the front door.

Chapter 36

Sean sat at the computer enjoying the quiet. Kate had taken Luke to Henry's birthday party and he had volunteered to look after Anna. She was a pretty good baby actually and the image of his own mother, he thought. Her arrival had been the best possible ending to the mess that had been their Amsterdam experiment. Until Lena's letter arrived. He took the photo of Sophia out of his wallet for the thousandth time and looked into her large, black eyes. She would have Lena's colouring, that much was obvious, but his features, probably.

In truth, he had thought of almost nothing but this child for the last three days. Every moment when his mind wasn't consciously engaged in some other task it returned, like a screensaver, to the image of the dark-haired baby in the fluffy sleepsuit. It was clear that he needed to come to a decision and the more he deliberated, the more he was inclined to conclude that Kate, Luke and Anna simply must not know. To tell them about Sophia would be to throw a bomb into their newly-mended family unit. He could easily imagine the emotional carnage that would ensue. The anger and blame that would be directed at him, Luke's justifiable sense of betrayal. Kate had been pretty good about an awful lot of stuff but he couldn't see her accepting this. He slipped the photo back into his wallet next to one of Luke and Anna taken at the hospital. He was being crap as usual. He needed to phone Lena and he needed to do it soon. She would be waiting.

And he would, he promised himself. He would do it this afternoon before Kate and Luke got back from Suffolk. But there was no rush, they would be hours yet. He still had time to finalise his strategy. Meanwhile, as Anna was asleep, he decided to flick through some photos of her and select a few to send to his parents, simultaneously taking the opportunity to delete any particularly unflattering ones of himself. He opened the pictures file, wondering, despite himself, if he would ever be able to include any of Sophia along with the other kids. But he must have opened the wrong folder because a picture of Kate appeared unexpectedly on the screen. She was standing in bright sunshine next to a wide river looking radiant, really incredibly happy. It was fairly recent, Sean could see that by the way she had her hair, but he didn't remember taking it. He scanned the image for clues.

Wasn't that a Van Gogh painting on that panel beside her? Presumably then, this was Arles and she had asked some fellow tourist to take the picture. She hadn't ever said much about the trip to Provence. In the aftermath of Luke's illness, all the stuff about Lena and the move back to the UK, Sean had never got around to asking her about her weekend.

He might as well have a look, he supposed. Perhaps they could go back together some day and finish sight-seeing. Hadn't she said she never got to see the sunflowers? With mild curiosity he pulled up the next couple of shots; a rather uninspiring bridge, somewhere that looked like a park, a Roman arena – all with the Van Gogh reproductions beside them. It was quite interesting, actually, to compare the two scenes, the modern and the one the artist had painted. And there was the *Café Terrace at Night*. This was the painting Kate had specially wanted to see at the Kröller Muller museum. Sean smiled to himself as he remembered how much Luke had enjoyed the ride on the white bikes. Kate seemed to have taken the café from several angles; presumably it was one of the more important scenes for Van Gogh buffs.

But hang on! He peered more closely at the screen. Who was the blond guy in the background only half in the shot? He seemed to be looking at the camera, at Kate. Sean had an idea he recognised him. Wasn't it that art-history lecturer? Luke had pointed him out once when they were wandering across

Museumplein. Kate had had been at home not feeling well or something. He zoomed in on the photo. Yes, it was indisputably him. He had really weird blue eyes. Sean swallowed the large lump that was forming in his throat and leant back in the chair, pulling out a handkerchief to mop the beads of sweat that had appeared on his forehead.

No wonder Kate had been so bloody good about Lena!

The baby alarm crackled and Anna's soft whimpers were broadcast into the room from upstairs. Sean pressed delete. This was one photo they didn't need. Was he sure, the computer enquired. Yes, he was. In fact, he doubted he had ever been surer about anything in his life. He clicked off the file and emptied the recycle bin. Maybe they wouldn't go and see the sunflowers after all. The baby's cries got louder, she probably just wanted a cuddle. He pushed back the chair and went up to her.

It was after six o clock when Kate and Luke finally got home and Anna was screaming. Sean had spent the previous hour pacing the sitting room trying to dribble milk into her contorted mouth. The noise was audible even from the driveway. Kate rushed in to rescue the distressed infant.

'She wouldn't take it,' Sean muttered, pushing her and the bottle into Kate's arms and retreating hurriedly to the kitchen in search of his son.

'Good party, Batman?'

'Spiderman,' Luke corrected, opening his jacket to show his father his tee-shirt. 'We got party bags with enormous, hairy spiders. See.'

Sean crouched down and together they examined the rubber arachnid.

'That is pretty scary,' he agreed.

'Very scary,' Luke beamed.

Eventually, Kate managed to feed Anna and, exhausted, the infant finally slept. Sean peered into the cot, slipping a finger into her tiny fist. Who was she? he wondered, chewing his lip. The evening ticked on. He supervised Luke's bath and read him a story while Kate chopped some chicken for a stir fry. The familiar smells wafting up the stairs seemed more pungent than usual as his brain flitted between the photo of Sophia on the sofa and the photo of the Yellow Café at Arles.

'Night, Dad,' muttered Luke from beneath the duvet. 'Are we going to football tomorrow?'

'Of course,' Sean agreed. 'Wouldn't miss it. As long as you're not too tired.'

'Course not,' replied Luke scornfully. 'Or at least, I won't be in the morning.'

'That's what I thought,' smiled Sean.

In the kitchen, Kate was tipping soy sauce into the wok.

'Nearly done,' she said brightly. Sean noticed she was wearing the gold earrings with tiny diamond chips he had bought her when Anna was born. He looked carefully round the kitchen as if fixing it in his memory; the baby paraphernalia, Luke's collection of snail shells that lived on a shelf above the sink; the daffodils picked from the garden, now wilting a bit in their jar but still colourful; photos – mostly of Luke – stuck to the fridge with fruit magnets. The miscellany of family life. It looked like the real deal, he thought. No one would guess. He took a bottle of wine from the cupboard and rummaged in a drawer for the opener.

'Kate,' he said.

She looked up sharply, hearing the catch in his voice.

He reached across and turned off the gas.

'That can wait. I'm not hungry just now.'

'Well if you'd said,' Kate began, 'I've been eating cake and sandwiches all afternoon.'

Sean shook his head.

'Come and sit down.' He put the Merlot on the table between them and rubbed a hand over the prickles of his hair. 'We need to talk.'

Uneasily, Kate slid onto the chair opposite her husband. Sean filled two glasses.

'No thanks.' She pushed hers away and studied the table top, tracing her finger along the grain of the pine.

Sean shrugged. 'Whatever.' He took a gulp of his wine and a deep breath. 'You need to tell him, Kate.'

He saw the finger pause, freeze momentarily on a knot in the wood, before continuing its path.

'Tell who what?'

'You know.'

She lifted her head and Sean found himself gazing directly into her clear, hazel eyes.

'Do I?'

He decided to change tack. He extracted the picture from his wallet and placed it on the table between them.

'This is my daughter, Sophia.'

Kate's gasp was audible.

'You bastard!' Her voice was as low and painful as the whine of a whipped dog. 'You had a baby with her!' She grabbed the picture and squinted at the tiny features, the soft down of dark hair. She was tense with fury. She felt as though part of her had slid from the chair and was lying, screaming on the floor. The life that she had thought she was living was a mirage. There was this other small person for Sean to love. Another sister for Luke. In fact, an entirely separate family set up from which she, Kate, would be forever excluded. She would have to welcome this child into her home and let her share Anna's room, Anna's toys. Sophia might join them on their annual holidays, she would come to family weddings. Kate fought the urge to rip the photo into miniscule pieces. Microdots. Fragments so small that there would be no chance, ever, that they could be reformed into a likeness of this child.

'It wasn't meant. It just happened.' Sean's glance flitted miserably from the photo to Kate and back again.

'Wasn't meant by whom?' Kate slammed her fist down on the table. 'My guess is that someone meant it. Bitch!' She rubbed her eyes fiercely. 'Couldn't she find a bloke that wasn't already married?'

Sean slid the picture back in his wallet. He'd been tricked, he knew that, but still, there was the baby. His daughter.

'I think,' he began slowly, 'things never quite worked out for her, for Lena. And maybe I gave her the impression our marriage was rockier than it really was.' He studied his trainers. Probably needed a new pair, especially if he was going to take up running again as he planned. He needed to get fit to keep up with Luke these days. When he looked up Kate was shaking, tears running through her fingers and down her cheeks. He got up and hugged her uncertainly. She turned and sobbed into his chest.

'Fuck, Babe, what have we done?' He lifted his glasses and rubbed his own eyes. 'But I'm right aren't I, Anna's not mine?'

'She's yours if you want her,' Kate replied, controlling herself. 'It's not like this...' she thrashed around for the word, 'this mess you've made.'

'Of course I want her,' Sean protested, wondering as he said it if this were true. He thought that on balance, it probably was, because she was Kate's and he still loved his wife, and because she was Luke's sister and there was a resemblance there, and because she was tiny and sweet and had mended everything.

'But how did you find out?' Kate asked.

'I was looking through some photos of Arles and he was in one of them. You went there with him.' It was an accusation.

Kate shook her head.

'No, really. It was just coincidence. I went alone.'

'You went alone? Christ, Kate!'

'I wanted to see what it was like, to be by myself again. He was there for some exhibition. Nothing was planned. And I thought...' she hesitated, swallowing hard. 'I thought I couldn't have any children.' She remembered the sparsely furnished flat overlooking the Rhone. 'It was like I was twenty again.'

Sean could relate to that.

'But still,' he insisted, 'you have to tell him. You have to give him a chance to know her.'

Kate thought of the picture on the shelf in Rudy's studio; the dark-haired woman and the boy. Did he have other children? Offspring scattered around Europe, seeds of the travelling artist? She doubted it somehow. He had used the past tense when he spoke of them, she remembered. His face had been closed, shuttered like the windows in an empty house. And the next time she went behind the screen to undress for the sitting, the photo had disappeared.

'I'll tell him,' she decided. 'And you, what are you going to do?'

Sean took off his glasses and polished them vigorously on his shirt.

'I'll send some money. I'll go and see her sometimes. I suppose, later on, I might even take Luke.' He looked across at his wife. 'I'm so sorry, Kate.'

She reached out a hand to him across the table.

'God,' she replied, 'so am I.'

Chapter 37

Sitting with her hands poised over the keyboard, Kate steeled herself to search for Rudy. She hesitated a full two minutes. There was a part of her that would have preferred to leave him in bed in the Arles apartment, slices of sunlight streaming through the shutters onto crumpled sheets. But now Sean knew the truth about the baby, leaving Rudy in the past was no longer an option. If he had been summoned once from loneliness and need, then she must invoke him again.

Finally it was all much simpler, more prosaic than she would have wished. She simply googled Rudy de Jong and he appeared on her screen together with a whole host of options for contacting him. He even had a Wikipedia entry! She sniffed at her own silly romanticism and clicked on a YouTube clip filmed recently in the lecture theatre of the Van Gogh Museum. Rudy was talking about Vincent's *Sunflowers*, about the artist's loneliness and his turbulent relationship with Gauguin. It was all just as she remembered. Was it really just a year ago? It felt like a lifetime. But, equally, like no time at all. She watched the film to its end. Rudy was as passionate as ever about his subject; his blue eyes flashed, his smile hovered, the lean, brown hands moved the baton to pick out points of interest on the screen. She remembered those same hands dangling a sugar cube over a coffee cup. Kate closed her eyes and took a very deep breath.

Hi,

She typed.

It's Kate/Kaatje. Hope you haven't forgotten me. We're coming over to Amsterdam for a short visit. I'd like to meet up if that's possible. There's something quite important I have to talk to you about. Just a quick coffee. Would that be okay?

K x

Quite important. She pressed send, marvelling at the myriad layers of deceptions and self-deceptions in which lives are wrapped.

*****

'Nice hotel,' said Sean, peering out of the window over the Prinsengracht. 'Good choice. Couldn't really tell when we arrived last night. And a truly excellent breakfast.' He patted his stomach contentedly.

'I know the city, if nothing else,' replied Kate, briefly. 'Though goodness knows how you managed to eat so much.' She threw him a searching look. 'Aren't you even a bit nervous?'

'Yes,' replied Sean. 'I am when I think about it.' The fact was, he reflected, he was able to focus on food in pretty much the same way he could focus on a work problem. Useful talent, all considered.

'So we can get to everywhere from here,' Kate went on. 'Though I don't know where you need to go.'

'Well, I thought –' Sean began.

'And I don't want to.' She flashed him a glance and continued unpacking Luke's case. She had absolutely refused to discuss Lena and her baby. 'Let's just wait and see,' was all she would say when Sean broached the subject. He supposed she wanted him to come to his own conclusions but he was finding this difficult. He was used to talking things through with her and he missed her input, her perspective.

'Should have talked it through before you got naked on that red sofa,' murmured a quiet voice in his head. Of course, but it hadn't been quite that that easy, had it?

'When's Tobias coming to get me?' Luke crowed, breaking into his parents' train of thought.

'He'll be here in about five minutes,' his mother replied, shutting the empty case. 'We can go downstairs and wait in the reception if you like. Daddy can watch Anna for a minute.'

'Yeess!' Luke shouted. 'I'm going to see the *oliphanten*, the *oliphanten!*'

'So you are,' Kate agreed, biting her lip. 'Lucky you.'

Kate let Sean leave the hotel room first. Despite his claims of equanimity he seemed to spend an inordinate amount of time in the bathroom and she caught him standing sideways to the mirror examining his stomach.

I would laugh, she thought, except that when he's gone I expect I'll do the same. How much have we changed in these months?

'Go,' she said, standing back, not touching him. 'You look fine. Anyway, the baby's only a few weeks old, remember. She probably won't be back to normal just yet.'

He nodded gratefully, not seeming to notice her detachment. Kate waited until the door had closed then crossed to the window. She caught a glimpse of him heading along Prinsengracht towards Leidsestraat. Presumably he was going to catch a tram. Then he was gone and she was alone with Anna. Her sense of remoteness, of anonymity, increased. She was just a woman with a baby in a city. She could be anyone. She could be Kaatje. With this thought came a sense of liberation, of having been released like a caged bird into the world. Her mouth twisted; it was a feeling she recognised from the trip to Arles.

'Walk out of your life,' came the whisper, and Luke and Sean would become like paintings on a wall, static figures in her past as she moved forwards. The sirens were calling, she should take care.

Outside on the pavement it was a perfect June morning; soft, warm air, a pale sun sitting in a sky of the same light, clear blue as Anna's eyes. The hotel, with its steeply gabled roof was mirrored perfectly in the almost motionless canal. Kate wanted to skip, to dance, but she forced her feet to move slowly, to stroll as she pushed the buggy.

There's no rush, she told herself. He lectures in the mornings. She deliberately ignored the rapid beating of her heart. It was a twenty minute walk at most. She could take her time, enjoy the city. She ambled along Hobbemastraat at a leisurely pace and instead of turning directly into Paulus Potterstraat, crossed onto Museumplein sauntering across the open expanse of grass past the paddling pool and the giant letters proclaiming 'I amsterdam'. All the while, Anna dozed, opening half an eye from time to time in response to a noise or smell, oblivious of her connection with the city. Kate checked her watch. Somehow she still had ten minutes to kill before Rudy would be free. She wondered fleetingly how Sean was getting on, then pushed the thought aside. Her palms were clammy. She took a breath, chose an empty bench and sat down in the sunshine, in the balmy air crowded with the sounds of birds, people, trams, and waited.

Chapter 38

'Hoi, Kaatje,' said Rudy, coming down the steps of the museum. She glanced up, catching the force of his look, that mineral-blue stare. Her hand tightened around the handle of the pushchair as she braced herself against the shock of his physical presence. He bent forward to offer the usual three kisses and stepped back to inspect the baby. Kate watched, trying to gauge his expression as he considered Anna. At length, he gave a brief nod, seemingly satisfied. In the same moment, the child opened her eyes and met his penetrating blue gaze with an identical one of her own. Rudy's face broke into a rare smile.

'She's beautiful,' he murmured. 'Hey, let me give you a hand with the buggy.'

The lady in the kiosk glared as he helped Kate and Anna past the queues and through the doors of the museum but he spoke to her in Dutch and they were allowed to pass.

'I explained we were only going to the café. I promised you wouldn't look at any pictures.'

'I would quite like to have a quick look in the gallery,' Kate protested.

'Of course,' Rudy agreed, amused. 'Frieda doesn't actually own the museum, she only thinks this way.'

It was the hour between coffee and lunch. The cafe was buzzing in a low-key way but wasn't yet crowded.

'This time it's my treat,' Rudy insisted, as they reached the counter.

'Coffee and one of those pastries, please.'

Kate noticed that his hand shook slightly as he passed across the note. It reminded her of the gardens of the asylum in Arles. 'He's just a man,' she told herself and felt immediately less nervous.

They found a table against a wall, away from the huge glass window where everyone else was sitting. The hum of conversation leant them anonymity.

'So,' he said quietly, 'you have come to tell me that this is my daughter.'

'Something like that,' Kate admitted.

'That is a big thing to say. Are you sure?'

'Fairly. At first we thought she looked like Sean's mother, but she doesn't really.'

Rudy bent towards the buggy and studied the baby. He smiled and said something softly in his own language. Anna cooed and waved her arms excitedly.

'It's possible,' Rudy agreed. 'She is a lot like my sister. What's her name?'

'Anna.'

'A good name.' He straightened up, the baby squarked a protest. 'So what do you want me to do? I don't have much money but you can have what I can give. Do you stay with your husband?'

Kate nodded. 'I think so.'

'Does he know?'

'He's pretty sure. But he will bring her up with Luke.'

'So, he's a good man.'

'It's complicated.'

'Everything is complicated. Always. Even what seems simple, like one of Vincent's paintings.'

'But don't you want to see her? To visit sometimes?' Kate was hurt that Rudy would give Anna up so easily.

'Maybe, but I can't offer her much? She is better to stay with her family, *nee*? She's my gift to you.'

Kate looked across the table at him. He was dangling a sugar cube over his coffee, letting the liquid seep into the grains. Kate's heart tugged at the familiar gesture.

'So it didn't mean anything, that night?' she asked.

'Of course, there was meaning. But I told you then, I had nothing to give you. Except, it seems, a child.' He paused, let the sugar fall, stirred the tiny cup and looked up. 'It wasn't quite a coincidence,' he admitted quietly. 'I followed you to Arles.'

Kate's forehead creased.

'But how did you know?'

'You mentioned it one day. Maybe you didn't even realise. Something unconscious, that could be true, I think. I thought maybe it was what you wanted. Or perhaps it was Kaatje.' He gave a little shrug. 'I was thinking I could make it possible. A possibility. And then see what happened.' He smiled. 'But it was good, *nee*, Kaatje?'

Kate blushed, remembering the flood of moonlight plating the world with silver, the huge bed with the clean, worn sheets, the man who had undressed her slowly and told her she was beautiful.

'Yes.'

'And because it was good, I think this child who could be mine, she will be golden. I think she will be loved.'

Anna was started to whimper. Kate gave her a dummy and the baby sucked hard, eyelids drooping.

'And who,' she said, plucking up the courage, sending him a shifting glance, 'who was the dark-haired woman with the boy? The one in the photo behind the screen. She was gone the next time I came.'

A tiny flicker, no more than a muscle spasm, contorted Rudy's face.

'She was for me alone,' he replied, shortly. 'I shouldn't have left her there.'

'Someone you loved.' It wasn't a question. There was no need to ask.

'The only woman I ever loved.'

Kate waited. Anna slept beside them in her pushchair. Rudy's eyes strayed to his daughter's face and softened.

'And your child?'

'No,' he shook his head slowly; a wayward dark blond strand fell across his forehead. 'No, not my child.' He sighed. 'Okay, so this is it: it happened, well, now twelve years ago. I was travelling round Europe, making paintings to sell so I could eat, studying all the great art. I found Celine in Rome. She was standing on a bridge, the Ponte Vittorio Emanuele, in fact, staring down into the black water of the river Tiber and the wind was blowing her dress, her hair. I suppose she looked a bit like you when you were standing on the Trinquetaille Bridge. It seems to be a theme in my life.' Here a small, ironic smile. 'She was fragile, tiny, like she might blow away. She looked very lonely. I had to talk to her.'

Kate's glance flicked from Anna to her mug of chocolate, she sipped slowly, listening without looking at him.

Rudy pushed the hair away, impatiently. His gaze was turned inside himself.

He is seeing her, Kate thought, on the bridge. That's where he is, on the Ponte Vittorio Emanuele. Now, when I think of Rome I will think of this.

'Later she told me she planned to jump off but couldn't summon the courage. She couldn't swim, hardly at all.' He half-smiled, shook his head, 'I thought that was sweet and romantic. All the Dutch women can swim since they are babies.'

'But why did she want to jump?'

'Because she was pregnant, she was Catholic and her married lover didn't want to know about it. Simple story. She was nineteen.'

Kate swallowed. 'But surely today people don't...'

'Do you know all the things that people do, Kaatje?'

Kate reddened.

'She was ashamed. Can you understand? Her family were very strict. She didn't think like you do.'

'Poor girl.' It seemed inadequate but she had to say something.

'Yes, poor girl. She was also mad. Mad like Van Gogh. This is another theme in my life. I think in English it's called bi-polar. So, she is pregnant, and Catholic, and ill. But suicide is also a sin so this is another problem.'

'What happened?'

'I married her.'

Kate gasped, pierced by the force of Rudy's cobalt stare.

'Of course. Of course you did. But where is she now?'

Rudy swallowed.

'Now she is dead. You see, the child drowned, in a pool for small children, in the garden of a friend.'

'A paddling pool?'

'Exactly. She went inside just for a second and she forgot he was out there. How did she forget? I don't know. But she was ill, remember. Eight minutes, that was all it took. And when she went outside again he was face down in the water. He was already dead. He was twenty months old.'

Kate threw a panicked glance at Anna. Despite the hot chocolate, the sweet warmth of the cafe, she felt icy cold.

'My God!'

'No God,' Rudy asserted. 'There was no God then. And Celine, she wanted to know how it felt, she wanted to know if he had suffered; if it had been easy for him to die. I couldn't watch her all the time. Two months after she went on a tourist cruise and she let herself fall overboard and into the Amstel.' He looked across at the large, plate glass window and his mouth twisted. 'The people watching said she disappeared like a stone. So it seems that it was easy for her, at least. They pulled her out two days later. Her dress was ripped, her face swollen. And sometimes I think, maybe it was their destiny. Tiber, Amstel, it's the same. I gave them just two years. That's how long I saved them for.' He chewed his lip, breathed hard. 'Now I don't love,

I work. But,' he looked across at the sleeping baby and his forehead cleared, 'I am happy to think perhaps I have a child. Keep your family together. I can offer her nothing, but maybe, I could be a Godfather. If only...' Once more Kate witnessed the small wry smile and her stomach contracted. 'If only there was a God.' He stood up. 'I'm sorry. I have another class, so, until next time. We will keep in touch I think.'

Kate nodded and took his outstretched hand, unable to trust herself with actual words. Rudy drew his finger lightly across the baby's velvet cheek.

'*Dag, schaatje,*' Anna opened her eyes and regarded him sleepily.

'Next time, perhaps I will paint her.'

'Yes,' agreed Kate, 'your very own *berceuse.*'

He lifted his hand in salute. She watched him as he left the café, a tall, loping figure with his shirt escaping from under an elderly jumper, splashes of paint on his jeans, unprepared for the knife twisting in her heart.

Sean was pacing the room when she and Anna arrived back at the hotel.

'Ah, there you are! Luke's still at the Artis with Tobias. They're bringing him back later. But I have good news. Let's go and have a beer and I'll tell you.'

Kate raised her eyebrows. His excitement was hard to square with the story she had just heard. She had been hoping he would be out so she could process everything alone. She wouldn't tell him. At least, not yet.

'So, what is it?' she asked, as they settled themselves in a café on Prinsengracht.

'Sophia is not my baby,' he said, beaming. 'I'm absolutely certain. I offered to take the DNA test, of course, but Lena's child is categorically not mine.'

'How can you be quite so sure?' Kate peered doubtfully into her glass of Heineken.

'Because she looks exactly like the Tunisian guy Lena went out with after me. Now she's a bit older it's clear. Even Lena was having trouble arguing about it.'

Kate felt something very heavy slip away from her, like a great cloak she had been forced to wear but could now remove. She looked about her; her husband, her beautiful baby daughter, the café they were sitting in, the hotel they could easily pay for thanks to Sean's new job, and Luke would be back soon with Tobias. Beloved Luke.

'I feel quite sorry for Lena,' she said eventually. Sean shook his head.

'No, she'll be fine. Really. Sophia's a cute kid and Lena adores her.' He smiled. A genuine, friendly smile. One of the things Kate had always liked best about him. The thing that had attracted Lena. 'How did your meeting go?'

Kate thought about Rudy. She had fallen more than a bit in love with him. She hoped it wouldn't matter too much. Her gaze slid to the baby and if Sean noticed her eyes were damp he didn't comment.

'It was fine. He would like to see her from time to time but he doesn't want to interfere.'

'Really?' His smile widened into a relieved grin. 'That's fantastic.' Kate stretched her hand across to touch her husband's and squeezed it gently.

'Yes,' she agreed. 'Yes it is.'

Chapter 39

The Sunday newspapers are scattered across the battered pine table. Kate and Sean sit companionably at opposite ends, sipping strong coffee. Anna is asleep upstairs but will shortly wake and want feeding. Luke is watching a film in the other room. Kate pushes back her long, red-gold hair and reaches for the Arts section. Her glance softens as it flickers across her husband whose brow has furrowed as he studies the performance details of the new Jaguar XE. She pulls the paper towards her, opens it at random and stops dead. There it is, the painting, the one she imagined no one would ever see, apparently star exhibit at some showcase for new artists in Belgium:

'A major exhibition of contemporary painting opens tomorrow at the Merle Gallery in Brussels. Attracting critic's attention is a stunning new work by talented Dutch artist Rudy de Jong. De Jong's painting, The Sonnet, *depicts a copper-haired nude reclining on a green chaise-longue. Although relatively small in actual size, this vibrantly sensual work dominates the exhibition. Painted in the style of Van Gogh and emulating his use of strong, contrasting colours, De Jong exploits the emerald background to draw the pale-skinned model almost out of the picture and into the room. Although it has been the subject of considerable speculation, De Jong has remained mysterious about his alluring muse.'*

It is her, Kaatje, she is out in the world, she has taken on a life of her own; she is flaunting herself. Kate swallows, turns the page before Sean can see it, not that he will be particularly interested, since it isn't a painting of a car. He looks up, winks at her, runs a hand across his shaved head. He is happy despite the broken night.

'Okay, babe?'

Kate nods. She is, really.

'Just a bit tired,' she replies. A wail from the baby alarm is broadcast into the room at foghorn volume. She moves to stand, but Sean is already on his feet.

'I'll get it.'

'Thanks.' As he leaves the room Kate reopens the paper. There is no doubt this is Rudy. Desire swamps her like a surf-wave, she rides it out, lets it ebb. Sean's voice comes over the intercom as he soothes Anna, a rustle as he changes her nappy. Perhaps, in the end, they all got lucky. She folds the paper and hides it in her bag. She'll show Paula, and that's all.

Acknowledgements

Firstly I would like to thank my friends at the Alès-en-Cevennes reading group for their encouragement and support through plot hitches and early drafts of the book – particularly Shelley, Vicki, Esther and Suzanne, who also corrected my Dutch.

Merci aussi, to Mark Gallant (and Marie Hill) for reading and re-reading various drafts way above the call-of-duty, for spotting inconsistencies and offering suggestions and valuable feedback. All mistakes now are mine alone.

And to my sweet daughters, Charis and Maddy Wheatley who have patiently supported my writing their entire lives and are now finally old enough to read, enjoy and comment (which they do). And my mother, Shirley Boulton, who has done the same.

Thank you to Matt Boulton for his excellent cover design despite the vagueness of the brief and the problems of working with limited resources and a tricky client.

Finally, and especially, to my husband Chris Burns, for doing all the things I didn't do because I was too busy writing; for the complicated discussions about plot and characters; and for bringing endless cups of coffee to my desk on winter mornings, thank you.

Van Gogh quotes from: Digital edition: Vincent van Gogh, The Letters. Ed. Leo Jansen, Hans Luijten and Nienke Bakker. Amsterdam 2009
1. 619, From Vincent van Gogh to Theo van Gogh
Les-Saintes-Maries-de-la-Mer on or about 3rd or 4th June 1888
2. 666, To Theo van Gogh, Arles, 21st or 22nd August 1888.
3. RM23, To Paul Gauguin, Auvers-sur-Oise, on or about 17th June 1890

Lightning Source UK Ltd.
Milton Keynes UK
UKOW01f0722300715

256044UK00002B/62/P